the bones of you

the
bones
of you

Laura Stone

interlude 🧩 press

ISBN 13: 978-1-941530-16-0
Published by Interlude Press
http://interludepress.com
Book design by Lex Huffman
Cover Design by Buckeyegrrl Designs
Cover & Interior Artist/Illustrator: C.B. Messer

*To Guy Garvey
for the irresistible inspiration.*

Chapter One

It wasn't a good morning for Oliver Andrews. In fact, it was a stressful, forgot to buy coffee, hit the snooze alarm too many times, tripped over a pile of textbooks and painfully fell to his knee sort of morning: a typical Tuesday for an overworked graduate student in a country not his own.

Oliver was struggling to get all of his things together to make it to a lecture on time; he sidestepped his flat-mate, Janos, who was also racing to get out the door. He didn't have to look up to know that Janos was still irritated with him. He'd only tried to reach out to the guy by speaking to him in Hungarian, and no, Oliver wasn't great at it, probably butchered the pronunciation, but surely he should have gotten some brownie points for *trying*. Oliver was positive that he'd used the right accents. Mostly positive. Well... pretty sure. He'd already had a few beers when he'd gone up to Janos and his soccer team to offer congratulations on their win that afternoon.

Then again, it wasn't as bad as when Oliver had first met the guy and wanted to give him a proper Hungarian greeting, a sort of verbal olive branch since they were both international students; that hadn't gone over well at all. Oliver knew he was using a formal greeting, but didn't realize that it was one only used for an elderly person; for an elderly woman, in particular. Janos had promptly informed him of his mistake. Then Janos had learned that Oliver was gay and spent the first two weeks avoiding any eye contact. Because sure, that's how Oliver liked hitting on guys: by politely referring to them as elderly Hungarian women.

It had been awkward living together the last several months and, from the look of things, it would continue to be. Janos grabbed his coat off the rack by their front door, knocking Oliver's navy wool peacoat to the ground and not bothering to pick it up, Oliver noted. Janos muttered as he raced out the front door. The cold wind whipped the research papers that Oliver had been trying to straighten into a jumble all over the floor.

"Son of a..." Oliver sighed and gave it up as a bad job for the time being. He was too overwhelmed by the sheer number of things going wrong, and he had a no-caffeine headache slowly building.

He was just having a bad morning, full stop.

He clicked on his email on his laptop and made sure there were no changes in the day's schedule before heading out the door. Finally, something positive: a new email from "Schreiber, Gustav"—an old friend from prep school with whom he'd not been able to connect in a couple of months. Gus was back stateside, busy with his final year of study for his law degree and about to sit for the bar exam. Slaving away to get his graduate degree in social psychology in the United Kingdom hadn't exactly left Oliver with a ton of time to stay in touch; drifting apart happened, unfortunately. So much of his former life seemed to have slipped out of his hands, and he knew that was on his shoulders. He had put his head down and plowed through his undergraduate degree and then dove headfirst into a master's at Cambridge only to look up and realize that while he was focused on his career, he'd let people who had been important to him fall by the wayside.

Great. Another thing to feel bad about. He made a mental note to sit down tonight and send a long email to Gus, catching him up on everything happening in England. Oliver clicked the link and saw that Gus had emailed him an embedded video with a note: "Hope this makes your day better."

Oliver could definitely use a feel-good something. He was steadily getting his ass kicked by his master's, even though it was everything he had hoped he would be doing at this stage in his academic career. He believed he had a lot to prove as an American student and, as a result, he was constantly behind on sleep from trying to stay on top of his reading and research.

Probably a dog dancing or something; he loves those.

He put the day's lecture and scheduled conformity experiment out of his mind by clicking play and then pause to allow the buffer to catch up. The Internet hated their building, the sort of cold stone affair common in town. At first it had been amazing to be living in a bit of history. Then the wet cold of autumn set in, and Oliver missed good ol' American sheetrock and insulation.

While he gave the video a moment to load, he tapped the stack of papers on its edge to straighten it, muttering his day's schedule to himself under his breath until he got everything just right. Then he clicked play, and the screen filled with an American morning show. Oliver rolled his eyes at the overly-peppy hosts and moved to grab his satchel to get the research papers safely stored, figuring that he'd listen to whatever whistling dog or stupid human trick was about to come on as he packed up to leave.

And that's when he heard it: a beautiful voice that was painfully familiar. *God, that sounds just like...* He dropped the satchel—the papers, thankfully, stowed away—and turned to his computer screen. It seemed as though time had stopped, that it took forever to see proof on the screen that he'd heard what he *thought* he had heard. And then he saw him.

Oliver immediately forgot that he needed to get to campus, that he had a mountain of work ahead of him, that he'd not even eaten yet. Seth. Seth, his first love, his first, well, *everything*, was on his computer screen, singing. And if he'd thought Seth had a beautiful voice as a teenager, it was nothing to how he sounded now. Clearly, his time at Juilliard and whatever he'd done after had developed his voice into something truly special, almost otherworldly.

Oliver gripped the computer with both hands, his face close to the screen, his breath trapped in his aching lungs. Seth, tall and lean, his pretty, still-boyish face aglow from the joy of performing, was in the middle of the studio, hands clasped in front of him, eyes closed and head tilted slightly as he sang a song Oliver wasn't familiar with. Oliver was transfixed by the lines of Seth's long throat, by the way the fitted shirt he wore accentuated the breadth of his shoulders, by the small smile on his face as he sang. It was Seth, but now so much more than the captivating boy he had loved all those years ago.

Memories came rushing back to Oliver, tumbling over each other as if trying to assert their dominance: Seth in his Bakerfield Prep uniform, sitting across from Oliver in their French class, smiling shyly. Seth's Adam's apple bobbing as he swallowed nervously before pushing open

Oliver's bedroom door after they decided to take their relationship to the next level. Seth's head thrown back, laughing at something his dad said at dinner, eyes sparkling with warmth as he turned to look at Oliver. A warm, sunny Saturday just after Oliver had graduated from Bakerfield when Seth, home from his first year at university in New York City, had managed to spend the night when Oliver's parents were gone for the weekend.

That was it. That was the day that would forever be branded in Oliver's memory: his hand running through Seth's thick, light brown hair. Seth, eyes closed and still sleepy, turning his head to press a kiss to the inside of Oliver's wrist. Seth falling back asleep and Oliver's arm going numb, him knowing nothing on earth would make him move and wake Seth. Because Oliver had known even then how precious and fleeting these moments were, even if the two of them didn't want to admit that things were changing, that life was moving too fast for them to keep up, that they were still kids and had no idea how hard life would get when they were finally on their own. He'd had that entire Saturday with the person he loved in his arms, unable to accept that it might be the last time he would get the opportunity.

Oliver swallowed around the lump that had risen in his throat at the first sound of the voice that belonged to the only person he'd ever really loved. He clicked on the pause button and tried to catch his breath. Seth was frozen in mid-action on his screen, turned to the left as if acknowledging the hosts of the show. Why was he on *The Today Show*? Why did Gus send him this? He scrolled back up to read the message of the email.

Hope this makes your day better.

Oliver attempted a laugh; a strangled, sad sound came out. He noticed the clock in the lower right-hand corner of his computer screen. "Shit," he muttered, flipping the screen closed and jamming the laptop roughly in his satchel. He would deal with this later, whatever that meant. For now, he had about three minutes to get fifteen minutes away. He stepped out onto the slick stones that made up the walkway to his flat and pulled the heavy wooden door shut. The icy cold wind cut through every layer he had on, and he tried to stop thinking of how beautiful Seth's bare skin had been with the midday sun shining on him at two in the afternoon on that warm and lazy Saturday, him spread out on Oliver's bed, smiling as if he weren't about to shatter Oliver's heart into a million pieces just a few hours later.

* * *

"... Determinants and consequences of adaptive and maladaptive parental behavior are the data needed in order to progress when confronted..."

Oliver saw a few dirty looks directed at him as he slipped into a chair in the back of the lecture hall. *Well, yet another black mark for American students, I guess.* One of his heroes in the field he was studying was giving today's lecture; he'd looked forward to it for weeks. And yet he could barely focus on Dr. Lan's real-world experiences in forensics psychology while his mind continued to bombard him with vivid memories, things he hadn't allowed himself to think about for years.

The look of pleasant surprise on Seth's face as Oliver moved in to kiss him for the first time. The triumphant happiness on Seth's face the first time Oliver held his hand in public. The devastation Oliver read in Seth's eyes when his father—his only living parent—was hospitalized after a motorcycle accident. How important it made Oliver feel when Seth came to *him* for comfort that day; how Seth held onto him, needing him and no one else. The first time they had sex, how trusting and happy they were. The elegance of Seth's long fingers. How their hands looked when they laced them together.

Oliver was getting angry with himself. He dealt with this *years* ago. Hell, before he moved to England he'd packed up all of his extraneous things for his parents to add to all of his trophies and report cards and whatever else they couldn't quite bring themselves to throw away. It had been a relief to add the mementos of his relationship with Seth to the other stored memories trapped in their expansive attic, to put those things out of his mind and thousands of miles away instead of letting them crowd space in the back of his closet and in his broken heart, choking him every time he came across them.

In those boxes was his framed picture from Seth's senior prom; they were the first male couple to attend in their school's history. God, he'd been so amazed by Seth that night; how proud he'd been of both of them for going. There was a small bundle of handwritten letters from Seth's first semester at university, tied together with a bit of blue satin ribbon. It hurt just knowing they existed (and the letters he'd written in turn, filled with his own longing and dreams for their future), knowing that those feelings so earnestly expressed by the boy he'd loved had changed. Also jammed in a box, as a last-minute thought, was a heather-green Larsen Custom Cycles & Repair T-shirt from Seth's father's shop that Oliver had foolishly worn to bed every night that first semester when Seth was studying in New York.

He pushed it all aside, frustrated that a song he didn't even know was capable of setting off all of these reactions in him, forcing him to remember things he had worked very hard to forget. He didn't want to think about the person singing the song. He wanted to focus on his studies. Well, he would just make himself focus. *This* was important, not ghosts from the past. He'd pushed them away before and he could do it again.

He set his jaw, and listened to Dr. Lan describe a session with a twelve-year-old who had almost committed suicide as a result of bullying by his peers. The session turned out to be very productive and had led to change in the boy's school in Manchester, fortunately, and Oliver scrambled to take notes on the various processes and tactics used with the school administration and the local government, knowing they would come in handy one day.

As Oliver walked to the research center after the lecture ended, he gave his brain permission to mock itself. The first paper of Dr. Lan's he'd read was during his senior year at Bakerfield. The psychologist had worked with an Irish high school boy—delicate features, a dancer, and out—who suffered horrible abuse from both his classmates and working-class father. The case had sparked a renewed interest in the "It Gets Better" campaign circling the Western world at the time, one Oliver used in his own student council campaign. Oliver had told himself that he was interested in it for the obvious reasons: He was gay and he knew how difficult it was to be out as a gay person in a conservative place. He ignored the fact that the boy bore a striking resemblance to his boyfriend who had just moved away—consciously, at least.

When he'd gone to visit Brandeis' campus that same year, excited by the close proximity of a cultured city like Boston and for all the potential the school year held, he saw a flyer on a bulletin board announcing that Cambridge University's Dr. Lan would be a guest speaker at the Heller School for Social Policy on sexual harassment of LGBT people. This dovetailed so perfectly with everything he'd experienced as a kid before attending a private high school that he gladly skipped an audition for the music department and sat in on the lecture, eyes wide and mind soaking up all of the ideas being presented.

His conservative father, a founding partner in a corporate law firm, was very happy with Oliver's decision to switch majors from musical theory to social justice and social policy. "It'll give you more options," his father said over the phone that night. "You can sing for others and go hungry, or you can have a career that feeds you and sing for yourself."

Oliver told himself that he simply wanted to have a hand in making the world a better place. It had been his mantra since coming out to his friends his freshman year in high school. He had so desperately needed someone to be there for him when he was struggling with his own identity that he'd make a point to be there for people when *they* were struggling. Like how he'd been there for Se—

He laughed bitterly at himself. His entire academic career was based on a person he thought he'd never see again. *It's taken five years and two countries to finally figure this out?*

But that was unfair—he'd always known why he began to pull away from music and sports to broaden his extracurricular activities as his senior year of high school played out. It was just that once he and Seth severed ties, he took great pains to convince himself that Seth had simply been a catalyst for him to finally make a choice, and that the desire to focus his life on specific things must have been buried deep within his psyche all along.

What a load of garbage. It had *always* been about Seth.

* * *

FALL, FIVE YEARS AGO

"You have to be kidding, Oliver." Disbelief dripped from Seth's every syllable. "Babe, you're in *Kansas*. I love that you're trying, I do, but you put your heart on your sleeve." Seth's voice changed to one of sweet sincerity. "I love that about you, but it's going to backfire. People there don't care about hate crimes. Hell, they don't even see bullying as a hate crime! It's that whole 'boys will be boys' bullshit. This isn't a good idea."

Oliver was glad he'd called instead of Skyping his boyfriend to tell him about the student petition he was starting; he was pretty sure his face would show how crestfallen he was. He cleared his throat. "I thought you would be happy about it. Proud, even. I know I'll get enough signatures here, and once other high schools see what I'm trying to do—"

"Oh, Oliver," Seth sighed. Oliver could imagine him rubbing his hand over his eyes in frustration. Seth tried again, his voice soft. "You and I both know how backward people can be. We had to fight to even go to prom last year, remember? High school students don't care about bullying; it's practically a school-sanctioned sport. I think it's okay to accept that the Midwest is jam-packed with the blissfully ignorant."

"Well, I disagree. I think they've just been too afraid to stand up to the status quo." Oliver couldn't understand why Seth wasn't being totally supportive. Seth had been bullied out of his high school until his father had sued the administration, landing Seth in private school, tuition paid, as a settlement. It was how Oliver and Seth had met.

"Babe, I think you're setting yourself up for disaster, and I just don't want you to be hurt. I can't see how this can end in anything but disappointment for you, and I don't want that to happen. But you know that I'll be here when you need soothing after this all stalls out. Trust me, I know how this story ends: with you hanging from a flagpole in your underwear. But I *have* to tell you about a class today where..."

Oliver sighed and sat back against his headboard, frustrated yet again by the distance between them. How their lives were slowly pulling away from each other as Seth became more and more enamored of New York City, his school and all of the possibilities stretched out before him. Oliver thought that his own life was in a constant state of limbo, with nothing to look forward to but Seth's trips home for the coming holidays—or months down the road, when Oliver finally graduated. He was beginning to feel that he had nothing of interest to offer. There were so many people Seth was surrounded by in New York who could sing, perform, be *interesting*. He felt small and stupidly provincial next to the glamour and excitement that came from living in the greatest city on earth.

And it wasn't that Seth made him feel insignificant. It was that Seth barely had any free time, with his demanding schedule, and Oliver felt guilty when he wanted to have a long conversation about the latest assignment in school or his student council campaign. Seth surely saw far more interesting things than his high school boyfriend back in Atchison, Kansas.

Oliver couldn't blame him. His life *was* boring. That's why they both wanted to get out of Kansas. But Oliver couldn't yet, and he worried that Seth would get tired of waiting for him to finally join him. After all, Seth had bigger things happening in his life. New York things. Things that had nothing to do with his lame high school boyfriend back in Nowhere, Flyover State, USA.

Later that night, while laying in bed, Oliver tried to let go of the earlier feelings of hurt. He didn't want to be upset, didn't want to have a knot of worry eating away at his insides about Seth's new friends, Simon and Geoffrey. Geoffrey. And Seth had pronounced it "JOFF-rey," as if it was the most amazing thing. No. No. He was *not* a jealous person. He wasn't going to *start* being a jealous person. Being jealous implied that he didn't fully trust his boyfriend, and he absolutely did. Seth was simply happy to have new friends who liked music and performing and fashion. God knew boys like them weren't easy to find in their hometown. Oliver was happy for him; he knew how hard it had been until they'd found each other.

He was happy for Seth. He was. He was just feeling sorry for himself.

Oliver went to sleep that night staring at their prom photo on his bedside table. He wanted Seth to be the first and last thing he saw each day.

* * *

Oliver went through the motions of collecting data during the experiment on conformity that he and his research partner were working on that year. Oliver had dubbed it the "Three Men Make a Tiger" project and one of his fellows, Moira Byrne, shortened it to TMMaT, or "team mat." Oliver would be the first to admit that he had not resembled anything close to a team member today. He was constantly distracted. Moira elbowed him at one point and muttered, "Pay attention, Yank."

Shaking himself a little, Oliver straightened in his chair and focused on recording reactions, feeling slightly ashamed at being called out for not being diligent. His team had devised a series of photographs of people, people who were dressed unobtrusively: office workers, teachers, shop owners; and people who matched LGBT stereotypes: women with severe haircuts, men dressed in flamboyant outfits, pre-operative transgenders, and the like. Groups of three, all people chosen at random, were shown the pictures together, and Oliver's team recorded their reactions when presented with the images and asked two questions: Is this person gay or straight? Would you be comfortable in close proximity to this person? After the group completed the test, the real test began: it was revealed that every photograph was of a person who identified as LGBT. The group's reaction to *this* was what they were studying.

Oliver sorted through the cards until one photograph jumped out at him: a slender young man dressed in pair of skintight trousers, his brown hair styled in a severe pompadour, a pale sweater hanging off one shoulder, a pouty, pink mouth and an almost coy look on his face. Oliver had chosen this particular person at the local LGBT center, thinking he would be a perfect example of how inoffensive a more effeminate gay man could be, a "See? See how charming and handsome and lovely? Nothing here to be offended by" sort of example. Surprisingly, it had turned out to be one of the more polarizing images—it and the photograph of a muscled woman, her breasts bound by an elastic bandage, staring defiantly back at the camera with her thumbs hooked through her blue jeans' belt loops.

He stared at the picture, not seeing the rounded cheeks of the young man whose name he didn't know, but superimposing high cheekbones and a full bottom lip and a faint spray of freckles across the bridge of the young man's nose. Just like Seth's.

Did he really think he was fit for a degree in psychology? Oliver scrubbed his face with both hands after putting the testing media away. What was the old saying, "Cobblers' wives go barefoot and doctors' wives die young?" Apparently people who studied the mind and behavioral patterns were idiots. Hmm, he'd have to work on the phrasing, give the saying more contemporary oomph, maybe make it rhyme.

Later that day he shouldered his way through the front door of his flat, shivering as he unwrapped his thick scarf and peeled off his coat. It was always freezing in this house. Kansas was no small shakes when it came to heavy-duty winter, but something about the cold in England sank right into his bones.

Janos looked over the screen of his laptop and jerked his head towards the small kitchenette. "Coffee is made."

Oliver sighed gratefully. "Thanks for picking some up."

Janos grunted, his eyes darting back to the screen after watching Oliver move toward the other room.

All right, that's enough.

"Janos?" Oliver leaned his weight onto his hands at the counter that divided the two rooms. This had the added advantage of showing off the muscles in his arms—sometimes, straight boys needed a reminder that Oliver had been an athlete and could hold his own. "I've offended you somehow, and I can't for the life of me understand why. If you don't tell me, how will I know not to do it again?"

Janos stared at him over the top of his laptop with a distasteful look on his face. "I am not interested in a relationship like you want, Andrews."

Oliver gaped at him, his face all confusion. "I don't—okay." He huffed out his breath, running a hand through his hair. He'd had odd roommates over the years; the guy who hid food in his bed "for emergencies" was definitely the weirdest, but Janos was quickly moving up the list.

Shaking his head, Oliver said, "Hey, I get it. Not everyone has to be best friends, but just because you don't want to be my friend doesn't mean we can't be friend*ly*, right?" He raised his eyebrows, hoping Janos would jump in and talk to him.

Janos crossed his arms in front of him and glared back. "I told you when I moved in that I am a Catholic."

"Yeah? And?"

"I do not do those sex things that you do. You are your own person; it is not for me to judge you. But *I* am not going to do those things with you."

Oliver was utterly gobsmacked. "Janos? And I mean this will all due respect: What the fuck are you talking about?"

Janos crossed his legs and looked back at Oliver coolly. "Clearly you desire me. But you cannot have me."

The sheer force of the laugh that exploded from Oliver should have made the windows rattle in their casings. He clapped a hand to his mouth, trying to stifle the noise, when he saw the look of anger that flashed across Janos's face.

"Janos, I don't know *where* you got that idea, but it never even occurred to me to *desire* you. Honestly." He rubbed the back of his neck and smiled. He noted that Janos was looking confused, so Oliver said in a teasing tone, "And just because I'm gay doesn't mean I want to hook up with every guy I meet. Sorry, you're not my type."

"What is this? Type?" Janos looked at himself and Oliver took a moment to really look at him as well. Huh. Janos was pretty attractive. Well-built from soccer—football, Oliver tried to remember—not as tall as Oliver, who stood at a lean six-two, but not too short. He had that pretty-boy, square-jawed fraternity-type look about him, also not unlike Oliver (or so he'd been told). It just wasn't something Oliver was attracted to; he'd had his fill of it back home.

Janos had an almost permanent sour look about him; he had a terrible personality, practically nonexistent. Oliver definitely favored someone who lit up a room when he entered, someone engaging and interesting. Someone witty and fun. Janos Feczesin was none of those things—at least, not with him.

Laughing a bit before responding, Oliver said, "It just means that I am not 'wanting to have you,' as you put it."

Janos settled back in the armchair and studied Oliver's face. "But you tell me things like a man does when they desire a woman. And you honored my... backside, my asshole last night. I cannot have that, Oliver Andrews. This to me is unacceptable."

Oliver bit his bottom lip for a moment, waiting for his brain to finally put the pieces together. "I did *what?* Look, I wanted to try and make you feel at home by learning some Hungarian, but I'll be the first to admit that my accent sucks. That's why I got some links off the web to show me how to pronounce conversational phrases. Here..."

Oliver grabbed his laptop and loaded the page in question; Janos, curiosity evidently getting the better of him, wandered over to stand beside Oliver and look at the screen.

"This is the website where you think you are learning my language?"

Oliver turned slightly to Janos before furrowing his brow and reading all of the fine print. Nothing looked weird. "See? It's free-translations-for-lovers-of-hungarian-dot-com. What's wrong with that?"

"Stupid American," Janos sighed, rubbed his face with both hands and then shook them at the ceiling. He pointed at the URL on the screen, his free hand on Oliver's shoulder, pushing him to look at the monitor. "Yes. For lovers of Hungarian. Hungarians. Me. I am Hungarian, Andrews, so you are telling me you love me by using this."

Oliver blinked at the screen for a minute and felt his entire face heat and flood red. "I am going to kill Todd," he muttered. He turned and darted around Janos to grab his cup of coffee. "So, are we okay?" Oliver made a thumbs-up with a questioning face. "Are we cool?"

Janos eyed him and then nodded once, tightly. "We are cool, Andr—"

"Oliver. Just call me Oliver. You don't have to be so formal."

"Okay." Janos turned on his heel and flopped back in his chair, his demeanor completely relaxed now. He picked up his own laptop and began typing speedily. "I am telling my teammates that you do not want to be with me sexually, so they do not need to find me a new place to live."

Oliver spluttered into his mug. "You told your team I was hot for you?"

Janos shrugged. "Now I tell them other. This is good, yes? Now we both do not have to find a new roommate to live with."

"You know what? I think I'm gonna call it." Oliver looked at the clock on his computer. "Time of death, 9:48 p.m. This day is officially dead to me."

He scooped up his computer and his coffee and walked straight to his room, shutting the door with his heel. If it slammed a little, it was just because it was a heavy wooden door, and he wanted to make sure it closed. He wasn't *trying* to slam the door. He set his mug on the small, wobbly table next to his bed and tossed his laptop carelessly on the duvet. After a moment of struggling with his clothes—remembering too late to remove his shoes before his pants—he moved to stand in front of the window, where half the panes of glass were wavy from so many years of gravity pulling on them, and looked out into the dark, shivering a little as the cold seeped through, purposely avoiding his laptop.

His fingers were itching to bring up his email. He didn't want to watch the video again. He *didn't*. What good would it do? It would just reopen more hurt, unlock more memories that didn't matter anymore. Except, he needed to email his professor. He'd send the email and that would be it. Just that one thing. He climbed into bed and piled the blankets over his cold limbs.

After he deleted some spam, the email from Gus was at the top of the screen. Oliver closed his eyes for a second and clicked it open. His index finger hovered over the trackpad as he worried his lip. He clicked play and waited for the video to load again. He opened a new tab and typed "Seth Larsen" into the search box on Google. Several news articles were listed.

"Wow, I'm really out of touch," he murmured.

Oliver clicked back to the video and fast-forwarded beyond the inane banter of the hosts to the point where Seth began singing. Now that some of the initial shock had waned, he was able to really absorb what he was seeing. Seth still had his amazing vocal range, but his control over it was even more impressive. His shoulders looked a bit broader, his neck was still impossibly long; the handsome angles of his face made him look masculine, and yet he was still, well, *pretty*.

No, that wasn't the right word. Delicate and easily broken things were pretty. China plates were pretty. Satin dresses were pretty. Seth was *beautiful*. He hit pause just as Seth looked directly into the camera and Oliver's heart thumped so painfully that it radiated out to every corner of his being.

Sighing heavily, he rested his head against the crumbly plaster wall behind his bed and just looked. A part of him was filled with such happiness. Seth had made it. He *made* it. The world was finding out how amazing he was. Is, Oliver corrected himself. How amazing he is. Oliver had fantasized about these moments years before: how he would bring Seth flowers, finding just the right color of golden yellow rose tied with a deep blue ribbon as a nod to their prep school's uniform, where they'd met. How Oliver would wrap his arms around Seth, so delighted and just plain happy for him. The fantasy was usually accompanied by Seth's Tony Award acceptance speech, but a performance on national television was pretty great, too.

He came crashing down from the elation of those daydreams. He wasn't there to do any of that. Didn't have the *right* to do any of that.

He checked the email one more time, looking for a clue from Gus. Why would he send this? As a reminder of how stupid Oliver and Seth had been when they were teenagers? Gus was the furthest thing from a jerk, so it didn't make sense.

"Keep-vid-dot-com."

Oliver hadn't noticed the URL typed in after the video. A quick Google search found it, and while he installed the program (well, Gus was right about that much, he would definitely want to watch it again and not be at the mercy of his slow Internet in this abominable Edwardian stone house) he clicked back to the news articles, rubbing his long feet together to warm them up.

"Understudy's Dream Come True!" was the title of one listed in the Theater section of the *New York Times*. "David Falchurch, star of yadda yadda," Oliver read, "inexplicably broke his leg in the closing number of the musical written by blah blah that specifically highlights his vocal range..."

Oliver skimmed the article looking for information about Seth. "Understudy Seth Larsen stepped in for the Saturday performance while production decided whether they would close the show until Falchurch had healed.

"As the saying goes, 'The show must go on,' and so it did to wildly positive reviews. Larsen is being referred to as the Cinderfella"—Oliver groaned—"story for modern times. With his vocal range exceeding even the jaw-dropping range of his predecessor and his angelic looks, more fitting for the part of Shakespeare's Fair Youth, the powers that be behind the show should consider dropping Falchurch completely and sticking with the real deal. The standing ovations after performances have become a test of endurance, it seems. New York is smitten. Let's see if we can't hold onto this gem as long as possible."

Oliver noted that the play's ad on the web page featured Seth, dressed in a simple linen Elizabethan-period shirt, on the cover of *Playbill* magazine. He clicked the image and realized after a moment that he was searching for available tickets after the term let out, the first week of December. Three short weeks away, and he was free for more than a month...

What, I think I'm just going to show up? This is stupid. This is also sold out. Damn it.

He couldn't find tickets anywhere. He told himself that was great, because it meant that Seth was shooting up the ladder to success. He worried his bottom lip with his teeth as he wracked his brain, trying to think of how he could get to New York.

What am I doing? The last thing Seth would want to see would be me. Hmm, still? I mean, I'm happy for him. I wanted this for him, and it's the right thing to do to let him know. Sending flowers or a note would be too impersonal.

His mind flashed to a letter, the first one Seth had sent from Juilliard, one that he had read every night for a week before going to sleep.

Dear Oliver,

That sounds so formal. Well, I suppose it doesn't get more formal than a handwritten letter, but don't you love getting things in the mail? That was a huge hint, by the way.

I already told you about my room—a.k.a. The Glorified Broom Closet—and my roommate when we talked this afternoon on the phone, so I just wanted to tell you in this, my first letter from New York City, that I love you. I miss you. I know, we promised that we'd be strong and not mope, but I'm not moping. I'm just expressing how I feel, in case there are times when you worry that I don't love you completely. Because I do. So, so much.

I spent the better part of the day walking through the city, imagining your hand in mine, me showing you my favorite café and the place where I love to sit and people-watch. I haven't found them yet, and people get very mad at me when I stop in the middle of the sidewalk, but when I do and when you're here, I'll show you how, on each and every corner of this city, I could pull you to me and kiss you. I could wrap my arms around you. I could hold your body against mine when I did. No one here would care. Or, if they did, they would get over it. Here we'll be safe.

I could say out loud, in each and every place we go, that I love you. And I do. More importantly, I will.

I can't wait.

Yours, Seth.

Oliver had wanted that so badly. He'd had dreams, that last year of high school, of the very things Seth described: the two of them, holding hands on park benches, laughing and kissing and being together; in a favorite café, where they could kiss and talk and love each other. He had wanted all of it so desperately.

Seth had loved him completely, had wanted nothing but a forever in which the two of them were together. Oliver had wanted that, too.

He opened a new tab and began looking at plane tickets from London Heathrow to Kansas.

Chapter Two

Nov. 20, 4:48 PM GMT
From: Oliver Andrews
To: Gus Schreiber
Subject: wtf

I had planned on a nice long email catching you up on everything, with hints of how I hoped you and Emily were still a thing in order to get you to tell me all about how happy you both are, but I think we both know that I just want answers to what that last email was about.

And I know you're home for Thanksgiving, so you have no excuse for not replying to me ASAP. We both know your parents will spend the vacation sitting quietly reading *Scientific American* magazines while you watch C-SPAN 2.

~O. A.

p.s. Tell your mother I said hello, please.

Nov. 19, 11:57 PM CST
From: Gus Schreiber
To: Oliver Andrews
Subject: re: wtf

It never fails to amuse me when I get an email from you with the time stamp a day ahead. It's like you're communicating with me from the future. If you could, let me know who wins the World Series and Preakness, thanks buddy.

Also, are you having trouble sleeping? No one should be awake at that hour.

The video? Oliver, don't you want to know that a fellow classmate is becoming a success? That should be enough of an answer.

…

Okay, I couldn't send this without adding more. We email every now and then, just like all the guys in choir and swim team. You should see the list of people I email from my frat. It's called networking—you should give it a try.

Let's just say that I thought it could be *interesting* for you to see how far he's come. And where he is. Specifically. For the next several months.

I'm going to bed now. Busy day tomorrow with all the watching my parents reading magazines coupled with the ever-riveting C-SPAN 2. And you're wrong; they'll be reading *The Economist*. It's like you don't even know us anymore.

Gustav Schreiber

"The real leader has no need to lead; he is content to point the way." —Henry Miller

Nov. 20, 3:22 PM GMT
From: Oliver Andrews
To: Gus Schreiber
Subject: re: re: wtf

Of course I want to know how all the guys are doing. Well, not all, because Bad Breath Brian was a jackass then, and he's probably a jackass now. I noted that you didn't send me any mention of Chance's engagement, so I have to wonder about your motivation in keeping me up to date on "everyone."

You talk to him? Rather, you email him? How's he doing? I mean, his father, that sort of thing. I don't want you to divulge any confidences, of course. Forget I asked.

And yes, it's incredibly helpful to know that he's in New York City in a sold-out musical. Especially as the only break I have is going to be six weeks spent with my parents in Atchison. And hanging out at your place, of course, watching your parents read *Harper's Bazaar*.

~Oliver

"Justice means minding one's own business and not meddling with other men's concerns." — Plato

Nov. 20, 11:33 AM CST
From: Gus Schreiber
To: Oliver Andrews
Subject: I hate all of the colons—too cluttered.
Nothing like waking up to a full inbox. There was this email, and another one from another particular friend. I had asked that particular friend a specific question, and he was incredibly helpful and gracious. You might take a page from his book, Oliver.

And I knew that *you* knew about Chance already, so why be tedious? Speaking of, my father wouldn't touch *Harper's Bazaar* with a ten-foot pole, and you know it. Now, if it were *Harper's Magazine*... this is fun, you getting things wrong and me pointing them out. I like this.

Speaking of fun, want to go on a little side trip with me over the holiday?

Oh, and because I know you actually do want to know, it seems His father is doing very well. Healthy and accounted for.

Gus

"A leader is a dealer in hope." —Napoleon Bonaparte

Nov. 20, 4:41 PM GMT
From: Oliver Andrews
To: Gus Schreiber
Subject: SIDE TRIP??
Your quotes are telling, but you haven't been. What side trip? Who was the particular friend?
WHAT SIDE TRIP, GUS?
~O
"You are most ungentlemanly to treat me this way." —Oliver Andrews

Nov. 20, 12:01 PM CST
From: Gus Schreiber

To: Oliver Andrews
Subject: Who has two thumbs and tickets to Seth's show
   This guy.

   I'll take it as an automatic yes that you'll come. Be at my place on Dec. 6th. Road trip! I'm in charge of all musical selections. You can sit and grin nervously. It'll be fun, like we're kids again.

   You're on your own for accommodations. I already have plans for use of my just-booked suite—and Emily says to tell you hello and that she recommends the boutique hotel around the corner from the theater. Small and intimate, good staff. And really, go for the Entertainment Suite if you do. Much more comfortable if you end up with an unexpected guest. In case you haven't put two and two together, we're staying there.

   Gus

   "Go confidently in the direction of your dreams. Live the life you have imagined." —Henry David Thoreau

Nov. 20, 5:05 PM GMT
From: Oliver Andrews
To: Gus Schreiber
Subject: re: Who has two thumbs and tickets to Seth's show
   If ever I have given you the impression that I do not admire the very ground you walk on, allow me to apologize for that.

   Okay. Yes. I'll touch base when I get my itinerary in order.

   ~Oliver

Oliver immediately hit "Undo" at the top of the email screen, which called it back before Gus could read it. What the hell was he thinking? So, what, he'd just drop everything and go see Seth? Someone he hadn't spoken with, let alone *seen*, in more than five years? He'd gotten a degree since then. He'd left the country. He was almost finished with *another* degree. Oliver was a completely different person now.

Well, there wasn't as much straight-acting to please his father since he wasn't in the Midwest any longer, and not having a piano meant no more playing music—he hadn't even thought of playing in ages. He'd always been athletic, so it had been easy to keep fit in college running or swimming, and he wasn't physically that much different than before: tall, lanky, but decently muscled. His black, wavy hair was longer, but truthfully he was too tired to bother with regular trips to the barber. He still dressed like a prep, but simply because it was comfortable. He was still fairly idealistic; he'd be the first to admit that. He still wanted to help people. He still tried to give people the benefit of the doubt and knew that it took something huge to shock him into seeing anything negative in a person.

Hmm. So he was still the same person, just older, hairier and less straight-acting. But he couldn't just show up. He couldn't just hop into Gus's sports car—Gus would want to listen to something like barbershop just to mess with him—and drive to New York City to see Seth perform.

Then again, his reaction to seeing Seth singing on a YouTube video was proof enough that there was still some hurt deep down, still some longing. But that was the purpose of a first love, right? To give your heart a few calluses so it wouldn't hurt like that ever again? And it hadn't; it hadn't ever hurt like that again. He'd hooked up randomly a few times before realizing he wasn't built for casual, had then dated a few men over the years. One time it was on the road to something serious, but that was more out of habit, he'd come to realize. Like it was what one did after dating the same person for several months. He'd caught himself saying, "I love you," and knew it was a lie as soon as it left his mouth. He knew what love was, and the basic familiarity he'd come to rely on with his boyfriend at the time wasn't it.

It *never* felt like that first time.

He leaned back in his chair, sighing as he buried his hands in his hair. He had to finish an outline for his report, he needed to email his parents his flight itinerary, and he needed to get some laundry done. Maybe get some sleep eventually. He *didn't* need to fixate on an ex-boyfriend in another country.

Oliver stared at a blank space on the wall. He couldn't control his thoughts; they veered back to the current possibility like a magnet pointing north. Say he *did* go. And then... what? If he went—and he wasn't committing to it yet, but if he *did*—then what?

"Hey, Seth, that was great! I know we broke it off years ago and we both cried and it was awful and I didn't shower for three days and I haven't been able to find anyone who could hold a candle to you since, but I just wanted you to know how wonderful your stage presence was tonight. Excellent choices you made in that second act. Well done. Ta!"

Take out all of the woe-is-me crap, and yes, that *was* what he should say. Except he wouldn't, because he wasn't going.

Oliver sat back at his desk, minimized his email and pulled up his spreadsheet. He got about halfway through his hastily scribbled notes before he groaned and pulled his email back up. Biting his lip as his fingers wiggled over the keys, he thought carefully before typing a reply. "Fuck it."

Nov. 20, 7:13 PM GMT
From: Oliver Andrews
To: Gus Schreiber
Subject: re: Who has two thumbs and tickets to Seth's show

First, I haven't agreed to going. I need to think it through. It's *Seth's* night, and I don't know if my being there will sour that for him. We didn't end as friends—you know that much. I don't want to give him any reason to be upset. That would be churlish of me.

Second, if I did agree, I'm not sure that I'd want him to know I was there. See above.

Third, you absolutely would *not* be in charge of music.

Let me think on it? I don't know how *I* feel about seeing him, either.

Thanks, Gus. I know you have my best interests at heart, even though I'm kind of really upset with you right now. We'll talk soon.
~Oliver

Oliver logged off the Internet and shut his computer down. There was no way he was going to get any work done tonight. He'd just not have another weekend—as had been the case all term, he supposed.

After brushing his teeth and pulling on some wool socks, he slipped into his bed, his glasses perched on his nose as he tried to read and fall asleep.

His thoughts kept drifting from the words on the page to memories of how excited he would get at the sight of a new letter, in Seth's distinctive handwriting, in his mailbox. The way Seth's blush went all the way from his cheeks to his sternum. How soft the scant amount of hair on Seth's pecs felt under his palm. How wonderful and warm Seth had felt in his arms as they danced to a slow song at Seth's senior prom, one of the few times they dared that night. How intense his hope had been of getting to slow dance with his love for the rest of his life when they lived in New York together.

Oliver let the book drop to his chest. He blinked rapidly and rubbed at his eyes. He wasn't crying. He didn't cry over that; he hadn't cried about that in a long time. Years. He was just tired and had experienced a shock; that was all. He folded down the corner of his page, set the book on the side table and switched off his bedside lamp.

He stared into nothingness in the dark. It took him a long time to fall asleep.

He woke up grumpy, almost disoriented, then showered and dressed quickly, loath to be without multiple layers in the drafty house for long. He spent a few minutes with the coffee pot, dumping the spent grounds into a composter Janos had brought with him ("Why do you throw these away? They are from the earth, so you put them back. Americans!"), refilling the filter to make enough coffee for them both. The warmer would keep it hot for Janos until he woke up.

While he sipped at his coffee, he checked over his plans for the day. He had to spend a lot of time on the computer if he wanted to graduate on time and not piss off his research partners. Fortunately, he could do that in the comfort of his own apartment.

He needed to be at the lab in an hour, leaving him with thirty minutes free. Just enough time. He let his laptop power up as he made a quick bowl of oatmeal. Pulling up a browser, he entered "hotels times square Broadway district" and spooned a little sugar over his oats. Just satisfying some curiosity.

The Paramount looks pretty swank.

There were lots of reasons to go to New York, after all. There was nothing like the city at Christmastime. He could do a little shopping for gifts; he'd have far more options than in Kansas, for sure. *The Lion King* was still playing. If Gus was going, there wasn't anything wrong with tagging along and maybe seeing some shows he really enjoyed.

And there was the latest revival of *Miss Saigon*, which was getting good reviews, he noticed.

Oliver casually clicked on the ad that popped up on the side of his screen and just happened to feature Seth's show. He had always known that Seth was destined for stardom. That is, he'd known it would be true if Seth were ever given the chance to show the world just how amazing he was. *Is*. It might be gratifying for Seth to know that someone who "knew him when" was proud of him. That he had always known Seth Larsen was a star in training.

He didn't have to speak to Seth, he realized. He could go and simply be proud that he'd once known this amazingly talented person onstage. Once upon a time Oliver had loved him, and he had loved Oliver back. Oliver could sit in the dark theater and just be happy for someone whom he'd always wished the best. Seth didn't ever have to know.

He pulled up his last email to Gus. After rinsing off his bowl and depositing it in the sink, he wrote a quick reply.

Nov. 20, 7:17 PM GMT
From: Oliver Andrews
To: Gus Schreiber
Subject: re: Who has two thumbs and tickets to Seth's show
   Okay. I'll go. But let's keep it between us, okay? I just want to be an anonymous admirer in the crowd.
   I'll see you on the 6th.
   ~O.A.

He took a deep breath and was surprised to feel a little tension leave his shoulders. He'd go. He'd be proud of Seth, see a great show and then maybe write a card telling Seth how great he'd been. That was a good plan. No stress. No need to worry about ruining Seth's post-performance high. This could work.

* * *

"Right, Yank. Spill."

Oliver, startled, clamped his teeth around his pen, his hum switched off mid-note. "Spill what?"

Moira narrowed her eyes, the look intensified by her thick, black eyebrows.

"You've been swanning about the place all morning. I just caught you humming what sounds suspiciously like a teenager's pop tune, and I daresay your eyes are fair sparkling. Positively crinkled at the edges. You, my dear boy," she sighed dramatically and patted his arm, "are clearly smitten. It's that or you've done me an unkindness and forgot to share the little green man."

Oliver laughed; he couldn't help himself. Moira's lilting Irish accent and random use of foreign slang always tripped him up. She spoke with a voice out of a fairy tale. Well, until she got drunk, which was often. Then she told the bawdiest, raunchiest stories he'd ever heard—and he'd gone to an American all-boy's school, so that was impressive. She was a teeny thing in her early twenties, same as Oliver, but could throw a punch and outdrink everyone he knew (barring the redheaded girl from New Zealand in his Childhood Development course—no one could outdrink a Kiwi, he'd been told), and was one of his closest friends.

He had been surrounded by serious people since he started college, and now in England there was a general air of stuffiness all around, a drawback of the department he was in, no doubt—not to mention his tendency toward a "corn-fed, American sense of idealism," according to one sharp-tongued professor. The first time he got drunk with Moira at The Eagle—not much of a feat since he was a bit of a lightweight—she told him a positively filthy story about her best friends getting the best of some sexually aggressive "posh wankers" that left him curled over the tabletop, laughing himself sick.

Now she winked at him and went back to her computer. "And if I didn't know you better, I'd say you got a leg over last night."

"Uh, no." Oliver affected disappointment to say, "Janos said that was officially off the table, unfortunately."

She brayed a laugh and turned in her chair to face Oliver. "He didn't! Oh, to be a fly on the wall for that conversation. Well," she huffed out a sigh, closed her eyes and held a hand over her heart, "there goes that fantasy. You've killed it dead for me. I hope you're proud of yourself."

Oliver laughed and turned back to face his computer.

"Hang on, you stupid article. You didn't tell me the tale of your footie tossing you over! How ever did *that* conversation come about? Finally tried to feel him up, did you? Obviously I wouldn't blame you; I'd climb him like a tree." She dropped her voice, whispering, "Sure, he's probably dumber than bottled shite, but I bet he's the mutt's nuts in the sack."

Oliver closed his eyes and dropped his face to his forearm. "I don't know *why* I'm friends with you."

"Sure you do: because I'm so fetching and sympathetic." She tapped the side of his leg with her foot. "And I picked up the slack at work yesterday when you were evidently mooning over some boy. You sure it's not Janos?" She poked him in his side.

"God." He scowled at her. "I never even thought about him like that, which is exactly what I said to him last night." He leaned back in his chair, rubbing his knuckles over his lip as he thought. "I'm looking forward to the break. I'm going to see some old friends, and I just made the plans this morning. That's all it is."

"Mm hmm. Not buying it, Ollie. He's got a name, and I'm going to figure it out one way or another. You've been warned, boyo."

She flashed him a huge grin. Oliver shook his head. Why did he think she was so much fun to be with?

Moira went back to entering data at a fast clip. She said, "Let's go out for a gargle tonight. I'll buy you a pint or nine in exchange for the story." She turned slightly and cast him a sweet smile, all teasing gone. "You look like you need to unload on someone that will tell you that you're fabulous and worth your weight in gold. I just happen to be that someone; would you look at that? Convenient, aye?"

Oh, right. That was why.

* * *

Moira teased him for the rest of the day, trying out names for his "mystery man" to see if they'd get a reaction. "Barnaby Rumplenutz, Esquire" was his personal favorite. He was able to actually focus on work with her teasing him; it seemed like any other day.

With her backpack slung over one shoulder, she asked, "Meet you at the pub later? Now that you've broken that footie's heart, do us a favor and bring him along, and let me ease him through the rough times that no doubt lie ahead, aye? There's a good lad." She chucked him on the chin, grinning hugely, and sailed out of the room—no small feat for such a tiny elfling.

As he logged off the university's computer and headed home for dinner, everything that work had pushed out of his thoughts came rushing back.

He didn't know what he'd do when he saw Seth. Yell at him? Cry? Babble like a moron and come off like a lovesick stalker?

But that was stupid, because he wasn't going to talk to Seth. What would they have to say that they'd not said already?

Oliver shrugged his shoulders up to his ears to try to keep the wintry chill from blowing through him and ducked into a café for some takeaway. The smell of curry and cinnamon dominated the room, making him feel homesick, somehow. He stared up at the board willing something delicious to make itself known.

* * *

Fall, Five Years Ago

"... I never thought I'd like curry, Oliver. I mean, please. You've seen the options available back home. But Geoffrey took me to this one place last night, and it was *amazing*. I hate admitting I'm wrong, because—as you know—I never am, but I practically moaned an 'I'm sorry' around the most delicious bit of saag paneer I've ever had in my life."

Oliver blinked rapidly, holding his phone with both hands. "You were with Geoffrey last night? You told me that you had to study, so that's why we'd talk today?"

"Oh! Well, I was. I did study, I mean. Geoffrey just came in and made me stop. He said I was working too hard, and we went out for a quick dinner. Is that a problem?"

Oliver bit his lip. He wasn't going to make a mountain out of a molehill. He knew better than anyone how hard Seth studied. That made sense. "No, sorry. Just...I've missed you, that's all."

"Mm, I miss you, too."

Oliver sighed on his end of the line. Seth sounded distracted.

"Hey, if this is a bad time, or you have too much work, I'll understand."

He could hear Seth shifting.

"Oliver, I just—I really miss you. There are so many things that happen every day, and I want to turn to you and tell you all about it, but you're not here, and it's just hard. And then I get onto myself for being melancholy when we promised each other we wouldn't mope, and then I feel guilty if I'm *not* thinking of you."

He needed to be glad that Seth was sticking to the plan. Oliver didn't need to feel depressed just because there were times when Seth didn't think of him. That was insane. He was being insane.

"I want you to be happy, Seth. I want you to enjoy this... this experience. My God, you're in New York! You're doing it; it's happening." Oliver sighed into the phone. "I just wish I could be there with you, that's all."

After a moment, Seth said softly, "I really love you, you know."

They could do this. They could make it work. All they needed was to remember that they were in love and were destined to be together, no matter what people said about high school romances never working out. Oliver knew they would beat the odds, knew it down to his core.

Oliver smiled against his phone. "I love you, too."

* * *

Someone behind him gave him a nudge; he realized he'd been standing in line, not ordering.

"Right. Sorry. Um, paneer, the cumin lamb chops, uh, two, please. And lentil cakes, thanks."

He stood off to the side while he waited for his order to be boxed up. He hadn't thought about *him* in years until yesterday, and here he was thinking about him again. *Geoffrey*. He sighed to himself. Geoffrey hadn't been the real problem with Seth, but Oliver's reaction to him hadn't helped their relationship, either.

Oliver had gotten pretty sick of hearing about Geoffrey that first semester Seth was away. Geoffrey was an amazing singer, had taken dance since he was a fetus, was *so graceful*, wore haute couture. And he always seemed to be wherever Seth was. What a dick. Oliver knew that he could trust Seth; that hadn't even been a question. He just hated the thought of this flashy dancing jerk fawning all over *his* boyfriend. It was clear to

Oliver that the guy was into Seth. But then, why wouldn't he be?

"Paneer, lamb chops?"

Oliver looked up and stuck two fingers in the air. "That's me." He laid the money on the counter, said, "Keep the change," and grabbed his food. He crossed over to the rail station for the short ride back to his neighborhood and walked the last two blocks at almost a trot.

Oliver fumbled at the door for his key, jostling his packages and messenger bag, until he was able to wedge his foot in the gap of the door and slither through. The heavy wooden door closed behind him with a solid thump. The house was completely quiet; Janos wasn't home yet.

Sighing, he unpacked his dinner. Which was already cold. He turned on the stove—*the cooker,* he reminded himself—and went about transferring his food to a pan. What a day this was turning into! While his food heated up, he unpacked his messenger bag and organized his papers for the next day. Tonight would be a good night to go for a drink with Moira; he could really use the distraction. Tonight she could be the perfect lifeline to pull him from the abyss of his painful memories. As he waited, he felt the draw of the worst of them, dragging him down into the dark.

* * *

MAY, FIVE YEARS AGO

"You live near Little Italy, but you want to go to Tony's Italian Palace in Topeka? Really?"

Seth laughed as he finished lacing up his boots. "For old times' sake. I'm feeling strangely nostalgic this weekend." He waved his hand in a flippant manner. "Now that I've had authentic Italian food, I want to see how it measures up."

Grinning, Oliver said, "It will be like comparing Boone's to a Rothschild."

"Well, aren't we the little bon vivant?" Seth's phone pinged with an incoming text, cutting off his laugh. He made an apologetic face at Oliver, who was trying to control his blooming irritation.

"Can we just have one night without him constantly interrupting?"

"Don't be like that, Oliver; he's my friend. Give me two seconds to tell him that my gorgeous boyfriend is taking me to dinner."

Oliver finished tying his shoe and tried to ignore the knot in his stomach, the one he named "Geoffrey." He just didn't want to share Seth. Not this weekend. He'd shared enough. "He does this on purpose, I swear."

Seth rolled his eyes, his thumbs flashing across the screen as he wrote out a reply. "Are we really going to have this conversation again? It's not like that. And every time you insinuate that it is, I feel like you're saying that I'm encouraging it. The 'it' that isn't there."

"I know. You're right. Just... I want you all to myself," Oliver said, smiling shyly. "And I don't want to talk about him, or whatever amazing thing he's doing in the Hamptons."

Seth finished his message, hit send, and raised an eyebrow. "Oh? And what *do* you want to talk about? What color we're going to paint the main room of our apartment? If you should bring those six hundred thread-count sheets of your mother's? Because the answer is yes, Oliver. The answer to that is always yes."

Oliver smiled, grateful for the levity. "That's kind of what I wanted to talk about tonight. Well... we haven't really talked about things since you got here. Future things. We've kind of been avoiding it."

His eyes flicked to the ground, a nervous habit he couldn't shake. It was the conversation he'd been dreading for weeks now, the one that he and Seth had been skirting anytime it came up. Well, Oliver was skirting it; Seth didn't actually know the topic was constantly being avoided because of an eight hundred-pound gorilla named Oliver's College Choice.

As soon as Oliver had mentioned the smaller university outside of Boston as a possibility back in February, the discussion about when Oliver was going to come to New York had become an "if." Oliver simply hadn't wanted to add to Seth's stress as his freshman year came to a close at Juilliard by hashing out pros and cons, so the topic had been dropped all spring.

Seth switched off his phone and set it on Oliver's dresser, whose edge he held as if to steady himself. His voice was quiet as he asked, "You're taking the internship this summer, aren't you?"

Oliver closed his eyes. He couldn't stand to see that look of impending doom on Seth's face, not after the amazing day they'd had—a day when they pretended that nothing mattered beyond them being together, touching each other again. Seth looked wounded, as if he'd held his hand out only to have it slapped away. Which, Oliver realized, was what he'd done. In a manner of speaking.

"It's an amazing opportunity, Seth. One I can't pass up."

Seth fussed with the cuff on his shirt, not looking Oliver in the face. "Which means you'll be going to Massachusetts in the fall, correct?" He looked up, then, and the last tendrils of warmth and security Oliver felt from the day faded at the enormous hurt in Seth's eyes.

"We talked about how this might happen."

"No, we glossed over it, once. Because I was led to believe that nothing would keep you from New York. Or from me."

"It's not about me staying away, Seth, or wanting to. You have to know that." Oliver blinked, trying to control his own emotions. He still wasn't ready to accept that they couldn't make it work. Deep down, he wondered if he were fooling himself just so he wouldn't have to face it dead on. "Look, I don't have the pick of schools I thought I would. Brandeis is amazing and they have staff that is at the forefront of the research I want to do. I—I have to go there. Columbia didn't want me." He smiled lamely, going for self-effacing but ultimately just feeling pitiful.

"*I* want you. But God, Oliver. Am I always going to have to work so hard just to *have* you?"

Oliver took a step forward and grasped Seth's bicep loosely, unsure if Seth would allow it. Seth didn't move closer, just kept his arms crossed and his eyes downcast. Oliver dropped his hand and pleaded, "You have me. You always will. We can... we can still get together on the weekends. We didn't have that before; we can—"

"And what about when I have a performance on the weekend? Or a project I have to work on? Or *you* have projects and research and whatever else it is that you end up doing? We've been drifting further and further apart for months. We keep pushing off Skype dates; we text on our way to other places with other people, and Oliver, I just can't keep doing this. It hurts too much."

He sounded so tired. Oliver wanted nothing more than to pull Seth to him, to rewind the conversation and make none of this happen. "I didn't want to bring any of this up until dessert. At least. One last dinner before—"

Seth looked up, his face stricken with grief. "Last? One last?"

"I didn't mean it like that! I meant one last meal before we talk about where we're going," Oliver said. "I have this week after graduation before I head out for the summer. I had plans for us, you know. Things we could do together before we have to, well, wait again."

"Plans I knew nothing about. So I don't even get this *summer* with you? The thought of that was all that kept me—" Seth dropped his head, his voice choked as he said, "I can't keep waiting for you to come to me, Oliver. To figure out that you should be with me. Do you remember Bakerfield? How many months I waited for you to just go out with me? To stop being afraid of your dad knowing you liked another boy? I've been waiting all year for you to get to New York, and now you're not even coming? Is it settled? Like you went ahead and registered? I told you about the place on Washington Square just three weeks ago, and *now* is when you're telling me this?"

Seth stared at the ceiling; Oliver fixated on how Seth's Adam's apple bobbed as he fought back tears.

Oliver's voice, choked with his own unshed tears, was almost a whine. He needed Seth to understand, to forgive him. He said, "A recruiter came out to meet with me when you were in the middle of rehearsals. They all but begged me to reconsider. I didn't want to upset you when I knew how stressful your class load was. I just—couldn't find the right time. Seth, it's—they have everything I want."

So quietly it was almost a whisper, Oliver heard him say, "No, they don't."

"Oh, no. No, I didn't mean it like that. Oh, please—"

Seth shuddered out a sigh. "I can't keep doing this. I can't keep waiting. I've waited my whole life in this fucking town to be free, to be myself and to be able to love *you* without worrying about getting beaten up for it, and I can't keep doing it."

"Yes, you can. We can. I mean, it's going to be hard, sure, but—"

"You don't know how hard it's going to be, Oliver." Seth wiped at his face, twisted with grief. "You've had your family and your things and your friends all year. You didn't have to find your way all over again, try to force people to take you seriously. Lie alone in bed every damn night, dreaming of a few more months down the road when your boyfriend would finally be there with you. And then your dream life of living in New York could finally—*finally*—begin."

Oliver didn't really know what to say. He stared at a spot just to the left of Seth's head, unable to make himself see what this was doing to Seth, to accept that he was responsible for the pained noises being wrenched from Seth.

"This can't be how I live my life." Seth yanked a tissue out of the box on the dresser, pressed it against his face and took a few breaths. "I'm not going to keep feeling this way, Oliver. It's not fair. Not to either of us."

Oliver's mouth was dry; he swallowed a few times. He noticed his hand was shaking. "Seth. What—what are you saying?"

"I'm saying that I can't do a long-distance relationship. It's *awful* wanting you and not *having* you. You can't keep doing this to me."

"I'm not trying to do—*Seth*. And—you left me! I was left here in fucking Kansas without you. Shit. I'm not upset you went to New York. Obviously that was the right choice for you."

"Just not for *you*. All of a sudden. After two-and-a-half years of building this dream together, since we first started *dating*, Oliver." Seth buried his hands in his hair as if he thought of tearing it out. "God. You... You just can't make me keep waiting. I can't keep feeling like this; you can't keep making me *feel* like this."

"This isn't happening." Oliver covered his face with both hands. He felt completely drained. They'd fought in the past: sometimes good-naturedly, sometimes not. But this was different. Seth sounded so *resigned*. This was why he hadn't wanted to bring it up. He couldn't stand the thought of causing this pain, not to Seth. But he knew it was a good decision for his future career, even if it was destroying his heart and Seth's.

"No, but—Seth, Boston isn't that far. We can do this. We can! It's so much closer than Kansas; it's just a few hours by train."

"It may as well be the moon. It's not New York. You'll get busy—you don't even *know* what it's going to be like. You promised me. Oliver, you *promised* me." Seth's voice broke.

Oliver looked up to see Seth, shaking, begin to cry; Seth looked as if he'd been betrayed, adding another layer of guilt and anguish to Oliver's shoulders. He reached out to pull Seth into his arms; this wasn't how it was supposed to be. Seth twisted out of his grasp. "Please don't touch me right now."

"Seth, I love you."

"I love you, too. But I don't love us. Not like this." Seth wiped blindly at his face. His chin jutted out, and his eyes were red and swollen. "Tell me you do. Tell me that you love this. You love the thought of four more years of nothing but emails, hurried phone calls, texts here and there."

It was as though the light was going out of the world; he couldn't *breathe*, this hurt so much. "Boston isn't—" Stubbornly, he huffed out a breath. "Seth, I can't go to New York. Not for the degree I want. Not for the career I want. NYU just isn't the school for my undergraduate work. I need—it's just not the right fit after all. Things just... changed."

"I can see that. And *now* is when you tell me, when you've decided everything without me." Seth's face closed down, and Oliver wanted nothing more than to apologize, to take Seth back to his bed, where they'd spent the day, and never let go.

Oliver knew that he was begging Seth to refuse to see the inevitable. He was begging himself not to see it. "My feelings haven't changed. I love you. I want to be with you."

Seth's laugh sounded hollow, like a clap in an empty room. "If you did, then you would."

"It's not that simple!"

"It is. It is for me, at least. You *could* be in New York going to a great school, but you won't—"

"Look, I changed everything for you, Seth." Oliver felt out of control, as if his future plans were roaring past, and he couldn't hold on to any of them unless he faced all of this mess that had been building up ever since the rejection letters had started to come.

"You know that when I came out and started dating you my dad cut me out. No more music lessons, no more family vacations, God, he wouldn't even *look* at me. My GPA was screwed, remember? Yeah, he came around after you left—"

Seth snorted. They both knew it was because Mr. Andrews didn't like how "effeminate" he found Seth to be. Nor did he approve of Seth's working-class background, or rather, Seth's rough-looking biker dad.

"I've had to add to my extracurricular activities so the colleges I wanted to go to would even bother *looking* at me. And NYU just doesn't have the curriculum in music theory and social justice that I need. It's not my dream school, Seth. This is how it has to be."

"Please." No venom. No anger. Seth was asking Oliver in his beautiful voice, so soft and so filled with need. Oliver wanted to tear his hair out, wanted to kick the furniture over, wanted to find a way to physically change geography, bend it to his will.

"I—I can't, Seth. I'm sorry, but I can't go to a school that doesn't offer what I need to learn just so we're close. I have to think about my future, too."

Seth clutched at his throat and swallowed convulsively to stop the broken sob he couldn't hold back. "I *was* thinking about your future. The one with me in it."

Oliver sank to the floor, his back against his bed. "Oh... Seth." His hands twitched, needing to reach out, to stop this.

"I can't stand another year, wait—" Seth laughed bitterly. "Another *four* years of seeing your life through Facebook updates. I know you don't want that either. You've been pretty clear on your feelings about my friends."

"Not friends, Seth. Just the one."

Seth shook his head, clearly angered by the turn in topics. He wiped at his face with the palms of his hands and attempted to get his breathing under control. As much as Oliver hated to upset Seth, he couldn't help himself; they were going to get it all out. Maybe if all of the puzzle pieces were laid out, they could find a way to put their relationship back together.

Oliver's head dropped, and he focused on his hands. He couldn't look at his boyfriend. "You took him to our spot, Seth. You took him to what was going to be our spot, the place you wrote about, and you took a picture in the crowd with your arms around each other." He held up a hand to silence Seth's protest. "Even though it wasn't sexual, I do know that. But *we* were supposed to stand on a corner with people all around us who didn't care. *We* were supposed to have pictures with our arms around each other, cheek to cheek, looking happy. And you've been giving all those firsts to someone else."

"Because you won't let me give them to you!"

Oliver rested his head against his bed and tried to stretch his throat, to push the lump that was choking him out of the way.

"It's not about that. It's... I can't. I can't be there. I'm not going to be there with you." He could barely say those last words, it hurt so much; but he had to say it, had to hear himself say it. No more pretending that it would happen at some far-off point in their future. Oliver felt the hot tears roll down his cheeks.

Seth covered his face with his arm, taking deep, shaky breaths. "I can't do this anymore. Oliver, I can't *breathe*. Oh, God... I have to go. I can't be here. I can't... It feels like I'm *dying*. I have to go."

"Wait. Seth, wait." Oliver's voice wavered from the sorrow that choked him. He scrambled to his feet as Seth randomly shoved his things into his bag.

"Seth." If he could just touch him, if he could just hold him, this would somehow be okay. It would be better; he knew it. "Don't do this."

Seth took a step backward as Oliver tentatively reached out, his hands clutching at the shoulder strap of his bag. "I'm not doing this. It's just... God, it's just happening, Oliver. I can't stay here, I—" Seth stumbled in the space between Oliver's body and the wall, moving away.

Oliver's chin dropped; tears ran freely down his face as his life crumbled around him. He looked up as Seth walked out the door and to the staircase. Oliver fixated on how Seth's shirt from last night was jammed in the bag, a sleeve hanging out. That Seth—overly fussy and hyper-vigilant about his things—hadn't carefully put his clothes into his bag... that little bit of disarray was it. This was really happening.

Seth flew down the stairs. Oliver remained frozen at the top landing, almost paralyzed by heartache and helpless to do anything about it. Seth paused at the front door, his hand trembling briefly on the heavy pewter door pull. His voice was pained, yet resolute. "I love you, Oliver. I always will."

The click as the door shut, closing off those parting words, was a like a blow to the solar plexus. There was no air, and the ache in Oliver's core radiated like a sonic boom, shattering everything in its wake.

* * *

The smell of curry, warm and enticing, pulled him back. Oliver realized he was clutching the front of his shirt and that his eyes were wet. That had been one of the worst days of his life, if not the worst. He had stood at the top of the stairs for a long time, willing Seth to materialize and take it all back. The next few days had been a hazy fog of heartache, a progression from laying in his bed, smelling Seth's aftershave on his pillowcase, to laying on the floor, unable to control the ache and the self-pity when he realized he would never have that luxury again.

He switched off the stove, pulled out the food and stared at it. He didn't feel hungry after all. And he certainly didn't feel like going to see the person whose heart he broke and who broke his in return.

Chapter Three

Oliver hunched over the bar, nursing his beer. He had managed to eat a little of his dinner, knowing that a drink or two with Moira tended to be six or seven, and it would be a bad idea to get drunk on a school night. He laughed a little at himself for that phrasing. Old study habits were hard to break.

Someone threw an arm around him and gave him a squeeze. "How's the talent tonight, eh?" He smiled at Moira, her cheeks pink from the cold, as she unwound her many layers. He signaled for a drink for her while she hung up her coat and scarf.

"Christ, it's as cold as a welldigger's arse in January out there." She climbed up on her bar stool and nudged his shoulder with her own. "Cheers," she said to the bartender, taking a long drink. She smacked her lips and fixed Oliver with a huge grin. "Right. Now tell me who's had your knickers in a twist the past two days?"

Oliver dropped his head to the bar and groaned a little.

"Oh, Christ." Moira crossed herself quickly as she muttered, "Forgive me." She settled more comfortably in her seat and laid her hand on Oliver's arm, giving him a little shake. "All right, Ollie, are we slagging off or mourning tonight? Give us a hint, would you?"

Still slumped forward on his arms, Oliver turned his head to face her. "I hadn't thought of him in years, Moira. Well, that's not true." He sat back up and took a long drink from his beer as Moira patted his back, all sympathy.

"He's always been in the back of my mind." Oliver laughed sharply, a hard and bitter sound. "You know Number Twenty-three?"

Moira looked confused for a moment, then brightened. "Oh, the sweet-faced dandy? The one bordering on twink? Oh, sorry, mate. I never can remember if that's offensive; you know the company I keep and the mouths on them."

Oliver waved her off. "I just realized yesterday that he's a lot like him. Like Seth."

"So we have a name!" She motioned for the bartender to bring Oliver another pint. "And just how is Number Twenty-three like this Seth fellow?"

Oliver fumbled with his smartphone and pulled up his email. He tapped on the video link in Gus's message and handed over the phone. It wasn't easy to hear over the din of the crowd, but she'd get the idea well enough. "Wait for the hosts to stop talking. That's him."

Moira held the phone close, her head cocked to pick up the sound over the bar's noise. Oliver watched her face, not the video. Her eyes widened as Seth began to sing, and after a moment she was smiling, entranced.

"Yeah, he has a tendency to do that to people," Oliver said softly, taking a long drink.

"Hmm?" She could barely tear her eyes away from the performance.

He toyed with the coaster under his beer as she finished watching the clip. She exhaled loudly and handed him back his phone. "You knew this bloke?"

"Knew him? Um, *intimately*. That's rude; I'm sorry."

She cackled. "And here I was wondering if you were a monk."

"Well, lately." He sighed again. "He's amazing, right?"

Moira fanned herself. "All that and looks, too? No wonder you look like your mam died. Oh, bollocks. She didn't, did she?"

At Oliver's eye roll, she continued. "So what happened there? I'm going to get it out of you, one way or another. The other way involves me getting you so shitted that you pass out at my flat. And I won't be held accountable for what I might end up doing to you in such a state." She winked.

Oliver didn't believe that wink, though. "I'm not going to forget that night when you tried to make out with me, you know."

She faked a pained sigh with her hand over her heart. "Ah, you can't blame a girl for thinking I could get you gee-eyed enough that you might forget I have the wrong bits, you handsome bastard."

He laughed. It felt good, the first time he'd felt relaxed in a few days.

He laid his cheek on his hand, smiling at her. "He's evidently the latest thing on Broadway."

"Oh?"

"And my friend back home got me tickets and is sort of forcing me to see him."

"Forcing you, is he? The bastard."

"Okay, so he's not *forcing* me," Oliver said. "I just don't know if I should go. He... Seth might not want to see me. I'm pretty sure he won't want to see me, actually. Or know that I was there. Or that I still exist."

"And what's wrong with this boy, thinking such things about you? If he does, he's clearly a bloody idjit. Not worth your time." She tried to hide a smile as she polished off her beer, but Oliver caught it.

"It's nothing wrong with him, and everything wrong with me." He took a deep breath and turned to face her. "Do you want the long or the short of it?"

She eyed their glasses, motioned to the bartender, and said, "We're not drunk enough yet for the long of it. Sum it up for me so I know how to wail properly when we're too fluthered to hold back."

"Flu..." Oliver shook his head. He wasn't drunk enough to understand her. "Well, once upon a time there was a young man—"

"It's you, isn't it? Got it in one." She laughed and took a drink of her new beer.

"*There was a young man,*" he said pointedly before laughing. This had been a good idea. He needed someone who didn't know the whole story to just listen and help him make sense of how he was feeling. "Who went to a very snooty but fair private school and was very much in the closet. When the cutest boy he'd ever seen transferred mid-term after being bullied out of his other school for being gay, that young man decided to 'mentor' the new kid to help him ease into prep school life by—"

"Snogging him senseless!"

Oliver sat back, a sour expression on his face. "Are you going to let me tell you the story, or are you going to just make one up?"

"From the sound of it, mine's going to be more exciting. Also, I thought we said the short of it?"

Oliver rolled his eyes. "Seth'd been viciously bullied at his high school. His dad—who is the nicest guy but looks like he eats metal for breakfast,

I mean seriously, he's the epitome of a biker—sued and got them to send Seth to my school because it had a zero tolerance policy for harassment. I was assigned to show him around the campus—"

"Lucky you," Moira chuckled.

"Exactly," Oliver said, grinning. "We got along great from the start. He really was my best friend. And I was young and stupid and too scared of my dad to come out beyond school, not to mention that I didn't want to mess up our friendship until I just couldn't help but notice how amazing he was. Talented, yeah. You've seen that for yourself. But... he was such an enigmatic person. Really self-possessed. And he didn't suffer fools."

"I like this bloke already! Life's wasted on the stupid."

"True. He's so funny. And smart. And he never let me get away with being full of myself, and I had a tendency to imagine that I had my shit together back then. Boy, I really didn't."

Oliver took a long drink, remembering how Seth's face had lit up as Oliver gave the school tour; how relaxed Seth had become when he realized Oliver was also gay; how Seth had opened up about what happened to him; how Seth was the most beautiful boy Oliver had ever seen; how he sounded when singing, his fierce, proud spirit clearing away the fog of fear in Oliver's brain, allowing him to finally defy his father's homophobia and give in to his feelings.

"We fell in love. We did everything together; that was when I knew you could be best friends *and* in love. That made it better, you know? There was so much trust and... I just knew I could be *me* with him. That even though I *was* me, he still wanted me."

Moira covered her heart with one hand and grabbed Oliver's with the other, giving it a squeeze. "You're about to make this cynical old cow cry in her beer!"

Oliver laughed, but it was wry, weak. "He was my first. I was his, too. Just... not just with sex, but with everything. My first love, my first true friend, my first honest critic. He always told me the truth, even when it hurt. But he wouldn't say things to hurt me, I don't mean like that. He just wanted me to be my best. I was. When I was with him, I was my best."

"Christ, lad, you're breaking my heart."

"Tell me about it." They were quiet for a moment, Oliver nursing his drink and Moira not wasting any time with hers.

Oliver continued. "He graduated—oh, he was a year ahead of me—and went to New York. The plan had been for me to join him. I wanted to go to Columbia; he went to Juilliard. And I just realized yesterday that the entire reason I took up this particular branch of study was because of him."

She hummed and made a "continue" gesture with her hand.

"I said that he'd been bullied, and God, it was terrible. I knew a little something about it, too." Oliver unconsciously rubbed at his side, where two of his ribs had been fractured over a decade ago, before he'd gone to Bakerfield. "And I wanted to know *why*. What makes people think it's okay to behave this way? To think this way?"

"Well, my reason's not as noble as your own," Moira said. "I just find it fascinating to know how people tick. Plus it does some good in the world, aye?"

They clinked glasses.

"So, he was in New York; I didn't get into Columbia and didn't want to go to another school in the city where I'd just be a number in a classroom. Instead, I chose to go to a university that was smaller and specialized in this field. It was a five-hour trip to New York, and that was unacceptable to Seth. Well, that's not fair." Oliver dropped his gaze to the bar top and nodded to himself. "It was too difficult for him. It was difficult for both of us."

Moira, already on her third beer, gestured with it toward Oliver's face. "So you didn't want a long-distance relationship, and you were young and foolish, is that the telling of it?"

"Well, I wanted it. He wouldn't do it. Couldn't," he corrected himself. "He couldn't." Oliver downed the last of his beer and thanked the bartender as he immediately set down another. They came here often, and the bartender knew Moira's habits.

"So, it ended. Neither of us wanted that, but what could we—" Oliver exhaled sharply and drew his finger along the old wood of the bar. "I was so glad to see him, though. Just... so *proud* of him." He swallowed past the lump in his throat and looked over at Moira, wanting her to understand that he really was. He truly wanted nothing but good things for Seth, even if he couldn't be a part of it the way they'd dreamed. Even if he still wished he could be a part of Seth's life. God, how pathetic. One look at Seth Larsen and all those feelings came rushing back, choking him with the force of how much he still cared.

Oliver ran a hand through his hair, trying to clear his head and get to what mattered. "Seth being successful, finally being seen as the talent that he is? It was so good to see that. For his sake, of course," he said, fixing Moira with a pointed look.

"You still love him, don't you? I can see it plain as the nose on your face." She gave his side a squeeze and rested her head on his arm; she was too short to reach his shoulder. "Oh, broken hearts... I'd rather a broken ankle, meself."

Oliver squeezed back and asked, "Who was he?"

She sighed, clutched at her heart and said dramatically, "The man I plan on marrying. I haven't any idea who he is, I just know the bastard's late in coming, and I'm fair sick of waiting."

He laughed as she nudged his shoulder. She smiled. "That's what I've wanted to see." She offered her glass up in salute. "For Seth and the unknown man who will have my heart one day. I've known many, liked but a few, and loved only one. This toast's for you." They clinked their glasses and as Oliver took a drink, Moira drained her entire glass.

She clapped her hands together while her empty was taken away and a new glass filled. "So, let's start the planning, shall we?"

"...What?"

"You'll be back in the States for over a month; are you daft? That's plenty of time to remind him that he still loves you, too."

"I don't think—"

"Exactly." She bumped him with her shoulder, tottering on the bar stool a little bit. Oliver wasn't sure how many beers she'd had, but she was still upright, which, Moira had once told him, meant that she wasn't drunk. "You're not thinking. So! Let me help you out there."

He propped himself up on the bar, his chin on his hand, and made a "go on" gesture with the other.

"The last thing you'd want to do is make a spectacle. Forget what the movies want you to believe; we hate that sort of thing. Sweet and heartfelt: that's the way to a person's heart. And when you've been wounded..." She looked off at the crowd, shaking her head a bit as she absentmindedly patted Oliver's knee. "You just want to hear that the other person was sorry. Even if they weren't fully in the wrong. You can't beat yourself up for wanting a proper education, Ollie. And if this Seth is as wonderful as you're painting him to be, and if he's an adult, he'll know it. It might take a lot of talk on your part for him to see it, but he'll know it."

"So, what? I just corner him and say I'm sorry over and over until he finally falls into my arms? You're a terrible planner." Oliver blinked a little. He was starting to feel the effects of the beer.

"Pfft, shut your hole, I'm not finished yet. No mind for romance, this one." Moira rolled her eyes at the bartender, who nodded briefly and moseyed to the other side of the bar. "Write him a letter. Use your best paper, your best penmanship, and tell him just what you told me. You'd make the devil himself choke up, you would. Have it delivered to him at the theater and be sure to leave him a way to contact you, but don't make it seem like he must."

Oliver stared at her for a long moment. "I am so sorry I told you that you were a bad planner. You are a really, really good planner."

"This is why I keep you. I love being showered with compliments. Give us another."

Oliver grabbed her hand. She was so warm and nice. He was so glad they were good friends. "I'm so glad we're good friends. You are *so nice*. You're like my own personal fairy of awesomeness."

She leaned back on the stool and laughed, giving his hand a squeeze. She had a nice laugh. "You're my own personal awesome fairy too, lad."

He laughed and then forced an angry look. "Hey, that's offensive." He leaned close to her and whispered, "You're not supposed to call me that."

Her face looked serious, and Oliver felt terrible for making his really good friend look serious. She was looking at him as if she was worried. No, that was wrong; he shouldn't do that to his best friend.

"Oliver, darling... I think you might be quite drunk."

"I am no-not," he hiccupped.

"Oh really? Ollie, me love?" She leaned in close and cupped his cheek. "Fancy a snog? Or we could pop back to my place for a shag..."

"What? Moira! I just told you about the love of my *life*! And I thought you were a good Catholic g-girl," he stammered, pulling back.

"Oh, good. I was worried you'd lost your tolerance. I don't want to have to go trawling for a new drinking partner." She ordered another round. "And as for the good Catholic girl, I am!" she said, playing at being affronted. "The Church says I must repent! So I'd better do something to repent *for*, aye? And why waste people's time with something nonsensical, that's how I see it. Give the priests something sexy to think about, and then I'm helping them follow the commandment to repent, too." She tapped her temple and fixed him with a shrewd look. "I didn't get into Cambridge just because of me looks, lad."

"You could have, though. You're really pretty for a girl."

Moira gave his knee a squeeze. She muttered, "Heavens preserve us... Oliver, if you ever think you'd like to try the other side of the playing field, promise you'll come to me first."

He took both of her tiny hands in his, blinking owlishly, and said with all seriousness, "I promise."

She howled with laughter, pushed a fresh beer toward him and held her glass in a toast. "Here's to hoping. And here's to me and here's to you, and here's to friendship and laughter. I'll be true as long as you, and not one moment after."

They clinked glasses again and drank. Moira pulled his arm down to keep him from drinking too much. "If the good Lord grants me wish, I'd rather not have the catch be you gacking all over me just when I get my knickers off."

Oliver thought he understood most of that. He took a long drink of water. Where did that come from? Moira was petting his hair. God, he loved that. "I love that. I love you, too. You're so nice."

Moira sighed. "Feckin' luck of the Irish..."

* * *

Oliver smiled, shushing himself as he stumbled out of his pants, trying to pull them over his shoes and failing. He knew he was leaning against his bed, but when did his bed get so low? He reached with one hand and concentrated on pushing a shoe heel off of one foot, then the other. He leaned back on his hands and flapped his feet until his pants worked their way off his long legs. He raised his arms in a victorious cheer, falling back and sliding to the floor with a thump.

He put his fingers to his lips, shushing himself again. He felt so much better now. Everything was spinning but in a nice way, like those swings at the fair. There were stars at the corner of his vision, and that was nice, too. He liked stars. Seth was a star now; Oliver loved him. Seth was a star and Oliver loved him and Moira—gosh, how great was she? She was going to help him put his life together. That was a good friend.

He nodded to himself. She was. He was going to write a letter. He would say all the things he had in his heart and he would give it to someone who would give it to Seth and then Seth would find him and they'd be happy again and there would be kissing and touching and loving and they wouldn't leave each other again and that was just the best idea ever.

Oliver knuckled away the tears under his eyes and exhaled slowly. "Okay. Okay." He rolled to his hands and knees, clutching at the side of his bed as he tried to pull himself back up. The blanket started to slide off the mattress and Oliver was sliding down, too.

"No!" he cried softly as he fell to the floor, the blanket falling on top of him. This was okay. This floor had been here for centuries; it was good to sleep on. It was a good foundation. Just as he would have with Seth. He slapped blindly at the bed until he felt a pillow and pulled it down to the floor, curling up inside his blanket to make a cocoon of warmth.

Moira was a good friend. But she drank too much. Oliver thought he should mention that sometime. Maybe he should call her? No, she was… where did she go? Oliver blinked, trying to think. Enough light came from the streetlamp outside the window for him to see the dust bunnies under his bed. That was funny. Bunnies. And gross. He was being gross and unclean and Seth was *so* clean all the time and maybe he wouldn't like Oliver being dirty, with dirty floors?

He thought about taking a shower, but he was so warm and he didn't think he could stand up even if he wanted to. Also, he could hear the shower already. He looked down at himself. No, he was still on the floor. Moira! Moira came home with him. And Janos! Janos had come to the pub with his buddies. And they did shots because Janos was happy that Oliver didn't love him. So dumb that *not* loving someone made him like you.

Oliver sat up, smacking his head on the edge of his table. "Ow." Moira! She was here! With Janos! Oh, that was nice. He wanted his friend to be happy. She had been *really* happy when they left.

Sinking back down to the floor, Oliver smiled to himself. He was going to be happy and Seth would be happy and Moira was happy and he didn't really care about Janos and was that mean? No, it was okay because he was just thinking it, not saying it to Janos's face. *That* would be mean.

He pulled his pillow against the length of his body, wrapped his long limbs around it and smiled. Warmth in his core and hope in his heart, he fell deeply asleep.

* * *

Winter, Five Years Ago
Dear Oliver,

I'm beginning to regret my previous stance on not being a stowaway in your parents' luggage. I miss you terribly. I wish that Thanksgiving had worked out, but the Andrewses' ski trip sort of ruined that. Not that I'm upset with you! Only that I had to wait longer. I just wanted to remind you that I am looking forward to seeing you over the Christmas break.

Looking forward. That's not right. I'm desperate *to see you. God, I want to hold you and kiss every inch of you, and we need to be together as much as possible. I don't care if it's at my home, your parents' house, in a car or on a haystack. Well, I do care about the haystack; that can't be as fun as Hollywood would lead us to believe.*

I just want to touch you, remind myself of how warm you are, the way your eyes flutter closed when I kiss you, your smell, the noises you make... God. I am going to need a new shirt of yours, babe, because the swim team shirt you sent me in October has lost its you-ness. It's hard to go to sleep at night without that smell. (Baby, I fucking love how you smell. God, I am so lucky.)

The last letter you sent me... I swear, Oliver, I miss being with you so much it's like a phantom limb or something. You know how hard it is for me to open up to people, but never to you. Not ever. Sometimes it's still hard for me to believe that you care. Not because of anything you do, but because I'm still just not used to it. People caring.

Oh my God, I love you. Just... I'll tell my dad you're going to pick me up at the airport, and let's just be somewhere, just the two of us. Can we? I'll even make a point of wearing a very simple outfit, hint hint.

Eight more days. God, I love you and miss you so much,
Seth

Oliver held the letter to his face and smelled the faint scent of Seth's cologne lingering on the paper. He checked his clock one more time, glad to see that it was finally time to head to the airport and pick Seth up. They had two whole weeks with nothing to do but enjoy each other. Seth's dad hadn't been too happy about missing the excitement of meeting him at the airport, but he'd relented after Seth had explained.

He wasn't sure how he would look Mike Larsen in the eye after today, sure that he would know that Seth just needed to "be" with Oliver. Well, at least Big Mike knew Oliver's intentions with his son were honorable. Maybe not for the next few hours, but big picture-wise he had nothing but the purest of intentions. He smiled to himself as he grabbed his coat and car keys. His parents were letting him take the big luxury sedan. He bit his lip and grinned as he thought about surprising Seth with the seat warmers.

At the terminal he tapped his fingers nervously against his leg and watched the doorway for any sign of perfectly coiffed brown hair. Seth had texted Oliver that they'd landed and to meet at baggage claim. Oliver read the message again, scrolling back up to make sure he'd not been mistaken about the carousel number. His phone buzzed with a new message. "Look up."

Seth was standing a few feet away, grinning hugely. Oliver pocketed his phone, his own face breaking into a wide smile. They met in the middle and hugged tightly, letting go after a moment and shifting their bodies away from each other. Kansas was still Kansas. Oliver kept grinning at him, looking down at his shoes as Seth bumped his shoulder.

"Please tell me you didn't check fourteen bags," Oliver said. "I have *got* to get you out of here and give you a proper greeting."

Seth hummed and tugged on his arm, leaning over to his ear to whisper, "Just the one. And I feel the same way."

As the light flashed and bags began to slide down the conveyor belt, Seth walked briskly to the carousel. Oliver laughed at the sight of a large plaid bag that came bumping down, covered in brightly colored ribbons.

"What?" Seth asked. "I heard that it helps you find your bag more quickly!"

Oliver grabbed the handle and tugged it off the belt. "That's only when it's a black bag, silly."

Seth laughed, practically bouncing on his toes as they wheeled the bag to the parking garage. Oliver got it situated in the trunk along with a carry-on bag as Seth climbed into the passenger seat. Before Oliver turned on the car, he checked to make sure the tinted windows were dark enough from the outside. He'd had the foresight to park the car facing the concrete wall so that the front windshield wouldn't be visible to anyone else in the parking garage.

Oliver clicked open Seth's seat belt and murmured, "Come here." They met over the middle of the console, lips tentative at first, both smiling too hard to kiss properly, until Seth slipped his hand into Oliver's artfully messy black hair and tugged a little.

"I missed this the most, I think," he said, pulling Oliver back for a real kiss.

Oliver held Seth's face in both hands, pressing their foreheads together gently. "I missed you the most. All of you."

Seth whined a little in the back of his throat as they came together again, savoring every touch, taking their time to reacquaint themselves with one another. Oliver slid one hand to the small of Seth's back and held their bodies as close as he could with the barrier between them. His mouth moved from Seth's to his ear and he whispered, "Missed you. So, so much."

Seth pulled back, a watery smile on his face. "Me, too. Please tell me you have a plan, or I'm going to tell you to just get in the back seat already, and damn the consequences."

Oliver laughed, feeling light and happy for the first time in months. "Oh, I have plans," he said, turning the car on. Seth settled back, squirming a bit to get comfortable in the deep leather bucket seat. He reached across and drew his fingers in patterns along Oliver's neck and shoulder as they pulled out of the parking garage and headed home.

＊ ＊ ＊

"Oliver…"

Oliver mouthed along Seth's neck, his hands working at tugging up Seth's sweater so he could feel the soft skin stretched over taut muscle. "Mm, yeah…"

"No, Oliver. *Oliver.*"

Oliver pulled back, hazy with lust. He was straddling Seth in the passenger seat, which was pushed back as far as it would go. They were parked in a secluded area of a state park campground. "What?"

Seth closed his eyes and laughed. "God, I missed you." He tugged on Oliver's hair, already going wild from being handled roughly. "My ass is on fire. The seat warmers were nice for a while, but I feel like I'm being charbroiled here."

"Oh! Oh, right." Oliver blinked, trying to remember what to do that didn't involve his lips on Seth. He twisted back to the dashboard and pushed at a few buttons.

"Thank you. Now get back here and show me how much you missed me."

Oliver grinned. "Yes, sir." He ran a hand through Seth's hair, relishing how thick and soft it was. How long it had been since he'd had the opportunity. Seth inhaled sharply, smiling at Oliver with nothing but love in his expression. Taking Seth's hand in his, Oliver curled their entwined hands up to his chest as he leaned down to press their lips together again. His lips parted when Seth moaned and ground his hips up against him, using the opportunity to slide his in tongue.

Seth pulled his hand away, still kissing him. As Oliver moved his mouth along Seth's jaw-line and down to his neck, he shivered briefly. He realized that Seth wasn't touching him. Seth was still smiling serenely, but was pulling back. He had nowhere to pull back *to*, Oliver thought, but that wasn't true. They were standing outside in the woods. That was why he was shivering; they were outside by the lake in December. He reached out—how had Seth moved so far away?—and the smile on his face wavered as Seth moved farther and farther into the distance.

Seth was calling to him, but Oliver couldn't hear what he was saying. The wind had picked up—because it was winter and it was cold; why weren't they inside where it was warm?—and it blew away Seth's words. He cried out, but Seth shook his head. He couldn't hear, either.

Oliver was shaking with cold and dread. Seth looked as though he was shouting. The wind picked up, and Oliver strained with everything in him to hear what Seth was trying to say.

"Don't leave me here—"

"Seth! I'm not!"

But Seth was practically disappearing into the background, and why the hell did they ever get out of the car? Oliver was beginning to panic. He couldn't see how to get to Seth, and now Seth was turning away and Oliver could barely see him anymore and he was so *cold*.

"Seth!" He was practically shrieking, trying to get Seth to listen, to stop, to come back. Oliver looked around, trying to find a way to him. There was nothing, no bridge, no ground, just Oliver and the car, and Seth was on the other side of the lake, and the wind whipped through and slammed the door shut—

Oliver jerked awake. He rubbed at his face. He felt like death warmed over. His bedroom door had slammed shut, waking him from his dream. But it wasn't just a dream; it was a memory, too. That day still clung to him, how much he'd just needed to hold Seth after being apart for so many months. But they hadn't gotten out of the car; they'd kissed and touched and brought each other off so quickly it would have been embarrassing if they weren't both so needy.

He lay back, shivering as he tried to push away the dread of the nightmare. "What the...?" He looked around and saw that he was tangled up in a blanket on the cold floor, only wearing briefs. He sat up and regretted it immediately. He grabbed his head, pressing at his temples to keep his skull from flying apart.

The wind blew through his window, ruffling the cover on his lap. A memory of prying open the window in case he needed to throw up—stupid drunk logic—came back to him. He crawled to the window on all fours and pushed until he could force the old thing to shut completely. He slumped back against the wall and breathed through his nose until the nausea wound down.

That day—that visit—was the last time they'd been together without the worry of the future pressing in on them. The plan for Oliver to join

Seth in New York after graduation was still the intention. Their families had given them the space to be together during the break, understanding that they were older and smart about their relationship. They hadn't given them the all-clear to be intimate in their respective houses, nothing like that, but they didn't harp on them to pay attention to the time or to leave doors open, just gave them room to love each other, whatever that meant.

Oliver smiled to himself briefly, thinking of the New Year's Eve party at Gus's house, how they'd slow-danced and held each other, not caring if anyone whooped or hollered at them to "get a room." They'd kissed languidly at midnight, knowing that the next year would bring them both to their final destination: New York.

Oliver's stomach heaved and he struggled to get to his feet, breathing hard through his nose. After a moment, the possibility of throwing up passed, and he staggered back to his bed and fell on it face-first. He wormed his way under the sheets, pulled the blanket off the floor and onto himself and stared at his side table, which was knocked askew from whatever the hell he'd done in the middle of the night.

Images from the bar came back: beer after beer, Janos showing up and giving him a tight hug, kissing him on each cheek and calling him "my friend Oliver." He thought wryly that Janos was being very affectionate with him now. Boys. Well, *straight* boys, he amended. Janos bought a round of shots, which meant that Oliver felt obligated to buy another round, and Moira kept encouraging them to "be hospitable to one another" to keep the booze flowing. Why the hell did he hang out with her, anyway?

The letter. She had the idea of writing Seth a letter. Now that he was sober, he thought about the merits of that. In a way, he still thought it was a good idea. Romantic. But he'd always thought that he was clumsy when it came to romance. Was this one of those crappy ideas? Say he did write a letter telling Seth that he's always loved him, that he was especially wrong not to have brought Seth into the decision. God, that had really been wrong. To just drop it on Seth as he'd done?

And... that's exactly what the letter would be, too: Oliver deciding to do something and dumping it on Seth. "Hey, I know you've probably not thought of me in years, but I want to mess up your life by making you focus on something painful and awful so I can feel better about it."

It was like that horrible trope in movies in which the person is advised by a well-meaning friend to tell his ex or friend or whoever that he's always loved him, and it's the other person's wedding day. That was just shitty. It was dropping your problem on the other person and waiting for them to fix it. He couldn't do that to Seth, not again.

His stomach lurched again. After his moans died down, he heard talking and laughing from the front room. "Moira!" he croaked. "I am going to kill you! I think you poisoned me!"

The laughing reached a crescendo for a moment, and then he could hear masculine muttering.

"What's all that stramash about in there? Quit being such a girl's blouse and come have some rashers and eggs before Janos eats them all. Oh, you're still hungry, are you?" she said. That last bit was clearly *not* directed at Oliver, if the deep chuckle was any clue.

He moaned into his pillow and pulled the blanket up over his head, whimpering and blocking out the noise of Hungarian-Irish flirting. He couldn't even comprehend how they understood each other. He flashed on a moment from last night, when Janos did a body shot off of Moira's neck. Right. They didn't need to understand much.

Less than two weeks and he could escape back home and never ever drink again.

* * *

After the term's end, Oliver found himself sitting on his parents' sofa pretending to read some boring book that they thought he would love while waiting for the sound of their car backing out of the driveway. Once he knew they were gone, he went upstairs to the attic. The entire open space had been lined with cedar, making it an excellent place to store his mother's furs, their off-season clothing and all the odds and ends they couldn't bring themselves to throw away or donate.

The past two weeks had been incredibly busy as the term came to an end and the team's research picked up. Moira had sent him a few significant looks in their makeshift office, but he just didn't know what to do about her suggestion. The more he thought about sending a letter to Seth, the more he thought how selfish it would be.

And he'd had a sickening thought earlier that day, prompting this little trip of his to the attic: what if Seth was in a relationship? And why wouldn't he be? Seth was amazing, loving, gifted and incredibly handsome and talented. Of course he'd have guys interested in him. Oliver had been in a few relationships over the years; it made sense that Seth would have, too. Or was in one now. Oliver didn't want to dump his own stupidity on someone's happiness.

Better to be stupid in the privacy of your own home, he thought as he switched on the attic light. He would allow himself one night to be pitiful; he'd sort through his things and see how he felt at the end of it. Mostly he just wanted to remember how much in love he'd been, how special that relationship was. With all of the painful memories that had come rushing back over the past few weeks, he wanted to remember the good things, if only so he could brace himself before seeing Seth perform. He still wanted to go to the show. Seth was one of the most talented people he'd ever known. This was a show not to be missed. It seemed right to add to the applause, to the accolades.

Even if he wouldn't have any contact with Seth on the trip, he still wanted to connect in some way. Maybe something here could help him make sense of what to do. He skirted a large armoire that had belonged to some random relative generations ago. Boxes with the words "Oliver's H.S. things" written in shaky handwriting across the labels were stacked neatly and out of the way. He dragged them to a clear space and lined them up side by side.

He sorted through them, lifting their tops until he found the one that mattered. He went still for a moment, holding the top, when he saw the silver frame around the picture they had taken at the end of Seth's prom. Oliver put the lid aside, sank to the ground and pulled the box between his legs. He smiled, tracing the edge of the picture frame. Seth stood proudly as Oliver, eyes shut, arms wrapped around Seth's slender waist, kissed his cheek.

Looking at the picture, Oliver could remember the excitement of getting ready, the fear that it would go wrong and how amazed he'd felt when their classmates let them have that moment. How Seth had walked into the ballroom defiant and proud, almost daring anyone to say anything about them as Oliver trailed nervously behind. How he realized in that moment that Seth was—had always been—the strong one in their relationship.

That was why he didn't need to bother Seth. Seth was strong. He was fine. He was making his dreams come true, and he didn't need Oliver to drop in out of nowhere and remind him of when life hadn't been good. Oliver blew gently on the glass to dislodge some of the fine dust that had accumulated and used the edge of his T-shirt to wipe away a smudge near Seth's face.

He pulled random things out of the box, looking for a small package tied in a pale blue ribbon. He found a manila envelope that he knew held ticket stubs from all the movies and concerts they had gone to. He saw a flash of green fabric and his heart gave a little lurch. After carefully tugging it out, Oliver fanned it out over the opened box. His old Larsen Custom Cycles & Repair shirt. It seemed so funny to him when he first met Seth's dad—they couldn't be more opposite if they'd tried. Where Seth was lean, stylish and graceful, his father was huge, barrel-chested, bald-headed, covered in tattoos and, at the time, sporting a long, braided beard. The first time Oliver saw him, he was terrified.

That is, until Big Mike ("Mr. Larsen's my old man. Call me Big Mike. Everyone does.") grinned at his son and pulled him into a bear hug, kissing Seth's temple. Oliver had offered his hand only to be pulled in for a hug of his own.

"So you're the one who's got my kid happier than he's ever been, huh?"

Big Mike loved his son with everything in him, and after Seth's mom— whom Seth looked like—died suddenly, Seth was the lone recipient of Big Mike's surprisingly tender-hearted affection. Big Mike couldn't care less about Seth being gay, aside from worrying about him being mistreated. Everyone who worked for Big Mike in his shop understood straightaway that a homophobic slur would not only get you fired, but also "get your ass kicked." One look at Big Mike in his leather vest, huge arms crossed in front of his chest, and Oliver felt pretty confident that the biker community in northwestern Kansas supported the LGBT community based on the force of Big Mike's love for his kid.

Oliver was incredibly jealous of Seth's relationship with his father. Fortunately, Mike had quickly begun to see Oliver as an extension of his own son and never left Oliver feeling like an outsider. Seth's house and Big Mike's shop had seemed more like home than his own did; he'd spent more time there, too.

Oliver held the familiar shirt in his hands. It was so soft; it'd been his favorite. He always made Seth wear it, whenever he came home for visits, so it would smell like him again: his skin care products, his cologne, his own smell. Feeling a bit foolish, Oliver held it to his face and breathed in. The familiar scent was long gone from the fibers. That it smelled like musty cotton—and only that—was heartbreaking. Just another reminder of what he'd lost for good. He carefully folded the shirt and set it aside. When he turned back, he spied what he'd been looking for: all of the letters that Seth had written him that first year in New York, carefully stacked in chronological order and tied in a blue ribbon from a gift Seth had given Oliver the summer before leaving.

The handwriting was so precise and elegant; he always got a thrill when there was something in the mailbox with that handwriting on it. When he mentioned, over that first Christmas break, that he was keeping all of Seth's letters, Seth had both blushed and beamed. Later that night he'd shown Oliver just how pleased he was. Oliver's breathing went shallow as he remembered the thrill of being in Seth's house with all of Big Mike's coworkers and friends celebrating while Seth had his hands down Oliver's pants and his mouth on Oliver's neck. Oliver had kept his fist pressed against his mouth to quiet his moans so they wouldn't be discovered in the laundry room.

He knew that Seth had felt neglected by most people for the majority of his life. It was something Oliver never could fully wrap his mind around, though. Seth was interesting, funny, talented and so, so handsome. Once Oliver had stopped worrying about how his dad would react (exactly as Oliver had feared) to his coming out, he let himself open up completely to this amazing, fearless boy who inexplicably loved him back. Of course he would want to keep Seth's letters. Seth told him later, brushing Oliver's hair back in place as Oliver did up the buttons on Seth's shirt, that he simply loved that Oliver thought they were something worth keeping. Which was crazy; everything about Seth was worth keeping.

Why didn't you keep him, then?

But... he couldn't. He wanted to. Did he try hard enough? He flashed back to the agony on Seth's face, the way his own heart felt as though it was shattering inside him. Why? They had loved each other so much. Oliver held the package of letters close, drawing the point of one of the envelope's corners against his lip. And he caught the faintest whiff of Seth's old cologne.

Something in his soul faltered, and he felt a sense of longing so strong that his eyes watered. What was he doing? Why was he doing this to himself? These were nothing but ghosts, tokens from a past love. He gave a bitter, sharp laugh. Past love? He was an idiot if he thought he could convince himself of that. He would always love Seth.

He put everything back, barring the packaged letters and the shirt. Those he carried down to his old bedroom. He just wanted to know where they were, that they weren't molding in a box up in the attic as if they had never mattered. Because they did matter. No one before or since had ever shared his heart with Oliver as Seth had in those letters. He fingered their crisp edges. Well, maybe rereading them wouldn't be a bad idea. They might remind him of happier times; that once he'd been a part of something amazing. That once he had been loved.

Once he was back in his room, Oliver set them on the edge of his dresser and forced himself to get back to the task of packing a travel bag for his trip with Gus. He pushed aside thoughts of opening the package and reading every one of the letters right then, or pulling out a pen and paper and writing one of his own. He didn't have the right to do that to Seth, to tell him how sorry he was, how much of an idiot he had been for not fighting harder, for not bringing Seth into the decision sooner so they could better plan their futures together. He didn't have the right to tell Seth that he never stopped loving him, not really.

He powered through the rest of his packing after making that choice. Finished, he couldn't help but look back at the dresser. He bit his lip, contemplating the small bundle with its blue ribbon. Then he carefully picked it up and wrapped it in a tie to keep the letters from getting bent or crushed, and put it in a corner of his luggage. He didn't want to leave the letters where the maids might mistake them for junk, or worse, ask his parents what they were. It was best to keep them close until he got back from New York.

Chapter Four

Oliver was biding his time; he'd stopped paying attention to the music one state back when he'd been proven right on the barbershop. Who the hell paid money on iTunes for that? Gus, apparently, and clearly just to use as a method of torture. Eventually Gus would slip up and Oliver could take over the music choices.

After a break in the noise Gus insisted on calling music, Oliver dropped the volume to a background hum and asked, "So how's Emily's internship going? She had to leave Boston, right?"

"Mm hmm. She's in D.C. full-time for the next year."

Oliver adjusted his seat to make more room for his long legs in Gus's sports car. Even with their stopover in Chicago, it was a long time in a vehicle. Somehow road trips had been more fun when he was a teenager. "That's rough. How are you doing with that?"

"It's hard, but long-distance relationships can work. And the train ride to D.C. is surprisingly pleasant. I get my best thinking done on that trip. Well," Gus paused, checking his rearview mirror and using his signal before changing lanes, "as long as I get the quiet car. We each get a lot done during the week, and the weekends when we get to see each other make up for everything else."

Oliver looked out the window as they drove, quietly growing irritated. Sometimes Gus was utterly obtuse.

"Oliver. They can work."

Maybe not so obtuse.

Oliver turned back to Gus's profile. "What are you getting at, here?"

"I—" Gus looked briefly at Oliver and seemed to think better of finishing his sentence. "Sometimes I just don't understand what happened. Sorry. It's not my business."

Oliver pressed his heated face against the cold window and bought himself some time to cool off and gather his thoughts. He didn't want to get into an argument.

"Look. We were kids back then. I mean, for God's sake, we met when I was a sophomore in *high school*, Gus. No one ends up with his high school boyfriend. It's a myth. We were good for each other, and then we weren't."

"Bullshit."

"Excuse me?" Oliver turned in his seat to face Gus straight on.

Gus straightened his spine and exhaled slowly. "There wasn't a time when you weren't good for each other. I can buy that things didn't work out because of distance, that you were both young and had a lot of life to get under your belts. That makes sense. But I know what I know: You were good for each other. Always were."

Oliver picked at the hem on the sleeve of his shirt, not trusting himself to look elsewhere. "Why are you doing this? I just want to be happy for him, okay? That's what this is. Let's get real," he said. He turned to face his friend, hoping he looked as if he meant it when he said, "Seth is probably in a very healthy relationship, and I truly wish that he's happy in it."

He was probably lying to Gus and himself about being okay with *that*, but he didn't need to tell Gus about his feelings now.

Gus gave a noncommittal grunt. They drove in silence for a bit, save whatever song was playing.

After a bit, Gus said, "I've known you since you were seven, Oliver. I know how important that friendship was. When Seth showed up at Bakerfield, you immediately knew that he got what it was like to be, well, treated the way you both had been. And I think *you* needed a friend who could understand you in that same way. We all welcomed him, obviously. I certainly count him as a friend, but you two were important for each other. Beyond the intimate relationship. I just worry about you."

"What?"

Gus sighed before saying, "You're letting people slip away, Oliver. Of course it's natural to separate from high school friends, but not all of them." He turned and flashed a quick smile at Oliver. "Obviously, our families' long history together and our fathers' partnership means that my obligation to you is a lifelong commitment—"

"Oh, *thank you*," Oliver laughed.

"But you've been holing yourself up in your research so much that we hardly talk anymore, either."

"Gus, I didn't mean to—"

"Stop it. I'm not angry. You think I haven't been buried in law books and studying these past few years? I understand completely. I just want to make sure that we don't lose touch. And I think it would be good for you to try and have a friendship with him again."

Oliver sat quietly for a few moments. Be friends? And only friends? Listen to him talk about dates or boyfriends? No, he didn't think he could do that. Not with everything that he'd been feeling these past few weeks. But was that childish of him?

Gus made a good point: They had been the best of friends. Oliver had never known anyone who got him the way Seth had, got his corny humor, his need to make people happy, his self-doubts. Seth was the only one who would tell him to stop being self-deprecating, to stand up to his father and stop trying to make his father accept him. Seth would have put Janos in his place right off the bat and had him eating out of his hand by the end of the first week.

He smiled at the thought of it. Seth would love visiting England and would most likely insist on visiting Buckingham Palace and stalking the milliner for the Royal Family. Oliver realized that he had no idea if Seth had even gone to England over the past few years. He might not be interested in the same things as when Oliver had known him; they didn't have that connection anymore.

There was that deep ache again.

"That's a tall order," Oliver sighed. "I don't know that he'd want to see me, let alone talk to me. And that's sort of important for forging a friendship, right? Being able to talk to each other?"

"Just think about it. That's all I ask."

They fell silent. Oliver turned up the music to hear some melancholy number playing. "Come *on*, Gus! Seriously. You've had nothing on but songs about breaking up and regret for the past fifty miles."

Gus bit his lip to hold in his smile. "Don't worry, the gangsta rap cycle is about to start after this song."

Oliver laughed as he rubbed his face with both hands. "As long as there's no more emo, I'm good."

Gus checked the rearview mirror and changed lanes. "Just be glad I didn't put any country on the list. Far less subtle."

"*Less* subtle? That's like saying a lake is less wet than the ocean."

"Technically, that's true. If you're talking about mean volume."

"Oh my God."

As Tupac blasted from the speakers, Oliver drifted off, thinking about whether it could ever be possible for him to have Seth in his life again, but only as a friend. Maybe Oliver just wasn't ready to be that grown-up about things, not when they involved Seth Larsen. And not when he was quite possibly still desperately in love with him.

* * *

The two checked into their respective rooms at the hotel with the intention of meeting up in the bar for a drink before the show. Oliver dropped his bag on the extra chair in his room and fell onto the bed with a groan. He didn't know what he was doing; he could barely keep a handle on his thoughts and his feelings, which vacillated between excitement and abject terror.

He lay there staring at the ceiling, trying to think of a way to get out of going to the show. It was cowardly, he knew. Well, maybe he wanted to be a coward. He groaned and threw an arm over his face. He'd already done the scared routine, when he kept his college plans a secret back then. It was time to face the music. In a dark room where Seth would never know that he'd been there. Like a man.

With a shaky breath, he sat up and got to the task of unpacking his suitcase. They'd be here for a few days; he could at least get some museum visits and good food out of the trip. As he pulled his sport coat out to be hung up, he spied the tie-wrapped package of letters. Was he really going to just sit in a hotel room and read old letters like some pathetic sad sack?

Yep. He unwrapped the tie and laid it flat on the bed. Off went the blue ribbon, and he flipped past the first letter; he'd memorized that back home all those years ago. He saw the mailing address on the second letter and laughed out loud. How had he forgotten that Seth made up names and businesses on some of them?

Cary Grants In Training Institute
c/o Oliver Andrews, President (and also a client!)
134 Nutmeg Ct
Atchison, KS 43081

And a later one:

Preppy Boys Inc. Clothing Warehouse
c/o Oliver Andrews (I can only assume it's in your closet)
134 Nutmeg Ct
Atchison, KS 43081

Oliver looked at the blue and green-striped tie, the shawl-collared sweater and dark gabardine trousers that he'd brought to wear. Well, at least he'd be predictably preppy tonight.

"I think a head start at the bar is in order for the evening," he muttered.

He wrapped the letters back up, grabbed his toiletry bag and headed to the shower.

* * *

When the trio rounded the corner onto Forty-fourth Street it hit him: this was real. Seth was actually performing on Broadway in one of the most beloved theaters in the district. A thrill of happiness ran through him as they walked under the large awning lit up with lights. He was just so damn *proud* of Seth for sticking to his goals and making it through sheer determination. Well, and a broken leg on the original star's part, but hey, that was how the business worked.

Oliver whistled at the poster out front. It featured Seth looking back over his shoulder with the chorus filling in the background. Oliver asked Gus, "So this play is modernized Shakespeare, homosexual, *and* has original rock music? Um... isn't that sort of what *Jesus Christ Superstar* was going for?"

Gus turned his head sharply as he guided his girlfriend, Emily Ishimoto, through the theater doors. "Don't you dare mention Andrew

Lloyd Webber to me, Oliver. The man wrote a musical with people on roller skates, for God's sake."

Oliver held up his hands in an apology, laughing a bit. "Sorry, sorry. But really. People are into this? I never would have guessed."

"It's sold out for the next six months, with every celebrity imaginable showing up for prime seats, so you tell me. We never would have gotten in without the comped tickets."

Oliver eyed the scalpers a few yards off selling tickets at ridiculously high prices and noticed the energy and excitement in the people standing in line. He guessed the theater-going crowd had decided jukebox musicals were gauche and wanted a little culture after all. He'd listened to bits of the soundtrack to get an idea of what the show would be like, and it was very Baz Lurhman-esque.

The buzz and excitement of the theater patrons seeped into Oliver, ramping up his already-heightened nerves. Emily led the way to their seats, followed by Gus, with Oliver bringing up the rear. They had excellent seats, courtesy of Seth, four rows from the front on the right aisle. Emily didn't want to sit at the end of the row, so that seat went to Oliver.

So much for being hidden in the back of the theater.

The loud noise of the crowd prevented him from being able to engage properly in conversation with Gus and Emily, so he left them alone and indulged in a little people-watching. The crowd ran from older Broadway patrons to middle-aged couples—both gay and straight, he was happy to see—to young people about his age and even younger, all thrumming with the excitement that only comes with the theater.

Oliver settled into his seat and flipped through the pages of his playbill, seeing mostly ads and kudos to various investors. He came to the page where Seth's bio was listed and his breath hitched just a bit. He traced the border of the photo with his fingertip. Seth wasn't really smiling; it was a hint of a smile, as if a wonderful thought was just coming to him. Oliver had seen that look more times than he could remember. Seth's eyes looked almost sleepy; his hair was perfect. He looked older, obviously, but he still looked like the boy Oliver had fallen in love with all those years ago.

Seth Larsen (*The Fair Youth/Willie Hughes*) is in equal measures shocked and overjoyed to find himself playing the role of Mr. W.H., making this his Broadway debut. (Get well soon, David! Hmm, not too soon, please?) From humble beginnings in Small Town, USA, a.k.a. Atchison, Kansas, he got his first stage experience while performing with his high school's choir. (Support the arts in schools!) Seth, a graduate of the prestigious Juilliard School, has performed in multiple off-off-off-Broadway productions (read: back alleys and the subway); as an understudy and swing for *Book of Mormon: The Musical*; and in the chorus of *Hairspray*, both on Broadway and in the national touring company. He would like to give the most heartfelt thank you to his loving and supportive father, Michael "Big Mike" Larsen; to the Steel Horse Riders, for sticking up for kids in need; to Bakerfield Prep's Choir for letting a contralto have a solo or five; to Professor Poynter, who always pushed him to hit High F in everything in life; and to his first duet partner, who made him believe he could finally get here.

Oliver's stomach looped a few times before dropping into nothingness, and his heart began to race as he reread the last phrase again and again, almost bubbling over from hope. He shook his head and told himself that Seth must be referring to someone else in choir back in high school. Then he forced himself to take a deep breath. He was being ridiculous. Why on earth would Seth mention *him*? There was no reason at all. Clearly it was someone else.

Except... Oliver was the only duet partner Seth had in choir, right? He couldn't remember. And Seth had mentioned everyone from his old life. Oliver ticked the names off one by one, trying to see who was left out. He didn't mean Oliver, couldn't. It would be incredibly self-centered of Oliver to think that Seth was talking about him. But he couldn't help the tiny thrum of want and hope vibrating in him as the lights dimmed, even though the thought gave him a queer little pang of homesickness.

Oliver murmured, "Here we go," under his breath as the audience quietened and the show began. Smiling, he thought about how Seth-like the bio had been. He loved that Seth hadn't let an assistant or an agent write it for him.

He's still funny. Oh my God... and still unbelievably attractive.

A single spotlight cut through the dark theater, highlighting where Seth sat on a wooden stool, the only decoration on the empty stage. He was dressed simply in period leather breeches and a linen shirt, open at the neck.

After the applause died down, Seth acknowledged the audience. "I just needed work. And Will–pardon—William. He just needed... me."

The crowd, the tiny vibration in Oliver's chair as Gus bounced his leg up and down in the seat next to him, hell, the entire *room* disappeared as he watched Seth bring his character to life. Oliver knew the story was based on the person to whom William Shakespeare had dedicated all of his sonnets, and that some people hypothesized that the mysterious "Mr. W.H." was actually Willie Hughes, a slight and delicate-featured actor from Shakespeare's theater company, The King's Men, and that the two were often lovers. According to this play, W.H., or The Fair Youth, served as Shakespeare's muse.

Oliver watched Seth take full command of the audience, his melodious voice setting the stage for them, briefly explaining how it was common for boys with fair complexions to take on female roles in the theater. He moved lightly across the stage, drawing the back of his hand down his cheek as he said, "A woman's face that nature's own hand painted is the, ahem, mistress of your passion."

Oliver sat transfixed as the Bard fell in love with Willie, who inspired him to write the great plays of his career. The more Shakespeare poured his adoration into Willie, the younger and more ethereal Willie became. One number involved a complicated tango as the two sang a modernized retelling of Sonnet 40 after Shakespeare found Willie flirting with another man. Oliver made a tight fist in his lap when the other man, a dough-faced actor, leered and made a pass at Seth, who was idly playing on a stringed instrument.

"Give the strings your fingers, and me your lips."

Oliver looked away as the two actors kissed passionately, feeling a little sick. He had no right to feel jealousy, and Seth was an actor; it wasn't the same, he reminded himself. Regardless, he felt for William as the actor stormed about, enraged and heartbroken at The Fair Youth's deceit.

"It hurts more to be injured by a lover than an enemy," William cried. "And even if you destroy me with these hurts, don't let us become enemies."

Oliver thought of the term Shakespeare had used only moments before, "lascivious grace," and how perfectly it defined Seth in this role. His linen shirt hung loosely off his shoulders, opened at the neck even farther than it had been at the beginning of the play, giving Oliver a glimpse of Seth's collarbone and the smooth expanse of skin on his torso, barely stippled with faint brown hair. His eyes shone brightly under the stage lights, making their hazel color even more prominent. He simply took Oliver's breath away.

The first act was drawing to its close with Shakespeare stalking about, quoting Sonnet 34, but in plain English. "Why did you make me a promise, like a ray of hope that could dry the tears from my aggrieved face... and what matters that when *nothing* can remove this disgrace? You say you're sorry, but that doesn't take away my pain!"

Seth stood still, his character taking the abuse hurled at him. Oliver couldn't watch the other actor; he only had eyes for Seth and the grief on his face. Oliver felt like he was reliving that horrible moment in his bedroom all over again. Seth's character was finally spurred to action when he realized that his lover was leaving him. "You gave me your heart!" Seth cried. "You... you cannot take it back again!" He collapsed to his knees, and the stage went black.

Oliver was breathing shallowly and keeping a tight grip on the arms of his seat, when he was shaken from his thoughts by Gus.

"You okay? Emily needs to freshen up."

"Hmm? Oh, yes. Sorry." Oliver stood and stepped into the aisle to allow Gus and Emily to use the intermission time as they needed. He sat back in his seat and thumbed through the playbill again, wanting to look at Seth. Not the actor onstage who was ripping his heart out—and God, he was so proud of him; it *hurt,* the sheer amount of awe building up inside him—but Seth. *His* Seth. Well, used to be his.

"He's very good, isn't he?"

Oliver looked up to see that Emily was back. She swept her long, shiny black hair over one shoulder and smiled at him.

"I'm blown away," Oliver said. "I've never really seen him act in a dramatic role. But this... wow." He shook his head and stood up, moving aside and allowing Emily and Gus to get back to their places.

The lights overhead flashed and the rest of the audience took their seats quickly. Gus used the moment to lean in and ask Oliver quietly, "Are you sure you're okay?"

Oliver let out a long exhalation. "He's amazing. I'm glad we came." He turned to give Gus a small smile. "Really. I'm honestly happy for him."

Gus smiled back and gently punched Oliver's shoulder as the music began to crescendo and the curtains pulled open for the second and final act.

William was at a writing desk, looking far older than he had in the first act. Seth looked impossibly younger by comparison as he bounded into the room, filled with life and energy and love. He promised fidelity, but William refused to leave his work and grew angry about the distraction that Seth brought.

Oliver squirmed uncomfortably in his seat at the flash of anger and sadness on Seth's face. Seth—as Willie—continued to press the issue until William pushed back from his writing desk in frustration. He held Seth to him and stroked his back. Seth melted into the embrace until William forced him back, keeping him at arm's length.

William said, "Darling. We two must part, even though our undivided loves are one. Circumstances are forcing us apart, but they cannot destroy what we have together—"

"*I love you, Oliver. I always will,*" Oliver thought with a twinge of misery.

"I may not evermore acknowledge you," William continued. "It would hurt too much to see you and remember the sweet hours we've shared knowing they can't be repeated. But know that my love for you is such that I will always be thinking of you."

A complicated but seemingly effortless transition on stage left it bare again, with Seth standing alone. The more William loved him and poured his love into words that would be remembered for centuries, the more ageless Willie seemed to become. Seth practically glowed with youth and beauty as the lights shone on him, leaving William in darkness. And now he was left alone, trapped by his youthful immortality and denied the person he loved.

Oliver was barely breathing. Every ache that Seth's character felt, he also felt; every high, every low. His eyes began to sting a bit when Willie was given the news of William's death "by fever." The Fair Youth scoffed at that, knowing William better than anyone. He'd drunk himself to death. Seth was handed a bound copy of all 154 sonnets inspired by and dedicated to him.

Not a sound could be heard in the theater but Seth's calm, soft voice as he read the dedication page. "To the only begetter of these ensuing sonnets, Mr. W. H. All happiness and that eternity promised by your ever-living poet."

Seth stood immobile, frozen as he turned the pages, tears freely running down his face. The lights dimmed and a thin fog rolled across the stage. William stepped out of the wings, but he was young once again. He began to recite the most famous of his sonnets, the one every romantic lover since has borrowed to express himself to the person he loves—it would have been sacrilege to modernize it.

"Shall I compare thee to a summer's day?
Thou art more lovely and more temperate:
Rough winds do shake the darling buds of May,
And summer's lease hath all too short a date:"

Seth smiled off into the distance; Oliver couldn't decide if this was a memory or a fantasy.

"Sometime too hot the eye of heaven shines,
And often is his gold complexion dimm'd;
And every fair from fair sometime declines,
By chance, or nature's changing course untrimm'd;"

Seth turned at this, acknowledging the apparition—or ghost of a memory, it wasn't yet clear. "But," William said, running the back of his hand down Seth's cheek. Seth sighed and melted into the touch; something in Oliver's heart fractured a little deeper at the sight.

"Thy eternal summer shall not fade,
Nor lose possession of that fair thou ow'st,
Nor shall Death brag thou wander'st in his shade
When in eternal lines to time thou grow'st:"

William ran his fingers down Seth's arm and laced their fingers together.

"So long as men can breathe or eyes can see," he held Seth's hand to his own chest, over his heart. Seth, smiling through his tears, reached out to cup William's cheek.

William continued, softly and with a bit of ferocity: "So long lives *this*," he kissed their joined hands, "and *this* gives life to thee."

* * *

They fell into one another's arms for one last passionate kiss as the curtain fell. Oliver sat back; he hadn't realized that he'd been leaning forward, hanging on every word. The crowd erupted into applause as the sweeping music from the final moments gained momentum for the curtain call. The bit players came out en masse, including the dough-faced letch who had tried to steal Seth. Oliver didn't really care to clap for him.

William came out, and the applause grew louder until Seth stepped out, giving an elaborate bow center stage, and the audience went nuts, getting to their feet. Cheers and bravos and loud clapping filled the air and sure, a lot of it came from Oliver, but Seth deserved it.

As the cheering continued and Oliver whistled once more, Seth looked in their direction, his hand at his forehead to block the bright stage lights from his eyes. Oliver panicked briefly, not wanting to be seen. He stepped sideways letting the person in front of him act as a shield, which was ridiculous since the old man couldn't have been more than five-and-a-half feet tall. Seth smiled in their general direction; surely he knew where their seats would be.

Oliver sighed in relief as the cast linked hands to bow as one. Seth directed the crowd's attention to the orchestra in acknowledgment, and then the cast stepped back as the curtain fell.

The audience began moving to the exits. Oliver's group hung back, waiting for the crowd to thin a bit before making their way out the door. Gus and Emily walked ahead, their arms around each other as Emily chattered excitedly about the production. As they exited the building, Emily tugged on Gus's arm to make a left.

"Stage door, sweetie." She smiled at Oliver. "He's your friend, right? He'd love to see you both, I'm sure!"

Well, a point to Gus; he hadn't told Emily all of Oliver's personal background with Seth. It was comforting to Oliver to know that privacy mattered. Gus looked over, and must have seen something on Oliver's face indicating that this was a bad idea.

Gus said, "If you'd like to meet him, Em, I'd be happy to stand here with you. I wouldn't mind seeing Seth again. It's been nothing but sporadic emails over the years. Oliver?" He turned and gave Oliver a significant look. "If you want to head over to the bar and grab a table, we'll join you soon."

Oliver was flustered; he wasn't ready to be face to face with Seth, especially not after that performance. He felt too many conflicting emotions. On the other hand, he didn't want to be a cowardly ass and run off. He bit his lip and looked around the street. Catty-cornered in the building across the street was an alcove with a large awning overhead; the bright lights didn't seem to reach that far.

"I'll just wait over there for you both. So I'm not in the way of Emily meeting a big star," he said, smiling with what he hoped was a bright and casual look.

Emily looked back and forth between the two men, confused but determined. "Sure, Oliver. That way we don't lose you. Gus?" They linked arms and continued down the block to the partitioned walkway outside the stage door where a small crowd of about fifteen people was gathered, all chattering excitedly. Oliver walked briskly to the alcove, hoping it was far enough for him to go undetected.

Seeing Seth like that, larger than life, in full command of everything around him... it was a lot to take in. His life was becoming what he'd dreamed it to be. So many nights they lay in each other's arms while spinning out their futures, and it seemed that for Seth it all was coming true. Well, the making it on Broadway and becoming a star part. Their small yet stylish apartment with a view, decorated in a tasteful palate that Seth could never decide on, that wasn't coming true. There was no apartment filled with pictures they'd taken on trips around the world. No large bed with enough room for both of them to stretch out on a Sunday morning with their computers and coffee.

There were no excited phone calls telling Oliver about getting a callback from an audition; no trips to the grocery store where they planned fabulous dinners for themselves. No huge shower large enough for both of them at the same time. No romantic strolls through Central Park at dusk, the two of them arm and arm. No coin tosses to see whose house they would visit for Thanksgiving and whose for Christmas. There were no New Year's Eve countdowns in Times Square where they could kiss freely, starting yet another year together.

Seth might be achieving his dreams for the future, but seeing him on that path just reminded Oliver of all of the dreams they'd shared that were lost.

With a shuddering sigh, he slipped his playbill into his front coat pocket and rocked on his heels, surveying the street and the passersby. He saw Gus smooth Emily's hair over her shoulder and give her a kiss. Oliver smiled to himself and looked at his feet. It would be intruding on their moment to watch.

The noise across the street picked up a bit; Oliver looked up and saw a few members of the chorus and the orchestra come out, carrying bags and instruments over their shoulders. They smiled and thanked the crowd for coming to the show. Oliver leaned against the stone blocks that trimmed the alcove where he was hiding. Standing. He was standing, not hiding.

The stage door opened again, and okay, he was hiding. It wasn't Seth, though, but the actor who played William. He had on a ball cap and a thick, quilted parka. A few women squealed with excitement (and a few of the men, Oliver noticed). He was a ruggedly handsome guy when not in costume. He smiled at everyone, and Oliver could hear his booming voice as he asked their names, moving down the partition to sign everyone's playbills. Gus and Emily chatted with him for a moment, he saw, but he was too far away to hear what they were saying. A security person walked over and whispered into the actor's ear; he nodded briskly.

"William" held his hand up, thanked the group for their support and gave a wave as he walked off down the street. The crowd shrank by a few people as more and more orchestra members came out, along with members of the crew. Oliver had a few scathing thoughts for those who peeled off before acknowledging the star of the show. Oliver could barely remember what half of the other cast members looked like; how could someone *not* wait?

He thought about going over and complaining about it to Gus when the door opened again and Seth stepped out. Oliver took a step back and pressed into the cold stone. Seth looked clean and freshly scrubbed of all stage makeup; his hair was styled and he wore an effortlessly chic-yet-casual outfit, including a beautiful scarf wrapped around his neck. Oliver knew that the look was anything *but* effortless. Years ago he'd sat patiently on the edge of Seth's bed, waiting for Seth to get his clothes to drape just so before he'd consider leaving the house.

He smiled a bit at that thought, even as he experienced another of those aching twinges that had been happening all night. He stayed back against the wall, hoping he'd been right about the awning casting enough shade under the bright theater lights for him to remain inconspicuous. Seth gave Gus a tight hug and then turned, all smiles; he was evidently being introduced to Emily. They hugged and seemed to hit it off well, chatting animatedly. After a moment, Seth looked confused. Gus turned to Emily—it looked as if he was sighing. Seth looked beyond Emily toward the place where Oliver was hiding. Standing. Whatever.

Oliver's heart began to race. Seth, with a slightly confused expression, looked right where he was standing. Okay, hiding. Where he was hiding. Oliver was frozen with the shock of being found out. Seth's mouth parted a little and... was he standing on tiptoe? He smiled slightly and gave a nervous-looking little wave, as if he wasn't sure if that was okay. Oliver's manners kicked in, and he smiled widely and waved back.

"Shit," he muttered under his breath, jamming his hands into his coat pockets, his eyes on the asphalt ahead of him as he jogged across the street to join his friends.

Seth inhaled, "Oliver." Seth had always managed to sound both surprised and pleased when he'd done that in the past, making Oliver feel like an unexpected yet welcome bonus. Oliver didn't know if he was just hoping that was the case this time, or if his showing up out of the blue might *not* be as unwelcome as he feared.

"Seth! Um, hello!" Oliver said, shaking his head a little as his stomach roiled with nerves. The last time he'd seen him this close... he didn't want to think about that. Seth had been such a commanding presence onstage. That was what he would focus on. "You were spectacular. Absolutely mesmerizing." He held his hand over his heart, hoping Seth believed his sincerity. Also, he needed to tone down the compliments so he didn't sound deranged.

"Really? Well, thank you very much." A bit of a blush was creeping up from under Seth's scarf. Oliver hoped that it was from post-performance excitement, not discomfort.

"To be honest, I'm still trying to process the play. I've always known you were unbelievably talented, but that..." Shit. He didn't mean to fawn. Was he fawning? No, he was just being polite. Manners help make difficult things pass, right? Keep it polite.

Seth smiled, though. "I forgot how good you were for my ego." The blush was steadily making its way up to Seth's cheeks.

Oliver didn't know if everyone could hear his heart beating like a trip hammer or if he had sweat on his brow. His palms were sweating and they felt clammy in his coat pockets, and his stomach was in knots, and his face felt as if it was on fire, and Seth was right there. *Right there.* Oliver laughed a little and looked at his shoes, trying to pull himself together. "Well, you should know that it was excellent. The whole play, really."

Gus coughed and said, "Seth, you were outstanding."

Emily reached out a gloved hand to grab at Seth's forearm. He smiled at her. "We have to take you out for drinks as a thank you!" she said. "We never would have gotten tickets otherwise. Right?" She looked at Gus and then Oliver for confirmation.

Yes. Come out for drinks. Wait, no! I don't know what I'd say to him. Don't be stupid; just say you're sorry and then ask how he's doing and—

"I would *love* to have drinks and catch up," Seth said. Oliver searched Seth's face to gauge how he was really feeling. Seth looked... regretful. "But this is the first night that everyone in the cast was free for a bit of a celebration. I'm so sorry!"

The dough-faced actor from the play showed up and took Seth's arm, pulling him close to whisper something in his ear. Oliver clenched his fists inside his coat pockets again as Seth smiled and gave a sharp laugh and a nod. Dough-Face winked at Seth and leaned in to kiss him on the corner of his mouth.

Oliver's stomach plummeted. Of course. Of *course* Seth had someone. He'd told himself to expect that, but being confronted with it was something else entirely. He knew he didn't have any claims, any *right* to be upset. Well, not upset with Seth. He could be mad at himself and planned on doing an excellent job of it at the bar later tonight. Where he *wouldn't* be forging a new friendship with Seth after all, because Seth had plans with this guy and the other cast members.

Oliver forced a neutral smile during all of this; he could be upset later, starting with a big "I told you so" to himself about why he shouldn't have talked with Seth at all. Even though he wished that Seth would ditch Dough-Face and everyone else and keep talking to him—because this was probably it, he realized. This was his chance to make things right.

Seth bit his lip and seemed to look at everyone but Oliver. His cheeks were bright pink by now. Oliver hadn't wanted to make Seth uneasy, but it seemed he'd gone ahead and done that, too.

"They're telling me that the other people in line are getting impatient, so I better go." Seth looked over his shoulder to where Dough-Face was walking backwards, grinning. Oliver realized that he was frowning at the guy and tried to force his features back into a more relaxed expression.

"It was *really* good to see you, all of you." He looked at Oliver with a sort of helpless "what can you do?" expression that was like a bucket of ice over Oliver's heart. Some woman jammed her playbill rudely into Seth's face and asked for his autograph, and that was that.

Oliver watched the crowd move down the partition, following Seth. He could see glimpses of Seth's profile, catch sight of his scarf, but he was walking away. Oliver didn't know why he felt so disappointed. After all, the plan had been to see Seth perform and support him, and that's just what he'd done. Yet now that he'd *seen* Seth and heard him speak and seen his face and been so close he could almost feel the heat pouring from his body, a part of Oliver wanted to be somewhere quiet with him, maybe even hold him and tell him they'd been stupid and he'd like to try to have a relationship with him again, even if it *was* just friendship. But it just didn't seem that would happen. Maybe it shouldn't.

It was like a dream in which he missed a step and the world came crashing down with a thud: the smell of the city streets, the incessant honking, the chatter of theatergoers on the street. He barely registered Gus's hand on his arm.

"Oliver?" Gus shot him a wry grin. "How about a drink?"

He saw Seth and Dough-Face walking briskly across the street to the corner, and then they were gone. That definitely wasn't the person he pictured Seth building a life with. If he was honest with himself, he couldn't see Seth's future with anyone but *him*. But he'd ruined his chance years before, and he really didn't have the right since to feel frustrated or upset about Seth's choices. He should be happy that Seth was happy; that was the right thing to do.

"A drink," Oliver sighed. "Yeah. That sounds about right."

Gus laughed and tucked Emily's hand under his arm as they walked along the length of the partition. A worker started folding up the movable gate and it was as if nothing had happened, as if he hadn't just finally seen Seth Larsen coming off of a Broadway stage to an adoring crowd.

"Hey! One of you Oliver?"

Oliver stopped and turned. One of the security guards saw him and headed up the block to him.

"Yeah, Mr. Larsen said to give you this."

The man held out a folded piece of paper that looked as if it had been torn out of one of the playbills. Oliver took it with a "thank you" and unfolded it as his heart jumped, somewhere in his throat, at the sight of that familiar handwriting.

Oliver—
Sorry—it's so crazy after! We're @ Hourglass on 46th, almost to 9th 3rd floor. Be great if you all joined us?
~Seth.

He read it a few times, making sure he wasn't missing anything. He didn't know how to take this. Was this a request to get together with old friends? An opportunity for Seth to tell Oliver off? Did Seth... miss him? Probably not that last one, much as Oliver would have hoped.

"Well?"

Gus held Emily close and looked at Oliver questioningly.

"Ah, yeah. It's from Seth." Gus made an impatient "obviously, Oliver" expression. "He says they're at Hourglass on 46th and for us to come."

Gus looked at him steadily. "Do you want to?"

"I—" Oliver exhaled, trying to get rid of some of the adrenaline that was thrumming through his body thanks to the whirlwind of unplanned events. "Maybe?"

"That's a yes."

"Come on, Oliver. I need booze. And nibbles." Emily bounced impatiently by Gus's side and gave Oliver a pouty face.

Oliver exhaled with a small laugh. "Okay. Sure. Yeah, let's go."

He thought about what Gus had said on the drive to New York, that he and Seth had been good for each other. Even before they fell in love, they'd been friends. The best friend Oliver had ever had, actually, with no offense meant to Gus. When they broke up he'd lost that, too, not to mention his relationship with Seth's dad. Seeing Seth, remembering how they had been friends, made Oliver think that it would be worth a little more heartache if he could have even that much back. No one had ever really understood him as Seth had.

And who knew, maybe he *wouldn't* be confronted with the reality of Seth in a healthy and fulfilling relationship with Dough-Face. Maybe he could get over his nerves, and they could really talk. For a solid year after they broke up, he had ached from not seeing Big Mike, who had become a stand-in father figure for Oliver, on a regular basis. His first year of college brought homesickness, but for the Larsens, more than for his own family. He still missed them. He missed everything that came with having Seth in his life. If he could only get back friendship, well, maybe Gus was right. It could be good for him.

Regardless, Oliver knew that he needed a drink to be able to deal with any of this. He thought of something Moira had taught him: "You can accomplish more with a kind word and a round of drinks than you can with just a kind word."

Chapter Five

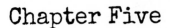

They walked the two blocks to the restaurant, Oliver growing quieter and quieter the closer they got. Emily linked her arm in his at the stoplight at 46th.

"Oliver?" Emily asked. "If we need to go back to the hotel, we can do that. I'm getting that something weird is happening here."

He huffed a laugh. "Well, it *is* weird for me, all things considered," he said. It seemed as though another person were saying it; he didn't think he'd ever get used to explaining who Seth was to him, who Seth had *been* to him. "It was years ago, but still."

She leaned back and looked over at Gus next. "Oh. Why the hell didn't anyone tell me?"

Gus and Oliver shrugged in unison.

"Boys," she muttered. "Okay, we can leave. Let's go. It's only a block and change back to our hotel, anyway."

Here was his out; finally confronted with it, he realized he didn't want it. He didn't want to hide; he didn't want to... well, not see where the night could go. "No, it's fine." He looked over her head at Gus and gave him a small but sincere smile. "Really. I think it'll be good."

Gus nodded at him. He nodded again because the road was clear and they were just standing out in the cold. Oliver led Emily across the street, her arm still tucked in his, and handed her off with a courtly bow once they were all on the other side. A quick hop around the corner and there was the pub. It was small, almost a hole in the wall, but it was packed. Seth had said in his note that they were on the third floor, so Oliver took charge finding where they were to go.

The hostess made sure that they were on the list for the cast party

("Oliver and two guests") and pointed the way up the narrow staircase behind the bar.

"I shouldn't have worn these heels," Emily complained.

"Yes, you should have. They make your legs look amazing," Gus said, scooping her up into his arms for the last flight of steps. Oliver smiled but still felt like a third wheel. He was glad they had each other, that they were having fun; he just felt awkward about the whole night—being solo, being confronted with his ex, showing up at a party last-minute. They could hear the cast whooping it up before they reached the top landing.

The upstairs was a good-sized room—well, New York City good-sized, at least. The walls were a dark gray, hung with musical instruments between the large windows. A smaller version of the downstairs bar was tucked in a corner; clusters of small tables with floor-dusting cloths draped over them filled the rest of the room. It felt intimate, but was large enough to hold everyone.

They stood awkwardly in the doorway for a moment as Oliver looked around, trying to find Seth. Someone Emily had chatted with extensively at the stage door apparently recognized her and called out, "Hey!" Emily waved back at him, dragged Gus over to say hello and the three of them began a lively conversation about the show. A waiter came between Oliver and his group; Oliver stepped back, out of the way, which pushed him into another group of people—none of whom he recognized from the show at all—leaving him feeling more awkward and out of place than ever. What was he *doing* here?

And then there he was, across the room: Seth, leaning against the wall with a highball in his hand, laughing with a group of people. Oliver felt warm down to his toes at the sight of Seth so happy. Seth went still and looked in his direction. They locked eyes for a brief moment before a smile spread on Seth's face and he waved Oliver over. Oliver's heart was pounding in his chest.

Don't make an ass of yourself, please. Be polite and cordial.

He turned to Emily and Gus and pointed toward the far end of the room. Gus waved him on; they were still talking to the chorus member. Oliver steeled himself and resisted the urge to smooth a hand over his hair. He wove through a few knots of people standing around the center tables and made his way to the back corner.

"Oliver! Everyone?" Seth gestured toward him with his glass as he addressed the group. "This is my old friend Oliver. Oliver? This is, ha, everyone."

They all laughed good-naturedly and a few nodded at him, smiling. The actor who played William was there, sitting in a chair in the corner with his arm slung around a pretty redheaded woman. He pointed to himself and said, "Jonathan."

Oliver pulled his hand out of his coat pocket to shake, but no one seemed to be the reciprocating kind. They were head-nod types. Okay, then. He cleared his throat and tried to keep his nerves in check; Seth was standing near him, and Oliver could *feel* his warmth and smell his cologne, and it was almost too much to just be standing there, after all these years, doing nothing more than watching strangers as they chatted amongst themselves.

Oliver had to say *something*; he couldn't just stand there staring like a buffoon. "Jonathan, you were excellent tonight. I was on the edge of my seat during some of your moments, truly."

"Oh? Well, thank you very much! Anything in particular stand out?" Jonathan asked with an artificially wide grin.

"Careful," Seth muttered, leaning in and almost causing Oliver to have a heart attack at the closeness. "He'll want you to tell him all night how fabulous he is."

Oliver was so surprised by the casualness of the statement and the proximity in which it was delivered that he almost sputtered a laugh. He made his best attempt at smoothing his facial features into a more benign amusement. "Oh, well, I have to say that I totally bought that you two were in love. It was... very impressive, your performance."

He could see, in his peripheral vision, that Seth had turned and was facing him; almost instantly, his face began to heat up. "Obviously, yours too, Seth." He knew he was blushing; he couldn't control that, but he could look at some point in the middle distance before smiling and looking at Seth in the eyes.

Seth hummed; he was amused, it seemed. "It's a long way from Atchison, huh?" he asked.

Oliver laughed and looked down, to the side, anywhere but directly into Seth's piercing hazel eyes; it was too much. They were too close, it had been too long, and he had been too overcome for the past several weeks by memories of looking into those eyes, of hearing that voice, of that boy. Man, now. He wondered if, in his mind, Seth would always be the boy he loved.

He clung to that; this was Seth the man. He was older, had lived a life separate from Oliver. Nor was Oliver the same person. He could do this. He could get to know who this new-Seth was.

"There's a coat check if you'd like to take off your things," Seth offered with a smile. "You look like you might be a little warm."

Oliver pressed his lips together, knowing that Seth was giving him an out for his blush. "Well, I didn't want to intrude on your party, but I didn't want to not come, either."

"Always the perfect gentleman," Seth said with a smile. He tugged on Oliver's arm—setting about a million butterflies loose in his stomach—and gestured to the other side of the room. "Of course you're not intruding. I'll be back," he mentioned to the cast members before leading Oliver away.

Oliver willingly followed Seth as he cut a path through his castmates. Seth stood aside as Oliver peeled off his coat and scarf, handed them over and took his ticket. Well, it looked as though he'd be here longer than he'd anticipated. He turned to find Seth watching him, a small smile on his face; it gave him a little hope.

"Let's get you a drink, and then I want you to tell me everything you've been doing."

Oliver shook his head with a little disbelief. "Um, okay. Sure. And the same to you; how are—"

Seth waved him off. "Let's get a drink and find somewhere to sit first, so we don't have to shout."

Seth pressed against the bar and made a little wave at the bartender to get her attention. She came over smiling at them both, looking at Seth expectantly. For the first time all night, he looked mildly flustered. Seth looked at the bar and then back at Oliver, his eyes a little lost for such a brief moment Oliver almost wondered if he imagined it.

"I don't actually know what you'd like. A snifter of brandy?" he offered, with a cheeky grin.

Oliver covered his face with one hand, laughing. "No, thank you."

He turned to the bartender, pulled his wallet out and said, "Wheat beer on tap? Thanks."

Seth rolled his eyes and pushed Oliver's arm down, giving him another little thrill at the touch even though he had a long-sleeved shirt on. "It's a cast party; you're not paying."

"Oh! Well. Thank you."

She came back with a glass of beer, and as Oliver took it, Seth asked, "Shall we?" He motioned toward a small table under a window at the back of the room.

"Yes. That's... yes."

He was in a bar in New York City with Seth. With *Seth*. He didn't know if he should laugh at the absurdity of it all or praise the heavens that he had the chance to rectify some of the mistakes he'd made. If ever there were a time for him to actually feel religious, this would be a good one.

There were only the two chairs facing each other; Seth rested his chin on his hand, smiling. He asked, "So are you still in Boston, or... ?"

Oliver toyed with the base of his glass, trying to control his nervous stomach. "No, actually. I'm at Cambridge. The one in England," he amended, smiling up at Seth and looking back at his beer.

"England?"

Oliver looked up; Seth was sitting back in his seat, a little shocked.

"I'm working on my master's there, thinking about a PhD there, possibly."

"Wow. Don't get me wrong," Seth said, leaning in toward the table. "That's amazing. I just... England. When you want to get out of Kansas, you really get out of there." He blinked a few times and then flashed Oliver with a wide grin. "Have you seen the Queen?"

"Of course! She comes round for tea every afternoon," Oliver said, speaking in a terrible British accent and earning a laugh from Seth.

How was this happening? He was sitting at a table with Seth Larsen and they were laughing with one another as if... as if nothing had happened. Well, that wasn't true, because if nothing had happened they'd be holding hands and talking with other people. They'd share secret looks, and Oliver would maybe wait for a prearranged signal from Seth to announce to the group that they had to head back home, and they'd laugh and kiss and be completely comfortable with each other. They'd *be* with each other—if nothing had happened, that is.

"So," Oliver said, trying to inject as much lightheartedness as possible into the conversation. "How's your dad?" He tried to not look desperate for information. He just wanted to hear that Seth and Big Mike were both doing okay.

Something in Seth's expression softened at that. "He's fine. In fact, he just recently opened a second custom shop near Fort Leavenworth—"

"Really? That's amazing!"

Seth ducked his head, smiling hugely. "It was my idea." Seth took a sip of his drink, a faraway look on his face. Oliver knew how important his father was to him; Seth probably missed him, Big Mike being back in Kansas. "Dad needed a new project when I started living here full-time," he said with a small shrug.

Oliver's ribs felt tight, as though he couldn't get a deep enough breath; he was so happy for them, that they were well, secure, thriving even. He just... he really missed them, both of them. They had been his family as much as his own was, and in some ways—acceptance, warmth, encouragement—even more so. Hell, Seth's father got choked up while taking their prom pictures. Oliver's parents hadn't bothered taking any, since Oliver didn't have a "real date."

"But your dad?" Oliver pressed. "He's doing okay health-wise? No more wrecks or anything?" He knew he looked concerned, but Mike Larsen had meant a lot to him. His hands were wrapped around the base of his glass; he wasn't quite ready to look up into Seth's eyes, not until he knew for certain that everyone—*everyone*—was fine and happy.

"He's really okay, Oliver. Dad's doing great. No health scares of any kind in over three years, actually."

Oliver let out the breath he didn't know he was holding and chanced a look at Seth. He looked... sad, maybe? Pleased, in a way? It gave Oliver a little jolt to realize that he didn't quite know all of the expressions Seth had now. In some ways it seemed as though no time had passed at all, but these little moments were a reminder that it had—there had been a lot of living since they'd known each other. And what were the scares *before* the three years? He had to remind himself that he didn't have the right to pry.

"I always smile if I drive past his shop when I'm in town," Oliver said. "He's such a good man, your dad."

"Well," Seth said, tearing at his napkin and clearing his throat, "I'll tell him you said so."

"And who's this tall drink of water, Seth? Don't be rude; introduce me to your friend!"

Dough-Face. He sat on the window ledge, practically in Seth's lap, and put an arm around his shoulder. Right. Oliver had let himself forget that little kiss. All of the warm, bubbly feelings that had been building up since he'd gotten the note were quickly doused by the arrival of Seth's... boyfriend? Oh, God, his *lover*? Oliver felt suddenly sick.

He slapped a smile back onto his face and turned to look at Dough-Face; he didn't think he could look at Seth just yet.

"Oh, right. Um, Oliver, this is Brandt Whitston." Seth cleared his throat and said, "You remember him from the play, right?"

"Of course he does! Hi, there. Oliver, is it?" Dough—er, Brandt—leaned against Seth *as if he was trying to claim him. Hmph, he doesn't know Seth* that *well if he thinks that's okay*—and held out his hand with a smarmy, smug little grin.

Oliver took it with a mental note not to try to prove anything with his handshake and was pleased when he realized he wouldn't have to. Nothing was worse than a limp-washrag handshake, and that's just what Brandt had. Oliver absolutely was not preening internally at how large his hand was in comparison to Brandt's, either. Okay, maybe he was, a little. A lot. Whatever.

"And how do you know our rising star here?" Brandt asked.

Seth jumped in before Oliver could answer. "Oliver and I have known each other since we were teens. We were in choir together." Seth smiled at Oliver, catching his eye for the first time since Dough-Face interrupted. "He's a pretty fantastic baritone. And he was my very first boyfriend, actually."

"Oh, that's so sweet! God," Brandt laughed, "I don't think I have any exes that I'd want to see again, let alone come to my show. That's so *nice* that you stayed friends."

Oliver was ready to go, ready for a hole to open up underneath him and just swallow him up. He couldn't look at that simpering jackass draping himself all over Seth. Okay, he just had an arm around him and was leaning against Seth's shoulder, but it *seemed* as if he was draping himself all over Seth.

"Actually," Seth said, "we haven't seen each other in years. I was pretty surprised to see you, Oliver." Oliver looked up at that. "It was a happy surprise." The heat in his face flared again as Seth reached across the table and patted the top of Oliver's hand, lingering for just a moment before he pulled it back.

"Pretty amazing how well our Seth has done for himself, hmm?" Brandt asked. Oliver got the impression that Brandt was trying to ferret something out of him, but Oliver couldn't figure out what. "I knew he was going to be something back when he was picked up as understudy."

Seth shifted in his seat, his eyes darting around the room as Brandt spoke. He looked incredibly uncomfortable, but Oliver wasn't sure if it was because of whatever relationship Brandt was trying to imply he had with Seth. When Oliver noticed Seth shift farther away from Brandt, he decided not to be just an observer.

Oliver looked into Brandt's face. "Seth's always been something."

Seth smiled and looked into his glass. He took a sip, carefully set the glass back on the table and turned to Brandt. "You know, Oliver and I really haven't been able to talk in years, Brandt, so how about I just see you tomorrow before the show?"

Brandt looked at Seth, shocked. Oliver wondered if he wasn't used to having people tell him to leave. Probably not. Brandt pulled himself together quickly and flashed them each an over-bright grin. "Oh, sure! Old friends, I get it. Well..." He leaned down as if to kiss Seth again, and Oliver felt a ferocious surge of pleasure when Seth leaned back and patted Brandt on the arm.

Seth isn't some kind of prize, moron. And if you don't know that by now... Maybe they aren't a couple after all.

Oliver watched Brandt walk back to the table where he'd initially found Seth. He turned back to find Seth staring at him intently.

"I'm sorry about him. He's..." Seth trailed off, seemingly embarrassed.

"A bit of a lech?"

Seth laughed loudly out at that and covered his mouth with his hand. "I was going to say obnoxious, but lech works."

"Seth, I know it's not my business. But are the two of you... ?"

Seth reared back; Oliver almost audibly sighed with relief at the disgust on Seth's face. "The two of—me and Brandt? Oh, no. Oh, that is a definite no."

"Oh! Well. I just meant to say that if you *were*, I would go. I don't mean to get in the way of anything, really." Oliver sighed and rubbed his thumb over the knuckles on his opposite hand. "I really struggled with coming. We always were honest with each other, right?"

Seth nodded, and Oliver hoped he wasn't just imagining the look on Seth's face, as though he really was okay with him just showing up.

"I really... worried that I would, well, mess up what you had going here. I didn't want to be something unhappy for you that just dropped in out of the blue." He circled the tip of his finger in the condensation ring on the table around his beer. "My plan was to support your performance and just be proud of you. I don't mean to upset you; I hope you know that."

Seth looked at him for a moment, his eyes searching for... something in Oliver's, Oliver didn't know what exactly. The longer the silence stretched on, the more panicked and worried Oliver became, fearing he'd said too much, sounded too desperate. Seth stretched his hand out across the table, palm up. Oliver's breath hitched a bit at that. Seth had done that over the years they'd dated: silently reaching out, waiting for Oliver to take his hand, acting as a tether when Oliver was filled with worry or self-doubt, quietly offering his love and support. There was no question now that Oliver would take it, even if it were just being offered out of friendship.

His hand slid into Seth's warm, dry palm; as he looked at their hands together he had a strong sense of déjà vu, which was silly, because of *course* they'd been like this before. He'd just never imagined that they'd be here again.

"Thank you." Seth said, sounding as if he meant it. "I—thank you for coming to see it."

Oliver finally looked up from their joined hands at Seth. "I would have come sooner if I'd known." He knew that was true, despite all the hemming and hawing he'd done. There really was no question now that he would always want to support Seth if the opportunity presented itself. "I've kind of buried myself in my studies these past few years. Gus says I'm letting things slip by."

God, that sounded pathetic. He hadn't meant to sound like that; he just was used to opening up to Seth about how he was feeling. Old habits die hard, he supposed.

Seth squeezed his hand. "I wondered if you were the plus-plus one, you know."

Oliver started.

Seth continued, "I didn't know Gus's parents, so I wasn't sure if they were both coming, but then he mentioned that he was excited for me to finally meet Emily, so that just left the one ticket. And he'd been specific about needing three."

Seth smiled at Oliver, giving his hand another quick squeeze before pulling it back and resting it in his lap. Oliver watched him pull his hand away and wanted briefly to clutch it back and keep it where it had once belonged: in his.

"Well," Oliver said, trying to buy himself a little time to gain control. He didn't want to seem a pitiful, needy twit. "I wasn't sure if I was going to be the, ha, plus-plus one."

He took a deep breath, steadying himself. *In for a penny...* "Seth—it's so great to see you. And it's amazing to see you onstage. It's where you should be."

Seth blushed, smiling bashfully. It gave Oliver quite a thrill to bring on that reaction after all this time.

"So, how are you doing with all of this?" he asked Seth. "The schedule alone has to be brutal."

Seth cleared his throat and leaned back, still a little pink-cheeked, but looking far more comfortable with the direction their conversation was headed. "It's a lot. I was used to it in a way, working as an understudy, but it's not the same. Yesterday we had the two performances, and we'll do it again on Saturday, so those are the days when I get just worn out."

"Oh! I'm sorry, Seth. I didn't even think of that. Here," Oliver pushed his chair back, feeling like a heel. "I can go. You probably need your rest; you don't need me keeping you—"

"Oliver," Seth laughed. "If I wanted to go, I'd go. Actually..." Seth stood up then and looked around the room. The crowd was smaller—Oliver hadn't noticed anyone coming or going; he only had eyes for the man across from him—and each little group was deeply involved in its own conversation. Oliver noticed Emily and Gus sitting at a table alone and felt a surge of guilt for having left them all this time.

Oliver got to his feet quickly. "You want to go, I completely understand. I can only imagine how exhausted you must be."

Seth smiled at him, his arms folded in front of himself. "What if you get your coat, and we see if Gus and Emily want to head somewhere quieter so we could all talk? Would that be that weird?"

"No! No, not at all."

That would be perfect, actually.

Oliver took a deep breath and tried to remember what he was supposed to be doing. Seth wanted to go somewhere and talk. They were going to talk and maybe make things okay again. Well, maybe not perfectly okay, but this was definitely a start.

"Coat. Right." Oliver dug in his pockets until he found his ticket. He made quick work of getting his things and met Seth at Gus's table. Gus looked up at Oliver and raised one eyebrow a fraction; everything fine?

Oliver gave Gus's shoulder a quick squeeze. He said, "So! Somewhere else, where we don't have to fight to hear each other?"

Emily pulled her coat on and said, "The bar at our hotel has nice, cozy booths. We could go back there?"

Seth held her cashmere scarf and her purse while she buttoned her coat. "Love the Kate Spade bag. And that's fine with me if... ?"

No one seemed to object, so they all moved to the door and the narrow staircase. Then Oliver realized something. He turned to Seth and asked, "Are you sure that you don't need to say goodbye to them? Um, to Brandt?" He didn't know what was going on there, but he didn't want to seem exclusionary or possessive. Just in case Seth had fibbed to spare his feelings.

"No, it's fine. I'll see them all tomorrow. We all see *plenty* of each other, trust me."

Seth sounded sure, so Oliver took it at face value; he could think about the emphasis on *plenty* later. He certainly didn't want to argue with Seth about spending time together. He hadn't let himself imagine that anything might happen on this trip; the hope of falling back into a relationship would be too painful for him when it inevitably *didn't* happen.

But. It seemed as though it was happening. Something was, at least.

* * *

"One day I'll be important enough to convince the house of Valentino to design a fabulous pair of sensible work shoes so the horror that is the Croc 'shoe'"—Seth made finger quotes—"can be banished from human history."

"They are unbelievably comfortable on hard hospital floors, even if they're unattractive," Emily said, laughing.

"Emily?" Seth took her hand in both of his. "And I mean this with all sincerity. They are a blight on mankind."

Gus sat back, a beer in his hands, and gave Seth a small smile—his version of being very amused—and leaned over to kiss Emily on the cheek.

Oliver was sitting back against the padded, curved banquette in the hotel bar, soaking up the conversation. It was easier for him to listen and let the others carry the weight while he reacquainted himself with grown-up-Seth.

There wasn't a huge difference—it was little things. He was looser-limbed, as if he were far more comfortable in his own skin than he had been back in Kansas. That made sense. He was still funny, still quick and sharp. He was maybe a hair taller, almost as tall as Oliver now. His shoulders were definitely a bit broader, his chest deeper. He was... more. Handsomer, cleverer, more talented. But in some ways he was, well, less. He was less nervous, less stiff, less cautious. Oliver assumed that living in a city where he was now not only tolerated, but celebrated, had a lot to do with that. Gone were the days of looking over his shoulder in fear while trying to keep his eyes on the future.

"The future is now," Oliver muttered to himself.

"Hmm?" Seth asked, turning his bright smile toward Oliver; it warmed Oliver's whole being, that happy, relaxed smile. He never thought he'd be in its glow again, and yet here he was.

"Oh, nothing," he hummed.

Emily and Gus had a silent conversation of significant looks during all of this; Gus took a last pull from his bottle, set it down carefully and said, "Well, gentlemen, the hour grows small. Emily and I are going to turn in, I believe."

"Oh, but it's only just after midnight!" Oliver said, his heartbeat picking up. It was what he wanted, to have Seth to himself, to talk openly and repair the damage done all of those years ago, but now that he was confronted with the possibility, he found that he was terrified.

The couple waved and walked away, hand in hand, to the bank of elevators opposite the bar's entrance. Oliver was fairly certain that everyone within a five-mile radius could hear his heart pounding. He and Seth looked at each other; Oliver quickly dropped his gaze, smiling. Seth looked a little nervous, too; he had that lovely tinge of pink high on his cheeks and started to fidget with the cocktail napkin on the table.

It was oddly comforting to Oliver, the old familiar gesture. Plus, if Seth was nervous, then he didn't feel blasé about their meeting again. Which meant that this meant something. What that something *was*, had yet to be determined.

"Would you like another drink?" Oliver asked, pointing to Seth's nearly empty glass and buying himself a little time. Seth sighed, visibly relaxing as he exhaled.

"Yes, thank you."

He could do this. He could be relaxed with Seth, who seemed happy to be with him. Somewhat nervous, too, but that was to be expected. And Seth was the one who offered to go somewhere where they could talk. That was definitely promising. Oliver needed to chill the hell out and stop worrying so much. Maybe Seth was even a little excited to be here with him, since he was the one who wanted to spend some time together. Huh.

Oliver hopped up and tried to play it cool as he walked over to the bar. He became oddly aware of his body; was he moving stiffly? He realized that he had really tight-fitting trousers on and worried that it might look as if he was trying to show off or something. But that was ridiculous; Seth wouldn't think that, wasn't thinking about Oliver in any lascivious way.

It was just that he was pretty sure Seth was watching him—as if the force of Seth's gaze was heating his skin.

He could do this. Be nonchalant. Relaxed. Use a little of the ol' heel-toe and not think about the unlikely prospect of Seth checking him out. Even if it did seem like the old days, before they'd become sexually active, when he could feel Seth watching him, trying to pick up cues for how they could behave. And maybe, back then, Oliver had purposefully done things to try to bring that particular topic to the table. Like maybe playing sexy music while maintaining a casual expression in their dorm rooms. Like pretending it was no big deal that Seth was laying on his bed—*on his bed*—watching him.

Jesus, why was he wearing such fitted pants? And why was he thinking about the past? The painful past, he reminded himself. The one in which he'd shattered their dreams for the future. Well, that thought worked to bring his mind out of memories he didn't need to revisit tonight. He could calmly bring drinks back to the secluded table where Seth was waiting.

And he wasn't here to flirt; he was here to make amends and regain a friendship. An important friendship. The most important of his life. One that had also featured kissing.

Nope, no, he wasn't going to set himself up for hope and want because as soon as he did that, Seth would say that he'd been waiting for years to tell Oliver just what he thought of him, tell him off and then leave him shattered, in pieces. So. No more thinking about his past relationship with Seth in any sort of sexual context.

It was just... Seth was sitting there right in front of him, being handsome and debonair and so very *him* that it was hard to remember how much time had passed.

Oliver carried back their drinks, trying to look around the room and not blatantly stare back. Because he had seen as he turned around that Seth was staring at *him*. God, he hoped his sweaty palms didn't cause the drinks to slide out of his hands and crash to the floor before he could get to the table.

"So!" Oliver said, forcing a bright, totally-not-thinking-about-how-hot-you-look-when-you-come smile on his face.

"So," Seth replied, tilting his head to the side as if Oliver were some amusing new creature he just discovered. "So... tell me what you're studying all the way over in England?"

"Bullying."

Seth looked taken aback. "Bullying? You're studying bullying," he said in a deadpan voice.

Oliver laughed nervously. "Well, yeah. That's obviously an over-simplification—"

"Oh, yes, *obviously*," Seth laughed.

"But that's what it breaks down to. I'm trying to figure out why people... hate us."

If Seth had looked shocked before, it was nothing to the gobsmacked expression on his face now.

"So, remember how I started that petition my senior year?" Oliver asked, nervous about treading dangerous waters. Seth nodded. He cleared his throat. "My first year at college, I sat in on a lecture about LGBT kids and bullying and how societal norms condition that response. It all just clicked. How much I hated how you were treated back in those days." He chanced a look at Seth's face to gauge his reaction. Seth still looked bewildered, so he powered on. "I knew what it was like, too; you knew about my troubles."

"Troubles," Seth murmured. "They were more than that, Oliver." He looked as though he was beginning to pull himself together. Oliver couldn't tell if he was fascinated or disappointed.

"I... people listen to me. I don't mean to sound full of myself, you know better than anyone that that's not true. I thought that if I could learn *why* people behave like they do, I could, well, help them not. Because—"

"Because they listen to you," Seth finished. He blinked rapidly for a moment, took a long sip from his cocktail and exhaled slowly. His face was still remote, but there was something burning in his gaze. Oliver didn't know how to interpret it just yet.

"And? Have you figured out why they act that way?" Seth asked.

Oliver gave a small smile. "Well... because they're assholes?"

Seth barked a shocked laugh, apparently caught off guard. They both laughed for a moment. Seth smiled at him—a real smile, not a polite small talk smile. He said, "Your parents sure spent a lot of money on an education for you to find that out. I could have saved them tens of thousands; I've known that for years."

He hummed happily and sipped his drink. Oliver couldn't take his eyes off of him. It was surreal; here he was with the boy he'd loved, now a man who was still so much like old Seth, but... better.

"So are you looking for a specific therapy for bullies? Or a magic pill? Tolerance pills—I like that."

Oliver laughed. "No pills. Right now I'm studying how people in peer groups behave when confronted with their own prejudices. It's pretty interesting, actually." He sat back, feeling happy and a little proud; he loved what he and Moira were working on. "Oh, my partner is just dying to—"

"You have a partner?" Seth asked lightly, even as he started to close himself off with his arms crossed tightly.

"Oh, yes. My research partner, Moira?" Oliver said. "She's Irish. You'd like her; she's spunky. Tells it like it is. Sometimes I think she's the illegitimate love child of John Waters and Kathy Lee Griffin, even though that's impossible."

"That sounds dangerous, honestly." Chuckling, Seth relaxed his arms' tight hold on himself. He reached forward, wrapped his long fingers around his drink and toyed with it.

"She's sweet, though," Oliver said. "Really sharp girl; I couldn't do this without her."

Seth regarded him for a moment with that faint smile still on his face, as if he was remembering something that had made him happy. "Is it hard?" he asked, quietly.

Oliver considered the answer before speaking. "Yeah, but—yes. It's hard, but it's challenging. I like it. I mean," he leaned his weight onto his forearms at the table's edge, "don't get me wrong, I never sleep, and I perpetually feel like I'm a week behind; I never have any free time and sometimes I just want to yell at people for being so stubborn. But... I really like it. I feel like I'm doing something that can be useful."

Instead of appearing focused on something far away, Seth's smile warmed as Oliver spoke and his bright eyes stayed solely on Oliver. It was as if Oliver were pulling him into what was now, what could *be* now: the two of them enjoying each other's company, supporting one another. The way it used to be, but it could be so much better. They were older, smarter, more aware of themselves. Oliver was, at least; he thought that Seth was, too.

Seth said, "I'm glad. You sound like you love it." He rested his chin on his hand and leaned toward Oliver at their small table. It was only a few inches, but it seemed to Oliver as though he'd moved a huge distance. He said softly, "I'm really happy that it's fulfilling you, Oliver."

"I think it is. I like the mental exercise it offers, for sure. It can be incredibly frustrating at times, dealing with prejudices and unable to say anything; makes me feel like I'm thirteen again."

"Ugh, that would be awful. It helps that I am, obviously, free of any and all prejudices. I hate everyone equally," Seth said with a grin.

Oliver felt warm all over; every nerve was standing on end in the best way. He was more aware of everything around him, the air, the sounds, the feel of his clothes on his skin, even. He was sitting and talking with someone who had always made him feel better, had always been there for him. They'd been each other's rock, their comfort, and in so many ways, Seth had been Oliver's inspiration.

Oliver felt as if his body couldn't contain all of the joy that was building inside of him, as if it radiated from his *skin,* his gratitude for this moment, this conversation, this *man.*

"I really missed you." Oliver sighed, and immediately went still. He said quickly, to cover his embarrassment, "You know, how funny you are."

"They don't have funny people in England?" Seth leaned forward against the table, his eyes narrowing. "Are you telling me that public broadcasting has been lying to me all along?"

Oliver exhaled, unable to wipe the happy grin off his face. "Well, I think we can both agree that there's no one quite like you anywhere."

"True, true," Seth preened. He laughed a little, as if self-conscious, and shifted in his seat.

A huge weight was beginning to lift from Oliver; this could work. They could laugh and joke and enjoy each other's company as they had in the past. He could do this.

Seth tried to hide a yawn.

"What are we doing? Seth, you need to get some sleep, I'm so sorry." Oliver braced his hands on the table and prepared to push back and get to his feet.

"No, it's fine!" Seth leaned forward, and folded his arms on the table. "So. Cambridge is filled with the humorless; please tell me you at *least* dress for dinner. If I find out it's anything less than Merchant and Ivory described, I'll be heartbroken."

Oliver laughed; he couldn't help it. "Then I won't say another word. I'd hate to crush your spirit by telling you how rare brocade waistcoats are on campus. At least in my department, people dress for work. It's not like at Brandeis, where everyone rolled out of bed and showed up to class."

Oliver mentally cursed himself for bringing up his undergraduate school, the cause of their breakup. Seth seemed to take it in stride, even if he pulled back slightly. Oliver didn't think it was a conscious act on his part; Seth just shifted in his seat, sat straighter in his "protect myself for what comes next" posture.

"I can't imagine you going to class in flannel pants, Oliver, I just can't." Seth shook his head, amused.

Oliver was grateful that he didn't look angry or upset. *Just relax. Don't make problems where there aren't any*. He said, "Well, that's good, because I didn't. I'm still an Andrews with an image to uphold, after all."

Seth's eyes flicked to Oliver's neck and then back to meet his eyes. His gaze was warmer, more intimate. "Still dashing as always, I see. I never did send your mother a thank you note for teaching you how to pull together an outfit," he said, grinning. "I was shocked by the lack of real knowledge about ties in the theater. Shocked. Don't even get me started on the fabrics; these boys buy *poly blend*."

He looked so horribly offended that Oliver couldn't help but laugh and say, "Savages." (And Oliver was glad that he had worn a silk tie in a half-Windsor, which showed under his pullover.)

Their eyes met again and Oliver had another one of those effervescent sensations in his stomach. He couldn't help himself; he would always be fascinated and captivated by Seth. He just lit up a room. And something inside of Oliver, he realized with a painful ache.

Seth was the first to break eye contact; he gave another yawn and tried to hide it behind his hand.

"Seth."

"Hmm?" Seth was resting his chin on his hand again; his eyes were getting close to half-mast. He still smiled back at Oliver, though.

"You *must* be worn out."

"I have to admit that I *am* pretty exhausted." Seth looked... disappointed? "I really have enjoyed catching up with you."

Oliver decided to take a chance; he knew that it was up to him to make any progressive steps.

"I'm going to be in town through the weekend with Gus, actually." He took a deep breath to quell his nerves. "Is there any chance we could meet up for coffee? Something like that? I know you're busy and this is last minute."

Seth wrapped his scarf around his neck and held his coat in his hands for a moment. It looked as though he was biting his lip. Great, Oliver had clearly misread the evening and was forcing Seth to have to shoot him down.

"I'd like that, but I don't know what your plans are," Seth said. "I mean, you know mine: perform tomorrow and for the next two nights. So any time before shows or after works for me?"

Not shot down then. "Yes, whatever works for you! I think my schedule is a bit more flexible than yours," Oliver said with a grin. "Oh, you know, hold that thought."

Oliver jogged over to the bartender to borrow a pen. He scribbled the hotel number and his room number along with his UK email address on a cocktail napkin and walked back to the table.

"Here. I don't have my cell phone with me here in New York. International roaming charges are ridiculous. But this will go straight to my room. Or you can email me; I'm pretty fanatical about checking it."

Seth read over the napkin and carefully folded it and placed it in the inside pocket of his coat. "I didn't expect that," he said, chuckling to himself.

"What?" Oliver felt like an idiot, suddenly. Was Seth just trying to be polite? He himself was being pushy. What was *wrong* with him that he couldn't pick up signals?

"I'm so used to the old days, when I'd text you and only have to wait a few seconds for a reply. But calling the hotel desk to be transferred is so old school." He looked pleased about it.

Oliver's heart skipped at beat at Seth talking of their past relationship so easily and with fondness. He needed to quit jumping to so many conclusions. Oliver checked Seth's seat to make sure he had everything; Seth smiled and looked away, seemingly touched by the gesture, and they began walking toward the hotel lobby.

"I'll call you tomorrow mid-morning and we can touch base?" Seth asked.

"Yes! Sure, that sounds fine."

Oliver knew that he wasn't ready for Seth to leave. He didn't *need* to show Seth out of the hotel, he just didn't want to part company: simple as that. He slowed their pace to drag out the inevitable. He wanted to lean in, to touch shoulders, hands, anything to make the reconnection feel real, and not leave it at just a pleasant conversation. He was being obvious, maybe, but Seth didn't seem upset. In fact, if Oliver wasn't mistaken, Seth seemed perfectly fine walking slowly and needlessly leaning over into Oliver's space to avoid bumping into someone.

Very promising. And very frustrating. Oliver just wanted... well, confirmation that they were okay, that they could be in each other's lives beyond just this night, this conversation. That Seth really would call him tomorrow. He didn't know how to *get* it, though, that was the thing. Not without being really forward and putting pressure on Seth to act. He would never do that.

A doorman held the front door as they stepped out into the cold air and promptly hailed a cab at Oliver's signal. Oliver opened the car door for Seth and was almost positive that it flustered Seth a little. In a good way. He liked seeing the blush high on Seth's cheeks, after all this time.

"I'll call tomorrow?" Seth said, sounding slightly breathless. That could have just been because it was freezing and a little windy outside.

"Looking forward to it," Oliver replied, rocking on his heels, knowing he had a huge grin on his face and not really caring. *That just may have been confirmation.*

Oliver shut the cab door once Seth was inside and gave a little wave as the car pulled off the curb and out into the never-ending New York traffic. He stood smiling and watching the cab until it turned at the end of the block, headed to wherever Seth lived. He gave the doorman a huge grin as he turned back to the entrance and whistled tunelessly on the way to his room.

He hoped that he had a big day ahead of him.

Chapter Six

Oliver was checking his email (two messages from Moira, both asking how things were going, and one from his department advisor, who wanted to track his schedule for graduation in the spring and remind him that he needed to decide soon whether or not to enroll in the doctoral program) when the phone rang in his hotel room. His hands hovered over the keyboard, frozen, as the phone continued to trill. He hadn't been completely sure that Seth would take him up on the offer to meet again. Now his heart hammered away and his ears rang faintly as he crossed the room, staring down at the small black phone with the red blinking light.

"I don't know why I need to get so nervous for a phone call," he mumbled, even as he smoothed his hair before picking up.

Calm. Don't be too eager. "Hello?"

"Hi, Oliver," Seth said.

"Hi!" He practically sang hello, for crying out loud. *So much for not sounding eager.* He could hear Seth's quiet laugh on the other end of the phone, an old, familiar sound that made him smile and flash back to late night phone calls when they had talked for hours.

Oh, who was he kidding? He sank onto the bed, holding the phone tightly, and hoped that he and Seth would get to spend some time together today.

"Someone's had their coffee, I hear," Seth teased.

"Oh, you know. Just a good, beautiful morning, that's all."

"Oliver, it's snowing outside. There's going to be icy slush everywhere."

Why was he blushing? "I'm pretty used to it. So! Did you get a good night's sleep?"

He settled in comfortably on his side as Seth rambled about his cab ride home and how good it was to fall into bed. Oliver could almost let himself forget that this was the first time they'd talked on the phone in years. A happy part of him that he hadn't realized was missing was beginning to make itself known as he listened to Seth's voice.

When there was a natural pause, Oliver decided to seize the moment. "You feel like getting lunch, maybe?"

"Well, that's why I'm calling, actually." He could hear Seth shifting on the other end, and the echo of footsteps on tile. "My publicist called me a few minutes ago—oh my God, can you believe I have a *publicist*? It's both fabulous and irritating. Irritating because she told me I need to do some PR stuff today. So there goes my free time."

Oliver's heart sank. Well, he knew he shouldn't have gotten his hopes up. As much as it stung, he didn't want to make Seth feel guilty, so he forced himself to sound as though his hopes hadn't just been dashed. "Okay, then," Oliver said, faking cheer. "You're too busy today. I understand."

"Well." Seth paused. "I was wondering if instead you'd like to grab a late dinner after the show tonight?" Oliver noted that Seth's voice was pitched a little higher and that he had rushed through asking the question. Was *Seth* nervous? Or maybe excited? Holy—

"Sure! Yeah, sure." Oliver cleared his throat to calm himself; his heart rate had doubled since he heard the first ring of the phone; the ups and downs of this conversation had kept it high, and Seth's familiar, richly-toned voice in his ear wasn't helping matters. He sat up and rubbed his palms on his pant legs. When did they start sweating? God, he was like a kid again. "How does this work, I meet you at the theater? Here?"

Seth was moving around on the other end of the line; Oliver could hear the sound of a sink turning on. "Why don't I meet you in your hotel lobby, and we can catch a cab to dinner? I know a great place that stays open late. Nothing in the theater district serves after the shows let out. Meet you there about ten-thirty?"

"Perfect! I'll, ha, be the one with the red carnation." *Good lord.* Oliver banged his forehead against the padded headboard, wishing he could just sound cool for *once* during this conversation. He couldn't help himself, it seemed. He was positively giddy at the prospect of dinner; it was hard to be cool and relaxed in light of the night's potential.

Seth chuckled into the phone, a sound that made Oliver's eyes close and his breathing hitch. "I'll see you then."

"Okay!"

Another soft laugh from Seth. "Okay, bye."

"'Bye." Oliver held the phone to his ear a bit longer, leaning forward and waiting to hear it disconnect before hanging up.

He flopped back on the bed with a happy sigh. It wasn't ideal; he *had* hoped that they would spend the day together, but dinner was fine. Dinner would be great. They'd talk and laugh—aside from Seth, only Moira could get him to laugh and break out of his thoughts—and he'd get to be with his friend again. He hadn't realized how big the hole in his life losing Seth had created until he was faced with the chance to fill it again. Not that he didn't enjoy himself or have friends; it was just that around Seth, life had always been... brighter. Better. He wanted it again.

He wanted his best friend back. His talented, funny, interesting and devastatingly handsome best friend.

Okay, okay. Don't push your luck.

He hopped to his feet, humming a song under his breath as he straightened his things. He hated to make more work for the maid service. He glanced at the clock—eleven more hours to go. There was no way he'd be able to focus on his work, and he knew that he wouldn't be able to sit and read a book for any length of time. He was practically bouncing on his toes, ready to go and make things happen. And since Gus and Emily were spending the day catching up with some of their old college friends, it looked as if he had the whole day to himself. This was unexpected, but not wholly unwelcome.

He needed to keep busy so he didn't sit and wait for ten o'clock to roll around. Oliver saw the wet snow blowing outside his window and grabbed his gloves, coat and scarf. It seemed like a good time to get a jump-start on his holiday shopping. And maybe he'd end up in Washington Square. NYU's Silver School of Social Work was heavily focused on some of the programs that Oliver was interested in; visiting might help to inspire him to get focused on what he wanted to do beyond his master's. He was beginning to be keenly aware of a need to sort out where he was going.

He sang a happy little tune under his breath as he entered the elevator.

* * *

Oliver couldn't stop fidgeting. He'd had a drink at the bar around nine o'clock, flipped through a newspaper, walked around the lobby to stretch his legs, apologetically turned down a nice woman trying to flirt with him, went for *another* walk around the lobby and now, at ten-fifteen, he flipped through a coffee table book about Swedish light fixtures as he sat on one of the sleek chairs near the front entrance. He assumed the hotel had it out because of its attractive, modern cover. He could either read that or the other one, a series of photographs of ashtrays.

"If you're too engrossed with your book, we can always reschedule."

Oliver jumped at the sound of Seth's voice. He almost dropped the book, but managed to get it closed and set aside without looking like a complete fool.

Flustered, Oliver asked, "How did you—"

"Valet entrance," Seth said, tugging at his gloves. He was grinning from ear to ear.

"Hmm. Well, this *is* pretty fascinating, you know. In fact," Oliver said, "did you realize that Swedish glass," he picked the book back up and flipped it open to read, adopting a lofty tone, "'had a major socioeconomic effect on the culture of Sweden after the first World War?'"

Seth laughed and nodded toward the entrance, still smiling at him. "No, I can honestly say that I did not know that."

While pulling on his coat and fishing his gloves out of the pockets, Oliver said, "Knowledge is important, Seth. And if it ever comes up as a question on a trivia night, you know who to thank."

Seth laughed again and bit his lip as if to control his smile; it was as if he was as excited as Oliver about having dinner and spending some time together. That was encouraging. Oliver tried to control the bubbling and fizzing in his stomach. He and Seth would have dinner and relax, and Oliver just really needed to keep it all together and not mess up his chance by being hyper.

Seth stood aside the revolving door to allow Oliver through first and even held the cab door for him; Oliver smiled at the gesture. They chatted comfortably about Seth's earlier performance on the cab ride to SoHo ("Would it have killed the guy to have brought a throat lozenge?

He was coughing up a lung during the entire first act.") and pulled up to a nondescript gray-fronted restaurant with a red awning.

Seth pulled off his gloves and tucked them neatly into his coat pocket before holding the door for Oliver again.

Okay, this feels like a date. No. It's not a date, and I need to stop it. He's just being polite and getting the door for me. Every time... It's not a date.

"I don't know if this sounds appetizing to you," Seth said, "but it's fabulous and what they're known for: oxtail marmalade and beef marrow bones." Seth showed two fingers to the hostess and turned back to Oliver. "This is a place where chefs come when they're off work. I hope it's okay?"

Oliver looked around at the cozy interior with low lighting, happy knots of people laughing and drinking, some more intimate tables in the corners and modern art hanging on the exposed brick walls. The smell was amazing: like a campfire with undertones of herbs. He saw that the bar along the far wall had a huge bank of micro-brews on tap.

I... think this might be a date. No, it just feels like a date because you're out of practice, dummy. Two people can eat in a small, quaint place with flickering candlelight without it meaning something romantic. Apparently.

"Wow, this place looks terrific," Oliver said, following Seth closely as they wove through the crowd to one of the smaller tables in a corner. Seth looked over his shoulder with a satisfied grin that almost stopped Oliver's heart.

"Even my dad likes it," Seth said. "He asks me to bring him here every time he visits. Oh," Seth stopped and put a hand on Oliver's arm, and the heat of his touch unfurled and rolled through Oliver's entire body. "Don't ever tell him what sweetbreads are."

Although he chuckled, Oliver still felt a twinge of longing at the mention of Mike. "Got it. Does he—do you get to see him often?"

Seth's expression softened; he had always looked softer, more protective when he spoke about his dad, but Oliver got the impression that it was also because he had asked. "Not as much as I'd like, but we make the most of it when he comes."

Oliver slapped his hand over his heart; he couldn't believe he hadn't asked yet. "Oh my God, how did he take the news about you getting this part?"

"I think everyone three counties over could hear his yell of excitement,"

Seth laughed, taking a menu from the waiter. He looked proud and pleased and a little shy. That little touch of shyness was something new. Seth had been the most confident person Oliver had ever known. It was just another tiny reminder that life had moved on since Kansas.

"I can just imagine how excited he is for you," Oliver said. He could almost hear Mike's deep, gravelly voice, soft and awe-filled whenever he spoke about his son. "Has he been here to see it yet?"

"Are you kidding?" Seth asked. "He came for the first week and to every single show. He pointed out to people that I was his son every chance he could get. It took me days to convince him that he needed to stop accosting the audience. Theater people were terrified of the giant Hell's Angel dude out in the lobby."

Oliver laughed, a little embarrassed by the hot-itch sensation of tears in his eyes. He could picture it: Mike in his one dress shirt and bolo tie, tearing up as soon as he walked into the theater, maybe looking around at the opulence in awed wonder. He probably had his playbill dog-eared at Seth's bio page, just so he could whip it out and point to Seth's picture. "That's my boy, right there."

Big Mike was just in love with his kid; he'd been the most loving husband to his wife before she died suddenly. After her loss, all of his affection was poured into their son—the spitting image of Renee Larsen, down to his eye color and the faint spray of freckles across his nose. Mike couldn't save his wife from the drunk driver who killed her, but he sure as hell could be there for his son, and had been. Oliver knew how much it meant to him for Seth to find a school that would not only accept, but embrace him. How proud and relieved Mike must be feeling now! Oliver fought the lonely ache for a relationship with his own father that was a fraction of what Seth had with his dad. And truthfully, a big part of that ache was from Oliver missing the relationship he'd built with Mike.

Seth told him stories about Mike's first show as they ate their meal, and how he had to get security to move his dad away from the poster out front; Mike stationed himself there before each show, listening in on people's conversations to make sure they were going to "be nice."

Oliver laughed at that.

"He was so ridiculous." Seth at first looked pleased and happy with his father's affection but now lowered his gaze and shook his head, as if he was embarrassed by it. Seth had never been anything but proud of the relationship and love he shared with his dad; something else was going on.

"Well, your dad has always known you were something special," Oliver said. "And with good reason." Seth looked down at his food, but Oliver caught the small smile on his face before it faded. "He didn't do anything... wrong, did he?"

Seth looked up at him in surprise. "No," he said, drawing the word out a bit as though he was hiding something. "It's more that he was so... vocal. I felt—" Seth sighed and looked off to the side at the other patrons. "Let's just say, the rest of the cast found it *hilarious.*"

"Oh." Oliver wiped the corner of his mouth and laid his napkin across his lap. "Is it because your dad is just, well, proud of you? Yeah, he can get a little... exuberant about things, but that's one of his charms." Oliver flashed Seth a grin. "Or do you think it's because *they* don't have supportive parents? Or maybe they think that someone who looks like your dad couldn't possibly appreciate the arts?"

Seth stopped fiddling with the base of his water glass. Oliver caught a flash of something in his eyes at the question, defiance, maybe? Straightening his posture, Seth said, "I think it's the latter, honestly. I just didn't—I don't like being a target of ridicule, that's all."

Oliver was shocked; he couldn't believe anyone would mock the Larsens. "Are you serious?" he asked. "What the—who? Who made fun of your *dad?*"

"Oliver. It's okay." Seth sighed, shaking himself a little before slipping back into his ever-composed self. Oliver watched, trying to take his cues from how upset Seth was, but not until Seth smiled at him, slow and sweet, did Oliver's temper cool. Maybe Oliver was just overreacting? Seth seemed to appreciate his defense of Mike, though.

"There are just some people in the cast who like giving off a very worldly air," Seth continued, rolling his eyes. "Honestly, they're not worth the energy it takes to be angry. There are times when I have to remind myself of that, that's all."

Oliver sat back in his seat, worrying the napkin in his lap as he watched Seth pick at his food, his smile benign and pasted-on, now, after the grateful smile he'd given Oliver just a moment before. Something was wrong, and it frustrated Oliver that *Seth* was frustrated. Something was different; old-Seth would have gotten into people's faces about this. New-Seth sighed and brushed it off. Who would cause him not to defend himself and his dad? It made Oliver want to defend them; even after all of these years, he still carried a feeling of family for the Larsens.

Oliver laid his fork across the outer edge of his plate and rested his weight on his forearms at the edge of the table, thinking for a moment. "Was it... wait, was it Dough-Face? I mean, Brandt?"

Seth laughed loudly and clapped a hand over his mouth. "You did *not* just call him that!" Well, at least Oliver had succeeded in getting Seth in a better frame of mind, if his amusement was any indication.

"Was it? It was, wasn't it?" Oliver couldn't help but feel a grim sort of satisfaction. He knew there was something creepy about that guy.

"He's one of the producer's brothers," Seth said, giving him a level gaze. "He's an ass, but he's an ass with important friends, something that he likes to remind everyone of. And ultimately, he's harmless. They're just words meant to get under my skin; I've dealt with far worse. It was just bad timing when I was nervous at the start, that's all."

Oliver matched his look and tried to find any tell on Seth's face; there had to be more to this than someone just suggesting Mike Larsen was small-town, or whatever rude thing Brandt had said. Seth dropped his gaze, shifted in his seat, played with his food, straightened the salt and pepper shakers and played with his food a little more. Seth was worried about something. He wasn't looking at Oliver anymore. As though he was hiding something, or embarrassed about something? Or... someone?

Oh.

Oliver took a deep breath and asked quietly, "What else is he, Seth? Brandt."

Seth didn't say anything for a moment; Oliver noticed his cheeks getting red. Finally, Seth looked away, straightening his silverware to make it just so. "An ex. Sort of," he trailed off with a dismissive wave of his hand.

Oliver felt sick to his stomach. It had been awful to watch Brandt drape himself all over Seth the night before, hinting at something, but to hear Seth say it... Oliver's heart rate picked up, remembering Seth saying that Brandt wasn't anyone special. Maybe things had changed during the day and they were growing serious? Okay, even he recognized that was a bit ridiculous. And he reminded himself that Seth had seemed so bothered when Oliver asked him if they were dating. But... was that because it was *Oliver* asking and Seth had been caught off guard and felt uncomfortable?

"We didn't really *date*. That's what I meant by 'sort of.' We—" Seth cleared his throat and took a moment to drink some water. "We fooled around a few months back. And now that I've made this incredibly awkward, how do you feel about dessert?" He directed a comically awkward smile at Oliver and ducked his red face behind the dessert menu.

Oliver certainly didn't like thinking of that simpering dolt with his hands on Seth, but he could hardly get angry about it having happened. Well, he *could* get angry that it happened, he just *shouldn't* be angry. He took a deep breath and let it out slowly. He could do this; he could be a good friend. Supportive.

Oliver said, "He has the handshake of a dead fish. I can't imagine what he must kiss like."

Some of the tension in Seth's shoulders dropped as he laughed again. "There's a very good reason why I'm not seeing him, Oliver."

They smiled in tandem as the waiter came to clear their plates, each saying "Thank you" quietly. From the corner of his eye, Oliver caught Seth smirking. He chuckled a little. "It's nice to see we're still in sync on some things."

Seth's smile faltered briefly before he put it back in place as the waiter asked if they'd like coffee. Oliver opened his mouth to say yes, but Seth spoke first. "Nonfat cappuccino and a brewed cup, black with two sugars, for my friend here."

The little wink Seth gave him sent a wave of heat through his body and pushed out the cold, negative thoughts of Brandt. It was both thrilling and comforting to be reminded of these little connections they'd had and that were still there. Oliver wanted to find out what else they still had together.

"Yep, still in sync on some things," Seth said, leaning back in his seat and crossing his legs primly.

* * *

They stood out front under the awning, wrapped up against the cold. It had started to snow heavily, fat, fluffy flakes that quickly coated everything in clean white.

"First snowfall of the year," Seth said, smiling at Oliver. "I always love how everything looks so new when it's covered, initially. You know, before it turns crunchy and gray and filled with trapped cigarette butts."

Oliver felt heavy and light at the same time. Light, because he and Seth had spent a great evening together, and the connection was still there. They were still meant to be friends. Heavy, because he didn't want the night to end and didn't want to presume that they would make this a habit while he was in town. He steeled himself and brushed some of the snowflakes from Seth's shoulder, still needing to keep some connection sparking between them.

Oliver watched his hand as it moved over the dark wool of Seth's coat. "It's too early for us to start thinking about it going wrong. We should be glad it's so nice now."

Seth sighed. "You're right." He reached out and brushed at the lapel on Oliver's coat, patting it smooth before putting his hands back into his pockets and hugging himself tight for warmth.

"Seth, I..." Oliver wanted to reach out again so badly, to just hold him and make what they'd had come back. But that wasn't how things worked; he knew that much. Well, he could reach out in other ways. "I'll be in town through the weekend, until Tuesday, if you think you might like to do something? No pressure, though. I know you didn't even know I was coming."

Seth twisted his torso in a little back and forth motion as he looked at the snow falling on the street. "I have plans this weekend that I can't change," Seth said, his voice quiet.

Telling himself to not get his hopes up was one thing, but the crushing blow of reality hurt far worse. Oliver tried to not let his features reveal how upset he was.

"So," Seth said, looking up at Oliver from under his lashes. "What if you come to the show on Sunday and we spend the rest of the day together?" He added quickly, "The show is over by four? And Monday is lights out, so it's not a work night."

"Yes! Sure, I'd love to see the show again." Oliver's heavy feelings blew away with the force of his excitement: He wasn't being shot down. "And leave the plans to me, is that all right?"

"Okay, then!" Seth straightened his posture and grinned. Oliver would have sworn that Seth looked a little... shy. As if he hadn't been sure of Oliver's answer and was surprised but also a touch bashful at the prospect of them spending the day—and possibly the whole evening, Oliver's mind happily offered—together. Oliver's excitement grew exponentially.

"I'll have your ticket at will call, and..." Seth bent a little at the waist and traced a line in the snow with the edge of his shoe. "I'll see you then?"

"Absolutely."

Seth jerked his head back. "I'm just going to take the train from here, if that's that okay? It's just that I'm only three stops from my apartment." Seth bit his lip nervously. "You don't mind finding your way back to the hotel, do you?"

"Oh! Oh, of course I don't mind. I'll just grab a cab, that won't be a problem. So..."

"So... goodnight?" Seth bit his lip and looked up through his lashes at him again. It sent Oliver's heart into palpitations to see that familiar look of excitement and nervousness on Seth's face; it had had the same effect on him when they were younger, too.

"Right," Oliver said, a little breathlessly. "Um, goodnight."

Seth seemed to debate something internally before he opened his arms and wrapped Oliver in a tight hug into which Oliver all but melted. Seth gave him a squeeze and let him go—far too soon, as far as Oliver was concerned. He was just getting the scent of Seth's cologne and marveling at how soft his cheek was when Seth pulled back.

Blushing, Seth waved goodbye as he walked away, backwards. "See you Sunday?"

"Yes, you will." Oliver was rooted to the spot. The spot where Seth hugged him. The spot where they became friends again. When he saw Seth's bright scarf disappear down the subway entrance he turned to look at the front of the restaurant and said its name out loud. "Blue Ribbon."

Oliver's first spot in New York with Seth. Somewhere they could wrap their arms around each other and no one would care.

On the drive back to the hotel he smiled and pressed his cheek against the cool glass of the cab window. He hoped that he would get the opportunity to have other firsts with Seth.

Chapter Seven

Oliver spent the weekend with Gus and Emily, wandering from museum to great restaurant to museum. In between some holiday shopping they ended up seeing the Kandinsky exhibit at the Guggenheim—surprisingly, at Gus's request. For all he was buttoned up and by the book, Gus was evidently a huge fan of what Oliver saw as nothing but chaotic shapes and colors.

"But look: Everything is precisely placed, Oliver. There's a reason for where everything is. The point of his work is to learn *why* it's there. How it affects what's around it. "

Oliver saw just a series of rectangles and lines. That is, until one painting that made him stop in his tracks: *On White.* He stared at it for several minutes, wondering why it looked both familiar and new. And then it hit him suddenly: It was... music. Or, it was like a physical representation of how he felt about music: that wonderful sense of creation building up inside of him until it just had to burst out, either through playing the piano or singing. Looking at the painting was like *seeing* the emotion that he didn't have a name for, the joy and noise and love for how it felt to share with others that precious *thing* that was inside of him. Or used to be.

He sat in front of the painting on a hard wooden bench for almost half an hour as Gus and Emily pushed on to look at the rest of the exhibit. Oliver ached. He felt both homesick and happy, and remembered moments of pure joy, the kind he only got from playing. When was the last time he'd played the piano? Sang out loud? Singing along under his breath in the shower or on a train didn't count. When was the last time he performed anything? He realized with a start that it had been since he'd graduated Bakerfield and moved away from the piano at his parent's house.

That long? That's not...

He moved through the rest of the exhibit, not really seeing it. It *had* been that long. He flashed on Seth in his show, how strong and beautiful his voice had become. How he was Seth fully realized, finally the person he'd set out to become.

While Oliver certainly didn't regret his course of study—he very much believed in what he and his colleagues were researching—he did feel regret at losing something that had once been so important to him, at *ignoring* something once so important. Part of him even felt a little shame at the thought of Seth discovering how much of himself Oliver had left behind in Kansas. He laughed that off; what, he was already imagining scenarios of closeness between the two of them? He wasn't even sure that Seth wanted his friendship.

Well, I can hope, he thought as he left the curved walkway and walked into the central rotunda on the ground floor of the museum. Emily and Gus were talking with one of the docents near the small gift shop toward the entrance; he shook himself to come back to the present and joined them. Unable to get the image of that painting out of his head, unable to shake a lonely feeling that had begun to creep out of a place inside him that had been closed off for a very long time, he bought a postcard of the painting.

Oliver left Emily and Gus to their own devices on Sunday after brunch and made sure that he had plenty of time to run a small errand before heading to the theater. He wanted to make a gesture toward Seth, one that expressed his gratitude for the tickets, the dinner and the conversation and would show that he would like this to turn into genuine friendship again. He'd agonized over the idea all night and throughout brunch. (Gus had called him out on his distraction by pointing out that he'd poured syrup into his coffee mug.)

It was important that Seth knew how proud Oliver was of him, and how much his friendship would mean. He didn't want to freak Seth out, though, and he *definitely* didn't want to pressure him into anything. Seth was just... someone special. Oliver's life could be nothing but better with him in it, and he wanted Seth to know that. He'd thought of the perfect gift, something he hoped would serve as a reminder of how close and supportive of each other they'd been.

He checked the business card in his pocket for the address the concierge had given him and whistled softly to himself as he walked through Hell's Kitchen toward his first destination on this bright and sunny and very cold day, feeling confident by virtue of having a plan. The hotel's concierge had gone on and on about the owner of this particular shop and how thoughtful he was at finding just the right match for the occasion.

Oliver chatted with the owner after placing his initial order, letting him know he had to make it to the theater for the two p.m. show. Richard, the owner, had also seen Seth's play and been impressed by his performance. He excused himself to find something in the back, leaving Oliver to wander freely and trail his hands lightly over the store's goods.

Richard came back, tied the gift with a simple silk ribbon and handed it to him with a wink. Oliver looked it over and noted that it wasn't exactly as he'd ordered.

"Trust me," Richard said. "It's kind of what I'm known for. I have outstanding intuition. Also, the meaning behind it is on the card; make sure you sign it!"

"Oh, right." Oliver borrowed Richard's pen. After a moment's deliberation, a huge smile spread across his face as he wrote:

> *To Seth:*
> *These are to celebrate you and everything you've become. I'm so proud of you.*
> *~Oliver*

He turned the card over and read the meaning of the various items, starting at the addition Richard had made. He looked up to find Richard smiling.

"It's a gift I have. Enjoy!"

Still smiling from ear to ear, Oliver left the shop with a friendly wave and practically floated to the theater a few blocks down. He got a few looks from people but couldn't have cared less; he held the gift proudly as he approached will call. The distracted girl behind the glass found his name and pulled out his ticket; as she handed it over, she finally noticed what Oliver was carrying and squealed. He made a shushing gesture and laughed.

"Don't ruin the surprise!"

She shook her head quickly, no. "Oh, he's going to love that. Hell, I'd love that!"

He ducked his head, chuckling, and made his way into the theater to his prime seat on the third row, orchestra aisle. He sat down, beginning to feel nervous. Maybe it was too much? Maybe it would send the wrong message? He shook his head; it wouldn't do any good to second-guess himself now. He set the present carefully across his knees and opened his playbill. He read Seth's bio through to the end once more as he waited for the show to begin, his heart racing as he read again: "to his first duet partner."

Whether Seth had meant him or not didn't matter; it bolstered his confidence. They'd always supported each other. That's what this gift was—a show of support with a nod to their former relationship. Seth should have all the support he could get.

Who made him believe he could finally get here.

For now he was happy to sit in the darkening theater as the orchestra cued up and let himself hope, just a bit.

* * *

Oliver stood at the end of the sectioned-off area outside the stage door, bundled warmly in his coat and scarf and holding both hands behind his back. He didn't want to be in the way of the other actors and fans gathered outside (a much smaller crowd, since it was Sunday afternoon and near the freezing mark).

Several of the supporting cast and orchestra members had already come and gone before Seth exited the building. Oliver's breath caught in his throat at the sight of him: freshly scrubbed face, hair styled, chic coat with the collar turned up against the cold, huge smile to greet the small but boisterous crowd. Oliver couldn't help but swell with pride for Seth and everything he'd accomplished.

He could remember their teen years; all of the crude and hateful slurs people in their backward, conservative town had flung their way, and how many times Seth had been told he was wrong or weird or just unusual, as if that in itself was something bad. How they'd said he would never amount to anything *because* of it. But here he was, surrounded by a crowd of people both young and old, the cultured and the newly-initiated to the theater, a crowd that clamored for his autograph and wanted nothing more than to simply thank him for their experience today.

Oliver rocked back and forth, smiling to himself, almost overcome with euphoric emotion on Seth's behalf. Seth glanced his way as he took a playbill from an older woman and shrugged happily before signing. Oliver laughed; he couldn't help it. He would have waited through a hundred signatures if it meant seeing that high color in Seth's cheeks and the joyful smile on his face at being surrounded by people who recognized and admired his unique gift.

The crowd began to disperse after Seth waved and told them, "Thank you for coming!" He headed down the walkway toward Oliver. "I still can't believe they're here to see me," he said, laughing.

"Don't be silly, of course they are," Oliver said, pulling one hand from behind his back and holding it out to Seth with a bit of trepidation in his smile. "Once again, you were... well, sublime."

His insides fluttered and twisted as Seth's face went still and his eyes opened wide in dawning recognition of what Oliver was offering him.

Oliver babbled, "Is it too much? I just wanted to do something as a thank you and congratulations, and I didn't know if—"

"Oh my God, they're *beautiful.*" Seth took the bouquet with both hands and buried his face in the blooms, breathing deeply. "Oh, *Oliver*, I..." Seth lowered the blue and gold flowers, eyes still on them, as a smile began to blossom on his face. "I can't believe you remembered these."

Oliver let out a shaky breath. Not the wrong gift, then. They'd worn matching golden rose and blue ribbon boutonnières to prom, to represent their school's colors and where they'd met. He leaned one shoulder against the brick wall and said, "How on earth could you think I'd ever forget the first flowers anyone ever gave me? I know it's not exactly the same; I had to fudge a bit with getting blue in there to make it right, but I tried."

Seth looked up. Oliver was desperate to know if he'd done right, if he'd pushed things too far too soon or if Seth really did simply enjoy the flowers.

"Yes, you did," Seth replied, warmly. His gaze was soft and he seemed pleased, so Oliver took it at face value. Relief spread through him.

"I love them, thank you."

"Shall we?" Oliver asked, motioning to the end of the block.

Seth followed along next to him as they walked down the side street, the roses cradled in his arm nearest Oliver. Seth touched one of the roses delicately with his gloved finger. "My dad gave me four dozen daisies after my first performance, if you can believe that."

Oliver laughed and saw through his peripheral vision that Seth was still smiling and biting his lip while he smelled the flowers.

Definitely the right choice.

"Why daisies?" Oliver asked.

Seth paused for a moment; Oliver stopped on the sidewalk and turned to look at him. Seth had that look of love and pride that was reserved for Mike Larsen. There was a touch of sadness in his eyes, though, something that sent a leaden feeling through Oliver's core and made him want to do anything to chase it away.

"Seth?"

Seth shook himself and laughed softly. "Sorry, I just miss my dad. He gave me daisies because he said they weren't 'too fancy' and would make me think of 'simple ol' Pop back in the sticks,' as he put it. And it was a dozen from each of them: him, the guys at the shop—John and Little Mike, you remember them?" At Oliver's nod, Seth said quietly, "And from... my mom."

Oliver smiled and looked off at the passersby on the street. "That's really sweet." Maybe it was just his close proximity to Seth after all these years, and all of the memories that came with it, but Oliver positively missed Mike. For such a simple man, he was capable of the most elegant and thoughtful gestures, and they came straight from his heart.

"So!" Seth said, putting a bright smile back on his face. "Where to?"

"Oh! Well, I have a reservation for an early dinner, is that okay?"

"I am absolutely *starved*, so that's perfect. But..." Seth looked down at his bouquet. Two dozen flowers were a bit much to carry around the city.

"I thought that we could leave those," Oliver nodded at the bouquet, "with the concierge at my hotel, since it's just around the corner, and then head out?"

"Excellent! Then again, you always excelled at executing elaborate plans," Seth said, a tiny smirk at the corners of his mouth. "Like that ride home from the airport my freshman year."

Oliver chuckled softly, his stomach swooping from the memory, as they entered the hotel's lobby.

Seth smoothed the front of his jacket, stopped mid-stroke and quickly looked up at Oliver. "Not that I'm always thinking of that."

The bare nervousness on Seth's face did more to encourage Oliver in this plan of getting his friend back than anything else.

After discreetly slipping the concierge a bill, Oliver had Seth's flowers taken care of. He turned to lead Seth back out to the street and hail a cab.

"I hope it's okay that I'm always using these," he said as he held the door for Seth to slide in. "Front and Beekman, please," he told the driver. "I don't trust myself with the trains yet. I'm sure I'll try to show off and take you north when I mean to go south."

Oliver settled in next to Seth, almost hyper-aware of the warmth pouring off of his body even though there was a respectable distance between them. He needed to act appropriately here and keep himself talking casually.

Seth shook his head. "South Street Seaport? If you wanted the tourist experience, we could always stay in Times Square."

"Just... trust me. Hey, I know some things," Oliver said, trying to give off an aura of casual city know-how. He was feeling a little on edge, worried that his choice for their outing was going to seem seriously uncool to Seth. "It's not touristy in the winter, and we're not going to the mall, I promise."

Seth hummed a laugh and patted him on the knee as they pulled away from the curb. Oliver felt the warmth of the touch all the way to his ears. He really needed to remember what Seth was possibly offering him: friendship. Oliver shouldn't treat this like a date or anything else. They were old friends, catching up. His stomach was already in knots as it was; he didn't need to put any extra pressure on the situation.

* * *

"And evidently I'd been hitting on him all term, no thanks to my friend Todd."

Seth sat back in his chair, laughing with his hand splayed across his sternum. "I can't believe you didn't pay attention to where you were getting your information, Oliver. And you, a researcher? That is *priceless*."

Oliver swallowed a mouthful of wine and set his glass back down carefully. "You can't imagine the looks I've been getting from his teammates."

The way Seth was looking at him—happy, interested, possibly even content—was doing insane things to his stomach. It looped and swirled with Seth's every laugh, his every casual touch to Oliver's arm.

They'd arrived at Harbor Lights for their dinner reservation just before the sun began to set over the water. The patio was enclosed with heavy clear plastic and space heaters were placed overhead; it was cozy, and they had an outstanding view of the Brooklyn Bridge, one of the prettiest views in the whole city.

Seth had raised an eyebrow at him as the hostess seated them on the patio; they were one of two couples that had chosen to sit outside. Oliver was sure that some people probably found this particular location terribly romantic; he just thought it would be a nice change of pace from where he'd been staying.

And... well, okay, it *was* terribly romantic when the bridge's lights came on, swooping along the suspension cables. The sun setting behind them cast a warm orange glow over the water. They'd taken their time with dinner, chatting about their days, Seth wanting to know every detail of Oliver's life in England. The conversation had been relaxed, natural, with not one awkward pause.

Oliver realized sometime after his second glass of wine that he could do this: simply be friends. It wouldn't be weird or painful—much—and he would have the benefit of his best friend to talk to again, someone who made him laugh like no one else, someone empathetic and kind and just... *Seth*.

He would do whatever was necessary to have this camaraderie in his life again.

Propping his chin on his hand, Oliver listened to Seth talk about David Falchurch, the actor who had originated the role of The Fair Youth before injuring himself and opening up an entirely new world for Seth.

"I think the only reason why I was able to resist brutally murdering him and certain other members of the cast was the diva training I got watching Chance back at Bakerfield," Seth said. He was resting his weight on his arms on the table, leaning into Oliver's space. "He was the gayest straight boy I've ever known, and I went to a dramatic arts college."

Oliver drifted off into thought as Seth explained the backstage politics that had existed prior to his taking the lead. Seth was so confident now; he'd always presented as confident when they were younger, but now it wasn't an act of defiance. He simply knew that he deserved to be where he was and that other people knew it, too.

Oliver wondered if he still bit the edge of his thumb when he was deep in thought. If he still liked the same cinnamon-flavored mouthwash. If his hands still trembled when he was kissed just at the base of his Adam's apple...

"But I'm boring you, I'm sorry," Seth said, blushing slightly. "This isn't interesting to anyone who isn't involved."

Oliver mentally cursed himself for letting his imagination carry him away. "No, no, I just got lost in thought, that's all. I'm sorry," he reassured Seth.

Seth raised one eyebrow in question as he took a sip from his wine glass.

"Oh. I—" Oliver wanted nothing more than to reach out and take his hand. But then, he'd always been physically demonstrative—even before they'd dated, he reminded himself. "I'm just so, so proud of you, Seth." Steeling himself, he reached out and laid a hand on top of Seth's, giving it a squeeze before letting it go and resting his own hand just inches from Seth's.

"Thank you." Seth kept his hand where it had been; Oliver wanted even more to take it in his, knowing how warm and smooth Seth's skin was, how their fingers looked linked together. A dull ache settled low in his belly. He wanted it so much, but knew he would be happy with another friendly hug at the end of the evening.

"Feel like walking? There's something I wanted to see with you, if you don't mind being a little cold?" Oliver asked.

"You're just full of surprises, aren't you?" Seth said, smiling.

Oliver laughed, feeling nervous and happy and all of seventeen again. He quickly took care of the tab and held Seth's coat for him to slip on.

"Always the gentleman," Seth murmured.

"Oh, um... habit. Sorry," Oliver said, rubbing the back of his neck. He felt shy and obvious.

"Don't be! It's a rare find in this day and age, believe me." Seth smiled and bumped his shoulder into Oliver as they headed outside. "Makes me feel special."

You are.

It was freezing. Fortunately, there wasn't much of a wind coming off the water, so while it was definitely cold, it wasn't bitterly so. The cold had the added benefit of forcing them to walk close together for warmth as they headed into Seaport. The sun had set, and the streets were decked with lit garlands hung from the streetlights, and other holiday-themed decorations. They rounded Fulton and there was a gorgeous tree, more than twenty-five feet tall, every single branch wrapped in warm amber light.

They stopped in their tracks, taken aback by its size and beauty.

"Even though I find the dogma ridiculous and insulting in places, they sure know how to decorate for a celebration," Seth mused. "Consider this hall decked."

Oliver chuckled and tugged on Seth's elbow. Then he stopped at a sign in front of the carpeted steps leading up to the tree.

Caroling every Saturday and Sunday until 4 p.m.!

It was close to seven. He had completely missed the carolers; there went the second activity for the night. He rubbed his hand over his face and tried to think of what to do.

"Oliver?"

He turned and pasted a smile on his face. "Well, evidently I can't tell time anymore."

Seth cocked his head in question, waiting for Oliver to continue.

"Oh. Um, they have carolers here on the weekend, and it's a crowd event. I thought it would be fun, but..." Feeling foolish, he pointed over his shoulder at the sign.

Seth rolled his eyes and walked up the steps to join him at the base of the tree. With their backs to it, they could just see the bridge lights dancing on the water.

"Like we need a crowd to sing," Seth scoffed. He pulled his hands out of his pockets and clasped them at his sternum as he took a deep breath. "Once in royal David's city," he began to sing.

Oliver went completely still. They stood shoulder to shoulder, Oliver aware of every small movement as Seth sang, the tiny shifts in his stature as he breathed deeply, his voice, as mesmerizing as ever but astoundingly controlled. Clearly his years of training had somehow managed to make his instrument even better. Oliver closed his eyes, a smile on his face, as Seth sang the first verse perfectly. He joined in the second verse, picking up the harmony. Seth bumped their shoulders together again, not missing a note.

Oliver had never been to this street corner before, had never sung this particular song with Seth, but it seemed like home. It was familiar and warm and *right* and he thrilled at the sound of their voices mingled in song once again. *This is how it's supposed to be*, he thought.

Seth leaned against him on the final repeated note and then laughed and stepped away. Oliver wanted to pull him right back and keep him there, warm and at his side, and sing every song he could think of. Seth walked around the tree, his hands back in his pockets and a bashful smile on his face as he looked at some of the utilitarian decorations hung here and there.

"Before people realized my voice wasn't going to get any deeper and it became something that made me an easy target, I always had the solo at Christmas at my mom's church. You know how I'm incapable of turning down a chance to sing in front of a willing audience," Seth said, laughing.

"They always gave it to you because you sound like an angel." Oliver went still and his mouth snapped shut. What was wrong with him? That was too much. He believed it to his core, but he didn't need to *say* it.

"Remind me to record some of these compliments so I can listen to them on days that bad reviews come out," Seth said, shaking his head. He turned back to the tree, but not before Oliver saw the high color on his cheeks; it wasn't from the cold.

"Since I didn't plan this portion of our evening very well, how do you feel about moving on to our next destination?" Oliver asked, hopping down the steps one at a time, trying to keep things light. When he reached the bottom, he turned to look up at Seth, who was still standing by the tree. "Oh, unless you're worn out and just want to call it a night; I don't mean to pressure y—"

Seth glided down the stairs and hooked an arm through Oliver's. "Where to, *mon Capitaine?*"

Oliver tried to control his grin—he really did—but at that simple gesture, the casual touch, he was filled with excitement. It was as if something within him had been asleep and was waking up again. He didn't want the night to end—he was just getting started.

They walked toward the main street to hail a cab—Oliver didn't want to give away their destination by getting Seth to help him with the subway, and he had the money—and when Oliver began to sing "God Rest Ye Merry, Gentlemen" as they waited for an available taxi, Seth joined in, not missing a beat as he threw his arm up in the air to stop a cab.

Oliver opened the door with a flourish as he sang "Comfort and joy," sliding in after Seth as they wrapped up the verse, laughing. If this was what friendship with Seth would be like, then coming to New York was definitely the best decision of his life.

This is exactly where I should be.

* * *

"I love these. *Love.* If I had the space, I would install one in my apartment," Seth said, running his palm lightly over the Japanese painted ferns. He looked over his shoulder at Oliver, eyes dreamy, his head no doubt filled with new décor plans. "My place is a shoebox, though. Not to mention the two hours of sunlight I get most likely aren't enough to keep this alive."

Oliver smiled at him and turned back to look at the patterns woven into the installation. The mass of plant material was as high as the vaulted ceiling and stretched along the entire wall. The atrium of the Lincoln Center was beautiful on its own, with the various sculptures and exhibits placed here and there, but the Living Wall was something unique. Oliver had seen one in London a year ago and had fallen in love with the idea of interior landscaping; it just made the room feel... warmer. Cleaner.

"I do have a fabulous view, though," Seth continued. "Huh, the opposite view of the one we had at dinner, come to think of it."

"You live in Brooklyn?"

Seth sat on one of the chairs near the wall and sighed. "I couldn't afford Manhattan anymore. I shared an apartment the first year after I graduated, but with roommates' weird schedules and my need for living in cleanliness, it was just a nightmare. I got a job in the chorus and was able to get my own place, so I jumped on it. Brooklyn's pretty great, actually."

Oliver took a seat opposite him, leaning on the table and ruffling the greenery with his free hand. "Did you get your exposed brick wall? Loft? Massive shower and—or—a claw-foot tub?"

Seth softly hummed a note of pleasure and looked away. "You remember that," he murmured.

"Of course I do," Oliver replied, just as softly.

Seth sat back in his chair, one leg crossed over the other, his hands in his lap. He smiled fondly at Oliver for a moment before saying, "No. No brick wall, no loft. And it has a stock shower-bathtub unit." Seth rolled his eyes playfully. "Very boring. No shower curtain on earth can change it from stodgy to fabulous, I'm afraid."

Oliver chuckled. "I actually have the claw-foot tub, and they're not all they're cracked up to be, to be honest. I've practically killed myself trying to get out of it, more than once."

"Do you like it there?" Seth leaned in and rested his chin on his palm. "In England?"

Oliver ran the pad of his thumb over a glossy leaf of trailing ivy, thinking. "Yes. For now, at least. There are too many things I miss back in the States," he said, looking directly into Seth's eyes. *People I miss.* "This has been the year of realizing just how much."

Seth looked down at the table and drew patterns on the Formica with the tip of his index finger.

"I hope you get it, Seth."

Seth looked up, confused.

"The brick wall? The claw-foot tub? The slate-stacked fireplace reaching all the way up through the loft?" Oliver added, smirking genially.

Seth laughed. "Ah, yes, that last one was during our mid-century modern period."

Oliver could forget that they were in a public place, surrounded by people. Forget the years that stretched between them like a black hole. He was flooded with such longing at the mention of their Palm Desert fantasy: they'd dreamed they had a beautiful home, warm and inviting, and planned dinner parties and holiday gatherings that all began and ended with the two of them, together.

Oh, he wanted that again. He wanted *all* of it: the friendship, the shared memories, the plans for their future. He wanted Seth to love him again—wanted that most of all. His chest clenched tightly at the thought of not ever having that, of not *deserving* it. It was almost too painful, sitting across from Seth with their futures unknown, their past both joy-filled and heartbreaking, not knowing where things could go or what was okay to ask of him.

Oliver must have been sitting and staring at nothing for a long period of time, because Seth cleared his throat and looked at him expectantly.

"I have a proposition," Seth said. He paused, and it seemed he was thinking carefully about his choice of words. "I don't know what other whirlwind activity you've planned for this evening, but to be truthful, I'd really just like to be done going from place to place and get these shoes off." Seth poked his leg out and tugged on his pant leg to expose the gorgeous brown leather of his boots. "They pinch like hell."

Oliver's heart sank. Of course Seth was tired. He'd had a show earlier, and Oliver was dragging him all over the island—

"So why don't we go back to your hotel, I'll make you order ridiculously expensive room service, I kick these shoes off and we... talk?"

That deep sense of longing within Oliver pulsed with the rhythm of his heartbeat, which was beginning to pick up speed, and he dared to let himself hope that maybe Seth wasn't immune to this... whatever it still was between them. For Seth it might just be a longing for friendship, for someone who understood him at the most basic levels. Or it could be more. Oliver didn't want to set himself up for disappointment; he had to tell himself that this was nothing but what Seth said it was, an opportunity to talk.

But Oliver couldn't help the little glimmer of hope for something more that refused to die, that told him maybe he *wasn't* reading the situation wrong.

"Okay," he answered, his voice soft, and nodded.

Seth held out Oliver's coat for him this time. He smiled as he pulled the fabric up over Oliver's broad shoulders.

The roaring of the water as it shot into the air and pounded back into the fountain outside Lincoln Center, couldn't match the roaring in Oliver's ears when Seth tucked his arm into his own again and led him to the cab stand.

Chapter Eight

They came to Oliver's hotel room to find Seth's bouquet displayed in a beautiful cut-glass vase with the card propped up against it, a bottle of champagne chilling next to it and a small plate of chocolate-dipped strawberries to round out the tableau. Worried that Seth would think he had planned it, Oliver stammered, "I guess this is a really good hotel, huh?"

Seth smirked, took one of the strawberries and settled onto the lone chair in the room, next to the table and opposite the bed.

Oliver excused himself to freshen up and took extra time to run cold water over his wrists in order to calm his racing heart and thoughts. It was freezing outside. They constantly had to bundle up to go from place to place. This was just a way for them to relax and catch up without all of that hassle.

In Oliver's hotel room. With champagne and strawberries. So, hey. No pressure.

He splashed cold water over his face and patted it dry. He found Seth still sitting in his chair, his fingers tracing the aubergine leaves of the filbert spray behind the roses. Their dark color was a lovely contrast to the golden-yellow roses and vivid bluebells. Oliver noted that Seth held the card, open, in his other hand.

Oliver searched Seth's face for any hint of what he was feeling and Seth looked back, breathing deeply. More than anything, Oliver wanted to lean forward and bury his hands in Seth's thick hair. He wondered if it still smelled of Seth's old shampoo. He wanted to press his lips to the warm, thin skin at Seth's temple, to hold him close, for them not to have lived these past several years apart.

Seth exhaled and shook his head a little—but he was smiling, Oliver was happy to see. It was a small smile, but it was warm.

"You didn't forget anything, did you?" Seth asked a little breathlessly, his fingers drawing over the message on the card.

Oliver shook his head. He didn't want to take his eyes off of Seth's face. They stayed that way for a while, their breathing in sync, their eyes looking for clues: where it was safe to take this... whatever was happening? Seth was the first to break the gaze.

"Feel like champagne?" he asked. "They went to the trouble to bring it up here, after all."

Oliver felt almost groggy, as if he had been shaken awake. He blinked heavily and forced himself to snap out of his reverie. "Uh, sure. Yes, let me get a towel." He grabbed a hand towel from the bathroom to cover the cork, focusing everything on the task at hand in order to keep his wits about him.

As Oliver unwrapped the foil on the bottle, Seth unbuckled his ankle boots, slid them off his feet and lined them up against the foot of the bed, out of the way. "Oh my God, that feels amazing," he groaned, flexing and pointing his feet.

Oliver wedged the cork out with a loud pop and set the bottle aside. "Here, Seth, this is silly. Stretch out and be comfortable," he said, gesturing to the bed. As Seth made himself comfortable against the padded silk headboard, Oliver poured out two glasses. He handed one to Seth and settled in the chair. It was only a few feet away, but suddenly it seemed like miles.

"To old friends," Seth said, holding up his glass.

"To old friends," Oliver murmured, taking a sip.

Seth laughed and his lips buzzed against the crystal of his champagne flute. "I remember you hiding your mother's crystal in your room so we could toast my being accepted at Juilliard."

Oliver chuckled at that memory as he settled comfortably in the chair. He felt warm again. How special it had made him feel to have Seth want to be with him, and only him, to celebrate.

"But that was diet soda we drank, not Veuve Clicquot."

Seth smiled and looked off into the middle distance.

There had been another celebration with champagne: their last New Year's Eve together, when Oliver was still a senior at Bakerfield. They had held each other for hours, their arms wrapped around one another,

Seth's forehead resting in the crook of Oliver's neck, while Oliver sighed contentedly with every warm exhalation of Seth's breath on his skin. They'd stayed that way until the final countdown. Seth had made sure their bottle of champagne stayed hidden so the other guys and their dates didn't empty it before midnight.

They had slipped into Gus's garage and made quick work of popping the cork as quietly as possible and pouring the champagne into plastic cups, toasting the New Year as the group inside screamed and whistled their excitement. Seth's kiss had tasted of fruit, the effervescent bubbles still sparkling and popping in his mouth when Oliver slipped in his tongue to taste both the drink and Seth.

Oliver blinked and watched the bubbles race to the top of his glass, their tiny fizzing noise the only sound in the room. To get to that place again—if it was even possible—Oliver knew he would have to bring up the past, and that part of his life that could still lay him low, make him ache as if a part of himself were missing. Which, in a way, it was. He looked up at Seth, so impossibly handsome: the sharp edges of his jaw-line and the faint stubble there, the breadth of his shoulders, his masculinity underscored by his flawless skin, his full lips, his elegant and effortless carriage.

He still looked so much like the boy Oliver had fallen in love with all those years ago, but he had become a man Oliver wanted to know—to love, given the chance. *Surely* Seth was feeling this undercurrent of longing. Surely Seth was not immune to the echoes of the love they'd shared that had been reverberating between them since they saw each other again.

They sat in companionable silence for a moment, sipping at their champagne as if to keep from saying something that might break the fragile bond between them. Oliver argued with himself: Should he bring up the thing he most wanted to say? It also was the one thing he really, *really* didn't want to talk about for fear of ruining the tenuous bridge he was trying to build back to Seth's life.

He sighed; he needed to man up, here. Seth deserved any and every apology Oliver could offer.

"Seth—"

"Oliver, you don't have to." Seth's smile was fading from his eyes.

Regardless, Oliver knew he *had* to get this out there. "Please just let me," he said quietly. "I am so, so sorry." He could feel the tears stinging his eyes. They wouldn't fall; he wouldn't let them. He didn't want to seem pitiable, just honest. "I want... Seth, I'm so sorry."

Seth slumped back against the pillows, his head against the padded wall, his face looking so sad. Goddamn it, Oliver had done it again. He was responsible for that shattered look on Seth's face yet again. His intention had been to make Seth feel better, somehow. He was just really, monumentally bad at this.

If that's not the understatement of the year...

"Seth, God; I didn't mean to make you—I was so stupid, so selfish. God, why am I so clumsy at this!" He ran his hands through his hair. Seth sat still, regarding him with a pained expression. Oliver had to make that go away; he had to get back to where they could laugh and joke and be Seth-and-Oliver again, even if it *was* just as friends. He'd happily accept that gift, and he knew that, after this week, he could never go back to not having Seth in his life.

"I still ache, thinking about hurting you." Oliver couldn't help himself, couldn't rein it in. Seth was right here and he just needed Seth to know that he'd been stupid and wrong to go about things the way he had and he just kept *hurting* him—

"I still ache thinking about that *day*," Seth said quietly.

Oliver hung his head. He felt utterly ashamed and awful. "I'm so sorry," he whispered.

"Just... let's not do that ever again, okay?"

Oliver looked up to see that Seth hadn't moved. He was still sitting back against the headboard with hurt and sadness in his eyes. But. He was still there.

"I wouldn't. Won't." He spoke quietly, but fiercely. "It's the biggest regret of my life."

Seth regarded him, breathing slowly and deeply but not moving. After a moment, he set down his glass and stretched his hand out across the duvet, palm up. A broken noise stuck halfway in Oliver's throat at the sight. He jumped out of his seat to sit on the edge of the bed and take Seth's hand in both of his.

Oliver could barely force himself to look into Seth's eyes; he was terrified of seeing something worse than hurt there. "I miss you," he whispered.

Seth tugged on his hand and shifted, making room for him on the bed. Oliver forced himself to look into his eyes—he had to know that he wasn't imagining this peace offering. Seth looked sad, yes, but Oliver hoped that he was also seeing a little longing, maybe a little loneliness for *him*, too. He sat on the edge of the bed, unsure until Seth circled his arms around him and rested his cheek against Oliver's shoulder.

He shuddered out a breath and tightened his own arms around Seth. "I missed you, God, I..."

Seth sighed, and the warmth of his breath on Oliver's neck sent tiny tremors down his spine as Seth whispered, "I missed you, too."

Oliver couldn't help himself; he felt a tear roll down his face. It was finally safe to let it, now that he was in Seth's arms. They held each other for a moment, Oliver running his fingers through the soft, thick hair on the crown of Seth's head, Seth rubbing small circles on Oliver's back.

Eventually, Seth pulled back, still holding Oliver's waist loosely. "Sorry, that was a little uncomfortable, twisting like that," he said with a sheepish grin.

Oliver got to his feet and tugged Seth gently into his arms again in one fluid motion. They stood like that, cheek to cheek, as Oliver rocked them gently from side to side and reveled in the feel of Seth in his arms again. He marveled at how light and relieved he felt, now that Seth had accepted his apology for not having included him in his decision all those years ago.

He shuddered, a chill running down his spine as Seth raked his fingers through Oliver's hair. Tightening his grip, Oliver buried his face in the hollow of Seth's neck, breathing in his clean scent and finally feeling whole for the first time in far too long.

Seth pulled back; Oliver could see that there were tears in his eyes, as well. Seth's gaze, both tender and anguished, bore into him. As Seth ran his thumb across Oliver's cheekbone, catching the moisture from his tears, Oliver's breath caught.

"Do you have any idea how badly I want to kiss you right now?" Seth murmured.

Oliver's heart gave an enormous, pained thump and with a choked cry, he leaned forward across the mere inches between them and pressed their lips together. He felt Seth's hand slide from his cheek and into his hair, felt Seth's strong, lean body pressed against his. Oliver held their bodies together tightly even as his mouth was still gentle on Seth's, sliding softly over Seth's lips. He was amazed that this was happening.

Seth pulled back and pressed their foreheads together, his hand massaging Oliver's scalp. "God, I've missed you so much, Oliver—"

"I know," Oliver exhaled and kissed Seth again, all wariness gone. He opened his mouth, moaning softly when Seth followed suit and splaying his hands across Seth's back when their tongues touched. Memories of all of the kisses they'd shared in the past came back and sped their reconnection.

They knew each other so well. They both knew that Seth loved his neck to be kissed and touched, knew that Oliver wanted to feel enveloped by Seth, hands in his hair, legs entwined; they knew that Seth would melt under gentle touches to his face and soft kisses to his eyelids and temple, and that he could have complete power over Oliver if he kissed and nipped at that one spot under Oliver's ear, his hot breath cooling the skin there.

Oliver murmured, "Missed you, God, so much," over and over like a mantra, a plea for this to be real, for Seth to be with him here, now, holding him, loving him again.

Seth kissed each corner of his mouth and slid his hand up the flat plane of Oliver's chest, up the side of his neck and into his hair. "I was sure that you'd forgotten me," Seth whispered brokenly.

"I tried, Seth; I did. I thought it might make the pain go away if I could forget how we were. I tried to forget you. You're just... unforgettable."

Seth held him tightly, his face buried against Oliver's neck. Oliver shuddered with the sensation of Seth's breath and the vibrations from the force of his voice against his skin as he spoke. "No one I've tried to fit into my life has *ever* made me feel as important, as wanted, as you did, Oliver. No one."

Oliver held Seth's face in both of his hands, thumbs softly working back and forth against Seth's cheekbones. He let himself look—really look—into Seth's eyes, wondering if he'd ever truly seen how beautiful their kaleidoscope of color was, how much of Seth's heart and soul he carried in them. His gaze fell to Seth's mouth, swollen and red from kissing.

"I remember this, you," Oliver murmured as he drew his fingertips lightly down Seth's cheek, his neck, and laid the flat of his palm against Seth's heart. It was beating fast, just like his.

"How you felt in my arms. God, your lips..." Oliver stared longingly at Seth's mouth until he heard Seth's breath hitch. Oliver took his time kissing Seth now, dragging his bottom lip back and forth along Seth's and lightly tracing it with the tip of his tongue.

Seth pressed their bodies together, gasping against Oliver's hair as Oliver dragged his mouth up the slender column of Seth's neck. Then Oliver felt Seth moving backwards, drawing him along. They broke apart as Seth bumped into the bed, sat down abruptly and blinked up at him. His hair was beginning to look wild, his cheeks were bright pink and his breath came short; Oliver never wanted this moment to end.

Reaching up to cup Oliver's face, Seth brought their bodies back together as he stretched back on the bed. They shifted awkwardly, unwilling to let go of one another long enough to move somewhere more comfortable, until they both were better situated. Pushing up on his hands, Oliver kicked his shoes off. When he came back to Seth, his weight now balanced on his elbows, Seth stroked up Oliver's chest to behind his neck and whispered, "I want to feel you."

Oliver closed his eyes, briefly. It was too much—too much want, too much need. When he opened them, all he could see was the soft brown-blue-green of Seth's eyes, heavy-lidded with his own want and need. Sliding his hands under Seth, his hips canted to the side, he sighed at the feeling of being so close; and as he held Seth's warm, firm body tightly, he knew he never wanted to let go. They continued kissing feverishly, Seth's burying his hands in Oliver's hair, his full lips kissing a trail along Oliver's jaw to get to that one spot that always made Oliver's toes curl.

It was almost sensory overload. Their bodies were so familiar to one another; yet enough time had passed, enough false attempts at love with other men, that Oliver couldn't help but notice tiny differences, such as the way Seth swirled his tongue against Oliver's neck before sucking gently. It made him ache for the time missed, jealous of the other person who had tried to love Seth in his place and desperate to please, to show Seth how much he wanted this.

Oliver rolled to his side, a little proud of the whine that came from Seth at the loss of his warm body weight. He began slowly to unbutton Seth's shirt, eyes on his to make sure it was okay. Seth's gaze was scorching; he arched his back and ran his hand through Oliver's hair over and over. The last button freed, Oliver ran the flat of his hand under one side of the shirt and slowly pushed it open. He'd been given a gift, this moment with Seth. He'd be damned if he was going to rush it.

Seth had more hair on his belly and pecs now: light brown, faintly dusting his pale skin, thickening under his navel and racing below his waistline. Oliver bent at the waist and placed a tender kiss over Seth's heart. "How did you get more beautiful?" he murmured, kissing his way up Seth's neck, his jaw and the corner of his mouth, following the blush blooming on Seth's face.

"Is this okay?" Oliver asked, drawing his fingertips up and down the trail of hair near Seth's waistband.

"Oh... *yes*, very," he breathed, already pushing up Oliver's sweater. Seth rose to his elbows, forcing Oliver back on his knees. "Will you take it off?" he asked, tugging on the soft wool.

Oliver pulled it off as quickly and smoothly as possible, even though his hands were beginning to shake. He went still, breathing heavily through his nose as Seth's hands caressed his firm stomach, higher, wanting to treasure every breath, every slide of a finger over his skin. He was almost unable to believe who was holding him, touching him.

He squeezed his eyes shut as the hot prickle of moisture built up. He didn't want any more tears, not when everything he'd dreamed of was finally happening. He could feel Seth go still, briefly, and then his strong, smooth hands at Oliver's waist, tugging him back down.

"Hey. *Hey.*"

Oliver opened his eyes, as he lay back down, to find Seth looking concerned. He kissed the worry line between Seth's brows and dropped soft kisses along his cheekbones, down his neck and over his shoulder.

"I'm sorry, you're just..." Oliver mouthed along the rounded corner of Seth's broad shoulders. "You're a little overwhelming."

Seth held Oliver's face in his hands, kissing him softly. "Same here. Let's just... enjoy that we're here, okay?"

Oliver looked down at him, at his messy hair, hazel eyes gone dark, shirt open to reveal his lean torso. "That's all I want right now, to enjoy this." He kissed down Seth's neck, breathing in his cologne and the natural smell of his skin. Memories of their last time together came flooding back: Seth on his bed, sleepy and spent, clothes thrown across the room in their haste to be together.

Oliver laid his forehead on Seth's sternum to catch his breath. It wasn't the same. This was now; he needed to make it count, to pour all of his regret and hope into this moment with Seth, to show him how much he still loved him. How much more he *could* love him, if given the chance.

His fingertips trailed down Seth's belly to his waistband. He looked up to find Seth with his head tipped back, both hands buried in his own hair.

"Seth?"

"Please," he groaned.

Oliver unbuttoned the soft fabric and slowly pulled the zipper down. He slid his hand in and felt the maddening sensation of Seth's erection trapped under another layer of clothing, hot and full to the touch. Seth moaned, and Oliver let out the breath he hadn't realized he was holding.

Pushing with his heels, Seth raised his hips off the bed to allow Oliver to pull his trousers off. Oliver carefully matched the pant legs, folded them in half and laid them on the chair at the foot of the bed, remembering how fastidious Seth had been with his hard-won clothes. Turning back, he caught Seth smiling softly at him.

"I told you I didn't forget anything about you," Oliver said, his voice thick with desire. Still on his knees, he unbuttoned his own pants, pushing them and his briefs down and laying back down beside Seth as he kicked them the rest of the way off.

Seth hooked his thumbs under the waistband of his own briefs and pulled them down just enough to expose himself. "I want your mouth on me," he said, his voice barely a whisper, low and rough.

Oliver crawled up his body, kissing him wetly, exhaling sharply into Seth's mouth when he felt their erections brush against each other. Seth pushed him up a bit, laughing softly. "Let me rephrase that. Would you suck me?"

Oliver dropped his head against Seth's neck and laughed noiselessly, his chest shaking with the effort. He felt full of adrenaline. It buzzed just under his skin from the desire coursing through him, the need for Seth to want him in return and his utter joy at being with Seth at all.

"My pleasure," he mumbled against the tender skin behind Seth's ear, smiling as he felt shivers course through Seth at the sensation. This was a bolder man than he was used to. It wasn't a problem; he just realized that it would take some time for them to find a new rhythm with each other. He would happily devote any and all time toward the task, he thought, as he slid Seth's briefs all the way down his lightly furred legs.

He had another moment of sensory memory as his mouth sank over Seth's cock—Seth's natural, clean scent, the weight on his tongue, the way Seth's hands immediately went for Oliver's thick hair, to pet and touch. Seth spread his legs, giving Oliver more room to work his mouth and stroke Seth's inner thighs. He was more vocal than he used to be; now he groaned loudly when Oliver did something he particularly liked.

It was heady; so much seemed like the past, the times when they sneaked off to love each other, taste each other. And still there were continual reminders that this wasn't the same, that *they* weren't quite the same. Oliver was more relaxed and confident in his ability to give Seth pleasure than he'd been as a teenager; Seth seemed to be more willing to open himself up to the physical sensations of lovemaking.

After a while—when Oliver's jaw began to ache slightly—he looked up to find Seth propped up on his elbows, breathing heavily and watching Oliver work his mouth and hand over Seth's dick. Seth moistened his lower lip with his tongue and when Oliver stopped, he murmured, "I forgot how good you were at that."

Part of him was pleased, and a deeper, darker part of him hated that Seth didn't remember. *It's just a figure of speech*, he told himself, allowing Seth to tug him back up for more kissing. His head dropped, all negative thoughts blown away when Seth grabbed his hips and ground their bodies together. Seth dragged his instep along the outside of Oliver's leg, and Oliver bit Seth's shoulder.

"Oliver, I want you," Seth gasped in his ear.

"Yes, but—" Oliver pulled back and nuzzled under Seth's jaw, his hairline, breathing him in. He held Seth's cheek in one hand, looking down and losing any remaining composure at the sight of Seth straining, trying to make their lips meet. He met Seth's gaze, saying intently, "I want *you*. Do you still... would you?"

Seth surged up and crushed their lips together, his tongue desperately seeking Oliver's. He exhaled into Oliver's mouth, "Yes. For you—yes."

Oliver's limbs felt loose and warm, even though his heart was racing a mile a minute as Seth rolled them over, pinning Oliver to the bed with his hands at Oliver's biceps. Seth drew the edge of his nose along the contours of Oliver's cheek and his hair tickled Oliver's skin as he kissed lower and lower, his hands soothing Oliver's overheated skin.

As Seth rubbed his cheek softly over the dark, coarse hairs on Oliver's abdomen, Oliver began to shake. His stomach muscles trembled at Seth's warm breath, at the nearness of him, the feel of his soft hair. Memories of love and trust crashed over Oliver; he wanted so badly to have that back, for this to go on forever. Seth must have sensed the change; he brought his weight down on the bed and wrapped his arms around Oliver's slight waist, pressing kisses just under his navel, holding him steady.

"We don't have to," Seth murmured against his skin.

Oliver ran his hand over Seth's hair, over and over, the softness so pleasant to the touch. "I need to. I need you," he said, his voice almost a whine. "So much."

Seth didn't look up, just held him tighter for a moment before saying, "Me, too." He pushed to his hands and knees and hovered over Oliver, rocking forward to press their lips together, leaving him feeling more centered and less likely to break and fly apart into irreparable pieces.

"But I don't want to hurt you, and—" Seth sat back on his heels, his hand making small circles on Oliver's hip as he began to blush, looking sheepish and adorable. "I didn't exactly bring anything with me, Oliver."

Oliver linked their hands together and smiled all the way from his heart at the sight of their fingers, entwined again. He gave Seth's hand a small tug. "I think I saw something here. Hang on."

He let Seth shift aside so he could get to his feet and felt momentarily self-conscious about being completely naked and walking around his hotel room.

Thank God I closed the blinds.

At the minibar was a "Courtesy Pack": an extra toothbrush, sewing kit, pair of socks and an "Intimacy Kit." Blushing and completely unable to control his grin, he grabbed the small packet and carried it over to the bed with a triumphant "Aha!" and an eyebrow-waggle.

Seth laughed and moved to turn down the duvet and sheets. Now that they weren't wrapped in each other's bodies, Oliver noticed it was cold. A quick glance down at himself to confirm that it wasn't *too* cold and then he slid into the silky sheets, legs gliding along Seth's, his warm hand seeking out Seth's waist to trace over the slight definition of his abdominal muscles and the strong curve of his chest, deeper now that he was a man.

Seth found his lips and kissed him sweetly, leaving Oliver breathless. He felt cherished, welcomed, wanted.

They broke apart after several heady minutes; Seth asked, "Are you sure?"

Running his hand down Seth's torso, Oliver said, "Completely."

Seth twisted away to reach the packet, opening it to reveal a small bottle of lube and two condoms. "This *is* a good hotel," he muttered, getting a deep, breathy chuckle from Oliver. Seth put the supplies within reach, shifted to Oliver's side and squeezed some of the lubricant onto his fingers. He watched Oliver's face as he stroked softly between Oliver's legs and behind his balls, pressing just enough to make Oliver's eyes flutter closed—this was a steady pressure for Oliver to get used to.

"Oliver, look at me. Don't close your eyes."

He felt overwhelmed by emotion as Seth looked at him, into him, touching his face and his hair as he stroked slowly inside him, twisting his hand just so to make Oliver gasp with pleasure, just as he'd learned how to do years ago.

When Seth added a second finger, his mouth dropped open, mirroring Oliver's open-mouthed gasps of pleasure. Oliver tried reaching up to kiss, needing Seth everywhere, but Seth pulled back. His dark eyes were exquisite. "No. I need to see you."

"Fuck... *Seth*." Oliver barely had the breath to cry out his name. He felt pressure, low on his spine, building in heat and electricity as Seth continued his stroking with both hands. He seemed to hold everything that Oliver was between them.

Oliver closed his eyes and turned his cheek into Seth's hand, kissing his palm until Seth stopped languidly thrusting his fingers into him and waited for Oliver to follow the rules.

I need to see you. Oh my God...

Oliver groaned and spread his legs wider, feeling his muscles tensing only to have Seth stroke him to a point of relaxation again. Seth shushed him softly as he pulled his hand away and reached for the lubricant again. This time he kissed Oliver as he slid a third finger in, his lips ghosting over Oliver's, whispering, "Want you so, so much," swallowing Oliver's throaty, broken cries as he was filled, stretched. Seth pressed the pads of his fingers deep inside while stroking the sensitive skin of Oliver's perineum with his thumb until Oliver was positively shaking under him.

"Please tell me you're ready," Seth moaned, sucking a spot high on Oliver's neck. Oliver didn't say anything—he didn't have the breath to form actual words to express his need—just turned his head, groped at the packet and pulled out a condom, trying to open it while ignoring the tiny tremors in his hands. Seth sat back on his heels, taking a moment to wipe his hand on a tissue, his surprised hiss turning into a moan as Oliver rolled the condom onto him.

Holding himself with one hand, Seth stroked Oliver's arm with the other and bent over to place a tender kiss just over his heart, almost breaking Oliver with the sweetness of it. He pressed inside, and Oliver moaned loudly at the stretching heat that filled him. They slowly built a rhythm. Oliver felt as if his skin was too tight, as if there wasn't enough of something. His hands found Seth's narrow waist and slid down until his thumbs pressed into the rounded bones of Seth's hips, pulling him closer, wanting more—more pressure, more heat, more *him*.

"Seth... I need you," he groaned. His lust-addled brain couldn't think of how to say that he needed Seth to be more forceful; he needed to feel claimed, taken. He knew that there was an overpowering sense of *must* building up in him; he ground his hips back against Seth roughly, trying to make his body say what he couldn't.

Seth stilled his movement and leaned forward to kiss Oliver slowly, as if he had all the time in the world. His hands soothed Oliver's heated skin as his mouth and tongue worked hot and wet on Oliver's. He broke their kiss and lightly traced his nose along Oliver's, shushing him quietly.

"Let me," he whispered, slowly pushing his hips forward again, and the slow, tight, wet drag of him inside Oliver caused him to arch up off the bed. Seth sat back, captured Oliver's hands with his own and held him down against the mattress, all while drawing out his pleasure with measured, almost languorous strokes, his hips moving slowly and steadily forward and back like pistons. He paused every few thrusts to kiss Oliver so deeply Oliver thought he would suffocate and then began slowly stroking deep inside him again.

"Oh my God..." Oliver moaned. Seth pulled away from his mouth after another searing kiss only to snap his hips forward again, slowly dragging them back and repeating this over and over. Oliver grabbed the sheets in his fists as Seth worked his body. After a moment Seth went still, closed his eyes and held himself tightly at the base of his cock. Oliver pawed at him, trying to pull their bodies back together as close as possible. He wanted Seth to keep moving inside him.

"Can't..." Seth moaned, his chin dropping down. "I'm going to come too quickly."

Oliver arched his back again, unable to stem his growing need to move, to belong fully to this moment and what it meant to him: being with Seth in every sense of the word. "I don't want this to end," he sighed, running his hand down Seth's arm and hoping he understood what that meant. "I don't want this to end."

Seth hung his head with a whimper, a sound that pierced Oliver's heart and sent a shiver of fear through him, though he couldn't say why. He pushed up on his elbows, canting his neck forward until Seth took the hint and began kissing him, greedily, and Oliver murmured sweet words of need into his mouth: more, want you, so good, please. He felt wholly surrounded by Seth, Seth's smell, his skin, his warmth filling Oliver, wrapping around him, giving him a sense of being a part of something again, something that had been amazing and special and *them*.

Seth's hand wrapped loosely around Oliver's cock and he began to drive his hips forward again, each thrust pushing Oliver through his own fist, until they were both panting. Oliver could feel himself about to let go as Seth snapped his hips more sharply, grinding deep inside and stroking Oliver just where he needed it most with every thrust.

"Oliver, look at me. Look—I want to see you come," Seth panted, and that triggered it: Oliver felt his orgasm building so quickly, his instinct was to close his eyes and give over to the physical sensation; but Seth had asked—no, *told*—him to look, and when he saw the longing in Seth's expression he cried out, reaching a hand up to hold Seth's cheek as he climaxed, pulsing over and over until he was spent, gasping with exhaustion. Seth surged forward once, twice, grinding and pressing deeply in a figure eight, holding Oliver's shoulders to stay buried inside as his own orgasm overtook him.

As Seth's breathing began to slow down, Oliver kissed Seth's hand, his palm, his knuckles and each finger. Carefully, Seth pulled out, murmuring, "Sorry," as Oliver hissed at the deep, aching and inevitable physical sense of loss. Seth reached for a tissue and carefully wiped off Oliver's belly and between his legs, kissing Oliver's knee, his hand. He made quick work of cleaning himself up, however, and collapsed at Oliver's side.

They held each other tightly. Completely sated, Oliver ran his hands up and down Seth's back, smoothing his hair, pressing kisses wherever he could reach. He couldn't help the tears: He felt utter happiness in this moment. How wonderful it felt to hold Seth again, for Seth to love him again, even if only physically. But that was just for now, he hoped; he was beginning to feel light and buoyant, imagining the things they could do now that they could be together. They could take walks, read side by side in a café, steal glances when they thought no one was looking, not caring if they were. They could share dinner and do errands and kiss and just be *together*.

Seth yawned against his shoulder; Oliver went still as Seth adjusted himself more comfortably against his side and threw an arm across his ribs. They pressed their foreheads together and breathed each other in, sharing soft kisses and exhausted chuckles.

Oliver flashed back to their very first time together: the feeling of trusting one another completely, the overwhelming joy of sharing that experience with someone he loved so deeply. How afterward they had tried to dress themselves, but had fallen back in the bed to simply be together, hand in hand, legs intertwined. Now Oliver's palm lightly ran over the flat planes of Seth's shoulder blades while Seth's long fingers drew new patterns on Oliver's chest. It all seemed both new and familiar.

Even though it was a second chance, to Oliver it seemed like a first time.

"Can I sleep for just a bit?" Seth mumbled against Oliver's neck. Oliver reached down, trying not to disturb Seth's position, and pulled the duvet up and over their bodies.

"Mm, me, too."

"Just for a bit, okay?"

Oliver nodded against Seth's head, yawning himself. He held Seth close and slowly drifted off, feeling complete again.

Chapter Nine

Oliver slowly swam to consciousness feeling boneless and warm. It took a beat for the unfamiliar sensation of something solid pressed up against him to register as Seth; he hadn't slept with anyone in such a long time. He smiled, stretched his legs and pointed his toes, tapping them against the backs of Seth's feet, burying his smile in the nape of Seth's neck.

"Mm, you sleeping?" he asked.

He heard a muffled, "Yes."

Oliver smiled against the warm skin of Seth's back at the sleepy-yet-aggravated tone in Seth's voice. He slipped his arm around Seth's waist, pulling their bodies flush, and kissed Seth's neck, cheek, wherever he could reach. "Sorry, go back to sleep."

"Can't sleep when you do that."

Oliver laughed softly and drew the emerging stubble on his chin over the ridge of Seth's shoulder with delicate strokes. "I know. I remember."

Seth clumsily rolled to face Oliver, closing his eyes against the light and burying his face in Oliver's neck. He pulled the blanket up high to cover himself. "Five more minutes."

"Only five? You can have as long as you want," Oliver said into Seth's hair, placing kiss after kiss in its softness. Seth mumbled something that Oliver couldn't make out; he just knew the hot tickle of Seth's breath as it buzzed against his skin.

"Hmm?"

Seth lifted his head briefly, eyes screwed shut, to say, "I'm about to completely fall asleep here," before dropping back to Oliver's neck with a tiny huff of breath. Oliver massaged Seth's spine and goosebumps sprang up over his skin at Seth's moan of pleasure.

"You can, if you want, it's not even midnight. But—" Oliver

continued stroking the soft skin of Seth's lower back under the duvet. "Well, do you want to shower or anything? I know it's been a long day for you."

Seth pushed himself up to look Oliver in the eyes. Well, *eye*; he only had one open. "Are you implying that I *need* to shower?"

Oliver hauled Seth on top of his body to better wrap his arms around him and hummed happily behind his ear. "No. I just thought you might be more comfortable if you'd been in some hot, steaming water and maybe had a little shoulder massage—and then sleep."

Seth groaned and squeezed Oliver tighter. "Oh my *God*. My vote is yes to all of that. All of it."

"Okay. We still have some champagne left, too. That should help you sleep." Oliver planted a sloppy kiss on Seth's cheek and wriggled out from under him. He headed for the bathroom and turned on the shower. While it heated up, he unwrapped the package of soap and made sure the shampoo and conditioner smelled all right. He knew how picky Seth could be about his toiletries. He smiled to himself, happy that he knew how to please Seth.

Once the water was nice and warm and there were fresh towels within reach, he adjusted the dimmer switch so it wouldn't be too bright when Seth unfurled himself from the bedding. He pulled the duvet off Seth, who groaned at its loss.

"Come on. Up. The shower's nice and steamy," Oliver said, tugging on the thin sheet over Seth to spur him into action.

Seth threw an arm out blindly, waving it until Oliver caught his hand and pulled him to his feet. Seth made a big production of stomping to the bathroom; he obviously wanted to sleep but was unable to deny the lure of a hot shower. The shower itself ran the length of the bathroom, with nice big slate tiles on the wall and floor, a massive shower head and a glass panel to keep the water from splashing over the low, tiled threshold. Seth moved under the spray and moaned again.

Oliver stepped in behind him, humming a song under his breath as he grabbed the bar of soap and lathered his hands. Seth threw his hands up against the wall when Oliver slid his along the flat planes of Seth's back, rubbing the tension out of his shoulders and the base of his neck. Oliver stepped closer and slid his hands around Seth's waist while hooking his chin over Seth's shoulder, eyes closed against the warm spray of water from above.

"Better?"

Seth sagged back against him. "So much."

Oliver kept one arm wrapped around Seth as he reached back for the bottle of shampoo. He squeezed some into his hand and held it up for Seth. "Good?"

Seth sniffed at it. "Mm hmm." He turned and rested his forehead on Oliver's shoulder and wrapped his arms tightly around Oliver's waist. "So good," he mumbled against Oliver's skin.

Oliver kissed Seth's temple and ran his hands through Seth's hair, massaging and kneading until a thick lather bubbled and ran down the back of Seth's long neck. He felt drunk, giddy and fuzzy-brained from the heat and steam and the nearness of this man he'd loved, from being in New York with him, holding him in his arms.

"Here, step back a bit and rinse off," Oliver said quietly. The moment they were sharing still seemed fragile and precious, as if he held a small animal in his hand and did not want to startle it.

Seth held onto Oliver's biceps and leaned his head back to rinse out the soap. He ran one hand over his eyes to wipe the water away and buried his face back against Oliver, snaking his arms around Oliver's waist once again.

Oliver took his time soaping Seth and himself as Seth continued to cling to him. Every inch of skin he was allowed to caress felt like a gift, every soft kiss Seth pressed to his neck was a confirmation that this was right; this was *real*. It was as if they were washing away the dark past that didn't include them being together.

His intention had been to offer a little soothing comfort to Seth in the form of a quick shower, so Seth could go straight to sleep. His intention went out the window when Seth began to mouth and nip Oliver's neck and his wet hands slid down to grip Oliver's ass.

"You still have the nicest," Seth squeezed, "roundest ass." He pulled back and kissed Oliver sloppily, needy and sleepy. Oliver couldn't get enough of Seth's hands on him, or Seth's mouth exhaling warm gasps into his.

Oliver reached to tilt the shower head so it warmed the tiles, before he pressed Seth up against the wall and sucked a trail down from Seth's jawline to his nipples, his sternum and the faintly protruding ribs at his sides. His hand slipped between Seth's legs to cup and stroke Seth's growing erection.

Guess he's not that sleepy after all. Oliver grinned into a kiss at Seth's clavicle, pleased that Seth was pleased. His grin turned into a shuddering moan when Seth brought his hand into play, linking their fingers together around his hard-on for a moment before breaking away to touch Oliver just as intimately.

He couldn't help the whine that escaped him when Seth shifted his thumb to make lazy strokes over the head of Oliver's cock, or when he sucked on a sensitive spot just under Oliver's jaw. Seth pulled back and looked Oliver in the eye, his own eyes glazed with lust.

"You still like that?" Seth grinned.

Oliver dropped his chin to Seth's shoulder and thrust up into Seth's hand. He was so hard it was beginning to ache. "Yes," he breathed. "But I meant," Oliver stroked the flat of his palm down the length of Seth, gently cupping him the way he knew Seth liked, and back up again, "to help you sleep."

Seth was flat against the tile, eyes closed, his hand on Oliver stilling briefly. "Keep that up and I will sleep like the dead, promise." Seth slapped at the shower head to push it back to center. Oliver quirked an eyebrow at him, and Seth laughed a little helplessly when Oliver brought his other hand to the task, lacing his fingers laced together and pumping with determination.

"Drowning. Didn't—ha! F–fuck, Oliver..." Seth clutched at Oliver's shoulders as Oliver sped up. "Promise I'll—Jesus, that feels—you, I'll get to, uh..."

Oliver huffed a laugh and nibbled on Seth's earlobe. He whispered, "You're close, huh?"

He stilled his hands and let Seth thrust up into them at his own pace, which was becoming increasingly frantic. Seth's face was flushed pink from the steam, his eyes half-closed, and he kept moving his lips as if he wanted to say something but couldn't. The way he clutched at Oliver, the way his body stuttered forward to keep them close anytime Oliver shifted—it made Oliver want to make this as good as he could for Seth, to see just how unraveled Seth would get before he finally came.

"You are so fucking beautiful," Oliver whispered into Seth's ear, biting his lip to hold back his moan at the tiny gasps Seth couldn't control. He felt a little out of control himself. "God, you feel so good."

Seth's hips jerked, his arms tightening over Oliver's shoulders to hold himself up, gasping as he began to climax. Oliver loosened his grip as Seth throbbed in his hand, holding him through it until Seth sank back against the wall, breathing heavily. Oliver nuzzled the hair behind Seth's ear, traced his lips along the tendon in Seth's neck, kissed Seth lightly on his swollen mouth and murmured, "So happy you're here. You feel so good to me."

Seth sighed and laughed. "I did not expect *that*."

Oliver chuckled low and smiled against Seth's lips. "Good surprise?"

"The best, even though I feel a little guilty, here."

"Don't. Just kiss me," Oliver said, leaning in for more. He pressed Seth up against the shower wall and held him there with his chest and broader shoulders, and his hand searched for Seth's, who took the hint; he wrapped his hand around Oliver's dick and helped to bring him to his own orgasm, whispering encouragement into his ear.

The hot water stinging his back, Seth's body warm and firm against his, their hands joined and "come for me" repeated like a mantra against his neck: Oliver arched his back and closed his eyes tightly as he came, pulsing hot, over and over, until he was thoroughly spent. Seth patted and stroked his back, keeping their bodies close so Oliver wouldn't collapse.

They each took a brief turn under the spray to rinse off, smiling shyly at each other and laughing softly. Oliver stepped out first and handed a towel to Seth, leaning in for a soft kiss before grabbing a towel for himself. He grouped a few of his skin care bottles together on the countertop and smiled at Seth. "Just in case you need anything."

Seth paused in the middle of toweling off his hair; a slow, surprised grin spread across his face. "You're still the most thoughtful boy I know."

Ducking his head, Oliver blushed slightly and laughed. "Well, I know how you feel about premature wrinkling." He stepped backwards out of the bathroom, smiling, unable to stop raking his eyes over Seth's long, lean, very naked body, a sense of pride running through him when he saw the faint red mark he'd left just above Seth's collarbone.

Oliver made quick work of yanking the fitted sheet off the mattress and tossing it into a ball in the corner of the room. The flat sheet he pulled taut for them to sleep on comfortably. He spread the pillows out and stretched out with a sigh, hands tucked behind his head, and watched Seth finish his grooming. Seth hit the light switch and came back to the bed, his jaw craning wide with a yawn. "Mm, sorry."

Oliver rolled to his side, propped his head up on one hand and smiled at Seth. "Don't be." He patted the mattress. "All nice and tidy."

Seth sat on the edge of the bed and turned to smile at Oliver, but then knit his eyebrows. Oliver reached out to touch the small of Seth's back. He wanted that tiny look of worry to go away.

"Oliver... I don't have to stay. I can catch a cab and be out of your hair."

"What?" Oliver sat up. "Why? Of course you can stay." A rush of panic began to ripple through him at Seth's hesitation.

"It's just..." Seth turned closer to him and bent his leg, tucking it under his body as he sat on the bed. His eyes were clouded with doubt as he asked, "Is this weird? This is a little weird. Isn't it?"

This was the furthest thing imaginable from the pillow talk Oliver had anticipated. He wanted to curl up with Seth—he didn't want to ever stop touching him—and talk about anything and everything, all of the little nothing-things said under whispered breaths before falling asleep. A dull pain began to radiate out from his center, and he felt echoes of his old loneliness. He knew he looked upset. He couldn't help it.

"No! I mean, not to me. Nothing about this is *weird*. Unexpected? Delightfully surprising?" Seth smiled softly, so Oliver pressed on. "That's what this is. I thought?"

Seth cupped Oliver's cheek and rubbed his thumb lightly back and forth. "I just... unexpected is the word for it. You're right." He leaned forward to press a gentle kiss to Oliver's lips, and it was broken by a huge yawn he couldn't control.

"Seth, just lie down. You're tired. I'm tired. Let's just go to bed." He didn't want to whine. He didn't want to beg. But not wanting to didn't mean he wouldn't. Fortunately, Seth took a deep breath and exhaled slowly. He nodded.

"I really am tired," Seth said, slipping under the duvet and curling on his side to face Oliver.

Oliver wasn't sure now. Wasn't sure if it would be okay to pull Seth into his embrace, to run his hand through Seth's hair. He was lost in this moment and didn't know how to find his way back to the happy place they'd been just minutes before.

"'Night," Seth whispered, cupping Oliver's cheek again and tangling their legs together. Something tight inside Oliver let go at that. Okay. It would be okay. As long as he could be with Seth—hold him, kiss him—it would be okay.

Oliver took one of Seth's hands and tucked it against his chest, willing his heartbeat to slow down. "Goodnight."

Seth fell asleep almost immediately; Oliver lay there in the dark room listening to the sound of Seth's steady breathing over the chaotic, jumbled music of Times Square just outside his window. He wanted to memorize Seth's every line of bone, every faint freckle; the full curve of Seth's lower lip, the barely-there scar on his left eyebrow. He had a sickening worry that he needed to store up these images for when the real thing wasn't there. He held Seth's hand firmly and pressed it to his heart, willing all of his love to come through with every beat.

Love you—love you—love you.

After a long while he finally fell asleep, still holding Seth's hand in his.

* * *

Oliver had fretful dreams of being locked out of his house, which then blended into a labyrinth he couldn't find his way out of. He knew someone was waiting for him, depending on him. He felt an arm snake around his waist and panicked for a minute until he forced himself to open his eyes and saw Seth's worried face next to his.

"Shh. Go back to sleep, babe."

Seth pulled himself up next to Oliver so that his head was cradled in Oliver's shoulder and gently carded his fingers through the hair on Oliver's pecs. Oliver held onto Seth's arm, rested his cheek on Seth's still slightly damp hair and fell back asleep.

* * *

Oliver could hear someone whispering, but they were supposed to be sleeping. He should tell them that. "No, no. No, shh," he grumbled, pushing his face into the pillow.

"Oliver."

The someone was running his hand over Oliver's back: Oh, he liked that. He rolled over onto his stomach, arching his back into the touch.

"You are utterly hopeless."

Realizing who was speaking to him, Oliver smiled into the sheets. He stretched his legs, feeling wonderful because Seth was there, and he was petting him, and that was so nice and—

He sat up and pulled the pillow off his head when he remembered. Seth wanted to go. Had seemed unsure about what they'd done.

"Seth?" Oliver blinked to get used to the light. Seth must have pulled the window shade up a few inches to let in some natural light. He rubbed at his face and turned to look at the clock. Eleven a.m. He saw Seth at the foot of the bed, pulling on his socks. Oliver moved to hug him from behind but was almost thrown off by Seth yanking his other sock on.

"Seth. *Hey.*"

Seth turned to look over his shoulder and then quickly turned back and buttoned his shirt. "Good morning, sleepy."

Oliver didn't miss the nervousness on Seth's face. He looked as if he was trying to bolt. All of the unease from before came rushing back; his skin felt cold and everything seemed as though it was just moving too fast. He needed *time* and he needed to wake up so he could figure out how to make Seth look at him the way he had before.

He wanted to tell Seth to stop, to stay, that he loved him still. What he said instead was, "Were you just going to leave? Just like that?"

Seth stopped buckling his boot and turned to face Oliver, taking one of his hands. "No, no. I... No. I wouldn't have left without saying goodbye, of course not."

Not once had Oliver thought that if he did see Seth, if he did talk with Seth—let alone have what they'd shared last night—there would ever be a goodbye between them, ever again. It was probably stupid of him, but it didn't change the fact that goodbye was the last thing he wanted as the result of their having come together again. He had thought—perhaps foolishly—that this was a sort of beginning.

"Can't we talk about—Seth, come on!" He ran his other hand through his hair, trying to calm himself, trying to slow his breathing and not think about Seth hurrying to put his clothes on and get out of here as though it was some kind of goddamn walk of shame.

"I just don't know how to process all of this." Seth pressed a hand to Oliver's shoulder, but before Oliver could catch it and hold it there, Seth motioned to himself and the moment had passed.

"God, and you think I do?" Oliver didn't want to *process* it. He wanted to *feel* it. He wanted to share the love and joy that had been building inside him again. And he never wanted it to be for anyone but Seth. That was what he wanted to talk about: How were they going to make this work?

He flopped backwards onto the mattress and buried his hands in his hair. It had been so amazing, just hours before; what the hell went wrong? "We always talked things through, Seth, always."

"Not always," Seth said softly, running the backs of his fingers along Oliver's leg.

Oliver sat back up and took Seth's hand in his. That seemed better; that seemed as though Seth wasn't going to disappear on him. If Seth let him hold his hand, he might let Oliver hold onto all of him. Oliver, so afraid that he'd see regret, couldn't look into Seth's face just yet; so he looked at their hands and willed himself not to beg, not to frighten Seth with the desperation that was about to swallow him whole. He forced himself to say, "Will you let me get dressed so we can go get some coffee, something to eat, and then we can talk?"

Seth squeezed his hand. "Yes."

He looked up, then. There was sadness in Seth's eyes, but he still gave Oliver a smile. At least Oliver had managed that much.

* * *

Oliver got dressed as quickly as he could and sent a silent prayer of thanks to the preppy clothiers of the world for using similar neutral color palettes and ensuring that most things he'd brought would coordinate with everything else. He didn't want to waste time. He also didn't want to look sloppy; if he looked pulled together on the outside, maybe it would hide that he was falling apart inside.

Seth used the spare toothbrush from the minibar. Oliver didn't think sharing was an option anymore. He didn't know why it hurt so much to look down at his toothbrush and see another one in the trashcan, but it did.

They stood awkwardly, shoulder to shoulder, as they waited for the elevator; Oliver's mind raced with all the things he wanted to say, to ask. *Did I do something wrong? Did I hurt you again? Are you just scared? How can I fix this?*

Seth seemed to be struggling internally as well, starting to speak but then snapping his mouth shut and biting his lip.

There was a coffee shop on every corner in New York, it seemed, so they walked into the first one ("New York's Best Coffee!"). Oliver asked Seth if he'd like anything from the case and quickly placed their order. Silently, they carried their mugs and pastries to a quiet table in the corner near the front window.

Oliver took a napkin from the small stack he'd brought to the table and handed it to Seth, just as Seth was doing the same for him. They both smiled sheepishly and looked back at their plates. Oliver didn't know how to begin. Seth tore off small bites of his croissant and stared intently at his plate, as if it had the answers and could explain all of this.

Man up. Oliver sighed softly, pushing his plate to the side.

"I... don't... regret last night at all," Oliver started nervously, worrying the napkin in his lap. "I'm getting the idea that you do? I..." He searched Seth's face, looking for any clue. Seth just looked nervous. Well, and a little sad. "Seth, you have to tell me what you're thinking."

Seth held his mug in both hands and slid it to the middle of the table. It was a familiar gesture that tugged at Oliver's heart, recalling days of homework after school, stolen kisses by the coat rack, shared brownies from the display case at their favorite café. He had watched Seth hold his mug just as he did now when he told Seth that he loved him for the first time. Oliver wanted to wrap his hands around Seth's and hold those memories, make this the moment when they decided to be together again. He wanted to hear a happy, "We'll make it work."

"I'm thinking," Seth began, and then sighed. "I'm thinking that I'm freaking out a little." He looked up at Oliver with a watery smile. "I think this is all surreal. Oliver, I haven't seen you since—well." Seth sighed out a long exhalation and said, "Are you going to tell me that over the years you didn't wonder what it would be like? If we saw each other again? What we would feel?"

Oliver gave in to his urge and cupped Seth's hands, his eyes closing briefly at the warmth. "Of course. Seth, of *course* I did. That's all I did for months after you left."

Seth looked out the window and bit his lip. He turned back to face Oliver, who felt gutted when he saw tears in Seth's eyes. He looked anxious and confused, exactly how Oliver was feeling.

Seth looked at their twined hands, pulled one away and rested it on top of Oliver's, stroking across his knuckles. "And did you think about what *I* would do? Would feel? Did you ever think about what would come *after*?"

Oliver swallowed thickly and tried to find his voice. He felt as if he was drowning in all the unshed tears that clogged his throat. "I... I hoped that after I groveled at your feet and asked for you to take me back, you would. And then you'd say that you felt the way I did. Do."

Seth cocked his head, his mouth open in apparent shock. Oliver watched his Adam's apple bob as Seth swallowed nervously before asking softly, "And what is that? After all these years... what do you think you feel?"

At the bewilderment in Seth's voice, Oliver felt about three feet tall, totally stupid and naïve. He really hadn't thought about what he would do if this went wrong; truthfully, he hadn't looked further than the moment. But he was sure that the love he still felt for Seth was something Seth must still feel for him as well. Something like what they had shared didn't just go away—at least, not for Oliver. He believed that everything he felt about Seth was completely and utterly true.

"That I still love you. That I never stopped."

Choking off a noise, Seth turned his head away. He pulled his hands back to bring them to his eyes, the heels pressing into the sockets. "Oliver, how can you say that? I'm not the same person."

Seth dropped his hands to his lap and looked so totally wrecked that it was hard for Oliver to not jump to his feet and pull Seth into a bone-crushing hug, kiss him fiercely and tell him that it didn't matter that time had passed: Seth was still Seth. He was still funny and clever and sharp and so goddamned talented and true to himself, it was breathtaking.

Oliver had learned more about how to be himself and own who he was from simply being near him, his presence—his drive, his passion, his determination—was that strong.

Back then, Oliver had been a stupid kid trying to hold it together, trying to please everyone from his homophobic father to his teachers, coaches and peers. But Seth had shown up with a black eye and a flinch from being bullied out of public school, still strong and defiant, and managed to crack through the facade of perfection that Oliver Andrews had been hiding behind all his life. Oliver had realized at sixteen that Seth Larsen was an immense personality, destined for greatness. He was also someone with whom Oliver wanted to spend every moment of the rest of his life: a person who challenged him, who was his friend, who made him want to drop all pretense of having it together and actually *be* someone who had it together—someone worthy of *him*.

And... God, that was how he'd felt as a teenager. Now? Looking at Seth and who he'd become—was still becoming—made him want to stretch himself again, try new things, *be* new things, try harder. He was only just starting to realize just how mechanically he'd been moving through life since Seth had left. Sure, he'd accomplished some good goals, but... it was as if the flavor had gone out of life. As if he'd stepped back into the farmhouse where it was all black and white.

He thought of blurting all of that out and making an ass of himself; instead, he took a shuddering breath and tried to keep his features calm as he exhaled and glanced out the window for just a moment's reprieve from the sadness in Seth's eyes.

He swallowed and said fiercely, "No, you're right. You're not the same person. You're even more."

"How can you *say*—" Seth hung his head but took one of Oliver's hands in both of his. Oliver's heartbeat matched the back and forth motion of Seth's thumb over his knuckles. "How do you always say these things that just cut straight—"

"I'm saying what's true. Seth, ever since I saw you on that stupid talk show—"

Seth looked up in surprise.

"And heard you—you, your voice, you *singing*—I haven't been able to stop thinking of you.

"I can't stop replaying that awful night. I—Seth, I can't stop remembering what we *were*."

He just needed Seth to understand. He made himself breathe before continuing. "I had every intention of leaving you alone, of not even interrupting your life when I came, I promise. But once we started talking... Seth, you were my best friend."

Seth whispered, "You were mine, too."

"You *still* are. Even if that's all I can have?" Oliver leaned forward and held Seth's hands tightly between his. "Seth, even if all I can have is your friendship, I would do anything to have that back. Anything. And if you felt that you could give me more..." Oliver tilted his head back and leaned away, trying to appear less aggressive. "I don't mean to pressure you. I just want you to know how I feel."

They sat quietly, Oliver searching Seth's face as Seth thought, took time, whatever it was that he needed to do for himself. Seth patted Oliver's hand and crossed his arms across his chest as if he needed to protect his heart physically.

He continued to stare out the window, biting his lip. Without turning to look at Oliver, he quietly asked, "What did you see happening between us? Today?"

Oliver blinked and looked down at his empty hands. "I have no idea. I just wanted to wake up and know you were there with me."

"Oliver," Seth sighed, looking so sad and confused and *lonely* that Oliver just hurt all the more.

"I don't know! I thought we could spend the day together. I thought we could have one last dinner before I have to go back to Kansas. I wanted to hold you, one more time. And... I thought about picking you up at the airport when you come home for Christmas. I could even borrow my parents' car." Oliver gave Seth a lopsided grin.

Seth smiled fondly. "Seat warmers."

Oliver laughed a little. He knuckled at the pressure building behind his eyes and looked out the window, aching when he noticed Seth's reflection in the glass, watching him. Window-Seth was undefined; Oliver couldn't see anything in his eyes, just people passing by on the street outside. He turned to look at the real thing, wanting to be lost in Seth's eyes again like he was last night, to see Seth for all that he was now, to learn who he was becoming. He wanted them to have that together, for it to stop being a mirage he couldn't help but long for and become *real*.

"I thought we could spend New Year's Eve together," Oliver said. Trying to keep his voice from breaking, he continued. "I thought we could spend all of them together, like we were supposed to."

"Oh... Oliver." Seth's eyes closed, his hand clutching at his shirt just above his heart.

Oliver couldn't stomach the idea that he might be hurting Seth all over again. He wouldn't. He wanted to do the opposite: prove that they were meant to be together. They were supposed to be the ones who actually got the happily ever after. They *belonged* together.

He wanted to make Seth hear him, to find just the right thing to say to make everything right again. "I thought you would love to come see me in England. How you'd love to see Buckingham Palace, and maybe you would come for graduation—"

"England, Oliver, you're in *England*." Seth rubbed at his face with one hand. "Instead of a noisy, crowded train for a few hours, we have an actual, literal *ocean* between us."

Seth sounded so tired. Oliver just wanted to rewind life back to them getting out of the shower, holding each other, whatever moment would reverse this current heartache.

"But I'm not always going to be there. Seth, I graduate in just months. *Months*. Seth, listen to me." Oliver was on the edge of his wooden chair, practically sliding around the table in his need to be as close to Seth he could get. He laid his hand on Seth's knee and sighed with relief when Seth let him leave it there.

"Can't you wait just a few months? I'm talking about us finally having a forever in exchange for just a few months. I still love you. I *know* you still care about me."

Seth looked up, looked right into him. Even though his gaze was tinged with hurt, Oliver could still see that Seth did care. And that it was still painful for him.

"Of course I do, Oliver. Of *course* I still care about you. It wouldn't hurt if I didn't."

"What? What wouldn't hurt?" The tiny glimmer of hope that was trying to stay alight in the darkness flickered, in danger of being put out.

"This. Not knowing what to *do*. Oliver..." Seth leaned back in his chair, eyes to the ceiling, blinking rapidly. "Babe, I don't know what to do here. You say you still love me, but you're going back to England. I'm *here*. You said the other night that you might stay in England for your doctorate, don't think I wasn't paying attention."

"No, I mean—it's not set in—"

Seth plowed ahead. "And how long is that? Six more years? And that's an ideal time frame, right? Six years?"

Seth seemed to be waiting for him to confirm this. Oliver nodded shallowly; Seth blew out a breath of frustration, his fingers tapping the side of his mug. "I can't believe this is happening *again*," he laughed, but there was no humor in it.

"I don't know that I'm going to stay in England after this spring." Oliver flashed on an email his advisor had sent him earlier. "I'm supposed to discuss all of this when I get back. Seth, please. *Please* give me a chance, here."

"A chance for what, exactly?" Seth leaned forward, earnest and hurt and open, and Oliver just wanted to make all of the hurt go away.

"A chance for us to be together like we were supposed to be. I want you in my life, Seth."

Seth dropped his head, shaking it a little. "That's... all I wanted. Oliver," He looked up and took Oliver's hand again. "That's *all* I wanted then. But I can't leave New York. This is where I belong. I can't be me anywhere else."

"I know. But I can be me when I'm with you."

Seth shook his head, but the tiniest of smiles was starting to bloom. Oliver thought he might be able to breathe again.

"This would be so much easier if you weren't so damn romantic," Seth said quietly.

They sat together in silence as Oliver caught his breath, trying to take in the possibilities. He hadn't been sure, on the way here, what his future could hold; now he knew he was looking at it. He had to make this work. He simply needed Seth in his life; fortunately, his future happened to be more portable than Seth's.

"You're going to have to give me time, Oliver. I... just you *being* here is going to take time for me to get used to. I've seen you for days now, and I still don't believe you're actually here."

"Okay." Give Seth time in exchange for a chance? Oliver was willing to make that deal without question.

"I can't believe I'm even having a conversation about any of this with you. That this isn't some crazed fever-dream." Seth groaned and covered his face with both hands. "I woke up no more than two hours ago and I'm already exhausted."

Oliver smiled, "Well, we can always go back to—"

"Oliver." Seth cut him off quickly. "I'm not kidding; I need some time to deal with all of this."

Oliver nodded. "Sorry. I was just trying to—"

"I know," Seth said, cutting him off again, but not unkindly. He went back to tearing what was left of his croissant into smaller and smaller pieces.

After a moment Oliver asked, "Are you going home for Christmas?"

Seth smiled then, with real warmth and relief. "Yes. I get in early on Christmas Eve and get to stay through the first. A whole week for my understudy to have fun with half-filled theaters."

"Will you let me see you then?" Oliver didn't want to sound plaintive; he just wanted to put the option out there for Seth to think about.

Seth exhaled, his "Yes" carried along with his breath. "I think I should go now, though."

It hurt, but Oliver knew Seth needed this. He had promised to give Seth time, after all. He moved to stand up, but Seth shook his head and walked over to where he was sitting. He kissed Oliver's mouth briefly, and then pressed a sweeter kiss to Oliver's temple, lingering. Oliver clutched at his arms. He was not ready to let Seth go yet.

Standing up and breathing deeply, Seth cupped Oliver's face and smiled. "I'll call you, okay?"

"Okay."

Oliver couldn't bring himself to turn and watch Seth walk out the door. He closed his eyes and focused on the lingering heat on his cheek from where Seth had touched him, telling himself that it wasn't over, he was just making good on his promise.

* * *

Oliver ran his key-card to unlock his hotel room and was confronted with the room cleaned and tidied, the bed made with fresh sheets and the empty champagne glasses gone. He walked into the bathroom and saw that all of his toiletries had been lined up and the garbage emptied. It was as if last night hadn't happened.

He leaned against the doorway, eyes sweeping the room until the bright color by the small table and chair in the corner caught his eye. Seth's flowers. He'd forgotten to take them. Oliver sat heavily in the chair and stared at them, touching one velvety petal with the tip of his finger. The card was back in its envelope, resting within the blossoms and the aubergine leaves of the filbert spray. He pulled it out of the envelope and read it again, remembering when Seth had pinned a similar boutonnière to his tux lapel on their hard-won prom night.

Printed on the back of the envelope were the meanings of the flowers in the bouquet. Yellow roses were for loving friendship, he knew. Bluebells apparently not only meant gratitude, which was why he'd picked them, but also eternal love. And a filbert spray, Richard's addition, meant reconciliation.

The air left him in one sharp exhalation. He'd put it all on offer: love, gratitude, a future together. And Seth hadn't said no. He hadn't said yes, either, but Oliver wanted to focus on the "I need time." He could do that. If it meant having Seth back in his life, he would.

The mistake he'd made years before was not going after Seth that night. Not talking to him the next day, not *trying* to make things right between them. He would have to finally learn from those mistakes and not repeat them. He slipped the card back into its envelope and set it on the table, grabbed the phone and dialed the concierge line.

"I need a box sent to room 822. The type for flowers?" He listened to the quick reassurance that one would be sent quickly. "Is there someone who can make a quick delivery as well? Great."

After hanging up, he pulled one of the yellow roses from the vase, fascinated by the velvet softness of its petals. For a moment, he thought about keeping one or two flowers for a memento. But these were Seth's. Oliver still had his, the small rosebuds from his boutonnière.

* * *

JUNE, FIVE YEARS AGO—AFTER

"Oliver, we're going to miss our flight if you don't hurry up!"

"Coming, Dad." Oliver looked around his room, ready to be gone for the summer and away from its mix of jubilant and heartbreaking memories, and yet reluctant to leave all the same. He was still holding out for Seth to come back. Any minute now he might open Oliver's door, drop his satchel on the floor by the bed, smile that slow, sweet smile of his and tell Oliver that everything was going to work out, that they would work it out together.

It had been four days since Seth left him with a shattered heart. Four days that Oliver had stayed in his room, only coming out from necessity and then going straight back in and burying his face in the pillow that still carried Seth's distinct smell: a combination of his aftershave, his shampoo and his own natural boy-scent. Four days of ignoring phone calls and texts from their shared friends, wanting to know what he'd done wrong. Four days of wondering if a person could actually die from a broken heart.

But his father, making a concession for Oliver since he would no longer be in New York with "that boy," had pulled strings with the director of The Stonewall Center in Amherst for an internship position; the director, a former client of Mr. Andrews, also knew most of Oliver's future professors at Brandeis. For Oliver to be given this opportunity when he wasn't yet officially a college student was amazing; Oliver was fully cognizant of that. And a distant relative had offered a rental property for Oliver to stay in while he spent the summer stuffing envelopes and learning the various aspects of keeping a nonprofit functioning. He'd been looking forward to it for weeks, excited for the chance to be involved with something important, to move toward a goal he'd not yet realized had been set in motion by the simple act of meeting a particular boy.

He'd wanted to surprise Seth with a trip to Amherst to visit him—they would have a house all to themselves. Oliver had daydreamed about them imagining it was *their* home and that they were finally living together.

He realized belatedly that he obviously hadn't thought that idea through. And when his father grumped at him that morning that

"Enough is enough, Oliver," pointing out that the world still carried on without "that boy" in it, he had to force himself to pack, to leave Kansas without the promise of Seth's phone calls, texts and letters.

Suitcase in hand, Oliver quickly glanced around the room. His eyes skimmed over the pillow missing its case on his bed; he knew he had it safely packed in his suitcase next to his favorite sleep tee, the heather green Larsen Custom Cycles & Repair shirt. His mother had made the gentle suggestion that he take down some of the pictures of Seth; that seemed like sacrilege, as if he was trying to forget Seth. He would never be able to forget Seth. Deep down he was sure that she would pack them away somewhere while he was gone, but it wouldn't be *him* doing it.

He grabbed the spine of a worn-out copy of Walt Whitman's *Leaves of Grass,* careful not to let the book open and spill its contents, and slid it into the front pocket of his rolling bag. He closed his eyes and wondered if he would still be able to smell the faint odor of the faded rose buds he'd pressed inside to join the underlined words he knew so well:

> For the one I love most lay sleeping by me under the same cover
>   in the cool night,
> In the stillness in the autumn moonbeams his face was inclined
>   towards me,
> And his arm lay lightly around my breast—and that night I was
>   happy.

Seth had given him the flowers a year earlier, pinned them on with shaking hands as Mike told them in a choked voice how "good-looking" they both were in their "monkey suits." He'd wanted to preserve the roses to honor how he felt and how much their relationship meant to him. One night when Seth had stayed with him—the first time they'd had sex, the night that changed their relationship even more than he'd imagined sex could—Seth had gone into Oliver's closet to get some sleep pants and found that book open, that passage marked. He'd seemed pleased by Oliver's bashful stammering about how it made him think of the two of them. And the morning after prom, when Seth had left with kisses and caresses that carried so much more meaning, Oliver had pulled out the book, found the passage and pressed one of each kind of flower there between the pages.

Looking down at his luggage, ignoring his father's grumbling at the front door, he knew that he had packed as much of Seth as he could—hoping that, if he surrounded himself with these tokens, they would show him the way to call Seth back.

* * *

A sharp double rap at the door caught his attention. Blinking away the last wisps of memory, Oliver opened the door to find a bellman holding a long, slender box. Oliver took it, slipped the man a bill and took a few minutes to carefully package the bouquet after blotting the cut ends with a tissue. He tucked the card under one of the stems to keep it in place.

He'd done nothing the last time Seth walked away from him. He wouldn't make the same mistake this time.

He tore a piece of paper from the hotel notepad on the side table and wrote a message.

Seth, take all the time you need, but please take these as well. You were wonderful, and that's what the flowers were for: a reminder that you are.
With love, Oliver

Smiling genuinely for what seemed like the first time that day since he and Seth had begun talking, he grabbed the box and quickly made his way to the concierge desk with instructions for it to be delivered to Seth's theater and the blossoms put in water to keep them fresh. Oliver was not going to make the same mistakes he made last time. He wasn't going to let Seth out of his life again without a fight. If ever there was someone worth fighting for, it was Seth.

Chapter Ten

Oliver spent the rest of his last day in New York wandering Seventh Avenue, watching people race by to work, to lunch, to meetings. For the first time in years there was nowhere Oliver had to be, and he felt a little adrift. He and Gus had decided to give each other space while they were in the city: Gus, so he could have the week with Emily before she headed back to D.C., and Oliver, so *he* could make repairs to his relationship with Seth.

He'd promised to give Seth time to think, and he would. He wouldn't push, even though everything in him was practically screaming to find Seth, hold on and not let him go again. What if he didn't call? What if he decided that there was too much distance between them, that too much time had passed and the connection for him wasn't what it had been for Oliver? For Oliver, this past week had meant *everything*.

But Oliver realized underneath it all that he'd had the luxury of time to prepare, time to know this trip was coming and daydream about what ifs. For Seth, this was all new. He didn't have the benefit of weeks to mull over the past, reliving their happy times and their worst, weeks to think about what had gone wrong and how to avoid making the same mistakes again.

So Oliver would give him time. Now that Oliver had seen Seth, had held him and kissed him, he was surer than ever that they belonged together. Even though a huge part of him worried that Seth wouldn't come to the same conclusion that he had, he told himself that he needed to be optimistic. It was either that or tear his hair out.

With anything else, it wouldn't have been a struggle. All his life, he had given people the benefit of the doubt; he approached problems hoping that things would work out in the end and believed that if he did everything he could to make something right, well, he could at least know deep down that he'd done his very best.

But this wasn't a public debate on policy. This wasn't an attempt to bridge differences between rival teams. This wasn't a proposal for a budget increase or a request for a larger lab space. This was Seth, and this was Oliver's chance to put what went wrong in his life to rights. And this time he would make sure to do anything and everything he could to make it work.

Walking around, he spied the MOMA gift store and slipped inside when he saw a pair of earrings his mother might like. He found a few other baubles to round out his holiday shopping for her. He had put his wallet back into his inside pocket and was tucking his packages under his arm when he was jostled against the granite block wall outside by a noisy group of people entering the shop.

As he waited for them to decide what to do, to come or go, he noticed an elderly couple sitting on a bench outside the building, leaning against each other and watching the people pass by. The husband held out a hand while still watching the street; his wife took it, laid it across her lap and idly stroked his palm. The old man sighed and smiled, something in his posture visibly easing.

It was something millions of couples had done for thousands of years, but the sight sent a bone-deep tremor of aching want through Oliver. Companionship: comfortable, tender, seemingly effortless companionship. He'd had it once, and he'd let it slip away. He would never take it for granted, if given the opportunity to have it again.

He smiled at the couple and headed back to his hotel, the sky darkening as night came on. He'd held out his hand; he would just have to be patient and see if Seth took it.

* * *

He had no idea when he'd hear from Seth again, but he clung to the knowledge that Seth would be home for Christmas, at least. Oliver had weeks to keep from climbing the walls at his parents' as they inevitably dragged him along to the neighbors' holiday parties, the office Winter Cocktail Hour and so on to make small talk and polite conversation.

No one was really interested in what anyone else had to say; they simply went through the motions of sipping just enough to stave off boredom, nibbling just enough to comment on the food and chatting just enough so his parents could be told in the coming months how "fine" and "handsome" Oliver was becoming.

But there was also work: research to sort through, programs to decide on, Moira pestering him via email three times a day until he finally sent a message in huge, bold type one night: "I am giving him space. Please give me some, too."

He tried to keep himself busy, offering to help decorate the house or run menial errands just to have something, anything to occupy his mind other than the constant dread that he'd never hear from Seth again. Nighttime was the worst, when he lay in bed with nothing to distract him from his memories and the fear that he'd had his one chance and there would be no more coming.

Seth called a week after Oliver had come back to Kansas. His mother carried in the old cordless house phone as if it was something she had completely forgotten they still owned. He smiled and shrugged at her as he took the phone, reminding himself to be calm and not overeager even though his insides thrummed with excitement.

"Hi, Oliver."

"Seth! Hello!" He settled into the easy chair in the living room, a knot loosening inside him. He called. He said he would; he did. "Were your flowers returned to you?"

Seth hummed pleasantly on the line. He sounded as though he was tucking the phone close. "Yes, and that was so sweet of you. I didn't mean to leave them behind, really. I'm so sorry; I didn't—"

"Seth, it's okay."

Seth sighed on the other end of the line. "Okay."

They sat silent for a moment, Oliver's heartbeat racing. He wanted to speak but didn't trust himself just yet. And Seth had called him; it would be rude to drive the conversation.

"So..." Seth drawled.

"So?"

"So, it was really surprising to see you. A good surprise," Seth quickly added. "Very good one. I'm just still trying to believe that actually happened." Seth shifted on the other end and dropped his voice in a teasing tone. "That happened, right?"

Oliver laughed, his nerves driving it to something almost manic until he tamped it down. "Oh, it definitely happened." *It could happen again...?*

"Mm," Seth murmured. After a moment he spoke again, all playfulness gone. "Oliver, it's—it's been hard this week. Seeing you, being with you like that—are we still always going to be honest with each other?"

"Of course; yes, always." Oliver gripped the phone close, cold dread trickling through him at the seriousness in Seth's voice. He felt like he was being shut out.

"I can't stop thinking about that last time—back when you graduated? How awful that was when you were just gone."

Oliver closed his eyes, all feelings of giddiness that Seth had called draining away. "Seth, I would do anything to take that back—"

"I know," Seth soothed. "Oliver, I know. I don't want to beat a dead horse, that's not why I called. I just meant that when you were here in New York, and I had the promise of actually getting to see you—"

A spike of thrill shot through Oliver when he thought of Seth wanting to see *him*.

"It was—well, it was wonderful. But then I realized later that night that you were just going to be gone after a few days. I don't want that again."

Oliver's chin dropped, everything inside him constricting all at once. "You... what are you saying?"

Seth sighed. "I'm not saying anything yet. I'm... I want you to know that I won't do a long-term long-distance thing. I'm just not built for it," he laughed, but with the furthest thing from humor. His laugh sounded somber and resolute.

Oliver forced himself to breathe deeply. "I wouldn't want that either. Long-term long-distance? No, I mean, I get it. What's the point? I'd want to be with you, not somewhere else wanting you."

Seth inhaled sharply on his end of the phone.

"Oh... I didn't mean to pressure you, I just meant—"

"Oliver, it's okay. We don't need to be coy. I mean, what are we talking about here, our philosophies on dating? We're talking about you and me, right?"

Oliver swallowed thickly before saying, "Yes."

Seth was silent for a moment, breathing softly and steadily on the other end of the line. If Oliver wanted to, he could easily imagine that they were still living with their parents, still in school, talking to each other until they fell asleep. Seth had almost always fallen asleep first, said Oliver's deep voice lulled him to it; and Oliver had listened as Seth's voice grew softer and softer and his breathing leveled out.

"You don't know what's going to happen, do you?"

Oliver started, blinking himself back to reality. "What will happen? With me? I have a fairly good idea, but..."

"Care to share?" Seth said dryly, sounding so much like the Seth he'd known that Oliver couldn't help laughing.

"Well, I'm going to have to continue playing nice with extended family for the next few weeks, then—"

"Oliver," Seth reprimanded.

Oliver sighed and rubbed his face. "My advisor is 'on holiday,' as they say, but when she's back—well, when *I'm* back—I'll be able to look at my timeline for graduation and make sure it's happening in June as scheduled. But from there... honestly, I hadn't thought that far ahead." He rubbed the tip of his finger along the base of the table lamp next to him, watching his own distorted reflection in the metal. "I haven't needed a reason to have it all figured out until now, truthfully."

"Babe, the last thing I want to do is pressure anyone into changing their life to suit me."

"That's not what this is," Oliver blurted, feeling panic creeping in on the edges of his thoughts. Was Seth already shutting down? "You're not pressuring me to do anything here." He forced himself to relax and to talk this out calmly. Seth was being rational; he needed to be rational, too. "I'm not going to change my plans. I'm still going back to England in a few weeks," Oliver said, trying to sound as though he wasn't about to fall apart if Seth pulled every option off the table. He needed to be reassuring, show that he was approaching this in a thoughtful way and not rushing in like a fool. "I'd be an idiot to throw away a degree from Cambridge, no matter how cute you still are."

"Mm hmm. Flattery is the act of the desperate, honey."

Oliver smiled to himself; he could hear the pleasure behind the snark in Seth's voice. "All I'm saying is that I want you to be a part of my life.

I know it's a lot to ask, given our past. I want you be a part of decisions I make for my future, or at the very least to know what's happening."

"Okay," Seth said, pausing for a moment before quietly saying in an uncertain tone, "I just don't know how to make you a part of *my* life yet."

Oliver wondered briefly if it was possible to have one's heart broken multiple times during one conversation. "I... Seth. I meant it, what I said to you before anything happened that night. About us being friends? If... if that's all you can offer me—" Oliver closed his eyes and forced himself to exhale slowly. "If that's all you're able to offer me, I'd happily be your friend. I just *miss* you, Seth. You. Your humor and how it feels to have someone who understands what it was like to grow up where we did, someone who talks straight to me and *gets* me... I miss all of that. And most importantly," he affected an airy tone, hoping to prove to Seth that he could do this; he could be just a friend. "I don't have anyone in England who will play 'porn star or newscaster' with me."

Seth laughed, sounding shocked into it. "Well, I am the reigning champion, it's true."

Oliver smiled. He felt a little less hopeless, hearing Seth's genial laughter. "You always were able to figure out who was who because of—"

"Fabrics," they both said in unison, and chuckled.

"It's so obvious, though," Seth said, sounding far lighter and more relaxed than he had when they first began talking. "Newscasters always have someone else dressing them, so they avoid the rayon blends. Puckered plastic stitching should be considered a crime against humanity," he huffed.

"I see two sets of false eyelashes and I automatically assume porn star," Oliver responded.

"It is pretty trashy, but that's Fox News for you. That and the baby blue eyeshadow," Seth snickered.

Even though it seemed as if something inside of him was slowly dying at the thought that maybe Seth couldn't love him in return, Oliver was still grateful that Seth would offer him this, that he could still laugh with and tease Oliver. He would give anything to have more, but it wasn't up to him. He would simply have to put aside his own feelings about Seth and take what was given.

They talked about nothing, really, but Oliver didn't want the conversation to end. Eventually, Seth had to get into costume for the night's performance, and Oliver needed to lay on the floor of his old room and stare morosely at the ceiling. Not that Seth needed to know that.

"So, will I talk with you soon?" Oliver asked.

"I... yes. I'll call you in a few days. To chat." Seth sighed on the other end of the line. "That's what friends do after all, right?" He sounded hopeful, as if he wasn't sure if Oliver had really meant it when he said that he could accept only friendship.

"Absolutely." Oliver held onto the note of promise in Seth's voice as they said goodbye, even though he felt a pang at the emphasis on the word "friend." He wanted more, believed he *needed* more than just Seth's friendship; but he'd made a huge mistake all those years ago, and it wasn't up to him this time.

As he sat in the quiet of the house, he stared at the pattern of brick over the fireplace and wondered if he would ever come to the end of paying for that one mistake.

Dec 14, 10:24 PM GMT
From: Moira Byrne
To: Oliver Andrews
Subject: yer fookin killin me lad

Your font-based screaming doesn't scare me, so you know. It might work on others, but I'm made of sterner stuff, aye?

It's been an entire two weeks since you left to regain your heart and not a word. Not a single bloody word for me? Ah, what's the point of being Irish if the world—you're the world in this scenario, boyo—doesn't break your heart?

I'm fair sick with worry about you, 'struth. Drop us a line, there's a good lad.

Moira

P.S. I owe you the chance to tell me "I told you so." Janos: such a looker. And thick as manure but only half as useful. Don't get me started on stamina. You'd think being a strapping athlete like he is, he would have it for days. You'd be wrong to think it. Lately the cat purrs to please itself. And I'm left pleasing me own puss. Don't pretend you don't miss me and all my feminine charms.

Dec. 14, 4:49 PM CST
From: Oliver Andrews
To: Moira Byrne
Subject: how are you actually typing in your accent?

It's like you're right here with me. Wait, that can't be, I'm not drunk. It's almost happy hour, though. And let's save stories about your sexual conquests with my roommate until I'm blitzed, if you don't mind. I need to be able to look him in the eye in a few weeks, if only to collect rent.

Seth. Well, it's complicated. It's just been a mess and...*fine*, here it is. Short story: I saw him. He's wonderful. We spent some time together. That was wonderful. He doesn't want a long-distance thing with me. Far less wonderful.

Eh, it's a few minutes early, but it's happy hour somewhere right? I'm toasting you with a bottled Guinness, wishing you were close enough for a hug.

~Oliver

P.S. Oh God, is it going to be awkward when I get back? I'm too much of a gentleman to say I told you so. But if I weren't, I would.

Dec. 14, 11:13 PM GMT
From: Moira Byrne
To: Oliver Andrews
Subject: re: how are you actually typing in your accent?

Christ, and I wish I were there to soothe you, too. It's probably my one chance, eh? ;) Sorry, can't help myself.

Don't ever fancy yourself a storyteller, for you aren't. Give us the details! I've been stuck listening to the family insult the English— they say I've got meself an accent, ye ken that gobshite?—for days now. Not to mention they're shoving every Connor, Jack and Sean in the village at me, and they're all a pack of mouth-breathers living for nights at the pub. No thanks. And I'm desperate for news of you and your man, if only to avoid the likes of them.

But also because I care about you, ye stupid git.

And I bet I'll find the holes in your logic, just like at the lab. ;)

Moira

P.S. Truly, I worry about you. Don't leave us hanging.

Dec. 14, 6:29 PM CST
From: Oliver Andrews
To: Moira Byrne
Subject: don't worry about replying tonight; you should get some sleep
   We went on a few dates. That's what I'm calling them, even if they were just as friends. And for me, it was like nothing had changed. How I feel, that is. (I still love him.) And yes, he's different, but not in a shocking way. Like he's magnified, if that makes sense? He's fantastic. And we had one pretty amazing night; that's all I'll say.
   I think he's worried about being hurt again. I can understand that. I told him that if we could only ever just be friends, I'd take it. He's so fun to be with; we laughed so much I think I hurt myself at one point. And he *gets* me. I haven't had a friend like him since (no offense, you know I secretly adore you), and I just miss him. I miss feeling the way I do when I'm with him.
   So if all he can give me is friendship, I won't say no. It's something, at least.
   Of course I want more. I want everything: him, the future we'd planned, all of it. But I'm in England, he's here and he just won't do that again.
   Basically, it sucks.

Dec. 15, 12:37 AM GMT
To: Oliver Andrews
From: Moira Byrne
Subject: Me get rest? Pah! I'll sleep when I'm dead.
   Oh, my heart is aching for you, Ollie. I can just see you sitting with poor posture, your chin propped on your hand and a look on your gob that would make a puppy cry. Nailed it in one, didn't I?
   Do you want to know what I'm reading between the lines? We ladies are good for analyzing things that don't get said, didn't you know?
   I bet you're way off on him not being interested at all, especially if you had as much fun as I'm thinking. Laughter? The surest way

to get my knickers off. File that away, just in case. ;)

You talked about what you wanted from him, eh? Hmm. And he had an actual conversation with you about the future and what *he* wanted?

And sure, he's protecting his heart, who wouldn't? Especially when they'd had the likes of you once and then lost you. He's bound to throw every barrier up that he can think of. I'd have a moat and dragons protecting mine if I'd lost you, and that's the God's honest truth.

Most people don't talk about their future wants and wishes with one-night stands even if it's someone they used to love. Don't think I didn't catch what you meant about one amazing night, you filthy bastard. I'm so pleased you got a leg over! But then, you always knew I was a helpless romantic. That's what you talk about with someone where there are still feelings, no matter how deeply they're buried.

And sure you're in England. For now. What about when you go back to the States? Did you talk about that?

For crying out loud. Are you doing the bloody PhD at Cambridge, too? Because if you are, then it's no wonder he's turning you away. Me darlin', *I'm* not even doing the PhD there. I've had my fill of the English turning their noses up at me for me accent—and if I hear one more person mispronounce the name of my village, I'll start screeching like a banshee–why do the English hate their language so much they don't properly teach it to their children? I want to work on more than just our project, I have to confess, and plan on doing a legger.

Did you know that Dr. Lan is possibly going on sabbatical? If he's doing a legger, then what the bloody fook am I doing hanging about?

Tell me you're not staying. Don't you want to work on something new? Be with new researchers, at least? Stop letting yourself get stuck in places because you don't know what to do with yourself. Just thinking of you bellyaching over the lack of your weird, icy cold prune fizzy drink for the next six years is enough to put me off my feed. ;)

Do you need me to have a word with this Seth? Because I can

be verra persuasive, especially if he canna understand most of what I'm saying. It's my charisma—gets you blokes every time.
Moira

Dec. 14, 7:22 PM CST
To: Moira Byrne
From: Oliver Andrews
Subject: ...charisma? That's what you're calling it?
Please don't track down my ex.

I had considered staying, but—Dr. Lan might not? Really? When did you hear that news about a sabbatical?—I wasn't sold on it, and I had a few schools back here in the States in mind, but still.

Do you know where he's going? Is it here? To the US, I mean. No one comes to Kansas unless forced to by their well-meaning family members.

I've been focused on this project of ours for so long that I haven't let myself think of what's best for me at the next stage.

Let's say, for argument's sake, that I did mention offhand to Seth that I might stay in England for my doctorate. That would have been before we'd spent time together and when I was incredibly nervous and trying not to sound like a moron to my ex-boyfriend who is the current toast of the theater world.

(Oh, Moira, he was so good. I'm not just saying that. He *really* was.)

Might. I might stay. If I did, it would be to continue to work on our project. I feel like we're finally getting somewhere great with it, and... I don't know, I can't think past it just now. I'm also still a little shocked that Dr. Lan isn't going to be there—he's the reason I came to Cambridge in the first place. He's an institution, you know? The whole department is amazing, but still. It's something to consider when I'm able to think clearly.

I did mention to Seth that it's just a few months before graduation, as long as that continues on schedule. Have you heard from Barbara? Because knowing that we'll graduate in June will be a huge help. I feel like I'll be able to start planning what's next.

I don't know. I just want to curl up and listen to sad songs and be pathetic for a bit. I'll snap out of it soon, I promise.

~O.A.

Dec. 15, 1:13 AM GMT
To: Oliver Andrews
From: Moira Byrne
Subject: swear to Christ they're about to start singing Danny Boy. I hate when stereotypes come true.

I want you to know that no matter how much of a sad sack you are right now, I still love you, ya cuss.

Even though I think you're an idjit for not knowing what your plans are and for mouthing off to him that you don't know yet.

Let me sleep on things, and we'll find a way to get you sorted out and find a way to make this boy of yours see that he can't do without you. I'll email my DoS and see what he thinks about our schedule for grads. Och, I'm already grieving the loss of you come summer, laddie! Do send us pictures on occasion. Preferably the kind that will get you in trouble, but I'll take what I can get.

First, though, I have to chase the neighbours away as they're still hanging about looking for a drink and a story, and I'm beginning to feel a half bubble off true.

Don't despair, love, we'll figure this out together, aye?

Moira

For the love of Mike, they're actually singing it out in the lounge. Kill me.

* * *

"Oliver. You're moping, aren't you?"

"Hello, Gus," Oliver said into his phone with exaggerated politeness. "So good to hear from you, too! Yes, the past week has been hectic. And how are you?"

Gus sniffed with derision. "I knew it. I'll be there in a half-hour; grab your clubs."

Oliver sat up and blinked as he looked around his dark bedroom. It was the afternoon, but he'd kept the shades drawn and hadn't felt like getting out of bed just yet. "What on earth are you talking about? My *clubs?* It's twenty-four degrees outside, one, and two, there's a good three feet of snow on the ground."

"It's indoor golf, dummy. And my swing has suffered this last semester. I should have gone to medical school—you can take golfing lessons for credit, I hear."

Oliver laughed. "I don't know about that, but I do know that you look better in a suit and tie than you would in scrubs."

"I do know how to wear a suit," Gus said proudly. "Come on, I need to work on my chipping, and they have a sand trap simulator at the place. And then you can finally tell me why you didn't say one word about Seth during the entire drive back to Kansas. Poor form, Oliver, poor form."

Oliver groaned. "I can't say no, can I?"

"Nope!" Gus answered cheerily. "Oh, and my mother complained that we've not seen you at all this week, which means you're staying for dinner. I think she misses her favorite adopted son."

Mrs. Schreiber was the ultimate hostess—she remembered every catered dish Oliver had loved and always had them on hand when he visited. Thinking of the amazing curried chicken on endive she'd served the last time he visited, he said quickly, "I don't need a full set, do I?" He got to his feet and rummaged in his dresser for clothes.

Gus laughed. "Chip, wedge, driver, putter. See you in twenty; I'm already in the car."

* * *

"Put your weight on your left leg for the follow-through, Gus."

Gus tapped his foot, leaning his weight on the handle of his driver as he controlled his breathing. "I'm about to put weight on *your* left leg if you don't stop."

Oliver laughed. He lined up his five iron with the course ball and got his feet into position. This had been a great idea; he just couldn't spend any more time with nothing to do but run endlessly on the treadmill in the family weight room. All of the holiday shopping and decorating was done. The only thing left to fill his time during the day was stare at nothing and overthink things. That and spend hours googling reviews of Seth's performance versus David Falchurch's and smugly mutter, "Ha!" every time Seth was praised more than his predecessor.

Gus never pushed. He wasn't the kind of guy to force a topic when Oliver wasn't ready to fully articulate his thoughts. So they'd spent the past hour just teeing off in the enclosed driving range. Oliver enjoyed the feeling of swinging and twisting into the follow-through, of having something to focus on and knowing how to fix it.

He could change his grip, he could put more weight on the balls of his feet, his posture could be adjusted, he could keep his elbows straight in follow-through—that was easy. It was satisfying to have a problem that could be solved quickly.

He let his body relax into the physical acts of line-up, backswing and follow-through, checking the screen over their dugout for the electronic stats on his yardage and whether or not he was still hooking the ball. No, that last grip change was what he'd needed—sometimes he didn't think the process through, just moved on instinct, and as a result held on too tightly. He needed to remember to think things through and let... go.

Well, fuck.

He stood up straight, rubbing the back of his wrist against his hairline to keep the kid leather of his glove from getting damp.

"What is it?" Gus asked, bouncing the sole of his club on the AstroTurf in a light, methodical manner.

"Oh, just realized that I'm a walking cliché, that's all."

Gus swung back and through, hitting the ball with a solid "thwack." His arms twisted up to the left as he watched his ball fly straight down the center.

"I could have told you that," Gus said, turning and flashing Oliver a quick grin. "But how do *you* mean?"

"Hey, you got three hundred yards on that drive thanks to me," Oliver huffed.

"Yeah, yeah, weight on follow-through. You're the Golf Whisperer. Are you going to answer my question?"

As Gus set a new ball on the tee and did his multi-step loosening up—posture check, bounce bounce bounce of the club—Oliver shifted his weight and leaned on the dark green wooden wall that made up their bunker.

"I may not be standing on a lunch table shouting for reform in my mini-politician phase back in school, but it seems that I still have that need for extemporaneous displays of idealism."

"Mm hmm," Gus agreed, swinging with another solid "thwack!"

"Three-seventeen on that one, not too bad," Oliver said. He sighed and looked out at the ball sweeper roaming back and forth at four hundred yards. "I need to learn to control myself, don't I?"

"You said it, not me." Shoulder roll, tap tap tap.

"You don't think I do?" Oliver turned to watch Gus line up. "Watch your left thumb."

Gus shot him a dirty look and adjusted his grip. *Thwack!* "There are people who happen to enjoy your... shall we say, joyful spontaneity. I think it's more than just simple control." He nudged the basket of balls aside and looked at Oliver straight on. "I think it has more to do with you living in the moment than anything else. It prevents you from seeing a bigger picture."

Oliver bent at the waist and snagged a ball with two fingers, placing it on the tee. It was Gus's turn to watch as Oliver settled into his stance and focused entirely on the ball in front of him. As he brought his feet into position, he realized that he should think about where he wanted the ball to go instead of just hitting it. The ball sweeper was just off-center to the right, like the eighth hole at his father's country club. Four hundred yards was a hell of a drive, though.

He looked left as he bent over the ball, marked the place he wanted it to land in his mind and adjusted his grip slightly. Then he swung up and back, his sides twisting with the effort, and came back down and through, arms locked straight, right toe pivoting and providing a point of balance.

Gus whistled appreciatively. "Nice, Oliver. Did you mean to slice it?"

Oliver smiled to himself, imagining that he could hear the metallic thunk as the ball hit exactly where he had wanted it.

* * *

With a smug grin, Annabelle Schreiber folded her arms across her narrow frame. As was usual for Gus's mother, not a perfectly dyed blonde hair was out of place and her jewelry gleamed just enough to draw attention without being garish. "No one cooks for you like I do," Mrs. Schreiber said. Gus and Oliver bit their lips and did not mention the high-end gourmet takeout containers in the kitchen. "Why don't you come visit more, Oliver?"

Oliver swallowed the bite of lobster and truffle-filled puff pastry she'd cooked—er, reheated—choking a bit as it burned the back of his throat. "I'm sorry; I've not even been coming home to visit my parents much these past few years."

She narrowed her eyes, still with her arms folded. "Mm."

Gus rolled his eyes and passed a small platter to Oliver. "Mother, Oliver has been busy getting his degree. Although," he leaned toward her, dropping his voice in a conspiratorial manner, "he did say something about loving the corndogs at the mall, earlier."

Mrs. Schreiber gasped and literally clutched her tasteful string of pearls. She covered her distaste by sipping angrily at her Pinot Grigio.

Gus laughed. "Mother. *Mom.* I was joking."

She made a dismissive sound and waved her hand at him. Then she refilled Oliver's wine glass and clucked her tongue at him.

"Thank you," Oliver said, helping himself to more food. "It's utterly delicious. Really."

She set the platter down and ruffled his hair. "You need to come over more. You know how I love to be surrounded by handsome young men." She smiled at Gus and said to Oliver, "You know he's top of his class?"

Gus smiled and dug into his food. Oliver grinned at him too. "I did. He's working incredibly hard."

"Are you?" she asked, leaning back in her seat to regard him. "You look tired. Worn around the edges. Even though I want you both to do well, you still need to enjoy life."

Oliver didn't have a response for that, so he filled his mouth with food.

Mrs. Schreiber chuckled to herself. "I see. So, Gus is going to marry his Emily," Gus sputtered, "someday, I'm sure. They'll live in Washington, where she will become a doctor and he'll be a good lawyer and they'll make me beautiful, smart grandchildren. What are you doing to do?"

That was the heart of the problem, wasn't it? Oliver was just beginning to realize just how in-the-moment he'd been living. Every semester was its own world, every project a contained universe. And when it was over... what, exactly? He couldn't build a fulfilling life on dreams of a magically perfect loft with Seth and nothing else. He couldn't be happy staying stagnant in a never-ending blur of academia, either.

Gus cleared his throat, a look of pure innocence on his face.

"Traitor," Oliver muttered. To Mrs. Schreiber he replied, "Beyond graduation, I can honestly say that I have absolutely no clue as to where my life will go. And I'm realizing that I need to figure that out. Quickly."

"May I make a suggestion?" she asked.

"Of course," Oliver answered. He wiped the corner of his mouth and placed his napkin beside his plate, giving her his full attention.

"Get a job. Get someone to love you. Done." She made a dusting-off motion with her hands.

Gus, his wine glass paused just at his mouth, his eyes sparkling with mirth, said quietly, "See, Oliver? It's easy."

Oliver figured he was due a little payback for the impromptu golf lesson earlier and made a point of emptying the wine bottle into his glass before Gus could.

Gus rolled his eyes. "You know she has an entire wine cellar of that, don't you?"

Mrs. Schreiber stood and smiled at them both. "I'm so happy you two are old enough, so I don't have to feel guilty about giving you booze anymore. No one likes to drink alone."

Dec. 25, 12:37 PM GMT
To: Oliver Andrews
From: Moira Byrne
Subject: Happy Christmas, mate!

Me mam got me a fifth of Jameson and a blind date for Christmas. I'm kidding. She didn't get me a blind date. We don't let the blind in our village. *Yes I am going mad being at home, why do you ask?* I hope you're having a lovely time of it in your Hallmark home surrounded by your loved ones. You have pets, right? No? Then surrounded by your family.

I have a bit of an extra gift for you: my DoS spoke with me two days ago to tell me that *I'm* on schedule to graduate, which means that as long as you mind yourself with our carefully constructed project plan, you will be as well. So there's a bit of holiday cheer, right?

I also asked him if the rumblings were true about Dr. Lan leaving, and he was verra cryptic. The mystery thickens... I'm slagging off for a few months after June and mucking about the countryside, so it's no skin off my nose, but I thought I'd mention it.

I'm saving a bit of mistletoe to bring back to Cambridge, so you know. Enough to cover every doorway in your house and the lab. ;)

Love and peace to you and yours, me ould segotia,

Moira

P.S. ...any conversations with a certain someone that you'd like to fill me in on?

P.P.S. I hear Hungary is lovely in the summer. I'm completely daft, aren't I? He's just so handsome when he's starkers, even if he is only as smart as a box of hair.

Dec. 25, 11:17 AM CST
To: Moira Byrne
From: Oliver Andrews
Subject: re: Happy Christmas, mate!

Merry Christmas to you, too! We all slept in here and had a nice brunch, and now I'm ready for another nap. My mother doesn't cook often, but for Christmas morning she makes these sausage rolls with brown mustard that are so good. I may have eaten my weight in them. It makes her uncharacteristically happy when I eat her food, so I'm more than willing to oblige her.

You'll note that I'm skipping over responding to the more ridiculous portions of your email, but I will say that it's a huge relief to know you're on schedule. I'll pull my weight, I promise, and I'll start making plans for getting out of my flat after the end of June. :)

I've been doing a lot of thinking over the past few days. I need to stop being so single-minded and hyper-focused. No, this is not about Seth. Well, partly. Remember my friend I told you about,

Gus? There was a group of us that were pretty inseparable. Once I settled into school, that was all I focused on, that and Seth. Then I went to college by myself, moved straight to Cambridge and... you see my point. Most of the friends from my old group still do things together. I haven't seen most of them in years.

I need to look up more. I need to figure out what the hell I'm going to do once I graduate. It's been this nebulous idea in the back of my mind for years, but I need to get it sorted out. And once I have *that* sorted out, I need to talk with Seth. No, we haven't had any conversations since that last one, but he's been performing and preparing to come home, so I'm not upset he hasn't called me yet.

This is what I'm telling myself—that is, after checking the phone to make sure it's plugged in and not in silent mode. Yes, I realize how pitiful that is.

What if I told you that I was deathly allergic to mistletoe? You didn't even think of that, did you?

Love to you, too, and even though I shouldn't encourage you, I can't wait to see you when I get back, either. I'm sure I'll regret saying that after a few minutes, but until then, I'll bask in happy thoughts of your wee elfish self.

~Oliver

P.S. You can't see that I read your postscript with my mouth hanging open. I just don't even know what to say.

* * *

Oliver was stretched out on the floor in front of the fireplace, half asleep, half listening to his parents playing cards in the other room, when the house phone rang. He slapped his hand around blindly, looking for the cordless. He'd brought it down there with him just in case. He hadn't been an official Boy Scout, but he did believe in being prepared.

"Hello, Andrews residence."

"Merry Giftmas, Oliver," Seth said. "Is this a bad time?"

Oliver could hear voices laughing and talking boisterously in the background on the other end. A weightless feeling filled his stomach when he was able to hear Big Mike.

"No, not a bad time at all. Everyone is in their post-brunch malaise here." With the exception of a few quiet exclamations over losing or winning a hand, his house was silent. "I assume you got in safely. Glad to be home?"

"I did! And I am," Seth laughed. Oliver could hear the sound of his hand muffling the receiver as he told his dad that he was on the phone. "Sorry. Little Mike brought over some movie for my dad that apparently involves a lot of shouting and loud engines."

Oliver closed his eyes, curled in on himself on the floor in his blanket and tried not to let memories of Larsen Family Movie Night get him choked up. He cleared his throat, saying with forced calm, "Your dad can't help but love anything with The Rock in it."

Seth hummed happily on the other end. "You remembered."

Oliver stared into the fireplace: It was a gas fireplace with a stone log. Nothing moved in this house, nothing changed. The fake log continued to glow red, barely putting off enough heat to be satisfactory.

"I bet your dad was ecstatic to have you back home," Oliver said, feeling a million miles away from pleasant memories of Seth's house all those years ago. He turned up the heat with the remote that controlled the fireplace. Maybe he could increase its warmth enough to forget it was artificial.

"Well, he does have a pretty fantastic kid to be glad to see. Or so I've been told. Repeatedly. He's been ridiculous about visits since I moved out." Seth's happy energy practically crackled through the phone line. "Oh my God, he, ahem, *reimagined* the basement. Total man cave. I'm surprised there aren't actual bloody pelts on the walls. It looks like his garage but with a ridiculously huge television."

Oliver remembered the Larsen house, simple, with mismatched furniture randomly collected over the years. It was clearly the home of a working man; not elegant by any means, but it was a home. It felt vibrant and lived in.

The sounds of people lovingly teasing each other seeped through the call. If he closed his eyes, he could picture himself at the dining room table with all of them: Big Mike, Seth and the guys from the shop who were Seth's honorary uncles.

"Okay. I don't know if you already have New Year's Eve plans," Seth said, sounding slightly coy and nervous. "But if you don't, we're having a party here at the house. Mostly Dad's crowd and their kids, so it would be great to have someone my age here who isn't in a biker gang. They're nice, but, well."

Oliver knew what Seth was referring to: Seth was a Broadway performer, tall, thin, well dressed and very, very gay. Standing out in a crowd for being fashionable was one thing, but standing out like a sore thumb was another.

"Are you sure you want me there?" Oliver sat up, momentarily over his longing for the past. He began to bounce his leg. Anxiety bubbled up in his chest, making it difficult to breathe. A chance to spend the evening with Seth and his dad? "I mean, your dad is okay with it?"

"Of course! Dad's wanting to see old familiar faces, I think." Seth's voice was softer. It was almost as if he had hoped Oliver would ask. "So... party starts around eight and goes until whenever. Do you think you might come at some point?"

"Yes, absolutely!" Oliver closed his eyes and mentally cursed himself for sounding too eager. "I mean, I've been looking for an excuse to avoid the party my parents are having."

Seth laughed, "Oh, Oliver, don't you want to make small talk about bland, uncontroversial topics all night?"

Oliver chuckled. "Not particularly, no. And for the past few weeks, I've been dodging my father's partner's daughter at all of the events they've dragged me to. She *really* doesn't believe that I'm gay, and apparently she's making it her mission to Bridget Jones me over the break."

The fireplace may not have put out much heat, but the joyful feeling that built inside of him at the sound of Seth's laughter was warm enough for now.

"But Oliver, she likes you just the way you are! You *do* have that whole clueless, adorable straight boy, frat-legacy vibe working against you. Girls can't help themselves," Seth teased.

It was incredibly satisfying to know that even after years of being apart, they could still laugh and tease one another. Maybe New Year's would be a chance to show Seth how perfect they still were for one another.

"Amanda is sweet," Oliver said, "but, well. A woman."

"Poor Amanda. I know what it's like to be struck stupid with a handsomely dressed Oliver Andrews, dripping with polite manners.

You sure do know how to turn on the charm, babe, and God knows you can fill out a tuxedo like no one else," Seth said, his voice going soft and intimate.

Oliver was filled with so much want he couldn't breathe. He couldn't help himself, not with an opening like that. His voice dropped to match Seth's as he said, "I'd much rather be at these things with you. We could play our 'Who's More WASPy' party game. Lots of corners and nooks at the country club for us to hide in so we wouldn't get caught..."

Oliver shook his head, remembering almost too late that he wasn't supposed to push anything. "Talking," he said quickly. "Caught talking."

Seth cleared his throat and teased, "Just don't offer to show her around any campus libraries or help her with her French homework, and you'll survive. That's always been your superpower, you know."

"What's that?" Oliver asked.

"Charming your way into someone's heart with your helpful earnestness. I'm surprised you didn't woo any of those English boys with your smile and manners, quite honestly. And don't get me started on that gravelly voice of yours; God, I loved it when we were paired up in choir."

Oliver's mouth hung open; he was unable to respond with anything quippy or clever. That niggling feeling he'd had in New York at the museum came creeping back. He'd all but stopped singing.

"Oliver?" Seth asked, concerned, all his former glibness gone.

"Sorry. I just realized that with the exception of our little caroling moment, I haven't really done anything musical in... years."

"Why?" Seth sounded positively horrified, and worried. "Oliver... okay, if you *do* come—"

"I'll be there, promise."

"Then know that John will make a point of getting you to sing with him; just be prepared. And knowing him, all the songs in his karaoke machine are Molly Hatchet or some other '70s rock band."

Oliver bit on his lower lip for a moment, his voice low as he asked hopefully, "Just him?"

He could hear Seth sigh, but it was meant to be silly. "If you want me to sing with you, I *suppose* I could be forced." Seth scoffed. "Like I need an excuse, please."

Oliver couldn't help the excited grin that spread across his face. He exhaled slowly and said, "I'll put you on my singing card, then. Can I bring anything?"

"Only if you want to. We should have plenty of food and drink, so just bring yourself."

"Can do. Eight o'clock?"

"Eight o'clock. And Oliver?"

"Yes?"

Seth paused for a moment and dropped his voice to a sweeter register than his earlier teasing, something more intimate. "Feel free to come earlier. I know Dad would love to see you. Unless that's weird for you, I don't mean to—"

"Seth." Oliver pressed his hand to his sternum as if to keep his heart from exploding. "I would *love* that. I'll call before so I don't just drop in unannounced."

"Okay. I'll see you then?"

"Absolutely. Yes. Wouldn't miss it."

Seth laughed on the other end as he said goodbye. Oliver sat back against the safety glass of the fireplace, the warmth seeping in through the back of his shirt as he held the phone to cover his huge grin. It seemed as though he had just made plans to come home. He looked around his quiet, sterile house and laughed dryly.

That was *exactly* what he would be doing: coming home.

* * *

A charity fundraiser, an award ceremony for his father's company and a bridge party later, it was finally New Year's Eve. Oliver had had his fill of talking about so-and-so's impending wedding, who had just gotten into medical school (Oliver remembered Kyle as having been the neighborhood's source for weed, so he had suspicions about any prescriptions Kyle would write) and the ever-present questions, "And do *you* have anyone special?" or "But what is it that you can actually *do* with your degree?" when they realized his intention was not to become a psychiatrist or a politician.

His parents' friends seemed to take in stride that Oliver would not be the one to take over his dad's law firm; that task belonged to the steely-eyed shark on the other side of the room that his father had an arm wrapped around. Oliver was just the spoiled, irresponsible child; evidently, getting a degree in social sciences at the best university in the world was a complete waste of time for this particular crowd of executives and lawyers.

Constantly defending his choices, and the ever-present one-upmanship that came with the Andrewses' social circles, was exhausting. He had spent the week after Christmas looking forward to the ease at the Larsens'. They weren't judgmental people. Well, not in the same way. They judged people by their character, not by how much money had been made and how many generations had been able to hold onto it.

He was a bundle of nerves all day Monday, wondering how soon "early" was. He didn't want to be presumptuous and show up midday, but if Seth had hoped he'd come a few hours early, he didn't want to arrive at seven-thirty and cheat himself out of one-on-one time with the family. *This is stupid; just call.*

He chewed on his bottom lip for a few minutes and stared at the handset. What if, instead of Seth, Mike answered, and he hadn't forgiven him for breaking Seth's heart years ago? Besides Seth, the only other person whose opinion of him mattered was Mike Larsen. He was direct, intimidating and absolutely worth having on your side. He didn't suffer fools; he was honest and compassionate and expected nothing less from the people in his life.

Oliver shook his head, smoothed the front of his sweater with his free hand and dialed. He knew how to be polite on the phone. This was silly; he could do this. It was just a phone call.

"Uh, hello?"

Oliver blinked for a moment, trying to place the voice until he remembered Mike's right-hand man at the garage, a short, heavyset guy with a thick handlebar mustache. Grinning, he asked, "Is this John Flores, by chance?"

"Yeah? Hey, dude, no offense, but I don't want to buy anything or do, like, a survey or whatever, so thanks and have—"

"John! It's Oliver. Um, Oliver Andrews?"

"No way! I almost hung up on you! Those salespeople usually call at dinner, but you never know. How are you? Huh, long time, no speak!"

Oliver leaned against the fridge in the kitchen, trying to catch the last thing John had said. His apparent excitement was the last thing

Oliver had expected. Smiling with relief, he replied, "It's been a while. How are you?"

"Oh, you know, just working hard and hardly working, same ol' same ol'."

Oliver laughed softly at the pat response John gave every time he was asked. "Good to hear."

"Right! Seth told us that he saw you in New York. Pretty cool, huh? Kid's like a huge star now."

"Seth's pretty amazing, you're right." Oliver had his eyes closed, and he pictured the kitchen at the Larsens'. The raw oak table with the eagle-footed pedestal that Seth hated with a passion. The baby blue calico chair pads, another sore spot for Seth. The list of foods Big Mike wasn't allowed to bring into the house that Seth had tacked onto the fridge.

"So, like... what's up?" John asked, sounding a little confused. True, that was a pretty typical sound from him, but this sounded more like nervousness. *Oh.* Oliver realized John might think he was being disloyal by their chatting.

"Well," Oliver exhaled. "Seth invited me to the party tonight; I hope that's okay with you guys?"

"Oh, sure. I mean—" John shifted, his voice muffled slightly, and Oliver had the distinct visual pop into his mind of John cupping the receiver with his hand so as to not be overheard. "You know that stuff isn't up to Mike. Seth's the one who makes the rules."

Oliver heard the sound of a door opening in the background and John saying, "Hey, man," before coming back to the call. "But yeah, that would be pretty sweet if you came."

"Is that Oliver?" Mike. Oliver could hear the sound of the phone moving around. He swiftly crossed the kitchen to sit on one of the bar stools at the kitchen island, worried that he wouldn't be able to stay standing if Mike sounded angry.

"Oliver?"

He felt like a string about to snap. "Yes, sir?"

"Don't you 'sir' me, are you coming tonight? You are, right? Of course you are."

Oliver felt as though like he was in the middle of conversational whiplash. So Mike *wasn't* mad at him. He slowly let his shoulders relax.

"Yes? As long as that's okay with everyone. Seth did offer—"

"Okay with everyone? Get your butt in your car and get over here now. I just got back from the store with the stuff to make those fancy sandwiches that you two love. I can't promise that Seth won't cut 'em into shapes, but they'll be ready and in the fridge before you hit the off-ramp."

"I... uh." Oliver pressed the flat of his palm on the cool granite, willing himself not to choke up. He *had* made a big deal about those sandwiches at Seth's graduation. They weren't anything special, but Mike had been so proud of himself for making something from one of Seth's cookbooks, and Oliver had been raised to be appreciative of any food someone made for him, no matter how simple.

At the Andrewses' house, there were always more beverages in the fridge than actual food. They ate out or picked things up on the way home from school or work, and his mother abhorred frozen dinners. But at the Larsens', there was always something to eat. Seth had made healthy sandwiches in bulk and wrapped them to deter his father from fast food drive-throughs, and Mike had always made sure there were plenty of snack foods for the guys from the shop and for Seth and his friends.

Such a silly thing, enjoying the ease of eating somewhere, but it added to the warm welcome that the house already gave. That and the priority Mike had made of having meals together, something the Andrewses rarely did due to everyone's busy schedules. The Larsen household had filled Oliver in more ways than one.

His smile trembled at the edges as he swallowed around the lump in his throat. "That sounds great, Mike, thank you. I do think I should double check with Seth, though."

"Have you not talked to him yet? John?" Mike covered the phone, but poorly, as Oliver could hear everything clearly. "What are you doing, not putting Seth on the phone? It's *Oliver*," he hissed. "Kid?" he said, back to him. "Give me just a second to round him up for you. And then get in your car and start driving."

"Yes, sir. It was..." Oliver cleared his throat. "It was really good to talk to you."

"Save it for here when I can strong-arm you into giving me a hug. Now let me go grab him."

Oliver rubbed at his eye with his index finger, unsurprised to feel moisture there. He loved his parents, of course he did. But a huge yawning hole in his soul had longed for a certain kind of affection his entire life. The kind that made it okay to pull someone into a hug, and for mothers to fuss over their children, touching and soothing and kissing them simply because they were close enough to do it. Okay for fathers to be okay with *themselves* even if they had gay sons and know that hugging their sons was not what had made them gay.

Shoulder claps, back pats. That was the height of affection from Oliver's father. It was different, he knew that: His father had grown up in a cold house with high expectations. He didn't really know any better. But Oliver thought about Big Mike, the most stereotypical "guy" Oliver had ever known in his life, and how Mike never hesitated to make sure the important people in his life knew that he loved them and didn't see anything weak about expressing it.

"Hello? Oliver?"

"Seth, hi!"

"Well, I see you've been properly accosted by everyone," Seth laughed. "Are you still coming tonight?"

"Oh, yes. Um, if it's still all right with you that I do?" He looked at the digital clock on the microwave: 3:57 p.m. Four more hours until people arrived at Seth's house.

"Don't be silly. Besides," Seth shifted at the other end, his voice dropping in false concern. "I think Dad would drive out there and kidnap you if you didn't visit."

Oliver wanted to lay his cheek on the cool granite. Heat was just pouring off of him. He wanted to rush to his car and finally be moving toward them and simultaneously felt nervous about seeing them after all these years. After all the hurt he caused.

"If he has those mint brownies, I would happily let him."

"Those are atrocious, and you know it. They're just from the grocery store with Junior Mints pressed into the top," Seth huffed.

"You're right," Oliver laughed. It was so surreal to be talking about these mundane things that were such a significant part of his life way back when. "The ones you make with crumbled Thin Mints baked inside are superior, but don't tell your dad I said that, please."

Seth hummed a little laugh. "Deal. So when would you like to come? Dad is shooting me looks from the kitchen."

Oliver traced an iridescent vein in the stone with his finger up to the place where it fractured into multiple lines that crisscrossed toward the edge. "I... don't know."

"Well, what are you doing now?"

This wasn't happening, Seth casually asking him over. "I'm looking at the clean kitchen where the caterers will be swarming soon and trying not to be bored out of my mind."

"Sounds *fabulous*. Well, you could come now, if you want? I... I would like it if you did. If you want to."

"Yes," Oliver breathed. "I would."

"Good," Seth sighed. "I'm looking forward to it."

"Me, too."

"I'll see you soon?"

"Yes, um, I'm just going to freshen up and then I'll head out."

Seth laughed. "Perfect."

They said their goodbyes and Oliver hopped off his stool, doing a little step-ball-change in his excitement. He was feeling energetic and really, really hopeful.

Mike and John were glad to see him. Seth wanted him to come now. He'd been back at his house for three weeks, but today it felt as if he was really here, as if he wasn't just bouncing from place to place.

The Larsen house was a place of so much joy. Not static and unchanging as his house seemed to be, but the physical embodiment of a feeling of happiness and support. It felt *alive*. He couldn't help but let the hope that he would be welcomed back there flood his entire being. It was enough to make him start singing some old-school love song as he ran across the wood floors, sliding on his socks around the corners before rounding the staircase. He threw open his closet doors, did a little James Brown move and laughed at himself as he picked out an Oxford and coordinating pullover.

It really did feel as though a new year was about to start—one in which he would no longer be afraid to look ahead.

There suddenly seemed to be a lot to look forward to.

Chapter Eleven

Oliver made his way carefully out of the car, trying not to tip the unwieldy platter of cut fruit he'd picked up at the market on his way over. He didn't want to show up empty handed, and fresh fruit was always a good option, he figured. He bumped the car door with his hip to shut it and carefully made his way up the narrow path that had been shoveled on the front walk. He pressed the doorbell with the edge of his knuckle and tried to keep the platter level while rolling his shoulders and forcing himself to breathe normally as he waited on the porch for someone to answer.

He'd been both excited and incredibly nervous on the drive over, especially as he exited the highway and took the familiar drive on auto-pilot. The streets were the same—except, that wasn't quite right. The second house on the right before he turned on Seth's street was gone, a new brick house in its place. The Larsens' neighbors seemed to have lost their giant maple, the one with the huge silver-backed leaves; he remembered drawing the edge of one along Seth's forearm one summer afternoon as they sat on the front porch.

"I've got it!" he heard, and then Seth was there, looking utterly gorgeous. It took a moment for the ghost of teenage-Seth to fade from Oliver's mind and let the actuality of Seth as he was now—slightly taller, broader, more relaxed, just *more*—sink in. "Oliver. Please, come in."

Oliver ducked his head as he stepped inside. "I brought this; I hope that's okay?"

Seth smiled back at him warmly as they walked to the kitchen, where Oliver felt both comfortably at home and *completely* foreign. Seth took the plate from his hands and set it on the pony wall between the kitchen and the living room.

A loud voice called from living room, "Is that Oliver?" John sauntered over, a huge grin on his face. "'Sup, man?" John said, his face open and friendly.

Oliver couldn't help but match his smile. John somehow managed to look exactly the same as he had years ago: short and broad-chested in his old leather vest with a Harley Davidson tee underneath. His kind, weather-worn face and relaxed manner put Oliver at ease.

"Well," Oliver laughed. "Not much, I guess."

John gave him a bro-five and pulled Oliver in for a pound on the back. Oliver wanted to tell John just how much he appreciated being there, that he was thankful John was still being so friendly and open toward him, but that would just make everyone uncomfortable. So instead he pounded John on the back in the manner of dudes, while still worrying that he might actually vibrate out of his skin from self-induced tension.

As John started catching him up on the shop and the "sweet setup in the basement, seriously, Mike's TV is freakin' huge," Oliver checked his periphery for signs of Big Mike, still unsure how he would react to Oliver being here. He wasn't sure how he would react to seeing Big Mike, either, and just hoped he wouldn't make a spectacle of himself by being overly complimentary in the hope of putting everyone at ease. Instead, he had the happy surprise of seeing Seth leaning against the door frame, arms crossed and smiling at him as Oliver continued to interject where appropriate in John's ongoing, one-sided conversation.

"Okay, John," Seth said. "I am *sure* that you are the very best shooter person thingy in your favorite game, but I have a feeling that Oliver doesn't have time to play video games at school."

Oliver smiled at the ground, huffing out a quiet laugh. "No, not a lot of time for XBox, unfortunately."

"Man, that sucks," John said, all apologies. Oliver absolutely loved that John was completely sincere.

"Okay, I'm going to have a little chat with poor, videogame-less Oliver now, John, if you don't mind."

"Oh. Okay. You're sticking around for later though, right? I just downloaded a bunch of Lynyrd Skynyrd for karaoke," John said, shooting a finger gun at Oliver, who nodded. "Cool." He gave Oliver one of his half-smiles, the kind that twisted up on one side with a nod, and Oliver realized just how long he'd been out of the country. John was such a... dude. And an American dude at that, he thought, remembering how Janos and his buddies slung their arms around each other easily and had no problem with big, face-grabbing kisses when their teams were winning.

"Come on, I'll show you the 'freakin' huge' TV." Seth nodded toward the basement door. "He won't stop talking about the Super—"

"Well, look who the cat dragged in."

Mike. A heavier paunch added to his already sizable presence of six-five, there was more gray hair in his beard—no longer in a braid, but trimmed—and the lines in his face were a bit deeper. Mike was a man who played his cards close to the vest and didn't give away any emotion until he was ready to, so the straight face he gave Oliver now as he stood stock still, big arms crossed in front of himself, had Oliver's heart lodged somewhere near his Adam's apple.

"Hello, Mr. Larsen, hi!" Oliver quickly wiped his palm on the side of his pants before sticking it out to shake.

Mike rolled his eyes and tugged Oliver in for a hug. Then he clapped his hand twice on Oliver's back and held him even closer. Another ball of tension Oliver that had been carrying around dissolved in the tight, welcoming bear hug.

Mike pulled away and pressed his hand against Oliver's cheek, holding it there and smiling. "You look good, kid."

"Thank you, sir." Oliver shook his head a little and gestured at Mike with both hands. "You look great, I have to say. Just like I remembered."

Mike smiled and ran one hand absentmindedly over his jaw. "Well, got a lot more gray in here," he laughed, tugging on his beard, "but you know. Life keeps on ticking. This one rides me about eating better, so that should tack on an extra six months at the end." He chuckled and gave Seth's shoulder a squeeze.

"Don't act like you don't love it, Dad," Seth said, rolling his eyes playfully. "I bet you love the attention you get at Whole Foods."

Mike crossed his arms again and leaned back with his feet splayed wide, glaring at Seth. "Hey. We'll see how you feel about getting checked out by old horny ladies when you're my age, huh?"

"Gross, Dad."

Mike shook his head at Oliver, like, "Come on; this guy."

This type of easygoing, playful banter happened every day in this house. Oliver had watched Seth and Big Mike tease each other—sometimes getting his share of it, too—more times than he could count. It was so normal and so, so long since he'd been allowed to be a part of it. He felt nothing but gratitude to be near them again, however briefly.

"You go see Seth in his musical? Broadway—that's the big time."

"Yes, sir, I did. Twice, actually." Oliver didn't know what to do with his hands. He could still feel the soft cotton of Mike's shirt against his palms, so he jammed them into his pockets, balling them into fists to hold onto the sensation.

"Twice?" Mike nodded his approval at that. "Pretty cool, huh?"

"Okay, Dad. I'm the best thing ever; Oliver is well aware of that," Seth said, rolling his eyes but clearly not upset with his father for heaping praise on him. It was something Oliver could understand; it was something he'd longed for in his own family, that type of easy affection.

Mike said, "Seth here tells me that you're living across the pond. They treating you right over there?"

"Yes, sir. It's a lot different from Kansas in some ways," Oliver laughed, rocking back and forth on his heels to dispel some of his nervous energy.

"You like it there?" Mike asked the question casually, but Oliver had the feeling that he—and his future plans—were being vetted. It was a little scary. Mike Larsen, no matter how much kindness he'd given Oliver over the years, and he'd given him plenty, was still an intimidating man as the father of his boyfriend. Well, former boyfriend. But it was also heartening that he wanted to know what was going to happen down the road. Like maybe this wasn't a one-time visit.

"I do," Oliver said carefully. "The city itself is great, not too big, not too small, lots of things to do. I've gotten into a bit of a rhythm there. But—" He looked Mike straight in the eye, wanting to convey all of his hopes for a future with Seth. "It's not home. I miss a lot of things from my life here. Things I just can't get there."

Mike regarded him for a moment, the tiniest of smiles crooking the corner of his mouth in a blink-and-you'll-miss-it moment. "I hear they drink their beer warm."

Oliver laughed. "Well, maybe in some places. But you can get a cold beer. When you hear that people in Europe drink their beer at room temperature, you don't realize that the room is at about fifty-five degrees. And I have to tell you, Mike," he shot Mike a wry look, "I've had better beer there."

"All right, now you're sounding crazy," Mike laughed and shook his head. "So you're just here for the holidays, huh? What's next?"

Oliver shot a quick look at Seth, who had gone still and was listening intently to their conversation. He took a deep breath; he had hoped for a chance to talk about this with Seth in private, but now was as good as any time, he supposed. "Well, it looks like I'm on schedule for graduation, barring a huge mistake on my part." Seth inhaled and straightened his posture. It was a tiny movement, but Oliver noticed it. He took it as encouragement. "That's in June. After that, it's wherever I end up for my PhD. I have some ideas, but I still need to decide on a school as soon as I get back or I'll miss the deadline to get my apps in for fall semester. I still need to talk all of that out."

"Hmm," Mike said, glancing at Seth.

Seth evidently took that as his cue; he pushed off the wall and said, "We were just on our way downstairs to do some talking, actually." He glanced at Oliver as he moved behind his dad, gently pushing on Mike's shoulders to move him away from the door. "Right, Oliver?"

Oliver nodded sharply.

Seth gave his dad's shoulder a squeeze, saying, "So if you don't mind," as he continued to push Mike along the corridor.

"All right, all right. But the door stays open... ha. Sorry," Mike said, laughing and shaking his head. "Old habit. You two have fun. You sticking around?" he asked Oliver.

"Yes, that's the plan."

"Good."

It was almost too much to process: Mike assuming he and Seth would fool around like they were back in school; the blush on Seth's cheeks (*Are we? Oh my God. No, he's just embarrassed. Oh my* God.); the feeling of comfort that was beginning to settle in him just by virtue of being in the place where he had so many wonderfully happy memories.

Seth stopped three steps down and turned and looked back at Oliver with an easy smile. "You coming?"

Oliver breathed in through his nose and slowly exhaled, feeling more of the tension melt away, even as his chest tightened with the force of his longing. He smiled back and said, "Lead the way."

* * *

"I will never understand the need to have speakers the size of buses," Seth said, sighing as he stood in front of the huge sound system in the basement. "I did make him let me pick out the sofa, at least," he said, running his hand over the leather.

Oliver held a large throw pillow that Seth had, clearly, bought and raked his fingertips through the fringe along the seam. While he didn't mind talking about the hassle of convincing a man who thought neon signs were the height of chic décor to buy things that were more tasteful, he really wanted to talk about *them*. And how to make them a "them," again. The problem was that he didn't know how to start the conversation in which he would convince Seth to love him again and to start apartment-hunting for his arrival at the end of June. He didn't know how to start, because he had no idea what he was going to do after graduation.

"I just don't understand the old metal motor oil signs," Seth said. "And I can't say anything to him about it because he's so proud of them. He even texted me a picture when he found them at a yard sale. I'm assuming someone helped him with his phone, of course."

Oliver propped his head on his hand and rested his arm on the back of the sofa, watching Seth, who leaned against the opposite side, legs crossed, fingers trailing the velvet trim on another pillow. Oliver's eyes tracked the movement of Seth's fingers. He wanted to feel them trail along his arm, his face, through his hair.

"Oliver." Seth's fingers had stopped; he was looking at Oliver with a contained nervousness. At least Oliver wasn't the only one who felt out of his depth here.

"So you're graduating in June?" Seth asked. "That's... interesting."

"I was going to talk to you about that tonight, if we got the chance." Oliver said quickly. He didn't want Seth to think he was hiding any details.

"It looks like we have the chance now," Seth said, smiling.

Oliver could hear the faint sound of footsteps on the upper floor, but all his attention was focused on what he thought might be hope on Seth's face.

"I heard from Moira, my partner?" Seth nodded and he continued. "She says we're a go, which is great."

"That is. It seems like a long way off, still." Seth toyed with the pillow again.

"It's not that far off. Honestly, after five years of school, it feels like it's rushing at me."

"Does it?" Seth asked, looking back up and then past Oliver to the doorway, which had been left cracked open; Seth had smirked at Oliver when he made a production of it. Someone was coming down the stairs.

"Everyone decent? I'm not looking!" Mike pushed the door open with one hand; the other hand covered his eyes, as if he was scared of what he may have just walked in on.

"Oh my God, Dad. No one is naked," said Seth, his annoyance evident. Oliver didn't miss the deep red blush blooming on his neck. He looked embarrassed, as if they were a couple of teenagers.

Oliver remembered the two of them hopping off Seth's bed and scrambling to pull up their pants when they heard the garage door begin to open. Smoothing their hair back into place after a quick grope in the hallway before walking into the living room. Mike loudly asking him if he'd eaten, when he came to pick Seth up for a date, because evidently the last time they'd gone out, Oliver was so hungry that he'd mistaken Seth's neck for food and gnawed on it.

Oliver's palms began to sweat just remembering the utter embarrassment he'd felt not only from giving Seth a hickey (so tacky), but being called out for it by his *father,* a man who looked like he chewed glass for breakfast. He wiped his hands on the legs of his jeans and glanced over at Seth. Seth's hand hovered at the neck of his shirt, which was still perfectly buttoned, and he looked at Oliver with such a familiar "we just got busted" expression that Oliver couldn't help himself. He started laughing and reached over to give Seth's hand a squeeze. They *had* only been talking, but it had been such a common occurrence back in school to be caught *not* talking that they had both easily slipped into their familiar roles.

Seth chuckled to himself and shook his head. "This is ridiculous," he muttered to himself. "Dad, I told you before that Oliver and I are just friends now. We weren't doing anything, for God's sake."

"Oh, I know what you *said*, bud." He shrugged. "You two getting hungry?"

Oliver smiled. "I'm not, but thank you very much. Oh, and the changes you made in this room are really cool, sir."

Mike positively beamed at him. "Thanks, kid. And stop calling me 'sir;' it's Mike, you know that."

Oliver nodded, a sheepish smile spreading across his face.

Mike looked around the room with pride. "All right, I know you two want to catch up. I gotta get John on grill duty."

"I hope there are turkey burgers waiting?" Seth said archly.

"It's New Year's!" his dad complained.

"And I'd like to see you make it to the next one."

Mike rolled his eyes. "You'd think I had a ticking time bomb inside me, the way he talks," he said, winking at Oliver.

Sighing in feigned annoyance, Seth crossed the room and pulled the door shut after him.

Oliver sat back on the sofa and tried to remember where they'd been in their previous conversation. He was still on the filial high that came from spending time with Seth's dad.

"Change of topic," Seth said breezily, flopping back onto the sofa and smiling. "Which means back to the original topic. June. You graduate. Good for you."

Oliver blinked for a moment, trying to catch up. "Yes. Check, check and check."

Seth looked back at him expectantly. "And?"

Oliver stared at the pale skin just above the collar of Seth's shirt. That had been one of his favorite places to kiss Seth, a surefire way to get him to make that wonderful throaty sound that curled Oliver's toes. Being in this house was making it difficult for Oliver to focus.

"And?" Oliver shook his head to clear it of thoughts of leaning forward to press his lips against warm skin. "Oh! Right. And... I'm not sure."

Seth briefly closed his eyes.

Oliver leaned toward Seth on the sofa, wringing his hands in his lap.

"I'm not sure because I still have to finish sending out my applications. I do have it narrowed down to two schools, though. Staying where I am or... one here."

"Here?" Seth asked, his brow wrinkling in confusion. "Kansas? Why on earth would you ever come back here?"

Oliver laughed and put a hand out to stop Seth. "No, not *here*, here. Here, the States here. Sorry. Um, NYU, actually."

Seth went still. His face did not give anything away. "Oh?"

Oliver bit his lip and nodded.

Seth suddenly seemed fascinated by the seam on one of the throw pillows. "But I thought you said that NYU was an inferior school for your degree."

Oliver took a deep breath. He needed to see how Seth was really feeling, to see if he himself wasn't about to make another huge mistake by jumping in with both feet before looking. He reached across and carefully took the pillow out of Seth's hands to make him look up. "It was. For my undergraduate work. Their doctoral program in social sciences happens to be one of the best in the world."

Seth stared back at him. His throat worked and he swallowed nervously. "Is it?"

Oliver decided he would go for broke. After all, they'd said they would try to be friends at the very least, hadn't they? And their first friendship had begun with Oliver taking Seth's hand and leading him through the school to show him around. Oliver stuttered in his movement for the briefest of moments and then took Seth's hand in both of his, something in him faltering at the small hitch in Seth's breath when they touched.

"It is. It's also in Washington Square. Well, one of the campuses. But applicants get to choose from four." He looked up into Seth's face. "That would be what I would choose."

Seth's hand convulsed briefly in Oliver's. When he spoke, his voice was high and breathy. "Is NYU your choice?"

Oliver sighed. "I have to see if they'll choose me, actually. As soon as I get back to England, I'm emailing them my CV and letters of recommendation, et cetera. I've already filled out the application."

"So it's not for sure," Seth said, leaning back and taking his hand out of Oliver's and dropping it in his own lap. It ached to see him so guarded, but Oliver understood why. A part of him was grateful that Seth had this reaction; it meant that a part of his heart, a part he needed to protect from hurt, still belonged to Oliver. He clung to that.

Oliver looked at his empty hand and closed it to hold the warmth that still lingered there from Seth's touch. "No, but I'm actually a really good student, turns out." He flashed an over-bright grin at Seth, who thankfully smiled back. "And I happen to be a really good student at a really good university, so my chances at being accepted are pretty high. I need to talk to my mentor when I get back and see what my options are for what I'm hoping to accomplish at the doctorate level."

Upstairs, the doorbell rang.

Seth rubbed at the edge of his thumbnail, staring at it. "So we continue to wait and see?"

"Unfortunately, yes. But at least the fork in the road is visible? That's a first for me in a long time. I've got you to thank for that," Oliver said, squeezing Seth's knee and wishing he could slide his hand to Seth's waist, pull him close and just *hold* him.

Seth looked back at him questioningly.

"I've had my head down, only looking at my feet, since the day you walked out, Seth. I guess I didn't see a reason to look toward the future when it was clear that I didn't have one anymore."

There was so much sadness in Seth's eyes when he said, "Oh, Oliver."

"Sorry. I'm sorry. I just want to tell you how important you are."

"Little Mike's here!" John shouted down the staircase.

Seth looked as though he wanted to say something, but snapped his mouth shut and got to his feet. He held his hand out; Oliver took it without question and was surprised to be pulled into a hug.

Seth wrapped his arms around Oliver's neck and pressed their cheeks together. "Thank you for telling me. I wish you knew more. I wish *I* knew more." His hands slid down Oliver's shoulders and he pushed himself back to look in Oliver's face. "It's good to know where my friend might be soon."

Every point of contact between their bodies was a point of radiant heat for Oliver. He wanted to be pulled back into Seth's arms, to feel his skin, to know that Seth was willing to wait for him to get his future sorted out. He told himself that Seth was being smart, though, by not jumping in. That was always Oliver's downfall: his lack of impulse control. He needed to follow Seth's lead so the night could be a happy one.

"Oliver's here?" they heard from upstairs, the scratchy two-pack-a-day voice indicating "Little Mike" Packard.

Seth gave Oliver's shoulders a squeeze and dropped his hands. "Promise me that you will not encourage him to pull out that ridiculous e-cigarette. I keep telling him it makes him look like a stupid teenager."

Oliver nodded, laughing. "Promise."

He followed Seth upstairs, bracing himself for the whirlwind of energy and noise that was the very essence of a Mike Larsen gathering.

Chapter Twelve

Little Mike raised his beer can at them, giving Oliver a significant stare while tilting his head toward Seth. It took Oliver a moment to figure out what that was supposed to mean, and then he gave Little Mike a tiny shake of the head and saw his smile deflate.

Little Mike also gave Oliver a bro-five, pulling him in close and whispering in his ear, "Don't give up."

It was hard for Oliver to keep the mantra of "we're just friends, we're just friends" reverberating in his mind as the night wore on. It seemed tough for Mike's friends—people who had always been in Seth's life, who had supported him dating Oliver—to remember that as well. John's longtime girlfriend, Natalie Greer—a tiny spitfire in skintight, broken-in blue jeans who favored sequined shirts and frosted tips on her short, dark hair—kept asking Oliver where Seth was, as if he would always know. He overheard one of the other guys from Mike's shop ask Seth how the two of them were "getting on" in New York City.

He tried to mingle with other people, to give Seth space, since he hadn't seen many of the night's guests in a while, either, but he couldn't help but notice how many times he looked up to find that he'd unconsciously moved toward Seth in the crowd. Seth simply had a sort of gravitational pull on him.

As much as he didn't want to spend the night making small talk, he knew that he had to continue to give Seth some space, to let Seth come to him. So he pretended to enjoy listening to Mike's employees from the shop (couldn't they leave work at work? What on earth were ape hangers?) and was grateful for Natalie and her girlfriend's banter about their new book club.

Little Mike spent a good forty-five minutes talking with Oliver about

England, asking him repeatedly about "what chicks are like out there," to which Oliver indicated that the *ladies* were just like anywhere else; they just had a different accent.

"Mm, stuck up, huh? Yeah, it figures."

Oliver rubbed the back of his neck and wondered if it would be the greatest match-up or the worst in history to introduce Moira to Little Mike. He kept coming down on the side of it being the worst.

"So what's up with you and our boy?" Little Mike asked, doing that guy head-nod thing. "Are you two—" He raised his eyebrows lasciviously. "You know? Back?"

"No, we're just friends," Oliver said, trying to not turn red.

"Shut up!" Little Mike looked around to see if anyone was listening in and dropped his voice. "You dudes totally hooked up!"

Oliver's jaw dropped. "What? I... how?" He also dropped his voice, and tried not to look shocked or caught out. "How did you know?"

Little Mike smirked. "I didn't. You just told me. Man, you guys never learn. Don't worry; I won't tell his old man." He pulled another beer out of a nearby cooler and cracked it open. "So? What's this 'just friends' stuff? I never took you two to be one-night stand kind of guys."

"I... Mike. *Please.*" Oliver felt hot all over. He was mortified, and worried that he would say something to ruin the delicate strands holding him to Seth for the time being. "It's just... no. No, I'm not going to talk about this. It feels like I'm talking behind his back, and I don't want to be that guy."

"No prob, bro. Just know that I'm kinda good at relationships, okay? I've had *hundreds.*"

He was completely sincere. Knowing that was enough to let off a little of the pressure that was building inside Oliver as he worried that Little Mike might run his mouth. The guy was true to his word. Most of the time. Well, often enough that people could be fooled. Oliver just hoped this was one of those times that proved Little Mike told the truth. "Well, thank you. And I'd appreciate it if you'd keep this between us."

Little Mike gently ribbed Oliver with his elbow, his half-empty beer can banging into Oliver's watch. "No worries, kid. I don't think anyone would get upset, but I can respect that."

Oliver sagged in relief.

"We're all pulling for you two to get back together, anyway."

Oliver turned to him. "What?"

"You two were meant to be together. You're like the gay Romeo and Juliet."

Oliver decided to not remind him how that particular love affair ended and take it for the sweet sentiment it was intended to be.

* * *

At various times during the evening, when Oliver found himself chatting with a group of people, Big Mike would walk past him on his way to the kitchen and give his shoulder a squeeze. And Mike sat down next to him for a brief period, as John told him all about his new apartment. After a few minutes, Mike patted Oliver's knee and muttered, "Real good to have you around again, kid." Then he went to tend to more guests.

Repeating the mantra was getting harder and harder.

John ran out to his car at ten-thirty to grab his karaoke machine and personal microphone; he had a stock mic for everyone else to use. John took karaoke very seriously and imagined himself to be Kansas's own Bon Jovi. Most of the party trooped down to the basement.

Oliver stood back against the wall as John and Big Mike moved the coffee table and small armchair out of the way, making enough room by the entertainment center for people to sing. Natalie perched on the sofa, whistling and catcalling at John when he bent over to plug things in.

"Do you think anyone would take a bet that he'll sing the first three songs?"

Oliver jumped at the sensation of Seth whispering in his ear. Their nearness sent a tingling shock across Oliver's skin. "Um, I think everyone will know that's a given, sorry."

"Mm." Seth leaned against the wall, arms crossed, his body angled toward Oliver's.

He could almost forget that they weren't a couple. That nothing was decided. That Seth hadn't said repeatedly, throughout the night, that the two of them were just friends. Almost.

By John's third song—Seth nodded knowingly at Oliver when "Blaze of Glory" queued up and John took a wider stance to belt it out—Natalie decided that a duet would be more fun and dragged Oliver onto the stage "for old times' sake." Oliver took the second microphone, worried that he'd make a fool of himself.

"Take it easy on me, okay?" he whispered to Natalie after she kissed John on the cheek and took his mic.

"Oh, honey, you know that if it's easy, I'm taking it twice," she teased.

Oliver groaned as she grinned and an '80s power ballad began to blast out of the floor speakers. Natalie winked and started singing, looping her arm through Oliver's when he joined in. He started to relax; the crowd was friendly and raucous, and they cheered and whistled as Natalie pranced onstage. He chanced a look at the back of the room where he'd left Seth and saw him still there, against the wall, biting the end of his thumb to hide his smile as he bounced his head along with the beat.

He looked at his own feet, dancing along with the music, and grinned stupidly. It just felt... good. Good to be singing, not terribly, as he'd feared; good to be having fun and helping other people have a good time by contributing to the energy. But most of all it felt amazing to see Seth smiling at him as he sang.

Oliver twirled Natalie as she belted out the chorus and then joined in, bobbing his head to the beat and letting go. To an outsider, he wouldn't fit: a stuffy-looking, well-groomed country club type hanging with folks covered in tats and studded leather. And yet this was where he felt most at home: with Seth's welcoming, fun-loving family, blood-related or not.

They finished the song to more cheers and whistles. Laughing, Oliver made a modest bow and motioned toward Natalie, who gave him a side hug and asked who was next. Oliver handed his mic over to her and did a little jog toward the back of the room. He was about to slide his arms around Seth's waist when he realized with a start that they didn't do that anymore.

He disguised the move by patting Seth on the arm awkwardly and asking, "When are you going up there?"

Seth gave him a questioning look and returned the awkward pat to his shoulder. "I don't know? Why are we doing weird patting things?"

Oliver hung his head and laughed. "Sorry. I just got caught up in the muscle memory, I guess."

Seth looked at him quizzically, and then his gaze softened. "Oh." He smiled and gave Oliver a one-armed hug. "It really has been a long time since you've sung anywhere, hasn't it?"

"Try high school choir," Oliver said dryly.

"Oh, we'll have to fix that right away," Seth said, leaning back against the wall and pointing his chin at the guy currently singing "Ring Of Fire." "Dad's friends are going to turn this into a country thing, and I just cannot start a new year with Billy Ray Cyrus in my head."

Laughing, Oliver pushed off the wall and tentatively held Seth's elbow for the briefest of moments. "I'm going to get a fresh drink; would you like anything?"

"I—" Seth looked down and laughed softly. He looked back up at Oliver, sweetly, nervously and with a touch of sadness. "I hid a bottle of champagne in the refrigerator out in the garage so no one else would find it." His expression was almost one of mourning, but that made sense to Oliver. He didn't think he would ever stop grieving their past relationship.

Seth touched his own neck, running his fingers along the edge of his shirt collar. "Feel like opening it up?"

Oliver forgot about the music, forgot about the crowd of people, most of whom he didn't really know, and stared at the pink flush of Seth's cheeks. Then he was drawn back to the movement of Seth's fingers, sliding back and forth over the crisp cotton of his shirt. At least Seth remembered that night, their last New Year's Eve together. How they'd slipped away to celebrate the clock striking twelve on their own and open their hidden bottle of champagne. How they'd kissed to ensure that the New Year started with their love for each other. How Oliver had unbuttoned the top two buttons on Seth's shirt, pulling it aside to kiss that sensitive spot where Seth's shoulder and neck met.

"It's just that everyone here is drinking beer, and that's never been my thing."

"Yes. Sure. Um, I'll be back?" Oliver stammered, and walked backwards to the stairs. Seth smiled at him and turned away, looking down and grinning. Seth could play it off like he just didn't want a beer, but Oliver knew Seth; even after all of this time apart, he *knew* him.

It wouldn't be the same as the last time, that was certain: Six years ago to the day, they were happily in love; they didn't leave each other's side all night; they danced for hours, swaying in each other's arms regardless of the tempo of the song; and they kissed each other with all the love in their hearts at the strike of twelve, murmuring "I love you" over and over. Tonight wouldn't be like that night.

But it was shaping up to be its own special event, all the same.

* * *

It took a while for Oliver to make it to the garage. Mike drew him over to a group of older guys whom he introduced as buddies from his fantasy football league, and while he was incredibly happy that Mike was introducing him and saying lovely things about what he'd accomplished ("This kid is something else, always knew it; he's going to school all the way over in England, you know,"), he wanted nothing more than to be at Seth's side and to see where the night would go.

He was finally able to slip away after telling Mike that he had been sent to get a drink for Seth, which earned him an impressed and happy nod. He found the bottle in the garage and helped himself to wine glasses in the kitchen. As he unwrapped the foil, Mike came in quietly with a beer in his hand. He set it down and ruffled his fingers through Oliver's hair, smiling at him in a fatherly way.

"We're all really glad you're here, Ollie. I missed ya."

Oliver couldn't help himself; he melted and smiled hugely. "I'm really glad to be here, too."

Mike held his gaze, softly smiling, before picking his beer back up and taking a sip. "Going well?"

Oliver was almost positive that Mike had an expectant look on his face. He tamped down his nerves to reply, "I guess so? I'm having a nice time. Thank you for having me."

"You talk like a stranger we picked up on the side of the road." Mike shook his head. "Kid, the number of times I thought about driving over to that mansion of yours and having a man-to-man with your pop—you're a part of the family. Of course we'd have you. We missed you, buddy. All of us."

Oliver flushed, not really sure how to absorb that Big Mike had missed him, too. Mike seemed to pick up on that as he patted Oliver's hand and grabbed a bag of chips off the counter.

Oliver watched him walk out of the kitchen and settle into his hideous easy chair, the one Seth had never been able to convince him to get rid of. Someone said something to make Mike laugh, and the ease in the man's face, the joy that poured from him simply because he was surrounded by his friends, made something ache deep inside Oliver. God, he just wanted to be a part of this family again. He wanted it with every fiber of his being. The ease with which Mike shared his love for his son, his friends—Oliver had never felt anything like it. Now that he was confronted with how bereft his life actually was without it, he couldn't stand the thought of not having these people, whom he still loved, in his life.

He took a deep breath and turned back to the bottle, popping the cork easily and pouring two glasses. He slipped the bottle into the refrigerator behind some condiments, hoping it wouldn't be discovered by someone else, grabbed the glasses and, unwilling to be distracted from his goal, made his way back downstairs with nods to people whose eyes caught his.

He had to push past a few people he didn't know who had strayed downstairs to listen to the karaoke only to find John back on the microphone, singing "Me and Bobby McGee." It was a surprisingly good fit for his voice. Oliver scanned the room, looking for Seth. He was across the room chatting with Natalie. John sang the part about trading all his tomorrows for a single yesterday and wanting to hold Bobby's body close; Seth looked up, a little scandalized, and caught Oliver's eye.

They grinned at each other, Seth shaking his head. He knew that Seth was wondering if John had ever listened to the words of that song before, or if he'd just become so comfortable with his own sexuality that he didn't mind singing about longing for a man to sleep with.

A thrill went through Oliver; it was such a couple thing to do, a conversation through nothing more than eye contact. He made his way through the crowd and handed Seth his glass. Natalie cast Oliver a sour look.

"You holding out on me?" she asked, her eyes narrowed.

Seth laughed but Oliver shrugged, worried that he'd just offended her. "It wasn't my bottle—" Oliver began to apologize, "and Seth asked for a glass, so—"

"I'm just joking; I'm designated driver tonight." Natalie winked and bumped him with her hip playfully.

Most of the crowd was singing along by now, so it was almost impossible to speak to anyone. Oliver stood near Seth and watched John sway on the stage, a huge grin on his face as he led the crowd. Seth clinked his glass gently against Oliver's and leaned in to speak directly into his ear. "Thank you."

Oliver flashed him a huge smile and mouthed, "Of course."

John handed the mic to Natalie when he was finished. She took a sip of her soda, blew a kiss to him and punched in her selection. The people Oliver didn't know were still talking loudly and not paying attention. John sat on the floor next to Natalie, looking up at her adoringly, and a few other people began to grow quiet and pay attention when Gladys Knight's "Neither One of Us" began to play and Natalie began to sing.

She was no Gladys, but she could carry a tune and did a good job inflecting the song with wistfulness, so much so that a hush soon fell over the room. Her voice was nice, but the song was painful. Oliver was keenly aware of Seth at his side; the few inches between their bodies seemed to grow into miles as the song went on.

Oliver dropped his gaze as she sang about old memories getting in the way of seeing reality, trying to tamp down the worry that somehow this song and its message of letting go was prophetic, that it would somehow ruin the mercurial strands of connection between him and Seth. Those fears, combined with the earnest voice singing of a relationship that had run its course, proved to be too much. A tear slipped down his cheek as Natalie, her head thrown back, belted out the part about a happy ending being impossible.

He felt a squeeze on his bicep and looked over to see Seth watching him, worry at the corners of his eyes and just maybe something else that Oliver didn't dare hope for.

Seth cleared his throat. "She's good."

Oliver nodded, unable to look Seth in the eye.

Seth smiled gently at him and turned back to watch her close out the song. He did, however, reach out and briefly hold Oliver's hand before he crossed his arms once again.

Natalie bent down and rubbed John's head, winking as she sang a final farewell to her love in the song.

It couldn't have hurt more if she'd reached inside Oliver and crushed his heart. Yes, it was a powerful, amazing song; but it also spoke to the fear that he was fooling himself into thinking that something permanent was happening between him and Seth.

The crowd applauded and whistled; Natalie feigned dusting off her shoulder and laid the microphone on top of a speaker. "Follow *that.*"

Oliver used the moment when everyone was focused on her to wipe his eyes. He needed to get out of there, needed to get his head clear and think. He wanted to make sure he wasn't projecting his expectations onto the night, no matter how badly he wanted it to end with Seth saying he was willing to try to be Seth-and-Oliver again.

He murmured, "Excuse me for a minute," to Seth, pushed through the crowd and climbed the stairs. The party was getting louder as it neared midnight; Oliver moved from room to room to find someplace empty and had to resort to stepping out onto the front porch.

It was freezing, and he wore just a thin cashmere sweater and a button-down. He huddled next to one of the porch columns, looking at the heaps of snow piled on either side of the sidewalk. The steam from his breath stuttered out into the cold night air, his lungs hitching with the force of his attempt to get some control over himself. He worried—was he just imagining signals from Seth, or the apparent approval for his return to the Larsen family? They might be just as happy to see him as they would any of Seth's old friends. Maybe the inherent romance of the evening was playing tricks on him.

Just because there was a sort of built-in promise in the night didn't mean it was for *him*. Just because Seth had champagne didn't mean he wanted to recreate their last New Year's together.

Just because he wanted Seth so badly he thought he would die from the ache of it didn't mean he would have him back.

He heard the door open behind him and slipped his hand to his face to wipe away his tears, saying in a forced-cheerful voice, "Just getting some fresh air."

"Oliver?" It was Seth. "Are you okay?"

Oliver's shoulders sagged, his eyes closed, and he was vaguely aware that he was shaking with the cold when he felt a warm hand on his shoulder. Seth said softly, "Oliver."

"Um." He exhaled. "Yeah! Yes, just... you know. A lot of people in there. I just wanted some fresh air for a minute."

"You're about to miss the countdown." Seth continued to stand behind him, rubbing calming patterns into Oliver's shoulder; Oliver's shaking intensified no matter how tightly he wrapped his arms around himself or how hard he tried to keep calm while Seth touched him, soothed him.

"Oliver. You're *freezing*." The apprehension in Seth's voice melted into something softer, as if he understood just how hard this was for Oliver and somehow wanted to make it better.

"I'm trying so hard," Oliver said, his voice barely louder than a whisper. "I'm trying not to push things, I really am."

"I know," Seth said softly. "I know." Seth sighed, his hand stilling on Oliver's back but not leaving. "This is really hard for me. I'm not trying to say it isn't for you, too, it's just—I see you, and my instinct is to act the way we once were. The last time I saw you—"

"Please don't bring that awful night up, Seth. Please." Oliver felt like he was crumbling to pieces, and his throat began to burn from the lump forming there.

"No, no." Seth started rubbing again, making a sort of figure eight across the expanse of Oliver's back. Oliver wondered briefly if Seth was aware that he was doing it.

Seth said, "I didn't mean *that*. I meant the last time I was *with* you." His voice grew soft and Oliver could feel that he had moved closer. "When it was just the two of us, together. That's what I keep thinking of. God," Seth sighed. "I loved you so much, Oliver. But we're not the same people, are we?"

Oliver didn't respond; he had already given his response back in New York, after all.

"But then we *are*, aren't we? It's so comfortable with you, and then there are moments when I don't understand how I'm in this situation again. I just don't know what to do, here, I really don't. I wish I did, though. I'm trying to figure it out, but... you're a little distracting. I—I don't think I can survive being hurt like that again. And I don't want to hurt *you* again, not ever."

Oliver tried to force his breathing back to something resembling normal, an almost impossible feat with Seth touching him; all Oliver wanted to do was pull Seth to him and promise they'd find a way to make things work.

The crowd inside grew impossibly loud. Seth pulled his hand away; the place where it had been felt icy cold as his warmth evaporated into the cold night air.

"It's almost the New Year," Seth said, tugging on Oliver's arm to get him to turn around. Oliver did so reluctantly; he was unable to look into Seth's eyes, afraid that he'd see "goodbye" there. Seth took him by both shoulders and shook him lightly. "Hey."

Oliver couldn't help himself. He slid his hands around Seth's waist and pulled him close, hooking his chin over Seth's shoulder. Seth wrapped his arms around him, too, rocking them gently from side to side. The noise inside exploded into cheers and the honking of plastic horns. It was the New Year.

Seth pulled back, a sad smile on his face. "Happy New Year." And then he leaned forward and kissed Oliver. Just a gentle press of the lips, but it was as if the noise and energy from inside the house were now housed in Oliver's chest, which threatened to burst open. He couldn't help the pained noise that escaped him at the warmth of Seth's body against his and the familiar scent of his skin. He wanted it to mean more; he wanted it to mean *everything*, but for now he allowed himself to fall into the wonderful sensation of Seth's lips against his and hope for what could be.

Seth held his face and pulled back slightly. His warm breath gently blew over Oliver's face. And suddenly it was just too much—the thought of losing him, the need for him to know without question how Oliver felt.

"I love you," Oliver breathed, craning forward just enough for his lips to brush Seth's. "I love you."

Seth pressed their foreheads together and squeezed his eyes tightly shut. "I'm leaving in the afternoon." His voice choked slightly on "leaving."

Oliver rested his hands lightly on Seth's waist. He couldn't help the tremors in his hands as he said, "I don't want you to say goodbye to me again."

"Oh, Oliver." Seth's voice broke on his name and he pulled Oliver back into his embrace, running the flat of his hand up and down his back, warming him, pressing his cheek against Oliver's shoulder.

Oliver didn't want to think about later. He didn't want to think about driving back to his house where the dregs of another Andrews party would still be there in the morning, waiting for the maids; where he'd go back to his bed, the one in which his whole life had been changed by the boy—man, now—in his arms; where he'd be all alone, fully cognizant of what he'd let slip away.

He wanted this moment to stretch on forever. Even if nothing was being declared, he had Seth in his arms, he had the taste of him on his lips and he had the hope of a brand new year stretching out in front of him, one with Seth in it. He wanted that most of all.

But. This might very well be the goodbye he feared the most. This might be the start of a new year without Seth. He held on tightly, as he held on to the possibility of having Seth back, for as long as possible.

The porch lights flashed on and off in quick succession before the front door opened and John shrieked, "Whoo!" out into the night.

Seth and Oliver, both startled, flew apart and turned to see what was going on.

"Oh! Whoops. Sorry, just..." John jammed his hands into his front pockets, horrified with himself. "You know. Happy New Year?"

Seth gave him a watery smile. "It's okay. But could you please give us some privacy?"

"Yeah, sure. No pro-blemo. I can totally do that." John's gaze darted back and forth between them and settled on Oliver. "You okay out here?"

"John," Seth said, firmly but not unkindly.

"Right." He pointed his thumb over his shoulder. "I'll just... right." He looked back at Oliver, gave him a sympathetic half-smile and went back inside.

Oliver looked off into the middle distance, knowing that he needed to close himself off from the flood of emotions that threatened to drown him, but finding it incredibly difficult. He asked quietly, "Is this where you tell me that we can't see each other again?"

"*God*. I..." Seth closed his mouth. His eyes brimmed with tears—seeing them sent a spike of agony through Oliver. Once again, Oliver had done that. He was afraid to ask again, but knew that he needed to. He couldn't continue to prolong these hurts; he couldn't do it to himself, and he certainly couldn't continue to do it to Seth.

Death by a thousand cuts.

"What do you want?" Oliver asked.

"I don't know about us being together like... that, Oliver." Seth reached out and held Oliver's hand in his. Oliver looked down, afraid to ask, afraid to *breathe*. Seth said, with a sort of ferocity, "But I do know that I don't want *that*—to never see you again?" Seth sobbed a harsh exhalation and visibly steeled himself. "I don't know about down the road, or what that means for us." He gave Oliver's hand a squeeze and waited for him to look up. A hint of desperation clouded the confusion that Oliver could see in Seth's eyes. "If there's an 'us' that can really happen beyond just being friends. If wanting it to work is enough to *make* it work, then you'd still be my... I *do* know that I like having my best friend back again. And I know how much I've missed you."

Seth dropped Oliver's hand to wipe at his cheek. "I really have, Oliver. I *never* wanted you to be unhappy. Not even when I was so miserable I couldn't—" Seth wiped at his face again, his voice soft and plaintive as he said, "I don't want you to be unhappy, no matter what happens with me. Don't you know that?"

"Seth..." Oliver was sure it had been foolish to hope for more, to hope for anything, really. But Seth pulled him back into a tight hug, and that's when he let himself go, shuddering both from the cold and the release of soul-crushing worry that this night would be it. He clung to Seth, who held on just as tightly to him.

Oliver wasn't aware of the cold. All of his focus was on the warm, solid feeling of Seth in his arms and the longing in his heart as his mind repeated "back in my life" over and over.

Seth eventually broke their hold on each other, running his hands over Oliver's shoulders to warm him. "I'm freezing, and I know you must be, too. Will you come inside with me?"

Oliver reached out and held Seth's face, his thumb drawing away the faint tear-track on Seth's cheek. All of his love for this wonderful, kind, amazing man was jammed inside him, trying to find its way out, so Seth would know just how much Oliver still loved him, what he meant to him. Seth closed his eyes, and a smile crept from the corners of his mouth, blossoming into something that filled Oliver with longing. Seth reached up and laid his hand over Oliver's at his cheek, his eyes fluttering closed briefly.

"Come on. Let's go inside." Seth laced their fingers together and drew him back into the house. Oliver closed the door behind him; Seth didn't let go of his hand.

It was a start. Of what still remained to be seen. But it was a start.

* * *

John scanned the crowd looking for them. Seth was turned away, speaking to a neighbor, his hand still linked with Oliver's. John caught Oliver's eye and gave him a questioning look. Oliver shrugged, smiling shyly, and looked down at their hands.

John's face broke into a huge grin and he gave Oliver two thumbs up. But Oliver didn't want to create the wrong impression, as much as he wished it was a sign that everything was going to be all right. He shook his head.

John scoffed and raised his beer in salute before turning back to some guy in the kitchen doorway.

Squeezing Oliver's hand, Seth whispered, "I'm going to freshen up a bit." He gave Oliver a shy smile and asked, "Meet you back here in a few?"

Oliver smiled softly back at him. The night would come to an end eventually; he wanted to enjoy the time they had now. After all, Seth had indicated that there was hope for more, of a sort. More time together, more talking.

Oliver watched him walk up the stairs. Then he turned and walked back toward the basement stairs, where he bumped into Natalie. She threw her arms around him, tugging him into a tight hug.

Then she pulled back, her arms still flung around his neck, and tilted her head to peer closer into his face. "Oh, no. You okay, honey? I got an emergency makeup kit in my car; I can go run and get it for you if you'd like?"

"Do I look that bad?" he asked, rubbing his face.

"No..." She hesitated. "You just look like you've had your heart scooped out and shoved back in."

"Probably because that's about what just happened?" He laughed. He felt wrung out.

"Oh. Were you boys talking?" At his nod, she continued. "So? You coming back?"

"Downstairs?" Oliver asked, flipping her hair back behind her shoulder. "I'm waiting for Seth to come back, first."

"No, dummy," she said, slapping him gently on the arm. "Are you coming *back*? To America?" She raised one eyebrow questioningly. "To Seth?"

He gaped at her for a minute. "I... don't know. I think so, eventually? We'll see if he even wants that?"

"You're never gonna convince that boy to live too far from his daddy, and his daddy would never leave the place where his wife's buried." She looked past his shoulder toward the living room and John. Her voice softened. "And I get it. When you're young, you're sure that you know what a forever love is, huh? Sometimes we get it right, too, even if we don't get to hang onto it."

He slumped against the wall, suddenly feeling very tired.

She pressed her hand against his chest, just over his heart, and rubbed her thumb back and forth before giving him a pat. "You know he spent all four years at college comparing boys to you?" At Oliver's bewildered look she shook her head and said, "Not realizing it, not every time. But that's what he was doing. Letters home just full of boys' faults."

They broke apart to let someone walk past.

"No one ever matched up to you, I think," Natalie said. "So—"

Oliver cut her off with a gentle squeeze to her arm. "Nat. You know I adore you. But I just can't right now, okay? I feel like I'm barely holding it together here. And I need to go wash my face, evidently," he gave her a pretend sour face. "And then find a place to sit and just be still for a bit. Is that okay?"

"Of course," she said. "I'll even let you go to the bathroom before me," she said with a wink.

He laughed; he couldn't help it. "Thank you, but I don't think I'm so down and out that I would cut in front of a lady. I'll just wait here." He bent to give her a kiss on the cheek and leaned against the wall near the bathroom door.

She beamed at him. "Lord, but I wish these guys would take some lessons from you boys in how to treat a lady."

* * *

After he had a chance to wash his face—and yes, he did look like he'd been dismantled and put back together hastily—he scanned the living room and kitchen for Seth and saw no sign of him. The crowd seemed to be thinning; it was getting late.

He went downstairs, wanting to find anyone he knew. Little Mike and John were talking with a small group of people he didn't know; Natalie was nowhere to be found. Big Mike wasn't anywhere he could see, either.

A couple got up from the couch, so Oliver sat down, leaned against one arm and fought off a yawn. It was a longish drive back to his part of town, and it was getting late. He should probably say his goodbyes, too, even though it was the last thing he wanted to do. He just needed to rest his eyes for a minute.

"Hey, Andrews." Oliver opened his eyes and looked up to see Little Mike. He said quietly, "You staying? John said you two might have worked things out."

He was looking down at Oliver with such a sweet and hopeful expression.

"We're... trying," Oliver said. "Trying to be friends again. So you can tell the rumor mill," he looked over at John, who now had his arm over Natalie's shoulder, "not to blow things out of proportion, please."

"All good, man. Just—the way you two are, even when you was kids?" Little Mike sat down next to him and narrowed his eyes in thought. "Coming from a busted up family, it was, you know, nice to see that people seemed to be able to beat the odds, that's all." He had a frank expression, as though he was explaining how pistons fired.

He slapped Oliver's thigh and stood up. "All right, man. Good to see you."

Oliver looked back at him with a dazed expression. "You, too."

Little Mike nodded and crossed to the door. Then Oliver heard him say, "Later, Seth. Congrats on being badass and stuff on Broadway." Oliver turned to see Seth awkwardly bumping fists and smiling his thanks.

Seth sat next to Oliver on the sofa, and their knees brushed. He laid his head on Oliver's shoulder briefly. Was Oliver tired? Because he suddenly felt very much awake in that buzzing-with-energy, not-enough-sleep kind of way.

"Are you getting sleepy?" Seth asked.

"I was."

Oliver jolted in his seat when John patted his shoulder as he walked behind the sofa. "Good seeing you, Mr. Fancy!"

Seth turned to shoot John a dirty look, which he ignored.

"You too, John," Oliver said.

The last crowd of people left; Oliver suddenly realized that it was just the two of them. Seth sighed and took his hand, shifting to face him on the couch with his leg bent between them.

"Oliver, I don't want to lead you on. By which I mean that I don't want you to think," he continued, "that everything is exactly like it used to be between us. That's too..." Seth shuddered out a pained sigh. "I'm not there, yet."

Oliver watched Seth's thumb work back and forth over his, utterly confused and completely exhausted.

"But I definitely want to be friends again. I miss that. I miss *you*." Seth gripped his hand tighter, his eyes pleading with Oliver to understand. Oliver didn't. Seth continued, "I want to take things slowly. I want us to talk, to share our lives a little and see how that works. Is that—can we do that, please?"

Oliver didn't answer; he pulled Seth to him, his eyes closing at the tingly feeling of Seth's nose brushing against his neck. He had asked for this much, to be friends as they'd once been, and knowing that he could have Seth in his life—even if as just a friend—was enough for now. And Seth had said he wasn't there *yet*.

Seth exhaled slowly, his arm draped loosely over Oliver's waist. "I just don't want to jump into anything and end up hurting you, or for me to get hurt and—" Seth sighed and rubbed the heel of his hand over his eyes. "I don't want to mess things up again, okay?" He turned to look up at Oliver, his face a plea.

"Okay." Oliver kissed Seth's forehead and tightened his grip. "I... yes. I would love to talk with you, and nothing would make me happier than to share my life with you. I know what you mean," he said quickly, squeezing Seth once. "I know you mean as friends. I do."

They held each other, using the quiet of the house to relax against one another. Learning how to share space again as friends was something Oliver would do willingly. Holding Seth would be enough. Talking to him again. That could be enough.

"You have a long drive," Seth murmured after a while.

Oliver glanced at his watch; it was after two. He groaned softly even as his arms held Seth just a hair tighter.

"You should stay here," Seth said quietly. "My dad won't mind. He'd rather you got home in one piece, I'm sure."

Oliver sat up as Seth pulled away. He rubbed at his face; he felt more tired than he could remember being. It wasn't a bad idea, but he didn't want to push his luck. "I'll just stretch out here for a little bit, if that's okay? Maybe catch a quick nap and then I can drive home—"

"Oliver, don't be ridiculous. Come on." Seth stood and pulled on Oliver's hand to get him to standing. "You can borrow a pair of pajamas. You're not napping in *cashmere*."

He sounded so affronted at the thought that Oliver laughed.

"And you can sleep with me. I mean—" Seth blushed. "You know, *actual* sleep."

Oliver cupped Seth's cheek, his smile turning into a jaw-cracking yawn. With the emotional rollercoaster that he'd been on all night, coupled with alcohol, he was barely able to stand, let alone get up to anything in the bedroom. And while he was close to passing out into a deep sleep, he wasn't so far gone that he didn't still fear Mike Larsen's possible reaction if he were to find out about any sexual activities in his house.

But, even the offer to stay? That was pretty great.

"Seth? As wonderful as I know it would be with you, I don't think I have enough energy to untie my shoes, let alone properly woo you. But I am flattered that you think I could."

Seth laughed sharply and clapped his hand over his mouth. "Okay, Don Juan, let's get you into some jammies and that sweater in some tissue."

Seth led them upstairs to his old bedroom, quickly set out clothes for Oliver and excused himself to go to the bathroom. Oliver looked around the room, recognizing a lot of the furniture and décor, but seeing hints of the past several years that he'd missed. The small loveseat was gone, maybe moved into Seth's New York apartment? A poster hung near the door from one of Seth's college performances. On his vanity was a picture of a cast with their arms around each other, Seth off to the side looking at someone and laughing.

The reminders of years he had missed out on made him ache. Nothing could be done about it, however. He needed to focus on moving forward. He stripped to his briefs, carefully laid his clothes over the back of a chair and pulled on the silk pajamas Seth had set out for him. He smiled. Of course they were silk. Anything that Seth thought of as opulent—the opposite of the "natural flora and fauna of Kansas"—was what he'd always gravitated toward.

Oliver sat on the edge of the bed, lining up his shoes, when it hit him. He was in Seth's bedroom. The place where they'd studied, where they'd talked about everything under the sun (oh God, their first sex talk when Seth had stammered his way through an explanation of what he was comfortable with), where they'd held each other and whispered their dreams for a future together. He sighed and ran his hand back and forth over the cool linen of Seth's duvet, one he didn't recognize.

Another giant yawn overtook him; he was too tired even to worry about brushing his teeth. It wasn't as though there would be any more kissing tonight.

He slipped under the covers on one side, remembering that Seth preferred the other, and moaned in pleasure as he stretched out his legs. He didn't want to be intrusive, but he also didn't want to seem indifferent, so he placed himself directly in the middle of his half of the bed, one arm behind his head and the other by his side. Blinking to stay awake and failing miserably, he began to drift off.

The bed shifted, and he turned to see that Seth had come back and was twisted away from him to turn off the light. His heart gave a little clench at the domesticity of the moment. He smiled softly, eyes fluttering shut.

"Thank you, Seth."

Seth hummed a quiet, sleepy note and whispered, "I meant it, earlier. I'm confused and I'm scared, but I know I want you back in my life." He shifted his limbs, swallowed thickly and let out a slow breath. "Goodnight, Oliver."

Oliver felt Seth's hand find his own, down by his side; a happy noise floated out on his exhalation as he fell asleep.

* * *

Oliver woke with the sun streaming through the partially opened slats covering Seth's window. He stretched his limbs and encountered a lot of empty space. Seth's side was still moderately warm, so he didn't have to panic that Seth had had a change of heart in the middle of the night or something drastic.

He opened the door to Seth's bathroom and saw a note on the counter propped up by a toothbrush.

Good morning, sleepyhead!
This is a spare—feel free to use it. We're downstairs about to have brunch, but please know you can take your time.
Seth

Oliver smiled at the thoughtfulness and decided to grab a quick shower before getting dressed. He made quick work of it; he didn't want to linger where Seth had spent so much time naked. He had no outlet for his reactions to the memory and sensory overload, and the smell of Seth's special shampoo was too familiar. It was the smell of holding Seth, of being quiet and intimate. It was the smell of bending to place a kiss on Seth's head as Oliver got up from studying to get a book in the school library.

He had to remember that they weren't in that place anymore. Maybe just for now, but maybe not. They needed time to ease into... whatever it was their relationship was becoming.

He dressed quickly and, as he looked around the room to make sure that he hadn't forgotten anything, he caught sight of a photograph in a simple black frame on a small bedside table. A lamp was partially blocking it; he walked over and picked it up to make sure he wasn't seeing things.

It was just after Seth's graduation at Bakerfield, a shot that Natalie had taken of them in a candid moment. Oliver smiled at the sight of Seth's hand reaching for his mortarboard—he'd spent a solid hour trying to make it just so without completely crushing his hair underneath— as Oliver enthusiastically kissed his cheek, his arms wrapped around Seth's waist. Oliver's eyes were squeezed shut tightly, an almost ferocious expression on his face, as Seth laughed, looking slightly embarrassed and nervous with the public affection.

But before the party Mike had put together—before they'd left the school, actually—Oliver had had his first taste of worry about Seth leaving more than just their small town, and for good.

* * *

SIX YEARS AGO, GRADUATION

"God, I am so relieved that I can finally close the chapter of my life labeled 'Kansas.' I don't ever want to even *think* of this place again," Seth had sighed, looking around at the crowds of people hugging and congratulating each other.

Oliver had gone quiet, though. It was finally, fully hitting him: Seth was leaving. He was going somewhere bigger and better than Kansas, where he would be around incredibly talented people and have the cultural center of the world at his fingertips. What if Seth decided that it was too much to keep in contact with his high school boyfriend? What if Seth realized that it would just be easier to cut all of his ties here? Well, Seth would never do that to his dad, Oliver knew that for certain. But how many high school sweethearts made it, really?

They may have been stupid fears, they may have been unfounded, but Oliver had them regardless.

"Ugh. Look at Bad Breath Brian's parents, acting as if he was salutatorian. I don't even know how he graduated, come to think of it. Money changed hands, I bet." Seth noticed Oliver's silence and laid his hand on his arm. "My normally jubilant boyfriend seems to have disappeared; any idea where he might be?" Seth teased.

Oliver picked at his pants leg, trying to control his rising panic. "I... I don't want you to forget me."

Seth laughed, sounding shocked and completely unaware of the dread filling Oliver's heart. "That's ridiculous! How on earth could I ever forget *you*?" Seth asked, running the flat of his palm across Oliver's chest and squeezing his shoulder. "Wait," he said, narrowing his eyes in mock suspicion, "is this some horrible way for you to back out of helping me with our crêpe brunch for ten tomorrow morning?"

"What I meant was that *I'm* still a part of Kansas." Oliver looked into Seth's eyes and tried to dispel the gnawing worry that Seth would soon realize he no longer wanted any ties here and was finished with *everything* that reminded him of Kansas, including Oliver.

Seth's face fell as he realized what Oliver was talking about. He reached out to hold Oliver's hand and pulled him away from the crowd, holding a finger up to his dad to ask for a minute. Instead, they spent five minutes behind a linden tree, Seth kissing every available bit of skin on Oliver's face, neck and hands.

"I could never forget you, Oliver," said Seth, kissing the side of his neck. "You're the first and last thing on my mind every day, and always will be." He held Oliver's face in his hands, brushed their noses together and kissed him on the lips, a kiss slow and sweet and full of promise.

Oliver looked at him, stupidly and completely in love; Seth chuckled as he fixed Oliver's tie and smoothed his shirtfront.

"Well, we'll just blame my hair on my graduation cap." Seth winked. "I'll kiss the other parts later," he said, his voice dropping with the hint of another promise. A wave of heat pooled low in Oliver's body. "Come on; Dad has dinner reservations, so we better hurry back."

Oliver tugged on Seth's hand, pulling him back for one more kiss. "I love you."

"I love you, too."

*　*　*

Oliver noticed that the frame had a little bit of dust on the top. He wiped it away with the pad of his thumb, flicking the offending material into the air. It had been there for some time, it seemed. Seth hadn't packed it away, thrown it away or burned it after their breakup.

He was amazed at how young they looked in the photo, and at how it was still them. And then it hit him: it was still *them.* They still had something, something that would never leave. Looking at the picture, seeing it right next to the lamp ("You're the first and last thing on my mind every day"), Oliver knew in his heart that every time Seth came home, he saw the same thing.

"You know he spent all four years at college comparing boys to you?"

Maybe Natalie wasn't the most reliable of sources, but it had been the same for Oliver. He had spent years trying to recreate the spark they'd shared, but constantly came up short. There was no one else for him. No one.

"I could never forget you, either," he murmured, putting the picture back on the table but in front of the lamp, in a more prominent position. He cast his eyes around the room, no longer afraid of the ghosts it held, but hopeful for the new memories he knew, deep down, that he and Seth would make in times to come.

He grabbed his keys and sweater and shut the door, smiling.

* * *

"Hey, toss me one of those oranges, Seth."

Seth passed one to his father and continued his story about the weird homeless man on the F train who had fixated on him a few months ago. Oliver sat comfortably in his chair, watching Mike make a face as he poured the sugar-free syrup Seth insisted on over his waffle. He felt the warmth and ease of the family fill the entire room with a sense of peace and comfort.

Mike had greeted him when he finally came downstairs with a nod toward the coffee pot and a "Hurry up, kid, these waffles won't last long."

"My roommate and I were singing scales—it was when I was going in to audition for understudy?" Seth asked, glancing at his father. "And he just... it was weird. He just stared. People in New York don't stare without expecting to be called out on it, you know?"

"Nope," Mike said blandly, pulling the peel off his orange. "But don't let that stop you."

"Ha. Well, *anyway*," Seth said, looking pointedly at Oliver, "it was creepy." He took a sip of his coffee. "But he's harmless, I think. It's been months, and I've not heard him once ask me to put the lotion on its skin, so I think I'm safe."

Oliver laughed at Seth's reference to *Silence of the Lambs*, even as he worried for Seth's safety. "You're sure he's harmless?" he asked, feeling Mike's eyes settle on him briefly.

Seth waved his hand dismissively. "I know this is going to sound weird, but—"

"It sounded weird at the lotion thing," Mike said.

Seth fixed his father with a droll expression. "As I was saying... I think he likes my voice. Which, that's weird, right?"

Oliver propped his chin on his hand, enjoying the banter. While Mike had a more blue-collar sense of humor, he was still quick-witted and dry; it was clear where Seth got his own sense of humor. Oliver felt that he'd slipped right back into the family dynamic, that they were *letting* him back in, and it filled him with such a sense of yearning: This was how he wanted his life to be for years to come.

Today he'd realized: It was only a matter of time before that happened. He just needed Seth to come to the same realization. He watched as Seth spread preserves on a piece of toast, telling his dad about a repair he needed to have done on his apartment back in the city. It was as though the previously unclear picture of Oliver's future was slowly coming into focus.

Seth turned and smiled at him, tapping his foot under the table in a genial manner. Oliver looked down at his plate, beaming and trying to keep under control. Seth took his hand under the table and gave him a squeeze.

He didn't let go.

* * *

"I could drive you to the airport and save you the trouble—"

"Oliver, it's fine," Seth said, laying his hand on Oliver's shoulder for a moment. "I'm not even letting my dad drive me. John and Natalie offered as well, but I assumed they'd be dealing with his hangover today."

They both smiled. Seth smoothed the lapels on Oliver's wool peacoat, keeping his eyes on his hands. "I didn't want any teary goodbyes at the airport. And the cab is already arranged. It's fine."

Oliver bit his lip. He didn't want to plead for Seth's attention. Well, he *did;* he just *wouldn't.* "You probably want a little more time with your dad, too."

Seth smiled in gratitude. "He's gotten more emotional the older he gets. Such a softie. You don't mind, do you?"

"Oh, no, no. I should go. I shouldn't have stayed this long," Oliver said, wondering where his manners had gone. He might feel as if he were a part of the family again, but the fact was, he wasn't.

"Oliver. If we didn't want you to stay for breakfast, you know that my dad would have said something." Seth busied his hands with precisely wrapping Oliver's scarf around his neck as Mike wandered into the entryway.

"You leaving?"

"Yes, sir. Thank you for having me."

"Anytime, Ollie. And I mean that," Mike fixed Oliver with one of those intense, "you can test me on it" looks of his; it seemed good, familiar. Then Mike pulled him into a hug; he held his mouth close to Oliver's ear, the one farther from where Seth was standing, and whispered, "You finally get your head on straight?"

Oliver squeezed his eyes shut and willed himself to maintain his composure. "Yes, sir."

"Good. Now let's get his."

Mike clapped him hard on the back, and Oliver had the wild thought that he'd done it to give Oliver an excuse for the sudden, stinging moisture in his eyes.

"All right. Good seeing you, Ollie. Tell your folks I said happy New Year."

"Yes, sir. I will." Oliver smiled as Mike retreated to his easy chair; it was almost time for the Rose Bowl.

Seth opened the door and ushered him onto the front steps, arms immediately crossing tightly in an effort to keep warm. "So, we'll talk soon, right?"

"Yes," Oliver replied, happy for the reassurance.

They stared at each other for a moment, smiling. Then Seth opened his arms, shivering, and made a "come here" gesture with his hands. Oliver wrapped himself around Seth, trapping Seth's arms against his body to keep them warm. Seth shuddered once in his embrace and buried his face in Oliver's scarf.

Seth pulled back and kissed him softly on the cheek, rubbing it with his nose. "Be safe going home. I'll email you soon, if that's okay?"

Oliver laughed. "I'd be upset if you didn't."

"Okay, then." Seth's teeth began to chatter.

Oliver let him go, backing down the steps with a huge grin on his face. "You should go inside."

"You should get in your car," Seth teased.

He looked at his feet, trying to fight down the exuberance welling up inside of him. It was just like when they'd first started dating and each would wait for the other to hang up first. "Okay, okay."

He circled the back of his parked car, gave Seth a little wave and hopped in. Seth still didn't go into the house; he kept standing there, shivering and clattering and grinning at Oliver. Oliver started the car and leaned over to wave again from the passenger side window. Seth returned the gesture and finally went inside.

They weren't going into this blindly. This wasn't one passionate night without promise for more. This was the building of something Oliver thought might actually last forever. With the promise of a truly new year before him, he turned on the radio and sang along happily on the drive back home.

Chapter Thirteen

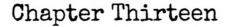

Jan 1, 11:23 PM EST
To: Oliver Andrews
From: Seth Larsen
Subject: La Guardia is the fifth circle of hell

I'm home, I'm exhausted, and I need to get to sleep—back on stage tomorrow. Just checking in so you didn't think I was abducted or something dire. :) I hope you get back safe and sound—I imagine your travel is a little trickier than mine was.

Talk soon?

S

Jan 3, 1:45 PM CST
To: Seth Larsen
From: Oliver Andrews
Subject: Hi :)

Hope your rehearsal and first performance went well. Can I say that? Or is it always "break a leg," even via email? Oh my gosh, is that insensitive, given David actually broke his?

I fly out in the morning. I don't know how I packed a month and change's worth of things in these two suitcases. I always lacked your superior packing skills. :)

I hope the rest of your performances this weekend involve a dozen legs being shattered. (Too much?)

XO

~Oliver

Jan 14, 2:13 PM EST
To: Oliver Andrews
From: Seth Larsen
Subject: re: Hi :)

Ahh! I'm so, so sorry it took forever to reply, but it's funny that you mentioned a certain someone's shattered leg in your email. Guess who seems to be making a full recovery? And who, apparently, has left the director for (omg) Dough-Face Brandt? And guess who—

Okay, this is ridiculous of me. David is all healed and has been released to physical therapy. He's hooked up with Brandt, whose brother basically owns us. He's the one that foots the bill, at least.

Rumor has it that David is looking to take his "written expressly for him" role back. I have a few more weeks as The Fair Youth before he's out of physical therapy, at least. :(

I'm going to need to channel my inner diva. I think that all of my spare time is going to be wrapped up in rehearsing, vocal coaching and Pilates. At least I'll look and sound great when I get the ax?

There was an old lady in the front row this week who kept asking her husband—equally ancient—"HUH?" loudly and *he repeated what the actors said, every time.* In his normal speaking voice. KILL ME.

S

Jan 14, 10:51 PM GMT
To: Seth Larsen
From: Oliver Andrews
Subject: re: re: Hi :)

Oh, Seth! You don't really think that they'd let the toast of Broadway go, do you? (It's you that I'm talking about, obv.) I'm so sorry that you're feeling stressed about this. Don't let it get to you, though. Don't give up hope *ever!* I can attest to this philosophy. :)

I remember when you didn't even think you'd be accepted at Juilliard, and look at how that turned out. It never hurts to be prepared, of course, but I've read scores of reviews where they've said how much better suited to the role you are than David.

Do you want to talk about it? I'm here for you.

OXOXO (I feel like you could use a bunch of hugs right about now)

~Oliver

P.S. You should have sat in her lap to deliver your lines. Maybe it would have saved time? ;) That actually sounds awful, though, I'm sorry.

Jan 15, 9:32 AM EST
To: Oliver Andrews
From: Seth Larsen
Subject: Well, that was dramatic of me.

I'm sorry I was so negative. I shouldn't just dump problems on you. It's going to be fine, one way or the other. And he's not going to take the part away from me without a fight. Also, he's still in physical therapy. I need to stay focused.

Anyway, thank you. It's just gray and awful outside. There's a stretch of weeks from January through February where it's cold and bitter and everyone seems to be sick, and I *cannot* get sick.

I'll stop grumbling, and thank you again. :) And yes, I could definitely go for a hug. You're very good at those, if I recall. It's those broad shoulders and long, strong arms of yours. I never did send your mother a thank you note for putting you in swimming and diving when you were young.

Enough about me, how are you doing? Everything on your— what do I call it? Schoolwork? Research? Anti-Bullying Experiment? Whatever it's called, is it still progressing? Moira still trying to get her hands on your Lucky Charms?

I'm going to be diving into more vocal work and such, so it might take me longer than I'd like to get back with you. So make sure I have a nice long email waiting for me, filled with what's happening in Jolly Old. :)

XO

Seth

Jan 20, 9:37 PM GMT
To: Seth Larsen
From: Oliver Andrews
Subject: I was buried under a mountain of research

Seth, I'm so, so sorry that it took me such a long time to reply to you. Moira was sick for a few days, so I had to pick up her end of the project. That's what you can call it. Or research. The Anti-Bullying Experiment makes me feel like Mengele.

Long story short, Moira does a lot. And she whines by text a lot. And she requires hot soup a lot. Apparently Janos isn't good at nurturing. I can't say I'm surprised by that. There were no manual manipulations of Charms, I'm happy to report. ;)

(The poor thing, she was really sick, too.)

And you don't need to apologize to me! I *want* you to talk to me and tell me what's happening. That's kind of the point. <3 I hope you're not running yourself ragged, though. That's a great way to get sick. And I'm not down the road, ready to bring you hot soup and warm blankets, so please take care of yourself, okay?

You said that it's gray and awful outside there? I took a picture of a foggy, tree-lined walk I take often just for you. Hope it cheers you up. I think it looks just like Narnia, personally, but it's actually a real place! I have to be careful that I don't keep myself from finding the real way in someday. That's how it worked, right? If you stopped believing? I'm no Susan Pevensie!

...I should have said Peter, huh?

XOXOX

~Oliver

P.S. And let me know how the vocal training is going! I don't think you need it, personally. :)

Jan 28, 10:31 AM EST
To: Oliver Andrews
From: Seth Larsen
Subject: my first day off in ages

Oh, *Oliver*. That picture you sent was amazing! That's a real place? And you get to see it? I half expected Mr. Tumnus to come dancing out. Siiiiigh. And I'm the Susan in this relationship, thank you. Wait—that means we'd be siblings. *Awk*-ward... scratch that.

It's an absolute pain in the neck to schlep to Central Park when it's nasty out, so thank you for the trees. It looks amazingly peaceful there. I can see why you like it. :)

And it's no longer a rumor: David is actively pursuing getting his part back and has Brandt telling the producers how much better their chemistry is. Jonathan—he's Shakespeare—did you ever meet him? I can't remember. I was a little preoccupied by a gorgeous *certain someone* who came out of nowhere. Well, he's on my side, so that's something at least. I have a few weeks until I have to worry that I'm being demoted, so I'm going to just focus on doing my best. I don't need any premature wrinkles.

Tell Moira that I hope she's all better! We don't need you getting off-track, now do we?

Speaking of off-track, are there any breaks or the like coming up for you? Do they even have Spring Break in England? What about Girls Gone Wild? Except I bet it would be called Ladies Who Have Gone A Bit Mad, Egads. Or maybe Knickers Down, Pinkies Up: Good Heavens, Girls!

I definitely could go for a hug from you today. :(

XO

Seth

Jan 28, 6:20 PM GMT
To: Seth Larsen
From: Oliver Andrews
Subject: re: my first day off in ages

I'll make a habit of sending you pictures/things to cheer you up, then!

Well... shit. Sorry, that's just aggravating, the thing with this David guy. That really pisses me off. Okay, so I'm starting to see what you mean about the distance being a pain. I really wish I could take you for a drink, or a walk even.

Seth, you're amazing. You're not going to lose your job. It's just not going to happen. I refuse to be anything but positive about this. And hey, who's going to go against Shakespeare? Fools, that's who. Or maybe Christopher Marlowe.

(And yes, I met him, er, Shakespeare from your play—Christopher Marlowe has been dead for centuries—but it was just briefly at that cast party you had. He wasn't the focus of the evening for me.)

You'd never wrinkle prematurely. You're as gorgeous as when we were teens, Seth. It's unfair how much you look like a model.

Our winter term ends the last week of March and I have most of the month of April off. Did you have some sort of idea for me? Or any general curiosity? :)

I laughed so hard at "Ladies-Egads" that Janos banged on the wall between our rooms and told me to shut up.

I definitely wish I could give you a hug.

<3

~Oliver (and I emailed you a picture of a pretty apple tree covered in snow outside my library. The grounds here at Cambridge are so beautiful and well-tended. Hope I get to show you in person someday!)

Feb 13, 11:22 PM EST
To: Oliver Andrews
From: Seth Larsen
Subject: trip?

So here's the thing, Oliver. This is what I hate: by the time I get home after a show, I'm exhausted and rarely check email. For now it seems they're keeping David as my understudy—oh, the bitter irony—so I've had nonstop rehearsals to get him up to speed on the off-chance he poisons me and takes the role, something I wouldn't put past him, and I rarely get to check in with my computer these days.

What I *do* like to do is have coffee with my friends. Or dinner. Somewhere I can talk to them face to face. And that's what I want at the end of the day: someone's face. I want those walks you mentioned. I want conversation. I want conversation with *you.* :(

I'm sorry, I'm just feeling isolated because I obviously can't talk about this with anyone in the cast. You did say that you wanted me to talk to you. Any regrets?

I know that you just came back to the States, but I wonder if you'd consider a return trip during your break? Might be fun to have a friend to go to museums with, one who actually understands the difference between a Manet and a Monet. Unless he has me killed, I should have David up to speed and have more free time than I do now.

Thoughts?

Seth

p.s. Thank you for the tree; it's very pretty. Architecturally interesting against the old stone building. That's a library? I thought it was a castle! I'd send you a picture of something outside my apartment but it would just be a pile of garbage bags with gray ice frozen on top. Yes, the garbage men are on strike again. No one told me there were less glamorous times in this city. =P

Feb 14, 11:18 AM EST
To: Oliver Andrews
From: Seth Larsen
Subject: You shouldn't have!!!

Ha, you know I don't mean that *at all*, and oh, *Oliver*! Thank you so much! They're so beautiful. And that they are a mix of flowers makes the bouquet all the more special. The delivery man said he got many jealous stares from women as he walked to my door. Yes, I'm preening quite a lot, but it looks good on me. :)

Really, Oliver. Thank you. They're beautiful. And don't forget to let me know what you think about my proposal? I want to see you more than ever.

XOXO

Seth

Feb. 14, 8:23 PM GMT
To: Seth Larsen
From: Oliver Andrews

Subject: re: You shouldn't have!

I'm so glad you got them and that you like them. I meant what I said on the card: you're the best thing that has ever happened to me. However you want to interpret that is fine, but just know that you matter to me.

Seth, I hate that I can't just reach over and hold you. Or take you out to get your mind off work. Or... just be with you. But it's not for always, please don't forget that? I'm focusing on my project not just to get everything done, but to make time seem like it's not dragging so much until I can see you again.

Speaking of, I would absolutely love to come back to NYC. Is there a time that you were thinking of? Even though it's a break, I would still be working, here, so I would love a hint in order to structure things. And I don't want you to think I'm being presumptuous; I would get a hotel nearby so as not to overburden you.

Seth, I would *love* that. Tell David that if he lays a finger on you he'll have to contend with me—*and* an irate Irish elf, for that matter. She seems to think you're best friends now; I guess I talk about you a lot. :)

And I don't have any regrets, either. Well, no regrets since I saw you again.

Love,

~Oliver

Feb 24, 5:22 PM EST
To: Oliver Andrews
From: Seth Larsen
Subject:

They're doing it. They're giving it back to him. I feel positively sick. I fucking hate that you are thousands of miles away and I need you and I have to wait to know if you are even going to get this.

I just

I worked *so* hard.

Feb 24, 10:53 PM GMT
To: Seth Larsen

From: Oliver Andrews
Subject: re:
> Oh, *Seth!*
> I'll have you know that I have notifications sent to my phone for emails from you, and ran back home (out with Moira) to reply.
> I hate being here while you're there and need someone to just tell you that it's going to be okay. God, I don't understand this. Seth, I've seen you. You're amazing. Breathtaking! They're being idiots; that has to be what's happening here.
> Please tell me what's going on—tell me everything.
> We'll figure something out, okay?
> Love you.
> ~Oliver

Feb 24, 6:10 PM EST
To: Oliver Andrews
From: Seth Larsen
Subject: re: re:
> Can we pretend I'm leaning against you? Because this is another one of those times when I could really use a hug from you.
> So here's what they said—before today's show, I might add. And don't think for one minute that I let it affect my performance—I've had a *rat* thrown at me when performing, for hell's sake. I'm going to turn the performance up to eleven just to spite them.
> They were so sorry, blah blah, but they felt they owed it to David to give him a chance yadda yadda originator of the role.
> So they're giving him a full week's run of shows to "test the audience" in April. A week during which I will hide in my apartment with the blinds drawn and no computer or television or newspapers, because I can't bear to see any praise thrown his way. Now I know how Captain Bligh felt.
> God, you should have seen Brandt. Such an ass. I'm so tempted to start calling him Dough-Face in public, I really am.
> I bit his lip during the kiss scene today. He's lucky I didn't bite his head off.

I miss you.
Seth

Feb 25, 12:29 AM GMT
To: Seth Larsen
From: Oliver Andrews
Subject: <3

Seth!! They're just giving him a week! It's not as bad as you think. Look at it this way: they might be trying to shut him up once and for all. I've been looking up things, and ticket sales went through the roof after your first week. David's shows never came close. He wasn't invited to be on *Today*, was he?

What if this is a way to make it clear to everyone that you're the right person? And April isn't really a hot time for ticket sales, anyway, so they're not losing money like they would over the holidays or summer.

Here's my proposal: for that week, you come here. You get out of the city, you refrain from torturing yourself with newspapers and all of that. I'll even take you to Buckingham Palace on a day trip, if you'd like. We can go punting! A punt is like a flat-bottomed canoe. It's really nice to do and is really popular.

I can take care of you. Make you feel better. It hurts me to hear how down on yourself you are!

What do you say? You and me and Moira makes three? We'll have to go out with her once, or I'll never hear the end of it.

I'd really love to see you. I can take you to my tree. :)

So? Will you?

Love you—it's going to be okay.

~Oliver

Feb 24, 6:40 PM EST
To: Oliver Andrews
From: Seth Larsen
Subject: <3 to you too

Really? REALLY? I could go there? I'm already envisioning where I might wear the cutaway coat I've been looking for an occasion to wear. And of course it would be wonderful to see you, too. :)

Yes, I will. I think I sagged with relief in my chair when I read your offer. And you're sure it won't be an imposition? Oh God, unless you mean for me to get a hotel, in which case, yes, I will, and I'm sorry that I assumed anything. And of course I'd love to meet Moira!

I'm so grateful for your level head. I've just been so angry about all of this that I couldn't think straight. Yes. One week. A week for him to prove why he's not right. Okay. I'm going to have to really shine for these next few weeks to make a point, then.

Thank you. Just, thank you. I feel so much better now, honestly. I just noticed your time stamp. I'm so sorry to keep you up late, and on a school night!

Let me get dates and things organized, and I'll email you so we can plan an itinerary? Is that okay?

You always did know just how to calm me down and make me feel better, didn't you?

<3

Seth

Feb 25, 12:51 AM GMT
To: Seth Larsen
From: Oliver Andrews
Subject: re: <3 to you too

Have you ever had a Hungarian yell in your face? I don't recommend it. I guess I was a little exuberant in my excitement for you to come out here. You're going to love all of the little shops in town!

Yes! Yes, come here for that week, just say when and it should be fine. It should be more than fine. Of course I meant for you to stay here! Unless that's weird? If it's weird, then we'll figure something out. I don't want it to be weird. Am I being weird?

No, it's going to be great, promise! We are going to have a great time, and oh, I can take you to Wren Library! (You thought it was a castle.) Seth, they have the original manuscript of Winnie the

Pooh there! Okay, that may not be exciting for you, but I loved that as a kid, and I was excited by it, and I promise that I'll think of more Seth-centric activities for you.

Um, just forget the Pooh Bear. We'll go punting! Have Merchant and Ivory-style walks in gardens! You're going to love it, I promise!

Well, you always did know the way to get me excited. ;)

Cannot WAIT.

Love you,

~Oliver

Mar 3, 2019 5:03 PM EST
To: Oliver Andrews
From: Seth Larsen
Subject: aaaaaaaand we have a schedule
They made an announcement after the show today that David would be given a "trial run" for the first week of April. I was more than a little pleased when there was only the tiniest of cheers for him, even though from his expression you would have thought he'd been thrown a ticker tape parade.

But I do not care (of course I do) because now I can plan my trip to see you! I'm looking at flights, and I could leave after my Sunday show, but that means I would get to Heathrow at just after 6 AM on Monday.

I'm all ears, if you have any suggestions for how to make this simple. Oh, but I don't have to leave until lunchtime the next-next Tuesday, because of the time difference. :) A week! More! I can't do calendar math right now because I'm so excited to go on a trip! Of course you know this means I get to buy a whole new travel wardrobe. I'm excited about more than just that, I promise.

And don't think that you'll have to babysit me the whole time. You mentioned earlier that you'll still be working over the break. I can keep myself busy; I'm good like that.

Jonathan told me as I was leaving today that he might undersell his performance while I'm off to make sure I come back. Isn't that just the sweetest thing? I never thought I'd actually inspire sabotage... *dreamed* I would, of course. But.

OMG I JUST REALIZED. Oliver!!! Please tell me I can have coffee while I'm there. I know they're a little fanatical about their tea, but if I don't get my Little Helper in the morning, you know just how ornery I can be. Should I pack a French press? *Mon dieu!* Suddenly four weeks doesn't seem like enough time to prepare!

Okay, let me know if those dates work and I'll book them ASAP. Yay!

XOXOXOX

Seth

Mar 3, 11:11 PM GMT
To: Seth Larsen
From: Oliver Andrews
Subject: AWESOME!

OMG, I don't know where to start. Wait, let's start with the travel, that way you can book that while you read. Does it work like that? I don't know. Anyway. Yes to those dates, that's fantastic. As long as you're not going to extra trouble by leaving from the show, I want you to be comfortable, okay?

Getting in at 6 isn't a problem for me. I can meet you at the airport and we'll take the train back. It's not a long train ride. We'll have to go to King's Cross—just like Harry Potter. :) And ha! I'll prove to you that I know how to use trains! Unexpected benefit.

Tell Jonathan that while I don't think it's very professional of him, I can overlook that in this particular situation. I don't think you'll have to worry too much. There's no way this David guy is half as charismatic as you are, Seth. I'd bet my diploma on it.

Babysit you? I think the word you were looking for was "entertain." I plan on making sure you have a great week. It's not a burden! You're never a burden. (That kind of hurts, to think you don't know that about me?)

Oh, and yes: you can have coffee. If anything, you can have it in my apartment. There are lots of coffee shops in town, and Janos took me to a Hungarian café not too long ago, and let me just say that there is *nothing* like their coffee. Oh. Do *not* call it Turkish.

Seriously. Even though that's exactly what it is. Really. I can't stress that enough.

Send me a copy of your itinerary when you get one, please. These next few weeks are going to positively drag.

Yay from me, too!

Love you! We're going to have so much fun!

XOXOXOXOXOXOXOX

~Oliver

March 6, 2019 11:29 AM EST
To: Oliver Andrews
From: Seth Larsen
Subject: Platform 9 3/4?

I'll be sure to keep my eyes peeled for any exuberant ginger children when we're at King's Cross. Are we really going there? Oh my God. Is there really a Diagon Alley? Don't answer. I'm embarrassed that I even asked.

I don't ever think anything bad of you, Oliver. How could I? You're Mary Poppins: practically perfect in every way. That was self-deprecation, silly. <3

I attached my itinerary, btw. Dough-Face tried to get under my skin last night by bragging about all of the extra rehearsal time he and David are logging. Hilarious! I just smiled back at him, serenely, and that drove him nuts.

It's starting to thaw here. Which means it's raining. Well, the streets will be clean for a while? I'm just waiting for it to be sunny for a few days in a row. I'm looking forward to wearing my new suede ankle boots. Butterscotch, monk strap—*trés chic!*

XOX

S

p.s. If I forget about the Turkish thing, is your roommate going to want to fight me? Oh my God, the only drama that should ever exist about coffee is to panic when there is none.

Chapter Fourteen

Over the next few weeks, Oliver made a point of emailing Seth positive reviews for his show to keep his spirits up. He was sure that this recasting stint was a calculated move on the part of the show-runners to take care of the David Issue (as he thought of it) by basing their ultimate decision on the public's reaction to the two leads.

Walking to the lab became more than getting from Point A to Point B; he took pictures of things he loved, of shops or cafés he thought Seth would find interesting. He began smiling at couples he passed, thrilling at the idea that soon he would have Seth here with him, and that there was a chance they would walk hand in hand down the street, too.

Slowly he began looking up at the world, looking at his life instead of just living hyper-focused on the moment. There was something exciting to look forward to, something more than just work or a degree. He threw himself into research as they neared the final stages before everything needed to be presented in his thesis. The original plan had been to spend the Easter break focusing solely on that, but Seth's visit had changed his plans. He couldn't have been more delighted.

The two weeks before Seth's arrival were spent looking over his apartment with a critical eye; there wasn't much he could do to make it look like anything but student housing beyond keeping his things immaculate—emphasis on *his things*. He'd fought with Janos for the better part of four months about not leaving his things in piles all over the house; it was as though he stood in the doorway and everything just fell away from him and into piles.

He really wanted Seth to be comfortable during his stay. Moira had promised that she wouldn't show up uninvited (she and Janos had cooled off to a sort of friends-with-benefits situation), and the weather was slowly getting warmer.

Oliver looked down at his bed, his hands on his hips. "Definitely need new sheets. And a couple of extra pillows." He would *not* repaint the walls. That was ridiculous. Possibly.

* * *

"When is your friend coming?" Janos asked for what had to be the tenth time.

Oliver sighed quietly and said, "In a week."

"Good. That is when I will be finished with open trials, so I will not be so tired when he is here." He crossed his arms and stared down at Oliver, who sat on the sofa. "I do not want to be awoken at night by... activities."

Oliver wanted to say, "Like you've done to me for the past year?" What he *did* say was, "Janos, I've told you countless times that he's just my friend." Oliver mentally crossed his fingers behind his back for the white lie. His current standing with Seth was no one's business but theirs. More important was the object lesson Janos needed to learn. "What did I tell you? That just because I'm gay..." He waited for his roommate to finish the sentence.

"*Igen*, this does not mean that all men are to your sexual liking, I know, I know this thing."

"Good." Oliver crossed his legs, turning a page in his binder and said coolly, "And if we *did* have 'activities,' we would be courteous enough to keep the noise down so you wouldn't be traumatized by anything you did hear, regardless."

The look on Janos's face was totally worth it. He fought the smile off his face and waited for Janos to leave before laughing.

* * *

Moira to Oliver: Are you going daft yet?

Oliver to Moira: Why are you IMing me when you are three computers over?

Moira to Oliver: Because I'm an excellent multitasker. If I stand

and talk to you then I can't verra well input data at the same time, now can I?

Oliver to Moira: ...

Moira to Oliver: I bet you're going mad. Five more days! I can't wait to see this Seth of yours.

Oliver to Moira: You promised that you'd give us 24 hours without interruption!

Moira to Oliver: And I'm a woman of me word. I can look without interrupting, can't I?

Oliver to Moira: I—WHAT?

Moira to Oliver: Ha. You're so easy to rile. I love it. Struth, I'll miss you next year.

Moira to Oliver: and I can see ya smiling at the screen, so don't try to lie and say you don't feel the same

Oliver to Moira: Yeah, yeah, I'll miss you, too.

Moira to Oliver: You'll be going to New York of course.

Oliver to Moira: I'm pretty sure. The acceptance letter just came for Silver. :)

Moira to Oliver: Go on with ye! Congrats on that! Well done, mate.

Oliver to Moira: I was also accepted here.

Moira to Oliver: Pfft. And?

Oliver to Moira: And nothing, it's nice to have options, is all.

Moira to Oliver: I'm going to break my multitasking rule now.

Moira shoved away from her station and stormed over to Oliver. "I don't even know this Seth, but I can tell you this: You tell him you want to have an option, and he'll gut you stem to stern. I'd bet my eye teeth on it." She poked him once, hard, in the chest. "And if he won't do it, I will."

Oliver looked back at her, terrified. She might be wee—an entire foot shorter than he—but she was fierce. "I'm not planning on it! Ow, by the way." He rubbed the center of his chest where she'd poked him. "But I can tell my children that I turned down Cambridge. Not many people get to say that."

She rolled her eyes, pulled a task chair over and sat on it backwards. "Sure they do; they're just liars. Now," her eyes glittered, "tell me what you plan to do with your man and be sure to tell me every filthy detail!

And how soon can I size him up?"

Oliver laughed as he saved his document in order to give her his full attention. "Well, some sightseeing when he gets here—I want to keep him up for the day so he can get over his jet lag. And you can see him on Tuesday. We'll meet up at the pub?"

"All right, then." She waggled her eyebrows at him and said, "I'll be looking to see who's walking funny."

"Moira!" Seriously, why the hell was he friends with her?

"You knew I was a foul-mouthed besom the day you met me, and you love it, you stuffy old owl. Christ, from the sound of it, the way you two make love must be giving each other intense manicures: lots of deep, passionate nail buffing across a table. Do you need to me to explain how it works? The whole bees and the bees talk?"

He scrubbed at his face before turning back to his workstation. A part of him was looking forward to Seth putting her in her place if she talked like that to him. Oliver smiled as he dove back into his work. Mostly he was just looking forward to Seth being here, period.

Mar 29, 3:17 PM GMT
To: Oliver Andrews
From: Mitchell Lan, PhD
Subject: The future of TMMaT

Oliver,

I know that you and your partner Moira have been working diligently on your research, and I have to say that the rough drafts you've shown me of your final thesis have gotten me very excited; and not just me, but others on the Board.

As you know, with the recent spike in news reports about LGBT bullying here in the UK, public interest has turned to try to understand what is happening. Projects like TMMaT can provide concrete data to help influence and educate public opinion.

I have a proposal for you. As you may have heard, I'm going on leave next year, and Dr. Callais has been lured to the Education department, which means the CSJ is going to be seriously understaffed. I did some checking and see that you've applied for the doctoral programme. I presented an opportunity to the Board, and they've agreed to it.

If you'll head the TMMaT programme in my stead—now fully funded by private enterprise, a huge coup for the department—the work you do will apply to your doctorate. You'll be provided with housing and an income. I don't have to tell you what a feather in your cap this is, I'm sure.

Please let me know your decision as soon as possible. I look forward to hearing from you!

Sincerely,

Dr. Mitchell Lan

Director of Social Justice and Social Psychology, Cambridge, UK

Oliver sat back in his chair, completely and utterly shocked.

Oliver to Moira: Did you see me drink anything unusual today?

Moira to Oliver: What are you on about?

Oliver to Moira: I just got an offer from Lan. To co-run the entire project next year.

Moira to Oliver: That's brilliant!

Oliver to Moira: Think really hard about why I might not be jumping.

Moira to Oliver: OOOOH. As we say in my village: fook.

Moira to Oliver: I'll bring the bottle and shoulder, me darling. Give me an hour to wrap things up and I'll come to you.

Oliver to Moira: I feel like I've just been hit by a truck.

* * *

The Sunday before Seth's arrival—seventy-two hours since he was offered an amazing job—was unbelievably stressful. Janos had a group of his teammates over, and they proceeded to undo all of the cleaning Oliver had done earlier. Janos insisted that they would clean things up when Oliver went to bed early. He had to get up and be out the door well before five a.m. to make sure that he was at the airport when Seth arrived.

Instead of getting any sleep, though, he tossed and turned, agonizing over what to do. That he wanted to be with Seth wasn't in question. But he didn't want to be with Seth just to hold his metaphorical purse, either. And Seth wouldn't want that for him—he'd want Oliver to pursue *his* own dreams every bit as much as Seth had done.

The chance to co-lead a government-funded research project in his field of study, with one of his mentors? A project that actually had the potential to make huge strides in the LGBT community? Not to mention the bonus of having that apply to his doctorate, having a place to himself (the staff houses were far more comfortable than the drafty old stone building he was currently living in) and an actual salary? His father would love that. He'd made a point of saving for Oliver's education, and that included graduate school, but to have it offset by an income? It was basically being paid to go to school.

But then there was Silver—it was an outstanding school, and it was in the heart of New York City. He'd be just another doctoral candidate, though. Not a bad thing, but in comparison? He was going to have to think long and hard. And he'd have to talk to Seth about it. He couldn't repeat the Brandeis fiasco. And maybe there was still the chance that they could make it work, regardless.

Oliver glanced at his clock: 1:42 a.m. Three more hours to try to sleep. *Yeah, right.*

He punched his pillow into shape, flipped it to the cool side and tried to turn off his racing thoughts.

* * *

Oliver pressed his cheek against the cool glass of the train window, his feelings alternating between excitement at seeing Seth after three full months apart and dread at his reaction to this newly offered opportunity. Seth wasn't selfish; he wouldn't want to be the reason Oliver didn't pursue a career path. But Oliver also knew that Seth wouldn't deal with several years of this back and forth.

And truthfully, *Oliver* didn't want to have a long-term long-distance relationship, either; the past three months had showed how limiting it was. If it was all he could have, he'd face that, but given the choice he would not pick long stretches without Seth.

Seth had been right: Oliver realized, that when he came home after his day, he too wanted to see a face. He too wanted conversation. He wanted to wake up with and make a home with and end every day with his boyfriend. And he wanted that to be Seth. But he didn't want to do without work that challenged him for the next forty years just for the sake of a face and conversation, no matter how wonderful the face or engaging the conversation. Seth wouldn't want that for him, either.

The last thing he wanted to do was spring this on Seth the second he stepped off the plane. They'd have a nice day and help Seth get used to the new time zone, and then they had an entire week to discuss future plans.

He closed his eyes and let himself feel miserable.

* * *

Oliver leaned against the wall across from the exit to the baggage claim and customs, waiting for a familiar face. Knots of people pushed through the open doors, a mix of tourists, regular travelers and people on business. As groups began to appear after a check through customs, he saw a perfectly coiffed head of brown hair and couldn't help the huge smile that spread across his face.

Seth pulled a large piece of luggage along behind him, his face impassive as he scanned the crowd. When he finally recognized Oliver, he broke into a big smile as well, ducked his head as if to hide how pleased he was and pushed forward through the crowd to Oliver.

Oliver, immediately forgetting any reason why he shouldn't be completely elated, took the luggage handle out of Seth's hand and asked, "You ducked into the restroom and fixed your hair, didn't you?"

Seth laughed, looking off to the side and composing his features. "Well, I didn't want to get off the plane with flattened hair. And a gentleman never asks for a lady's secrets, Oliver."

Oliver pulled him into a tight hug, noisily kissing his cheek. He couldn't help himself. "You aren't a lady."

"You noticed that, did you?" Seth was positively sparkling.

Oliver couldn't bring himself to move just yet. It was just... Seth. He was here. He was going to be in Oliver's home for an entire week.

Seth laughed, "What?"

Oliver shook his head, chuckling a little in embarrassment at being caught staring. "Nothing, sorry. It's just really good to see you."

Seth preened. "It's nice to be seen." He inhaled deeply, eyes sparkling with excitement, and as he let out his breath in a deliberate manner, he held his hand out toward Oliver.

If Oliver had thought just a moment before that he was excited by Seth being here, it was absolutely nothing compared to how his heart was thumping now. His whole being seemed to glow from Seth's gesture. Seth was willing to try. God, that's all he wanted. Well, not all, but that was huge, and he knew it.

Oliver gave the back of Seth's hand a kiss, earning him a pleased noise, and then tucked Seth's arm through his to lead them toward the exit.

They chatted about the flight as they rode the tube to King's Cross. ("Who brings a baby on an international red-eye flight? More importantly, who doesn't prepare to keep the baby happy on an international red-eye flight?")

Oliver tried to convince Seth to take a picture in front of the Platform 9 ¾ monument, but he immediately turned red and pushed Oliver into the station.

"It's okay to still like those books, Seth."

"We are *adults*, Oliver."

"So's J.K. Rowling."

Oliver led the way to the train and helped Seth stow his bag before they took seats at the back of the car. It was seven forty-five in the morning, so the train was packed with people heading to the university. Oliver didn't mind, as it meant that Seth was next to him, squeezed up against his side.

It was hard to carry on a conversation with all of the noise, so they sat in companionable silence, looking out of the window. They rocked gently against each other with the steady motion of the train. That, coupled with the warmth of Seth's body pressed against him, created a sense of tranquility that Oliver had not felt since he was a teenager, and he felt himself drift into a haze of sleepy contentment. Just as unconsciousness began to tug at him, Seth jostled his shoulder.

"If you fall asleep on me, *I'm* going to want to fall asleep, and we'll end up in another country, Oliver."

"It's an island," he mumbled.

"Scotland is another country."

He burrowed up against Seth and buried his face in the crook of Seth's neck. Just a few minutes, that's all he wanted. A few minutes when he could be without any worries beyond which stop was the correct one (there was only the one stop on the express) and forget that he needed to decide what would be happening in a few months, whether he would be in New York or staying in England.

"I am going to give you such a pinch if you don't wake up, Oliver Andrews." Seth's voice was low and sounded nervous. That did it. Oliver sat bolt upright and forced his eyes wide open as he inhaled strongly through his nose.

"I'm up. I'm up."

"Did you stay up late last night?"

"Couldn't sleep." He nudged Seth with his shoulder and smiled. "Too excited, I guess."

Seth rolled his eyes, but Oliver could see the pleasure in his face before he turned away.

Finally, they arrived in Cambridge, and as they had to go west of King's College to get to Oliver's apartment, Seth was able to see the spectacular view of The Backs. He gasped more than once, Oliver was happy to hear, even if he tried to play it cool—because of course Seth was a New Yorker now and had "seen everything."

Finally, they made it to Oliver's flat. Oliver led the way to his bedroom, where he'd set up a small table to keep Seth's luggage off the floor.

"So," Oliver said, trying to not sound nervous or expectant, "I cleared out a drawer for you to keep socks and things in, and I'm sorry that my wardrobe isn't large, but there's enough room for you to hang some of your clothing. But just know that I've tried since I moved in and still haven't found a way into Narnia, so give me a shout if you do." He smiled at Seth, who was laughing behind his hand, and said, "I assumed you'd prefer that to living out of a suitcase for a week."

Seth positively beamed at Oliver, sending a thrill of pleasure through him. "That was very thoughtful of you, thank you. Ever the gentleman." Seth trailed a hand down Oliver's arm and turned to lift his suitcase onto the table. Oliver showed him his drawer and pointed to the closet and en suite bathroom before backing out of the room.

As he stood just outside the doorway, sort of swinging in and out of the space, he asked, "Coffee here? Or do you want to go to the city center to that café I mentioned?"

Seth paused, holding a perfectly folded stack of undershirts, and replied, "Café, if that's all right? I'd love something to eat, too."

"Absolutely! I'll just wait out here and give you a chance to breathe."

Seth smiled up at him and went back to unpacking his suitcase. Every hair was in place, his eyes were bright and eager, and somehow none of his clothes even looked rumpled from his sitting in an airplane for hours. How could he travel for hours after getting off *work* and still look so pulled together?

"Oliver, thank you for letting me come stay with you."

Oliver laughed, because really? Was Seth serious? "Seth, believe me when I say it's my pleasure."

"Well, I hope that your roommate will feel the same. I know you said he's not... tolerant of gays."

Seth made a face, but Oliver said, "He's rough at first. Janos likes to test people, I think. But he'll see how great you are, don't worry."

They smiled at each other, Oliver feeling a little shy and a lot excited. He pointed over his shoulder and said, "I'll go ahead and leave you to unpacking. Take your time."

It was easy to imagine more of this, like Seth moving his clothes into their shared space. Well, they would probably have to convert Janos's room into a closet to hold all of Seth's things. But how sweet to get a taste of the domesticity he'd envisioned as a lovestruck teenager: sharing space, getting morning coffee, walking to work, doing all of it together. Turned out he could easily imagine it as a lovestruck adult, too.

Oliver flopped onto the well-worn sofa, making a point of sitting on the far end so he wasn't staring right into his bedroom at Seth; that would just be creepy. He laid his head back against the sofa with his hands folded across his belly and hummed a tune, completely and utterly satisfied with the exciting normalcy of Seth in his house, unpacking his things, singing something under his breath as he hung his clothes in Oliver's wardrobe. It was just a perfect moment. He tried to tamp down the giddiness building up in him at having Seth here and getting a full week to spend with him. Oliver knew that they'd have to have some serious discussions, but for now he just wanted to enjoy the moment.

* * *

Sitting together in a café halfway around the world from Kansas, talking about everything under the sun (the atrocity that was the mock turtleneck, the dangers of Auto-Tune, Mike Larsen's slow slide into acceptance that his future tasted of broiled chicken breasts and not the fatty death patty that was the hamburger) was absolutely surreal. Every now and then one of them laughed at how absurdly familiar it was.

"It shouldn't feel this normal, right?" Seth asked on a few occasions. Oliver just smiled back and shook his head a little, not in disagreement but to keep from blurting out, "It feels normal because it's *right*. What we feel is right." He needed Seth to come to that conclusion on his own, as much as he wanted to press the issue.

They spent the afternoon wandering the Back Lawn and people-watching. Seth was too jittery on coffee and lack of sleep to go on any in-depth tours, he said, so they strolled about near King's Chapel and along the King's Parade to window shop and make a trip to The Haunted Bookshop. Seth had rolled his eyes at the legend but bought a book on paranormal activities to bring back to John and Natalie.

Oliver led the way back to his apartment, feeling pleasantly exhausted. Before they hopped on the bus, he made a point of getting some takeout. Seth stood at Oliver's elbow as he paid, disappointed that Oliver used a bank card instead of actual British pounds.

"But their money is actually attractive; why *wouldn't* you want to use it? Oliver, it has *the Queen* on it."

After they climbed onto the bus and got settled, Seth reached into one of the bags to grab a piece of bread. Oliver playfully grabbed the bag back. "You'll ruin your dinner."

The sense of contentment that he'd felt on the train from the airport had continued to build throughout the day until Oliver had almost forgotten that this was temporary, that Seth would eventually go back to New York. That they might not get together in the end.

They hopped off the bus, Seth thrilling at the "Cheers!" the bus driver called out to Oliver; he chattered the entire way down the street, charmed by the buildings, the accents and how "cozy" the city seemed in comparison to New York. Oliver had enjoyed all of this when he'd first moved to Cambridge, as well, but for all of its charms, it had never felt like home to him. It had always felt temporary; Massachusetts had been the same, and if he were honest with himself, so had his own home.

He looked sideways at Seth, who was happily pointing out different elements of the cottages he found attractive, and Oliver realized that he knew where his home was. It was just a matter of whether or not he'd be allowed to come back to it.

They walked into the house, laughing ("I haven't seen one tweed cap, Oliver. I feel cheated."), and realized that Janos was home. He was watching a football game and looked over the back of the sofa at them and held a hand up in greeting before turning back to the television.

"He's not what I expected," Seth whispered as they moved into the kitchen with their food.

"Oh? What did you expect?" Oliver asked, pulling out two plates and silverware.

"Viktor Krum."

Oliver grabbed the edge of the counter and burst out laughing.

"American television has done the Iron Curtain a major disservice," Seth whispered, jerking his head in Janos's direction. "I expected a sallow complexion and a black unibrow, not, well... *that*. Why are the good-looking ones always the homophobes?"

Oliver bit his lip to keep from laughing again and motioned for Seth to take his plate to the small table against the far wall. "Janos," he called out, "there's enough for you, if you want any?"

Janos turned and looked their way, giving Seth a thorough once-over. "No, thank you," he said; his voice sounded mildly disgusted.

Seth went still briefly and bristled with visible indignation. "Don't worry. We didn't order it with a side of homo, so you should be fine. Although it seems like you had a helping of jackass earlier; no wonder you're not hungry. Must have had seconds."

Janos twisted on the sofa, his arm draped over the back as he gaped at Seth. Oliver was momentarily shocked into silence, but Seth had never really needed assistance in the face of bigotry—only support.

"*Van egy nagy heréje, akkor a buzl. Én szeretem.*"

Oliver and Seth both narrowed their eyes at him, Oliver trying to figure out what the hell Janos just said.

"Translate. Now." Seth's voice was positively icy; he vibrated with anger. "Or you're going to learn in a very painful way that I'm a hell of a lot tougher than I look."

Janos seemed to pick up on this and answered quickly, with his hands up in surrender. "I say: for a f-, uh... homosexual? You have... what, balls? Testicles." He grabbed his crotch and continued. "I say I very much like this about you."

With as droll a voice as Oliver had ever heard, Seth replied, "Isn't that interesting that you're fond of my testicles so quickly; normally it takes until the third date for me to hear that."

Janos laughed. He *laughed*. Oliver had worried that the two might butt heads; he knew that Janos, while not necessarily antagonistic toward homosexuals, was definitely not a fan, either. Seth wasn't one to shy away from defending himself; Oliver had learned that about him years ago (and he'd taught Oliver how to truly stand up for himself, as well). But to crack Janos up? Oliver had never made Janos laugh, and not for lack of trying.

"I like your friend, Oliver. He is a good guy, this Seth."

Seth rolled his eyes. "Oh, thank you."

Oliver smirked. "You'd better watch offending him, Janos. His dad could crush you with one hand. He's in a biker gang," he added, leaning in. "Real tough guy."

"Biker? Like... motorcycles?" Janos said, sounding skeptical.

Seth fixed him with a droll look. "Yep," he replied, popping the "p." He pulled his phone out, flipped through his pictures and handed it over. Oliver stood next to Janos to see which picture he had called up: Big Mike, all six-foot-five inches of him, in full riding leathers, black skull bandana tied around his head (Oliver knew that Seth allowed it because of his appreciation for Alexander McQueen) and mirrored shades, his beard steel-gray and full and a stoic expression on his face, sat astride his massive custom-built bike.

Janos whistled. "That's your father? *Your* father?" He looked Seth up and down, both shocked and impressed.

Seth gave a smile that didn't quite reach his eyes and turned to Oliver, signaling that his conversation with Janos was over. Janos shrugged and went back to his game on the television.

"So I see why you never tried to hook up with him. Looks, sure, but what a jackass," Seth muttered.

Oliver chuckled. "That's just what I told him when he thought I was 'into' him."

Seth, his tongue in his cheek to fight off a smile, said, "You better not be." Then he looked down at his food, blushing as if it were the most fascinating thing; but Oliver caught his smile.

After they finished their dinner, it was clear that the travel had taken its toll on both of them. Oliver showed Seth the guest towels in the small bathroom and the trick to climbing out of the claw-foot tub without slipping and cracking his skull open on the hard stone floor. Oliver took the few minutes during Seth's shower to wash the dishes and answer work-related emails. His plan of having a full day with Seth without worry about future plans was quickly trashed when he saw his inbox.

Apr 1, 10:43 AM EST
To: Oliver Andrews
From: Jones, Maeve MSW, PhD
Subject: Why Silver is the best program for you
Dear Mr. Andrews,

Thank you for your interest in the NYU Silver School of Social Work Doctoral Program. As head of GALIP (Gays and Lesbians in Psychotherapy Study), let me first say how delighted I am to have someone of your background joining us. TMMaT has made waves in the community; you and your team should be proud of your excellent work. I could tell from our phone interview last month that your excitement and passion for your work would make an excellent addition to our doctoral program.

As you are well aware, I'm sure, the time for accepting or declining graduate programs is almost at a close, April 15th. If you have any concerns about what you'll be involved with here, or need assistance financially, I would be pleased to offer help and/or guidance. And if you would prefer a closer look at the school and current research, we would love to fly you to New York next week and let you see firsthand.

You may know that I'm a board member for the Foundation for

Research and Experimentation. We've had a significant shift in our funding and are prepared to increase your original offer to a three-year fellowship, followed by a three-year assistantship.

I look forward to hearing from you soon,

Maeve Jones, MSW, PhD

Associate Professor of Social Work

* * *

Oliver sat back in his task chair, hands in his hair, his mind racing. They were offering him a free ride for three years and a job plus school for three more. Cambridge was also offering him a fellowship, but it was only for one year. But here, he would publish an important paper with one of the most respected members of his field and co-run a research program that was beginning to have real effect on public policy in England.

He had pursued this particular field of study because he wanted to make a difference. He wanted to help people find their own strengths and do for others what Seth had done for him. But now he had absolutely no idea which choice to make in order to do just that.

He heard Seth moving around in the bedroom, apparently finished with his shower. Oliver planned to sleep on the sofa—he hadn't wanted to presume anything—and wanted to grab a pillow and blanket before Seth turned in. Then Janos stood up, cheering loudly at the television as whatever team he was pulling for got close to scoring.

Oliver anticipated a long night.

"All yours!" Seth said as he folded his clothes to be put away in his suitcase.

"Thanks, I'll be quick. Let me just grab a pillow so if you fall asleep before I'm finished with the bathroom, I won't wake you up."

Seth turned in confusion, his jeans perfectly folded into thirds in his hands. "Grab a pillow? Are you planning on sleeping with him?" Seth cocked his head toward the door, where Janos was moaning in Hungarian—apparently some athlete had done something stupid.

Oliver laughed, "No, on the couch."

Seth turned back to his suitcase, slipping his dirty clothes inside. "That's silly. I thought you were going to sleep in here. Oh!" Seth turned back to face Oliver, looking concerned. "Unless that's awkward for you? I'm sorry; I just assumed. Here, I should be the one taking the couch—"

Oliver stopped Seth by holding both of his biceps. "Seth. It's fine. You can't possibly think I'd let a guest sleep on our old sofa. It won't be the first time I've crashed there, believe me."

Rolling his eyes, Seth said, "Just sleep in here; we managed just fine at New Year's, didn't we?"

Oliver's breath stuttered at the memory of that night. How they'd kissed, albeit chastely. How he'd said he still loved Seth. How he knew the next day that it would be just a matter of time for them to work out their relationship. He *knew* that; they belonged together.

He bit his lip, watching Seth's face for any signs of reluctance. "You're sure it's okay?"

"We'll be fine. And it's just like that night," Seth said, smiling. "I'm way too exhausted to get up to any shenanigans. And it's not like we haven't done this before as friends, back when we were at school."

Friends. Right. For now they were friends. Oliver could believe they would get back together eventually all he wanted. But without a solid plan, nothing could move in that direction. Oliver had to remember that Seth wouldn't commit to anything more until Oliver's future was settled.

Too bad he had absolutely no idea how to solve that problem.

By the time Oliver had taken a perfunctory shower, brushed his teeth and changed into his pajamas, Seth was sound asleep, curled on his side facing away from Oliver's side of the bed. The few times they'd found a way to sleep over at each other's houses, they'd teased each other about who would get to be the "the little spoon." On rare occasions, Seth wanted to be; sometimes he felt claustrophobic, he'd explained to Oliver one night. Years of fight or flight had ingrained that in him, unfortunately.

Oliver slipped under the cool sheets, quietly moaning at how good it felt to be prone and almost asleep. He curled onto his side, facing Seth's back. There was a reasonable amount of space between them to maintain the delicate balance of friendship they were attempting, but there was something about watching the gentle rise and fall of Seth's shoulder as he breathed deeply that soothed Oliver into his own state of blissful unconsciousness.

* * *

Oliver opened the door to his New York apartment, still thrilling that they they'd done it—they'd found a wonderful home together and were going to make life work. He'd finally finished school and had prospective jobs lined up—all in the city, so there was no need to commute long distance.

He dropped his satchel on the floor by the console in the entryway, his keys and wallet going into the bowl that sat there for just that purpose. Except it wasn't there. Huh. Maybe Seth had decided to switch it with something else? He was always doing things like that, changing the décor to keep things fresh. It was something Oliver loved about him.

He turned to hang up his jacket in the front closet, but the door opened the wrong way and it was already full, practically stuffed with coats and jackets and umbrellas and a host of other items that Oliver didn't recognize. He draped his coat over his arm and called out, "Seth?"

Instead of seeing the handsome face of his boyfriend (fiancé, soon—he patted the box in his front pocket, sending a wave of excitement and nervousness careening through him), he saw a strange man standing in the doorway between the entry and the kitchen.

"Are you lost?" the man asked. He looked tense, even if his tone was helpful.

"Uh, I think I could ask the same of you?" Oliver said, his voice rising in an incredulous tone, wary of this guy. What the hell was he doing in his house?

"Seth? Seth!" The man twisted behind him, trying to keep his eyes on Oliver but throwing his voice back into the apartment. "Look, I don't know what you're doing here, but we don't want any trouble, okay?"

What—why was he calling for Seth? And where the hell were this guy's shoes?

"Daddy!" A little boy of about three or four came bounding in from another door and wrapped his stubby arms around the strange man's leg. "Who's that?"

Oliver laughed and rubbed at his face. "Oh my God, I am so sorry. I'm clearly in the wrong house. I don't know how..." His voice trailed off as he looked back toward the door. There was a picture of Seth hanging there.

And the strange man was in the picture. They were holding hands and running as a group of friends—those are *my* friends, Oliver thought—threw confetti after them. Something in his heart twisted and coiled up as anxiety began to build in the back of his brain, pushing out all rational thought.

"Seth?" Oliver practically shrieked his name, confusion and fear taking over.

"Hey, hey—you're scaring my son. Can you calm down and tell me what you need? Are you lost? Did... something happen to you and you need help?"

Even as he began to tremble, he recognized that the man was trying to be helpful. Oliver, his chest heaving with the force of his breathing, tried to calm himself and figure out what the hell was going on; why there were pictures of Seth with someone else on the wall; why there was a man barefoot in *his* kitchen; and why the little boy had thick, soft brown hair and hazel eyes and a tiny spray of freckles scattered across his chubby cheeks.

He looks just like...

"*Seth!*" Oliver backed away from the man, who had gotten down on his knees to hold the little boy, now crying, and began to shout Seth's name, over and over.

The little boy turned his face against the man's body and cried, "Why does he want Daddy?"

Then it was as if the room contracted, making everything small and close before pulsing back out; Oliver was being pulled away from what was happening but somehow was still unable to escape the clarity of the situation. He began to realize what all of this was, what it all meant.

A door opened from the back and Seth came into the entryway, concern on his features. Oliver sighed, feeling relief at the sight of him. Seth would tell him what was going on. He would make this okay; he would say he loved Oliver, that this was their house, that the other man and the little boy—he looked *just like* him—would disappear and they could have the dinner that Oliver had planned, and he would wait for just the right moment and pull out the small velvet box and everything would be the way it was supposed to be. Their lives would move in the direction they were supposed to; he just needed Seth to come take his hand.

But Seth didn't come to him. Seth went to the man and wrapped his arms around him and the little boy, looking back at Oliver as if he was intruding. As if he was dangerous. "What do you want? You're scaring my family, and I want you to leave."

It was as though an icy knife plunged directly into his heart. "What? Seth... But I came home. I came home, and I wanted to ask you a big question and these people are here in our house, and I don't *understand*. Why are they in our house?"

"I'm sorry, but you need to leave." Seth turned back to the little boy, scooping him up into his arms and patting him on the back. The strange man put his hand on Seth, leaned forward and whispered in his ear. It was wrong; it was awful, and the man shouldn't be touching Seth, shouldn't be standing in Oliver's house, in his *kitchen* and in his fucking bare feet as if he belonged here. As if it were—

"Seth?" Oliver couldn't help that his hand trembled as he reached out toward him. If he could just touch him, if they could just be by themselves, he could explain. He could tell Seth his perfect plan, and they would be happy and... then...

This was Seth's family. This was their house, not Oliver's. Never was Oliver's. That was their child, these were their clothes, their furniture. That meant that the picture was of their wedding.

"Oh, God—" he choked back a sob as the realization hit him. He was the intruder. The little boy buried his face in Seth's shirt as the strange man—his husband?—rubbed his son's back, whispering sweetly, "Shh. He'll be gone soon, it's okay."

"I'm sorry. I'm sorry, I'll just—" He turned and yanked the door open and started running. The streets were close, and the buildings towered over him, blocking out any natural light. His breath was tearing out of him, but he couldn't run fast enough.

* * *

Jerking awake, Oliver clutched at his chest. He was on his back, staring at the ceiling in the dark room. Seth had rolled toward him, still mostly asleep, and his mouth was trying to work and shush Oliver. Seth reached out and fumbled along the bed, looking for Oliver's hand. He murmured,

"Shh, shh; it's okay." He pressed a sleepy kiss to the back of Oliver's hand, said, "I got you, babe," pulled their joined hands up under his chin and fell right back to sleep.

Oliver stared at his sleeping face and tried to reorient himself. His heart rate began to drop to normal and his breathing leveled out. The pale moonlight coming in through a crack in the closed curtains fell across the bed, illuminating Seth's profile. Oliver settled back onto his side, facing Seth and holding onto his hand as if it were a lifeline.

He turned his face into his pillow to wipe off the moisture and wanted more than ever to pull Seth into his arms and just know that it would work out between them. He wanted that surety from New Year's Day back desperately. The worry about which school to choose, coupled with his elation at having Seth so close, kept him from feeling any peace.

He closed his eyes and tried to will himself to fall asleep, but his brain kept replaying images, keeping him awake. He couldn't get over how *happy* Seth had looked in the pictures from his dream.

Chapter Fifteen

"Good morning," Seth said, stretching his arms over his head and pointing and flexing his feet.

Oliver was laying on his back again; it had taken a while for him to fall back asleep, but he had fortunately slept dream-free for the rest of the night, comforted by the warmth of Seth's body. Oliver knew that they needed to talk; he couldn't make this decision on his own. The last thing he wanted to do was revisit past mistakes.

"Mm, morning," he replied, curling up, flipping over onto his face and burrowing into his pillow. "I want, like, five more hours of sleep."

Seth rubbed Oliver's back soothingly, causing him to shiver. (*"Why does he want Daddy?"*) "Rough night?" he asked. "You were tossing for a little while. Bad dream?"

Oliver turned his head to face Seth, who was propped on his elbow, looking down at him with concern. "Yeah, I— it was just something stupid." He slid his foot across the mattress and poked at Seth's calf with his toe. "Thanks for making me feel better."

Seth's cheeks flushed. "Sorry. Old habit, I guess."

"That's a good habit," Oliver said, grinning back at him and then burying his face back in his pillow. He loved how caring Seth could be for those he loved; his heart skipped a beat thinking of it, thinking about how *he* wanted to be loved and cared for by him. Echoes of Seth soothing a strange man and child made his heart clench.

Seth groaned with another wide stretch, shaking Oliver out of his thoughts to ask, "Coffee here? Or...?"

"Or." Seth stretched again and smiled through a yawn. "Definitely 'or.' You were right, that place was fantastic. Don't tell anyone I said this," he said in a conspiratorial manner, "but I think it might be the best coffee I've ever had."

Oliver grinned back at him. "Your secret's safe with me."

Seth pushed himself up to a sitting position, twisting left and then right to crack his back. "No offense, but this mattress is medieval."

Laughing, Oliver replied, "Given this old house, that's a possibility." He stood. "Hey, go ahead and take the bathroom first. I need to reply to some of yesterday's emails, if you don't mind."

Seth looked at him, one eyebrow raised in question. "Oh? Anything interesting?"

Oliver tried to control his face; he didn't want Seth to see any remnants of nervousness or dread from his dream and start their day off on the wrong foot. "Could be. Let's get cleaned up and we can talk in depth over some strudel, if that's okay?"

Seth narrowed his eyes, but it was obvious that he meant it to be playful. "Strudel, hmm? You must be sweetening me up for something if you're going to steer me away from my granola."

Oliver laughed and then cringed inwardly at how forced and worried it sounded. But Seth didn't seem to pick up on it and began gathering up clothes and toiletries. Oliver left him to it, putting on a pair of slippers and shuffling into the living room. Even though it was officially spring, the old stone floors never seemed to warm.

He pulled up his email, agonized for a few minutes, and then replied to Dr. Jones at Silver with his thanks and a range of dates when he could come to New York. Anxiety twisted his insides as he hit "send."

* * *

They carried their coffee and pastries to a sunny table in the corner where they could sit comfortably. It had taken Seth longer than he'd expected to get ready and out the door ("You poor thing. You have zero water pressure in that shower."), so by the time they'd arrived, the morning rush had mostly come and gone. They hadn't talked much on the way over, had just exchanged pleasantries; it was if the words "The Talk" were hanging over their heads and they were waiting out the impending downpour.

Oliver took a deep breath and folded his hands together at the edge of the table. He glanced up to find Seth looking back at him expectantly, albeit guardedly.

"Before you say anything," Seth said, nervously picking at his napkin, "I get it. I get why it's a big deal to be here. It's the school of Watson and Crick. Darwin. *Tilda Swinton.*" He swept the tiny pieces of paper into a pile with the flat of his hand. "I mean, I haven't done more than just walk past the buildings here and... I get it."

Oliver opened and shut his mouth a few times, trying to process what Seth was saying. Heaving a deep breath, he pasted a nervous smile on his face and said, "Okay. Uh, thank you for that. I got a very interesting email late yesterday from Silver, though. A pretty outstanding offer from their doctoral program, a part of NYU—remember me telling you their graduate program is one of the better ones in my field?"

Some of the worry in Seth's face melted away as he nodded; his shoulders even relaxed enough to give Oliver encouragement.

"Please explain?" Seth asked. He raised his eyebrows and stared at his fingers as they flicked torn pieces of napkin back into a pile.

"I, um, may have been a bit too preoccupied with you being in my basement on New Year's, looking so very handsome," he said, grinning, "that I didn't take in all of the changes regarding your school choices since the last time we tried to talk about this." Seth gave him another silly sort of half-grin and folded his hands primly in his lap.

Oliver could feel the table shake with the force of Seth's bouncing knee. He took a steadying breath and said, "NYU's undergraduate program? It's good. However, their *graduate* programs are excellent. Silver is one. That's the one I brought up on New Year's Eve."

Seth looked as though he was going through a complete thaw. Oliver hoped with everything in him that he was seeing excitement and possibility glimmering in Seth's eyes. He still didn't know what to do, but the very large "maybe" was definitely something Seth needed to know about.

"What sort of offer did you get?" Seth asked, leaning forward to rest his weight on his forearms.

Oliver sighed and ran a hand over his scalp. "They want to pay me to go to school there for three years. Then I'll be a research associate—like working there—to pay off my last three years."

Seth's jaw dropped along with the bite of strudel he'd picked apart. "Oliver, that's amazing!"

But Oliver had meant it when he said that he didn't want a repeat of their first talk about schools. He needed Seth to know all of it. "Wait."

Seth slowly sat back in his chair, his eyes shuttering any excited emotions.

Shit.

"Cambridge made me an offer, too." Oliver closed his eyes, not wanting to see Seth's face just yet. Cowardly? Yes, but he needed to be a bit of a coward to get it all out. Then they could look at the situation together and work through it. He needed to be smart; he needed to be thorough, just as much as much as he needed Seth.

"They'll pay for a year and offset the remaining five with work. But the thing is," he finally looked up, "they're handing me the keys to the project I've been running. A private company is funding it, and the government wants it. It's kind of a big deal. I'd be publishing with one of the most renowned scholars in my field. That's... well, that's the hard place, and Silver is the rock. And here I am..." he trailed off, his hands twitching in his lap.

"Stuck in the middle with you," Seth sang quietly.

Oliver couldn't help but laugh. "Oh, please don't sing that! I always think of Mr. Blonde and the ear." He shuddered and made a face.

Seth smiled as he sipped his coffee. "This is why I've told you for years that you should stick with the Golden Age of MGM instead of Tarantino. Greta Garbo and Fred Astaire would never have given you those nightmares."

They smiled across the table at each other for a moment. Oliver's feeling that his lungs were trapped in a metal cage was lessening; he took a deep breath and told himself that it was good they were being smart about this, that they were being adults. That they were still smiling.

"I—" Seth started but snapped his mouth shut. He started bouncing his leg again and looked out the window. Oliver could understand him needing to gather his thoughts, since his own were too numerous and scattered. It was like trying to grab mercury.

"I don't want to tell you what to do here, Oliver. I don't think it's fair for me to do that to you." Seth sighed and picked at his strudel with long, delicate fingers. Oliver watched his hands, flashing to the feeling of a box in his pocket from his dream, and shuddered briefly.

"And I don't know enough about what you do, who's important, why one school would be better over the other." Seth looked back at Oliver helplessly.

Oliver breathed deeply, reached across the table and took one of Seth's hands in his. He stroked along its back with his thumb, gave it a squeeze and forced himself to let go; he needed to keep his wits about him.

"Well, that's where I am, too. Except for the knowing who's who." He watched as Seth looked down at his hand, as if he were seeing Oliver still holding it. "Think of it like this: Cambridge is the best place for research. That's what they're known for. They produce scientists and Nobel Prize winners in math and physics."

Rubbing the back of his neck, Oliver continued. "I would get to do more research and publish a paper. Everyone who is anyone would see my name next to Dr. Lan's, and that is some serious clout. Governmental policy-changing clout."

Seth looked thoughtful; he also went back to eating, which Oliver took as a good sign.

"It would almost be like you doing a workshop with Neil Patrick Harris, knowing he was eventually going to pull strings and get a show for you."

Completely still, hanging on his every word, Seth finally gave a nod of understanding. Oliver sighed in relief: Seth was on the same page regarding how important all this was.

"And Silver," Oliver continued, "would be more hands-on application, less research. Which isn't a bad thing at all. It's just, well, different. The head of the program is seriously phenomenal. Her whole thing is working with LGBT kids and their families directly, something I've thought about doing. I just don't know what—" He exhaled harshly. "I just don't know."

Seth let out a shocked, dry laugh. "I hope you don't think I do?"

"No... well, I might have hoped you would have something pithy to say that would make it all clear?" Oliver said, giving Seth a dopey grin. He sighed in frustration. "Okay, so *that* deal would be like, hmm, performing a supporting role with Neil and hanging out with him afterward." He dropped his head onto his forearms and groaned. "It's like an embarrassment of riches. And once I choose, that's it. I can't change my mind later," he said, his voice slightly muffled by his arms.

Seth patted his elbow, leaving his hand resting warmly on Oliver's forearm. They sat in silence for a few moments. Oliver's thoughts were all over the place, refusing to slow down and look at the problem head on; it was like trying to catch sight of dust motes in his peripheral vision—as soon as he turned to look at them directly, they disappeared. He sat back up, jammed the last bite of strudel into his mouth and hurriedly chewed and swallowed it, chasing it with his coffee. "Let's get out of here. I do my best thinking while moving."

Laughing softly, Seth finished his coffee and stood up. "Where to?"

Oliver wiped his mouth with his napkin, stood and led Seth to the door. "Somewhere special." He turned and smiled, walking through the door backwards. With a panicked expression, Seth jerked his hand forward and pulled Oliver toward him in a jumble before Oliver could back over a tiny, ancient woman trying to walk in. Sighing, Seth covered his face with his hand.

The old woman shot Oliver a look and said over his profuse apologies in a calm voice, "I believe we're meant to go the other way, young man."

"Um, yes, ma'am. I'm so sorry."

"Thank you," she said, smiling up at him.

He smiled back and turned to Seth, who was waiting with his arms folded and a hand covering his mouth.

"Unbelievable," Seth chuckled.

Oliver's blush felt like it had started in his cells.

"You know, if that had happened in New York you would have found that the lady had an Uzi in her bag, and she would have shot you in the kneecaps."

"Good thing we're not in New York, then, I guess?" Oliver said, holding the door open for Seth, and instantly regretted it. He didn't want to set the stage for talking this through with Seth as if he already had prejudice or preference.

Seth shook his head and didn't make eye contact as they took a right out of the café and into town. They walked in silence for two blocks, except when Oliver pointed out directions. Eventually Seth sighed and reached out to take Oliver's hand, giving him a squeeze before dropping it. Oliver didn't know if it was a "we'll figure this out" squeeze or a "let's enjoy this last bit of time we have together before it's all over" squeeze. They continued on, Oliver's insides twisting, Seth walking a half step behind him as he led the way for them to hop on a city shuttle.

They rode the short distance into the city center. As Seth climbed off the bus behind him, Oliver took him by the elbow and said, "You understand why I haven't made the final choice, right?" God, he hoped Seth understood; once committed, there was no going back. There was no second-guessing—all that would be left was regret. The last thing in the world Oliver ever wanted was for Seth to regret having Oliver back in his life. And quite honestly, Oliver didn't want to regret not going to a grad school that could affect the rest of *his* life.

Seth blinked and looked off at a random building for a moment, seemingly to collect himself. He turned back to give Oliver a watery smile but stiffened his spine. "I do understand. I don't ever want there to be any resentment between us, Oliver; I couldn't take it if you felt that way about me."

Oliver's heart felt as if it was constricting in the center of his chest, the pain went so deep. "Never," he said, quietly. Seth patted Oliver right over where the ache was the strongest. Oliver held it there for a moment before saying, "Just... please don't count me out already. Okay?"

"Oliver, I want..." Seth looked upset again, so Oliver took his hand and led him up the road. He didn't want to have an emotional breakdown in front of the campus bookstore.

"Just let me take us somewhere and we can talk without interruption, okay?"

Seth nodded and followed alongside him, still holding his hand. Oliver showed the man at Trinity Gate his university card to gain entrance, and they walked past the expansive green courtyard to the far building.

"Come on, it's just down this hallway." Because it was Easter break, the college and Wren Library were mostly empty. Oliver, excited to take Seth to "his spot" and desperate to sit and talk this through, tugged on Seth's hand and jogged down the hallway with him in tow. Seth gasped and stopped, dropping Oliver's hand.

He turned to see why Seth had stopped; it felt the way his heart had, when he saw that Seth had pressed the heels of his hands to his eyes and was breathing deeply.

"Seth?" He ran his hand down Seth's arm, giving his bicep a squeeze. "Are you oka—"

"Are you doing this on purpose? That's not *fair*, Oliver. You can't— God!"

Oliver's heart was somewhere in his throat, pounding so loud his ears were ringing with it; he had no idea what on earth was going on.

Seth dropped his hands. His face was filled with so much misery it tore at Oliver as if he were watching Seth be physically hurt. He pulled Seth into his arms and patted his back, trying to soothe him and get him to talk.

"You can't honestly tell me this place doesn't remind you of anything," Seth said, his voice filled with pain.

Oliver pulled back, completely confused. He looked around, and the world seemed to tilt on its axis. He could see that the marble floors at Trinity were a similar pattern to those at Bakerfield. He looked at the rich wallpapers, the ornate chandeliers, and he was seventeen again, his heart in his throat and excitement pounding in his veins as he crossed the expanse toward Seth so they could slip away to "their spot" in the library. He knew that he would whisper "Tonight," to Seth, that tonight they would take their expression of love beyond mere words and kisses for the first time.

The building wasn't exactly the same, but it was unbelievably similar.

"Oh my God." Oliver turned and pulled Seth into his arms, holding him so, so tight. "No, I didn't even think. I just—I don't know; this building has always felt good to me, familiar, I guess." He looked down the long, narrow aisle between the books and pairs of leather chairs and shook his head. "I guess I know why."

Seth was taking huge breaths in and out, his hands in fists at Oliver's back. It just killed Oliver that Seth couldn't bring himself to touch him now. He pulled back and cupped Seth's face with his hands, his thumbs lightly stroking Seth's cheekbones, and let himself breathe when he felt Seth lean into his touch.

"Hey. *Hey*. This isn't even where I meant to take you." He laughed, but it was more sorrowful than humorous. "Let's go, okay?" He smiled encouragingly. "Let's go outside and sit in the sun and talk."

He tried to name what Seth must be feeling, but couldn't. There was too much—too much pain, longing, fear and worry happening, and all too quickly. It was too much for him, too, now that he'd been reminded of the first time they'd decided to take advantage of Oliver's parents being gone for the weekend. He remembered how Seth had gasped when Oliver had taken Seth's hands in his, completely earnest and sincere, how Seth had laughed softly before nodding and saying, "Okay." Every time he saw Seth in the hallways that day, he had been unable to stop looking at the beautiful, ethereal boy who had come into his life and changed everything for the better. He had been so excited for that next step.

"Let's get out of here?"

Seth glanced around the building, looking as brittle as spun glass, and turned back with a determined, almost grim look. "Yes."

They walked without talking the rest of the way; when they passed the A.A. Milne exhibit, Oliver remembered one of his lines: "How lucky I am to have something that makes saying goodbye so hard." He had no intention of saying goodbye to Seth, but the sentiment rang true, regardless. As they walked, Oliver left his hand open near Seth's on the off-chance Seth would take it.

He didn't.

Finally outside and facing the river, Seth seemed to relax by a few degrees. It really was beautiful in this part of the city. Oliver thumbed over his shoulder toward a massive weeping willow, its newly budded leaves an almost electric lime green against the dark blue water. Seth stood still on the lawn, his hands tucked into his pockets as he surveyed the area. A smile began to bloom on his face; Oliver couldn't remember ever being more grateful for a smile.

"It's your tree. It's a bit different than the picture you emailed me," Seth said.

Oliver chuckled—it helped to dissipate his nervousness and worry. "It's that whole lack-of-snow aspect." He walked on to the low stone bench that separated the lawn from the river. As Seth approached, he made a point of dusting off the stone next to him.

That earned him another smile and another few degrees less anxiety. Seth sat carefully with his back stiff and straight, pulling on the knee of his pants as he crossed his leg. He looked away from Oliver, at the river and the punts on the water.

"Wow. It *is* just like Merchant and Ivory. Well, minus the tourists in their mismatched clothing."

Oliver smiled down at his empty hands. He would let Seth drive the conversation, even though it was killing him to sit and wait.

"You know I can't make this choice for you, Oliver, if that's what you're waiting for. You get why I can't?" Seth was still looking out at the water, away from him. "What if Silver is wrong, and you hear about something amazing happening here, or however it works. That would mean your career wasn't all that it could have been, which we both know would eat you up inside." He sighed, his breath shuddering as he held himself together. "Then the next, what, thirty? Forty years? You hate what you're doing. You're not helping people like you want. You're not making the difference that you imagined. Oliver, I don't want that for you. I don't want to be the reason you miss out on everything your life *should* be. I couldn't take it."

"Seth, no—that's not how it would be," Oliver pleaded.

Seth turned to face him, a sad smile on his face. "Yes it would, Oliver, and you know it. That's why you haven't made your decision."

Oliver sighed and rubbed the back of his neck, thinking. "If that did happen—hypothetical, here, okay?" he asked. "If I did choose New York, and something amazing happened here with my project..." He was *going* to say that he would be happy for the new head. Happy for whomever ended up with the accolades for the good achieved by his study. That he could be at peace with it even though the vast majority of the project was his idea—with help from Moira, of course. He wanted to say that he'd wish them well, because that's what he should say. That's how his parents had brought him up.

He couldn't bring himself to finish the sentence, though. A rare spike of anger flashed through him; he was really good at what he did, he'd worked hard to get to where he was, and to throw away all of his work, his blood, sweat and tears? He couldn't see that happening, and he sure as hell couldn't see himself feeling happy about it.

It would be a waste of five years, not to mention a tremendous waste of money. But neither could he bring himself to believe he'd be "throwing it all away just for Seth." That didn't sit right with him at all: there was no "just" about Seth Larsen.

Seth gave a sardonic laugh—evidently Oliver still had not mastered the art of the poker face. "Remember: I know how much you hate to let anyone down," Seth said.

Oliver looked over at him. He seemed to be resigned, bordering on crestfallen.

"No." Oliver shook his head. "Don't go ahead and assume, okay?" He had to just put it all out there. "Seth, the thought of not having you in my life... it's like losing a limb. That's how much a part of me you are. That's how much I need you."

Seth shook his head and looked out over the water, his jaw flexing as he worked it back and forth. "You've done just fine for years now, Oliver."

Oliver had done well in one area of his life, true. But. "Look," Oliver said, an edge creeping into his voice. "I'm not ready to quit on this, on us. I never was."

"What's that supposed to mean?" Seth whipped around to face him, his eyes glacial and his posture severe. "Are you trying to blame *everything* on me?"

"No—"

"Because that's what it sounded like. I didn't 'quit' on you or on our relationship. It was just what *happened*. And it happened because you were scared and didn't give me any time to prepare for the huge life change you planned without me." Seth's crossed leg bounced at a furious pace.

Oliver raked his hand through his hair, trying to keep up. "So if... what? If you'd had advance notice, that would have made everything completely different?" Oliver was confused, he was angry, and he really didn't want to fight about this. "Seth, I have no idea what to think about all of this, about you and me. I mean... are you giving me a chance or not? What the hell is going on?"

"I am, once again, waiting for you to decide that I'm worth picking. And you know what? I'm not going to do this again; it took me *years* to get over—Jesus," he muttered, getting to his feet.

Oliver stood up too and grabbed at his hand to stop him. This was really not going as he'd planned. Where did he go wrong today? His stomach roiled from the massive adrenaline dump of stress into his system.

"I have *always* wanted you, Seth. Don't make this about me not loving you enough."

Seth pulled his hand away, crossing his arms. He didn't leave, however. "I'm not saying that." Seth groaned and rubbed at his face. "I'm saying that I don't matter enough to you for you to know without question that you want to be with me. *That* is what I'm saying."

Oliver's heart gave a lurch at the waver in Seth's voice.

"Oliver, you say that you love me. Still. You say that you want us to have that magical future that we daydreamed about when we were kids." Seth jutted out his chin and wrapped his arms tightly around himself again as he inflected the word "magical" with sarcasm. Oliver knew that his words and his posture were his armor; he knew that Seth used them to protect his battered and abused heart. He just never thought he'd be the one on the receiving end of it. His gut felt as if it was made of lead, heavy and cold.

"You say you want all of that, but here we are again! God, I am so stupid to have flown out here just to have my—" Seth inhaled sharply through his nostrils, looking up into the branches of the tree and blinking quickly. "I can't believe I let myself hope that we could really... *God*."

"Seth, this is my *life* we're talking about here!"

"It's mine, too! The one where you're finally in it!" Seth, his voice growing louder, pressed a hand to his sternum. He was furious and upset and holding nothing back. Oliver could almost forget that they were in a public place. A few punts were on the water, but the tree and the stone bench must have been keeping their voices from carrying too far.

"Hey, I wasn't the one who wouldn't think of options, okay? I was *always* willing to find a way to make it work." Oliver was getting angrier by the minute, too. It was irrational and stupid that they were fighting at all but he couldn't just take it. Not when he was *trying*.

"That's because you're the eternal optimist. Everything always works out for you, Oliver. Lucky little rich boy. You weren't constantly hoping for life to finally give you a stretch of goodness only to be reminded that, once again, you didn't get to have the happy ending. You didn't grow up wishing to be noticed, then terrified for your fucking life when you were.

You haven't lost almost everything and had all that was wonderful and special in your life ripped away. And you can never see any bad coming down the road until it's thrown right in your face. You're always shocked that bad things ever happen outside your perfect life," Seth hissed. "And look at where that's gotten you."

Oliver stuck his own chin out. It stung, being reminded of how different their backgrounds were, how different being gay had been for each of them, he more straight-appearing and Seth more effeminate—practically a death sentence in Kansas. Right now, though, it didn't matter if Seth was right; Oliver was hurt, and he was sad, and he just wasn't thinking about his words. "Yeah. It got me to the best schools and at the top of my class." If he sounded a little smug, well, it was because it was true.

Seth, his voice bitter, sniffed and said, "And you're all alone."

"So are you." Oliver instantly regretted saying it. He couldn't take it back. He couldn't take back the pained look on Seth's face. Couldn't make this stupid, childish argument go away.

Seth drew himself up as straight as humanly possible, and his face closed off. He was icy and rigid and completely and wholly hurt, and Oliver had to take responsibility for his part of that, he knew he did.

"Let's make that literal." Seth turned on his heel and began stalking off the way they'd come.

"Seth, wait—"

Seth held up a hand; he didn't turn—Oliver assumed Seth couldn't bring himself to look him in the eye—but said, "I need space. I need air. You can give me this much," and continued walking.

Oliver sank back down to the stone bench, his hands buried in his hair and his heart breaking.

* * *

Oliver sat under his tree for a while, watching boats pushing up and down the river, hearing the groups laughing as they tried to punt in a straight line or the undergraduate students giving guided tours, explaining the different points of architecture. His body was tense as he waited, listening for the faintest sound of Seth coming back. He began to get worried after an hour had passed with no sign of him. Oliver hadn't brought his cell phone along; he didn't want the distraction.

He turned away from the water and the smiling couples to stare at the empty lawn that stretched all the way to the library. There was no one. What if Seth had made his way back to the apartment? But that was ridiculous; he wouldn't go all the way back there to sit alone. What if he was there and was packing? He could easily travel to London, to Timbuktu if he was angry enough.

His stomach in knots, Oliver told himself to calm down and be rational. Seth was most likely *not* packing his things to run off to Africa. He probably just got himself lost. Well... shit.

Oliver pushed up to his feet, checked his pockets to make sure he had his keys and wallet and walked swiftly back to the library. Maybe Seth was simply inside the building, thinking? Oliver just wanted to know where he was, that was all. He'd check on Seth, make sure he was okay and then give him the space he wanted until they could talk about this whole mess like reasonable people.

Walking quickly, he looked down each aisle, checking corners where he remembered chairs and sofas tucked away for quiet reading. Then he raced down the empty hallway and felt a pang, again remembering the excitement he'd experienced years before in a place so very similar and the pain on Seth's face just hours ago from the memory of it.

Bursting back out into the sunshine, he walked toward the statue in the center of the courtyard and hopped up on the low wall that surrounded it to survey the entire area. No sign of Seth. He asked the gate custodian if he remembered seeing anyone who matched Seth's description. Yes, but quite some time ago. He did, however, know that Seth had turned down south on King's Parade, so at least Oliver had a direction.

He couldn't run down the sidewalks without raising concern, not to mention that the streets were full; the day had turned into a gorgeous celebration of spring—warm, sunny, a gentle breeze in the open spaces.

Sunny. Seth would go inside, somewhere, since he hadn't brought any sunscreen with him. Oliver's breath hitched, thinking of Seth telling him that he hadn't because he'd always been told that "you can't get tan in England."

He forced himself to stop and think where Seth may have gone, what shop he might be in, and rubbed his forehead, trying to keep his panic at bay. Oliver walked the full length of King's Parade, ducking into shops and cafés looking for a familiar head of thick, perfectly styled light brown hair and coming up empty each time.

His heart was positively racing, and as he started back on the other side of the road, he wondered if maybe his first instinct was right. Maybe Seth had somehow found his way back home and was packing. Or had already left? He barely checked cafés at this point, only looked into the windows as his fear welled up thick and acrid in his throat. He turned down a side street where he thought he remembered a series of interesting shops and, after passing a few, moving deeper and deeper into the alley, he began to feel a prickle of recognition ripple over him.

He stopped still, his chest heaving from the half-jog, half-brisk walk he'd kept up for an hour or more. The sun did not shine brightly in this narrow corridor—the buildings were close and cramped on either side of him, blocking the light. He flashed on his nightmare ("Shh. He'll be gone soon, it's okay."), and honest-to-goodness fear poured into his veins as he turned on his heel and ran out of there as fast as he could.

He probably looked like an idiot, but Oliver just couldn't deal with anything that resembled his worst fear. He stopped when he felt the sunlight on his shoulders again and bent at the waist, hands on his knees, as he caught his breath.

"Are you quite all right?"

Oliver stood up and saw an older woman with a look of concern on her face. She reminded him of his mother, not because of her looks, but because of the reserved concern in her expression.

"I'm sorry, just a bit winded. Thank you, though."

She nodded warily and moved off slowly, as if she didn't quite believe him but didn't know what to do about it. He stepped back against a building and looked at his watch. Christ, it had been three hours since he'd seen Seth. He saw the woman turn back and give him a small smile, and he flashed on something his mother had taught him when he was little, to stay in one place so he could be found.

It was worth a shot.

Oliver crossed the street, his hand out in apology as he ducked around cars in the oncoming traffic and made his way back to Wren Library.

The gate custodian was talking with a group of tourists, so Oliver flashed his uni-card and ducked back inside, running full tilt across the lawn and through the maze of buildings until he emerged on the back lawn.

Someone was on the bench, obscured by the shadows of the large tree's branches. Oliver's heart thumped loudly, and not just from the exertion of running; it was Seth, sitting where he'd been earlier, looking out at the water.

Oliver gave a sob of relief. "I thought... I thought you'd left."

Seth turned and looked at him over his shoulder. His eyes were red and swollen, but his face was clear. "I did, remember?"

Oliver dropped heavily into the empty space next to him and buried his face in the crook of his own elbow to wipe away the sweat and give himself a moment to calm down.

"No, I mean I thought you *left*." Oliver drew in a shuddering breath and dropped his arm. "Like, the country. Or the city, I don't know."

Seth looked at him, his breathing hitched once, and then he reached over and took one of Oliver's hands. "I don't like fighting with you." Seth's head dropped and he turned it slightly away. "I'm sorry."

Oliver dropped his hand and instead wrapped his arm around Seth to hold him close. "Seth, just—goddamn."

They sat there for a moment as Oliver got his breathing under control.

"I hate feeling like this." Seth's voice was so quiet that if Oliver hadn't been right next to him, he may not have heard it at all.

"Like shit?"

"Like I did when I drove home from your house that night, almost too blind to see because of how hard I was crying. God, I had to pull over every ten minutes or so."

Oliver laid his cheek against Seth's shoulder, his heart twisting painfully.

"Like a part of me died. Like the future didn't seem all that exciting anymore, because you weren't going to be in it."

Oliver squeezed his eyes shut. He was at a complete loss for words.

"And yet here I am again, wanting and waiting." Seth sighed and sat up, dislodging Oliver and shifting his body to angle toward him. "I've tried telling myself this whole time that this won't actually work." He looked off into the lawn and trees. "I didn't want to get any hopes up. Just... I thought my heart stopped when I looked up and saw you across the street in New York, Oliver. I'd wanted it for so long that I thought it was something like a waking dream, I don't know."

When he finally brought himself to look at Oliver, there was nothing but emptiness in his eyes, their hazel color faded as if all feeling had finally just drained out of him. Oliver was devastated; he took Seth's hands in his.

"We said we'd talk this through, and we're *not*." Oliver wasn't above pleading at this point. "You're talking to me as if it's over. I don't accept that, Seth." Seth breathed out sharply in disbelief, his shoulders hunching with the effort. Oliver ignored it, insisting, "I don't. Why are you automatically assuming the worst?"

Seth pulled one hand free and tenderly cupped Oliver's cheek. "Because that's what usually happens to me."

Oliver covered Seth's hand with his own. "No. It doesn't. Seth—" He laced their fingers together. "The best things happen, too."

He waited for a moment and watched Seth swallow convulsively, wanting to stop Seth's lips from trembling with his own, but he knew that he couldn't. Not yet. He hoped.

"I have two weeks, exactly," Oliver said. "Two weeks to figure this out."

"Well, I'll be here for one of those agonizing weeks. Yay." Seth gave a halfhearted cheer, but his smile, while diminutive, was real.

Oliver hung his head and gazed at their hands. How perfect they looked, linked together. "They want me to fly out there and visit the campus, talk with the professors, that sort of thing."

Seth's head jerked up; he was fully focused on Oliver now. "And you didn't think of telling me that *first*? Jesus, Oliver."

"I was going to tell you that part after I'd said all the rest, we just got... distracted," he finished lamely. "But yes. They're flying me out; I just have to say when."

"So they *really* want you?" Lost in thought, Seth looked at nothing in particular.

Oliver exhaled through pursed lips, giving Seth's hand a squeeze and bouncing it on his leg to keep Seth's attention. "Yeah. I think stealing me from Cambridge would be a coup."

Seth looked over at him, smiling. "Someone thinks a lot of himself."

"Well, you know... some people think I'm a catch." He waggled his eyebrows to be silly, but when he saw the heartbroken look on Seth's face, he stopped.

"Come on. Let's go somewhere else." He pulled Seth to his feet. "I don't know about you, but I'm starv—"

Seth pulled him into a tight hug, cutting off whatever he was going to say. Honestly, his brain shorted out at the sensation of Seth, firm and real and holding him. He snaked his arms around Seth's waist and buried his face in Seth's neck. He wanted to stay as close as possible.

"Sorry. I really hate fighting with you. Always did," Seth mumbled against Oliver's shoulder.

"So let's stop?" Oliver's voice was muffled by Seth's collar.

Seth gave him one last squeeze, pulled back and smoothed Oliver's shirt at his shoulders and chest. Everywhere Seth touched sent a wave of warmth through Oliver, chasing away the chilly anxiety that had been pulsing through him since Seth walked off. It was an olive branch, Oliver knew. The past hurts couldn't be taken away, but they could try—*he* could do his damnedest to make sure that there would be no more.

"Just don't do anything stupid," Seth said, affecting an excessively prim tone, "and I won't have to yell at you for it, okay?"

Oliver grinned at him, relief dragging his smile to almost ridiculous proportions. "Deal. So... food?"

"God, yes," Seth sighed, smoothing his own clothes and dusting off his backside. "Ugh, my ass is frozen."

"Well, I can—"

"Do not finish that sentence, Oliver Andrews."

* * *

They found a great place to eat and kept conversation to lighter topics. Oliver was still feeling quite raw from the day and knew that Seth had to be feeling that way, too. As Oliver took care of the check, Seth watched the passersby on the street through the window and then gasped and stretched his hand across the table to grip at whatever part of Oliver was accessible. Fortunately, he found Oliver's hand and not, say, his nose.

"Oliver. There's an Anthony's right across the street." His voice was almost reverential.

"I... okay? Do you want to g—"

"Yes!"

Oliver laughed and sat back in his chair, watching Seth light up at the thought of custom-made clothes. Of *course* Seth wanted to go.

"Didn't you say something about your friend wanting to meet up?" Seth's eyes were positively sparkling with excitement.

"Yeah, Moira wanted to meet later at our pub. It's a great place, kind of well-known, but not stuffy or anything like that."

"Perfect!" Seth stood, carefully pushed in his chair back and strode toward the door. "This way I can be sure I look my best for you."

Oliver smiled and just tried to keep up. That seemed to be the story of his life.

* * *

In Anthony's, Seth almost dropped to his knees and wept over the fabric choices. "Oliver, I can choose the color of the *lining!* From over twenty colors!"

Oliver hated to admit that it had been so long since he'd needed a full suit that he was almost out of practice. A fine sports coat or two, that was all he'd brought to England; there hadn't been an occasion for more, not to mention that he just didn't have the closet space or leisure time to be as well-dressed as he'd like. He was beginning to think of himself as looking a little shabby, quite frankly, when next to Seth, who was always pulled together.

After watching Seth get fitted for a full suit (to be handmade and sent to his New York apartment when finished) and a few dress shirts, Oliver decided that he too might need to spruce up. He pulled a few shirts off the rack—still exquisite—and had the onsite tailor hem them just so.

Seth gave him the final seal of approval by doing a double take when Oliver stepped out of the dressing room in a dress shirt and finely cut jacket in coordinating tweed, the fabric Anthony's was best known for.

"Yeah?" he asked Seth, smoothing a hand down his shirt front.

Seth raised one eyebrow, smiled slowly and sweetly and said, "Very yeah."

The tailor, his mouth full of pins and the tape measure around his neck, turned to look and nodded his approval as well. As if Oliver cared about his opinion; he'd just gotten a compliment of the highest magnitude from Seth "even my underwear coordinates with my socks" Larsen.

A full two hours later—the shopkeeper, pleased to have a Broadway star buying up half the store, had come out with two flutes of champagne for them—they finally left. Seth carried a few bags with him; the rest of his purchases were to be shipped to New York once finished.

"I might as well enjoy my steady employment while I have it, right?"

Oliver gave him a shoulder squeeze in sympathy, but he was certain that this week would not signal the end of Seth's burgeoning career on Broadway.

"When are we supposed to meet Moira?" Seth asked as Oliver shouldered open the door to his flat.

"After eight? She won't mind if we're a little late. She um, has no problem with making new friends."

Seth gave him a questioning look.

Oliver laughed and shook his head. "You'll see."

Seth deposited his bags next to Oliver's wardrobe and stretched his arms out. "That gives us a few hours. Mind if I take a nap?"

"Mind if I join you?" Oliver bit his lip; he hadn't meant to say it, it just slipped out. He was tired, it had been a hell of a day, and the food they'd eaten had made him pleasantly drowsy. He would sleep on the sofa if Seth still needed space.

"Not one bit," Seth replied casually, turning to pull out some of his new things and hang them in preparation for the night.

"Okay." Oliver had his shoes off and was on the left side of the bed faster than Seth could button his newly purchased shirt onto the hanger. He folded his hands over his belly and tried to exude a sense of relaxed friendship; he didn't want to do anything to ruin the peace treaty they'd established.

The problem was that Seth, after slipping off his shoes and climbing onto the bed, immediately curled on his side facing Oliver and wrapped his hand around Oliver's bicep. Not that it was actually a problem for

Oliver. Not at all. He cracked an eye open and saw Seth with his eyes shut, a wistful sort of smile on his face. It wasn't exactly what Oliver wanted to see, but it was far better than the gut-wrenching pain that had been on his face earlier.

"Just an hour, okay?" Seth mumbled.

"M'kay," Oliver agreed. He laid his hand over Seth's and smiled at the warm smoothness of it, sighing as Seth laced their fingers together. He immediately felt slightly less off-kilter, and while the apprehension that everything could still go wrong remained, a part of him simply refused to give up hope that they could find a way to make it work. Their laying together in a moment of unconsciously declared truce fed that tiny ember of hope. And it wasn't anything world-changing; it was just a nap. Oliver stroked his thumb over Seth's hand, smiling as Seth moved just a touch closer and at the hum of pleasure he made.

Oliver was out like a light in two breaths.

Chapter Sixteen

When Oliver woke, the room was dark, save for a sliver of light coming from under the bathroom door. He could hear Seth humming; he must be in there getting dressed, Oliver thought, and pressed the heel of his hand to his eyes, rubbing the sleep out, pushing himself up to a sitting position. It had definitely been more than an hour.

He glanced at his clock: seven-fifty p.m. He quickly pulled out something to change into. Seth came out of the bathroom, all ready, and Oliver couldn't help but let out a low whistle. Seth looked amazing: tailored, together and utterly handsome.

Seth preened a bit, dusting his shoulder in an old, familiar gesture that tugged at something not quite healed over in Oliver's heart. "Not too much?" he asked, a little worry in his expression. He smoothed his perfectly tailored waistcoat over one of his new shirts.

"Not at all. In fact..." Feeling like a tightly wound thread, vibrating and filled with the potential to snap from their proximity, Oliver fished one of the many pocket squares Seth had purchased out of one of his bags and tucked it into the small front pocket of Seth's tweed vest. Seth's chest was solid and firm under Oliver's fingers, his breath warm and sweet against Oliver's cheek.

Oliver took a step back to clear his head and see his handiwork. Seth was breathing slowly, but his eyes were filled with heated longing, and it thrilled Oliver that he could still elicit that reaction.

"Better?" Seth asked, his voice quiet but slightly husky.

It took a lot for Oliver to resist pulling their bodies closer there in the dark room, but he controlled himself. He needed Seth to say it would be okay. "Perfect." Almost overwhelmed with longing, Oliver was the first to break eye contact. He looked over at the clock and made a noise.

"I better get a move on; Moira will be halfway into some stranger's lap if we don't get there soon."

Seth cocked an eyebrow but didn't say anything. Oliver's face heated; he knew it sounded bad, but Seth would soon see for himself what Moira was like.

"I'll, um, just be a minute."

"Take your time; it might be more interesting if your prediction comes true," Seth laughed. He grabbed a magazine from Oliver's dresser and left the room.

Oliver shut the bathroom door and exhaled. In the tiny room, he was immediately surrounded by the warm, spicy scent of Seth's aftershave. He groaned quietly in frustration. He didn't know how he was going to be with Seth for the next week and keep his hands to himself. Of course he would never push anything. But God, the desire to be with him again...

"Why can't he dress in flannel and stained jeans?" he mumbled as he stepped into the shower.

Of course, knowing Seth, he'd make even *that* look good.

* * *

"Ah, there she is." Oliver waved his hand high in the air until he caught Moira's attention. She was in their usual spot at the end of the bar; she'd once told him, "Where the till is, the bartender will be. And where the bartender is, there you'll find me." He had learned early on that the more she drank, the more she had a tendency to rhyme.

He made his way through the crowd of patrons with Seth close by his side, holding his forearm, and his nerves thrummed with pleasure at having Seth so near, holding him. He was nervous and excited for Seth and Moira to meet. They were different, but they had similarities, too: They both spoke their minds; they were both dramatic. Seth was just more, well, buttoned up, whereas Moira would happily pop open every button within reaching distance.

Mostly, he wanted these two people who had meant so much to him over the years to simply like each other. If anything, it would be great to have someone close by to talk with about Seth once he'd gone back to the States.

"Would you get a load of this pack of temptation! Dressing up for me? You flatter me, darlin', but we both know it won't happen." Moira wore the high pink of a few beers. She flashed Oliver a brilliant smile and reached up, wrapping an arm around his neck. "You gorgeous beast, you did this on purpose."

Oliver laughed and self-consciously fussed with his hair and shirt collar. He couldn't accompany Seth for the night and not make an attempt to keep up, so he'd taken a little extra care with his clothes, choosing colors he'd remembered Seth favored on him. Before they left the apartment, Seth had looked at him so appreciatively that he'd begun to blush after Oliver asked if he looked okay.

"Yes, very," had been Seth's breathy reply. The little side-glances Seth had given him on the way over had given him a little boost of confidence, too. With the exception of his trip to see Seth on Broadway, it had been a while since he'd had the chance to dress up, or to go somewhere that wasn't the library or lab.

Oliver leaned over to give Moira's cheek a peck.

"Now, out of my way and let me get my hands on this lovely creature you've brought to meet me," she said.

Seth laughed, a warm liquid sound that made Oliver's stomach loop.

Oliver made the introductions. "Seth? This little elfling is Moira; Moira, this is Seth."

Seth stepped forward, smiling, with his hand out in greeting. "It's very nice to meet y—"

"Enough of that, give us a kiss." Moira grabbed his hand and gave it a tug. Stunned, Seth allowed himself to be manhandled in her strong grip as she pulled him close and kissed each cheek.

"There. Now you've had a bit o' milk, time to focus on the rest of the cow." She waggled her eyebrows at him. "Take a seat, take a seat," she said, motioning to the chairs on either side of her with a shooing motion.

"Uh, Moira?" Oliver leaned in and whispered into her ear. "You're laying it on really thick."

She fixed him with a stare. "Of course I am!" She leaned in and whispered back, "He'll be so terrified, you'll find him shivering in your lap in five minutes, mark my word." She winked at him and hopped off her stool, pushing it out so they sat in more of a triangle than a straight line. At least that way Oliver knew she wouldn't be able to steal a kiss from either of them if they had to lean across her to talk.

"Okay, now that you've given me the tourist version, how about I get to know the real you," Seth said with a determined smile. "Hi! I'm Seth Larsen."

Moira laughed and squeezed his knee. "Excellent. And fine, no more Plastic Paddy." She offered her hand and said, "Moira Byrne, and believe me, the pleasure's all mine."

"That's probably accurate," was Seth's dry reply. Fortunately, Oliver knew that Moira had a liking for a dry sense of humor. He allowed himself to exhale and told himself to not worry that they might hate each other after all.

"So you're a huge star in America, I hear," she said, her eyes glittering with mirth.

Seth tugged on his cuffs, and to Oliver it looked as if he was fighting off a smile.

"Sounds like you've met my father," Seth said.

"Nope! But if he looks like you, I'd like to. Ah, cheers, mate." She took a new beer from the bartender and set it in front of her. "I've just heard you off this one's phone. Beautiful singing voice; matches the rest of you."

Oliver looked around her to send Seth a "please don't hate me?" expression. Seth asked the bartender for a vodka tonic with a lemon twist and said, "I see why you keep her. Where can I find one?"

"We'll set up a loaner system later," Moira said. She bumped her shoulder into Oliver. "And how are you? Any, well... interesting tidbits of information you'd like to share with the class?"

Oliver fixed her with a sour expression and said, "Well, I think Seth and I would like to have a drink or two before all of that, so why don't you tell us what's been happening with you, instead?"

Seth made an excited noise, put his drink down and gave her his full attention. "So! I met Janos. A little birdie told me that you happen to know him *very* well." He made a production of folding his hands in his lap and giving her a massive grin.

"That I do," she said, giving a saucy shake of her head and cackling. "Biblically, you might say. Now, don't go looking at us like that, and you just meeting me and all!" She shook her finger at him when Seth wrinkled up his nose at her confession.

"He's handsome, sure, but..." Seth shook his head a little bit before asking, "Hey, wait a minute. Aren't you doing the 'anti-bully, love the gays' thing with Oliver? Why on earth did you hook up with a homophobe?"

Moira twisted in her seat to give Oliver a turn at her full attention. "Anti-bully, love the gays? You changed the name without telling me?" She rolled her eyes playfully and turned back to Seth. "You do have eyes, don't you?"

Seth, looking slightly wary, answered, "Yes, but—"

"And you're a real live boy with urges and needs, right?"

"Um, I don't think that I—"

"Because let me just tell you. That was an itch I didn't know needed scratching." She kept eye contact with him as she took a long pull off her drink. "Oh, he's thick as mud and half as useful, but Christ does he fill out a pair of trousers."

As she fanned herself, Seth leaned behind her to get Oliver's attention. He mouthed, "Oh. My. God."

Oliver just laughed.

"But you're right, he's a smart as a sack of hammers and as open-minded as a shut door," she sighed.

"Does this mean the backpacking across Hungary is a no?" Oliver asked.

"We-ell," she teased, wriggling in her seat a bit and shoving on Oliver's forearm. "Ask why. Go on."

"Why?" he laughed.

"Oh, that's because I'll be busy, you see." She opened her eyes wide and took a dainty sip from her beer. She even held out her pinky.

"You've worked it enough. Spill," Oliver said.

"I accepted a four-year fellowship at one University of California, Berkeley just this morning, that's why."

"That's wonderful!" Oliver exclaimed, pulling her into a hug.

"Congratulations!" Seth echoed.

She leaned back, beaming at them each in turn. "I was sold on it because it's the school of free love. That sounds perfect for me." She winked at Oliver.

"Oliver still hasn't decided where he's going," Seth said, swirling his glass. He looked at his drink as if it was the most interesting thing in the world.

"He hasn't, has he?" She gave Oliver's knee a squeeze, then motioned for the bartender to bring another round by circling her finger overhead. "Well, Seth, I'll tell you—it's maybe the most difficult decision I've made in my life yet, struth."

"We don't have to do this now," Oliver said, trying to get Seth to look up at him.

Seth sat up, squared his shoulders and took a deep breath. "I want to hear about Moira's choice, though. It'll be interesting to hear how it all works from someone who isn't likely to use Broadway understudies as an example."

Moira looked totally confused at that.

"I don't know this Broadway thing, but I do know that at first, and Oliver will back me up." She turned to face him and rested her arm on the back of her bar stool. "Or he'd better—I was going to take some time off. Travel, that sort of thing. I've been going at it hard for five years, and the thought of another six made me feel melted."

"So what changed that?" Seth asked.

"I went home for the holidays," she laughed. "My da went to university, but no one else in my family did. At first they all teased me, said I was puttin' on airs." She took a long drink after that, pressing the back of her hand to her mouth to wipe away the moisture. "But this last time going home... oh, the stupid articles they pressed at me. They just want me to get married and make babies. I'd rather skip all that and just practice at it, personally."

Seth hummed a little laugh at her. Oliver had known about her family's background, but thought most of it was put on for his benefit: the "Plastic Paddy" act.

"So, my mam pulled me aside and said enough was enough, it was time to stop *thinking* I was smart and 'do the smart thing.'" She shrugged but smiled. Oliver noticed the smile didn't quite reach her eyes. "So I am. I'm doing the smart thing. Making sure that I will always have the credentials to have the life and respect I deserve."

Seth reached over and delicately patted her arm in sympathy.

"And it doesn't hurt that it's the top-ranked graduate program in the whole world, and don't let this one," she pointed her thumb at Oliver, "tell you otherwise."

Oliver rubbed her back with one hand. "I'm really happy for you."

"Prove it by buying a round! What is this, a funeral?" She polished off her beer. "Christ, I've seen livelier wakes than this. Lots more nudity, too."

Seth choked on his drink as she laughed and pounded on his back.

* * *

Seth swore that Moira had drugged him, because in twenty-plus years not even his own *father* had ever gotten him to play darts; but she had managed it somehow. He also told Oliver later that he was not surprised to find that he was excellent at it.

"With all of the daydreaming I did of throwing sharpened pencils into the faces of bullies in middle school, it just felt natural."

He also swore to Oliver that he didn't drink much that night, but she somehow managed to get him tipsy. Not drunk, just loose-limbed and laughing. After the day they'd had, Oliver was glad to see him relaxed and happy.

As the night went on, the bar began to get crowded, and the table they'd moved to near the dartboard became hot property. When Seth moved to sit down after a turn at the board, someone had taken his chair. He raised an eyebrow at Oliver, who immediately made to stand up and give Seth his seat. Seth rolled his eyes, pushed Oliver back into his seat and then perched on his lap sideways, draping one arm over Oliver's broad shoulders, his fingers trailing over the thick, rounded muscle as Oliver held onto his waist.

"You were right. She's fun," Seth said, his mouth close to Oliver's ear to make sure that he could hear over the din.

Oliver's eyes closed and he shivered from the sensation. His hand naturally migrated to the side of Seth's thigh to hold him in place, and he pressed his face into Seth's chest, just breathing him in. Seth's fingers on his shoulder sent electric pulses shooting through him, centered at his aching heart.

It was like being a teenager again, the way his stomach bubbled and fizzed, and yet he felt tied up in knots, wondering where the night could go. He had the hyper-aware feeling that Seth wanted him, and knew that the possibility of intimacy was becoming more likely as the night went on. And he had that amazing sensation of time, which seemed to race at breakneck speed and yet in certain moments almost froze in flashes, like snapshots for him to dream over later. As when Seth, impeccably dressed, laughed at something flattering that an older gentleman said to him regarding his waistcoat; and when, his familiar fashion-fervor lighting up his eyes, he admired the man's Donegal newsboy cap in turn. Like when Seth turned to look at Oliver over his shoulder, having made three bullseyes in a row. He looked proud, a little surprised, and pink with both excitement and drink.

"Oliver?" Seth's fingers had moved to twine and ruffle the shorter hair at Oliver's nape by this point, and Oliver wanted to sit in the silly pub forever if it meant Seth never stopped what he was doing.

"Mm?" Oliver tightened his arm around Seth's waist when he rested his cheek against Oliver's hair. Seth was close enough for his body heat to seep into Oliver's skin, for the delicate scent of his cologne to be evident, for Oliver to be soothed by the gentle rise and fall of his breathing.

"I want us to have a special place together."

Oliver's chest constricted painfully; Seth sounded so... despondent. Suddenly, he wanted Seth to turn back into the laughing, joy-filled person who, just an hour ago, had praised an old man with a pipe, saying that he was the "epitome of the classic British gentleman."

"I don't want to visit your tree. I don't want you to visit my corner." Seth sighed and ran the flat of his hand down Oliver's back and up again, curling his fingers at the nape of Oliver's neck and tangling them in the hairs there. "Are we just not meant to have something that's *ours*?" Seth's voice broke at the end. He turned to kiss the crown of Oliver's head and said, "Is that what we're not admitting ourselves?"

Oliver squeezed the leg that Seth had draped over him and held him just so. It didn't matter that they were in a public place; Oliver could barely hear the buzz of the crowd over the pounding of his own heart. He shut his eyes tight and pressed his face into Seth's side, the silk of the pocket square momentarily cooling his heated cheek. "I want us to have that, too. I always have."

Seth kissed the top of his head again and leaned back to his ear. "I want so—this might be it, this time together. Let's enjoy it. We don't know what's going to happen, and I just really need to have this time with you. Let's just enjoy this, please?" It was the please that broke him. For Seth to plead with him—for him to think that there was anything Oliver wouldn't give him...

But that wasn't exactly true, was it? He wasn't able to give Seth a definitive answer to the most important question for their future. He gave Seth one more squeeze. He needed to hang on to this moment, to burn the feeling of Seth holding him into his memory before he finally looked up to say fervently, meaning it with everything in him, "That's what I want, Seth."

"Oh, and don't I hate to break up this pretty picture!" To her credit, Moira truly looked flustered. "But if you don't take your turn, Oliver, I think these old geezers are going to break our kneecaps." Moira pointed over her shoulder at the group of men who had edged closer to their table over the past half-hour.

Oliver looked up at her; he must have looked either exhausted or devastated, given her reaction.

"Screw the darts; let's take a bit of a break, aye?" She cupped both of their faces and jerked her head toward the other corner of the bar. "There's a sofa in the corner that's free; grab that while I nick us a round."

She hurried off to the bar before they could argue. Seth got to his feet and held out his hand, a sad little smile on his face. "Come on. I'll let you be the little spoon."

Oliver dropped his chin and smiled against the hot prickle building behind his eyes. "You know that's my favorite."

"I do indeed," Seth said, tucking Oliver's arm around his and leading him back to a well-worn Chesterfield. Seth sat against the arm and patted the space to his right, sliding his arm along the back of the sofa as Oliver slipped in next to him.

Oliver noted that the crowd was the usual mix of students, older academics who lived in the city and locals. People from all over came to this particular place, but it had a homey air about it and, for all its notoriety, it was still a neighborhood pub. And while it wasn't quite the same as New York, it also wasn't unusual for same sex couples to be out and about in Cambridge.

Oliver reached his hand up to clasp Seth's, just at Oliver's shoulder, and Seth linked his other hand with Oliver's, pulling him back against himself. They sat quietly, wrapped in each other, pressed temple to cheek. It was undeniably bittersweet. Every time the "this could be it" thought rose up, Oliver quashed it with a counter-thought, "but this could be how it always is," and let hope have its moment for a change. Seth was right; they needed to enjoy this time together, regardless of the outcome, and stay positive and hopeful.

He turned his head and pressed his forehead into Seth's neck, breathing him in. "I still get to go to New York next week, remember."

Seth inhaled slowly, deeply. He squeezed Oliver's hand in his. "How long are you there?"

"I don't know. They just said to come." Oliver leaned back, searching Seth's face for just the slightest hint that he'd not given up yet, that this wouldn't be it. "So that's something we can plan tomorrow, maybe? We could see if there's a seat free on your flight back?"

Seth smiled at that, a genuinely warm and happy smile, and buried his face in Oliver's hair once again. It went a long way toward soothing Oliver's bruised and aching heart. Seth nuzzled behind Oliver's ear and murmured, "That would be great. Let's look at that first thing tomorrow morning, okay?"

"Whatever you want."

Seth's body briefly went rigid around him and his smile faded. He buried his face in the back of Oliver's hair again and shuddered. Oliver realized that it was a lie—it *wasn't* whatever Seth wanted. He needed to control his impulsive habit of saying whatever popped into his head. He pulled Seth's hand to his lips and placed a chaste kiss on it in apology. It wasn't enough, he knew, but it was something.

Moira arrived, balancing two huge pints and Seth's highball in one of her tiny hands like a professional.

"You either were a waitress or a world-class juggler in a previous life," Seth said to her.

She laughed. "I've four brothers, and guess who's expected to keep them in beer when the telly's on? And why do you suppose I want to get to California so badly?" She gave him a wink and sat in a deep wingback chair adjacent to the sofa.

"Oliver? You know I love ya dearly, right?"

"Of course!"

"And Seth, I have to come clean. If given the chance, I'd wrassle you to the ground with my legs for a chance at him, I would."

Seth laughed loudly and sharply, completely caught off guard.

She sat back in the chair, looking pleased with herself. "So with all of our late-night confessions out in the open, making us all nothing but the very best of friends, allow me to give you a bit of advice without actually being a wonk and telling you what to do."

Oliver and Seth shared an "uh oh" look and turned back to her.

"A pair of gorgeous idjits, the both of you." She sighed and leaned forward, her hands on her knees and a sweet smile on her face that made her look older and wiser than her twenty-five years. "Sure and I'm Catholic," she rolled her eyes and crossed herself, "but I know this in my gut: This is it, this life. You make the most of what you have, because you just never know. Life isn't measured by the number of breaths you take, but by the moments that take your breath away. Don't forget to leave room for that, my doves."

She gave Oliver's knee a squeeze and Seth a cheerless wink. After sitting back and watching them for a moment, she tilted her head and said, "Boys, you're terrible company tonight. Go on with you and get someplace quiet, and leave me to checking out the talent here before I call the night a waste." She smiled at Oliver to show that she wasn't angry in the slightest and rose to her feet.

"Seth? Lovely to meet you." The boys broke apart to get up and hug her goodbye. She gave Seth a tight squeeze while Seth looked over her head at Oliver, befuddled and bemused, and then hugged Oliver. She got up on tiptoe to get close to his ear and whispered fiercely, "Wise up, you gack! He's struck dumb with love for you, and a blind man could see you feel the same. You should find a way to make it work, lad."

She pulled back and held his face in her hands, clucking her tongue sadly. "Give us a kiss and off with you, then."

Oliver chuckled a sad laugh and obliged, kissing her cheek, but the laugh turned into a genuine sound of amusement when she made an angry noise at not getting a proper kiss. She shoved him at Seth, shaking her head and walked off to the bar, laughing. Toward a group of moderately attractive guys, he noted.

"I bet if scientists studied her for a year, we could solve the world's energy problem," Seth mused.

Oliver took a moment to just look at Seth. His clothes and hair were perfect, of course, but that wasn't what Oliver wanted to brand on his memory. It was the way the far-off look in Seth's eyes as he watched Moira walk away changed into something intimate and charged, something that left him feeling slightly breathless as Seth's heated gaze drifted back to him. That Seth could still look at him as if he wanted everything Oliver was and could be warmed him to his core and reminded him that he shouldn't even think of giving up on this chance they had.

Moira was right. He was stupidly, completely and woefully in love with the man. It could be argued that this made their unsolved problem worse, but it was true. Oliver loved everything about him: his proud and determined spirit; his long, lean frame; his graceful movements; the tilt of his head as he thought; the smile at the corner of his mouth when he was amused. The way he kept himself back to keep from being hurt, because when he let himself relax—when he let himself relax with *Oliver*—it was a gift. It was Seth trusting him, and Seth didn't trust just anyone.

"Ready to go home?"

Seth sighed around a smile. "No. I still have a week, remember?"

It was a painful but necessary reminder that this would never be Seth's home. Oliver's breathing went shallow; it hurt too much to breathe deeply and force his lungs to press against his aching heart. "Ready to come back to my current home with me, then?"

"You had me at current." Seth slipped his arm in Oliver's and allowed himself to be led outside.

Oliver didn't have a response, but he gathered that Seth knew that. They walked out together to hail a cab, not speaking except for Oliver giving directions to the cabbie. Seth held Oliver against him for the short ride back, and with his cheek pressed against Seth's, their hands woven together, Oliver allowed himself to simply appreciate the moment. His worry over the unknown was like acid eating away at him, and he wanted something to just feel *right* as the day came to a close.

After paying the fare and quietly entering the house—Janos had practice early in the morning—Oliver closed the door to his bedroom and reached out for Seth's hand.

"Can I just... can we just hold each other tonight? I'm not asking for you to do anything more. I just want—I just want to hold you." He felt desperate and needy, but he also thought Seth might not refuse him, not after the overtures Seth had made to him all night.

With a shy smile, Seth answered, "Please."

Oliver swung their hands between their bodies and smiled. "I'll meet you in bed?"

Something painful moved behind Seth's eyes; Oliver was aware of his own throat constricting. "Deal."

He made quick work of changing into something comfortable to sleep in and brushed his teeth in Janos's bathroom. He slipped into the cool sheets of his bed, arms crossed behind his head, and waited for Seth.

He knew that this was what he wanted; he wanted every night to end this way, with Seth climbing into his bed. He wanted to wake up every day with Seth at his side. He wanted to come home and have holidays and Saturday trips to the market and Sunday brunch in bed and all of it with Seth. He still held the belief that even if he stayed in England, it would just be a few years apart and then sixty or more together. It was foolish, given how Seth thought about his own ability to endure a long separation, but he just couldn't see a future that didn't have Seth in it.

Stepping out of the small bathroom, Seth shut off the light and quietly made his way back to the bed. Oliver flipped down the blankets and patted the mattress. Seth sat on the edge of the bed, staring down at his hands.

"You okay?"

Seth kicked off his slippers, slipped into bed and wrapped his arms around Oliver's sides, burying his face in Oliver's neck. Oliver pulled the blankets up to cover them, wrapped Seth up in his arms and drew warm, soothing patterns on his skin.

"When did it all get so hard?" Seth asked, his breath hot and ticklish against Oliver's neck.

Oliver looked at the ceiling, his throat working to swallow the bitterness of not having an answer.

Seth curled in tighter and tangled their legs together. "Tomorrow. That's when we look at flights, okay?"

Oliver buried a hand in Seth's hair, grateful that, for all of his dumb mistakes, for all the ways their lives hadn't gone the way they'd dreamed, Seth was still willing to try. "Yes."

They held each other there in the dark. As sleep began to pull at Oliver, he kissed Seth's forehead and whispered against his skin, "I love you." It was how he'd imagined every night ending before reality had pulled the two of them apart.

Seth kissed his shoulder and, his voice endearingly earnest, he whispered back, "I love you, too."

This is how every night is supposed to end, Oliver thought, as a few tears slipped down his face.

Chapter Seventeen

Oliver slowly rose to consciousness the next morning, a gradual awareness. And he was aware that he was warm and tangled up. He blinked his eyes open to see blue silk—Seth's pajamas. They must have switched positions in the night; Oliver was laying sprawled across Seth's torso while Seth worked his fingers through his messy hair, lightly scratching his scalp. He murmured quiet happy noises and buried his face under Seth's chin, squeezing tight when Seth laughed.

"That feels good," Oliver moaned, curling his shoulders in and flexing his feet. "Have you been awake a long time?"

"No, just a few minutes. I started to get out of bed, and you launched yourself at me. Pretty impressive given you were still snoring."

Oliver pushed up on his hands. "I don't snore!"

Seth barely held back his smile. "No, you don't, I'm just teasing. You *do* smack your lips and mutter, though." He ran the flat of his hand over Oliver's hair, pushing it off his forehead. "It's pretty cute."

Oliver blushed, groaned and smiled all at once, and he pressed his face back into Seth's neck. The tiny vibrations from Seth's laughing throat sent shivers down Oliver's body. It was a pretty terrific way to wake up.

"As much as I enjoy your human blanket, I really need to use the facilities."

Oliver laughed and rolled off him, starfishing in the bed as Seth stood. "Sorry about that."

"I said I enjoyed it, Oliver," Seth replied, smiling back at him as he shut the bathroom door.

This was a big day, Oliver knew. He might not be able to give either school a definitive answer today, but he and Seth could plan his trip to New York, and then he could let Dr. Jones know when to expect him.

And he needed to make sure Seth understood that, while this decision was important, he was too. Oliver was beginning to realize that Seth had held back not just because of the potential of being hurt, but because he saw this as an either-or situation. That was the *only* way Seth could see it. Cambridge or Seth, not New York and Seth *or* Cambridge and Seth in a few years.

Which was exactly how Oliver had seen it: He could have his Seth and academics too, even if it involved a long wait. "Ever the optimist," Seth had called him, and it was true. He'd been blinding himself to the reality that he wouldn't always be able to make things work. That the compromises that he'd come up with weren't always acceptable to others, no matter how willing Oliver himself was to bend for them.

A few years ago, fresh from the heartbreak with Seth, and this decision would have been easy. Love; always choose love. But he'd lived enough life and come to enough realizations about his parents' relationship and about himself to know that being miserable with a career or from taking the wrong path could be destructive to a partner. Regret—he never wanted to live with regret. Mistakes could be remedied, but whole-life changes weren't the same thing.

Seth—who had lost a parent, almost lost the other and was forced into an adult role far too early—had realized this a long time ago. With a sickening feeling of shame, Oliver finally understood how cruel it had been, for these past few months, to entertain the idea that it would be okay, no matter what, and just expect Seth to go along with either decision. Oliver was a bit of a people-pleaser, though he didn't think of it as a negative characteristic, as he knew others did; and he finally got just how arrogant it was to have thought Seth would be willing to be dragged along in the hopes that possibly one day Oliver could make him happy.

He ran the flat of his hand over the still-warm pillow on Seth's side of the bed. Seth was even more remarkable than Oliver had given him credit for. He was still the boy who would patiently wait for Oliver to choose him over his own fear, patiently wait even as his own heart was aching. He had become the man who would put that same aching heart on the line for a chance to be with Oliver again.

It was beyond humbling. Oliver covered his face with both hands and let himself feel the shame—he deserved it. He finally understood what Seth had meant all those years ago: Oliver was always making Seth wait. It had taken him forever to recognize how amazing Seth was when they were teenagers, and that being in love openly was better than hiding from his father and being miserable. While Seth was struggling with his first year in New York, waiting for Oliver to come, Oliver had been comfortable at home as he took his time with his decision about Brandeis, and then taking even longer to bother to tell Seth about it.

And now Seth was in his house, in England for crying out loud, waiting once again to see if Oliver would make him a priority.

He had never felt lower or angrier with himself than he did in that moment; he wanted desperately to tell Seth that they would be together from that moment on, and he knew that he couldn't say that.

Seth was definitely the more realistic man in their relationship, but Oliver would gladly spend the rest of his life making up for his own lack of foresight if given the chance.

After a moment of wallowing, he got to his feet and pulled an outfit out of the wardrobe. Today would be all for Seth. Oliver would do just about anything to show him how grateful he was for the chance to love Seth as he deserved.

* * *

Oliver wouldn't let Seth get on his laptop after they'd had coffee and pastries. Janos had brought some back after his first morning practice, telling Seth to "Eat, eat!" and making an assured thumbs-up at him. Seth was reaching for his fourth and trying to snake Oliver's laptop off his legs at the same time.

"*No,*" Oliver laughed, twisting away and taking his computer with him. "You just want to look up reviews for David's performances."

Seth grumbled and shoved a bite into his mouth.

"We decided that Saturday would be our day of joyful mocking at how he flopped, and I'm sticking to that plan," Oliver said.

"We might be looking up notices for auditions instead of mocking, you know."

Oliver took the last pastry out of the paper box, tore it in half—well, sixty-forty—and gave the larger piece to Seth as a consolation. "Now let me check flight seating."

Seth gave him a look and shoved the whole thing in his mouth, crossing his arms and working his toes under Oliver's leg on the sofa. "Is this place ever warm? I didn't think I'd need to pack toe warmers."

Oliver laughed and scrolled through the screen to see all of the available seats on Seth's flight. Then he pulled up his email and began typing a response to Maeve Jones, letting her know that he would be available to fly to the States on the upcoming Monday, arriving in the early evening, if that was acceptable.

"I'm going to go ahead and book it, I think. There are only a few seats left on your flight. Is that okay?"

Seth wrapped his arms around his knees and smiled at him. "Very."

Oliver exhaled, feeling energized at the idea of going back to New York together and getting closer to making an informed decision. "So, let's see..." Oliver checked his watch and did a little math. "It's not quite six o'clock in New York, so we have a few hours to kill before I get a response." Oliver set his laptop on the coffee table and stretched his arms high overhead, arching his back. "Any ideas?"

Seth coughed, turning away; he'd been staring at Oliver.

"What?" Oliver asked, tugging his shirt down.

Seth shook his head and smiled.

"Whaaat?" Oliver asked, nudging Seth's leg.

"Nothing," Seth said, turning his head away to laugh softly. He cleared his throat and turned back, the color high in his cheeks. "So! A few hours to kill?" He thought for a moment before getting excited and asking, "Could we do one of those flat-bottomed canoe tours?"

"Only if you asked the rental desk for a flat-bottomed canoe," Oliver teased. "Want to make it a full-fledged picnic?"

Seth brightened and squeezed Oliver's forearm. "Can we?"

"Of course; whatever you'd like. But the important question is this: Hire a student, or try to do it ourselves?"

"Oh." Seth seemed to take this very seriously, resting his arm on the back of the sofa and thinking. It was adorable. It was just punting; plus, the tourist season hadn't really started, so there weren't many people expected on the water, especially not on a weekday.

"I have absolutely no idea how to drive one of those things," Seth said, tapping his chin. "Do you?" He looked expectantly at Oliver.

"I've done it a couple of times. I mean, I'm no expert, but I think I can manage to not bang into anyone else."

A slow, saucy smile spread on Seth's face. "Will you wear a striped shirt and a straw boater? Sing me songs in Italian?"

Oliver laughed at that. "One, those are gondolas, not punts, and two, I'm pretty sure that I've never owned a straw boater."

"Party pooper. Can we bring a blanket and a picnic basket? Oh." Seth leaned forward and placed his hand on Oliver's forearm, concerned. "Do you *have* a picnic basket?"

"Sadly, no. But the place we'll rent the boat from has a ready-to-go picnic. I assume you want the full English experience?" Seth nodded, beaming from ear to ear. Oliver was feeling better about things just watching Seth's growing excitement.

"Of course!"

"Okay, then. Will you trust me?"

Seth stretched his legs out, hopped to his feet and held a hand out to Oliver to pull him up. "That sounds like the start of every wacky rom-com adventure movie ever."

"I promise," Oliver laughed, "there will be no kidnappings by dimwitted pirates, no secret agents planting microfilm on us, and no getting swept up in a failed jewel heist."

"Too bad about that last one."

Oliver graciously offered Seth first dibs on the shower. He used that time to call Granta Moorings and make sure that they would be able to get "The English Hamper;" Seth was going to get the full UK experience, with Pimm's and a few other key items.

"Thank you very much," Oliver told the clerk, and hung up. He whistled under his breath as he dug around the bottom of his wardrobe for his well-worn boat shoes, grinning in anticipation of a great day.

* * *

Having hired the punt and gotten the blanket and cushions situated just so inside the boat, Oliver knelt down and began rolling up his pant legs.

"Are you planning on getting wet?" Seth asked, twisting from the bottom of the boat as Oliver stepped off the dock and onto the boat's stern. He grabbed the pole and grinned down at Seth.

"Hush, it's tradition."

"Mm," Seth hummed, but Oliver could see him smiling.

"Plus, I happen to have it on good authority that you like my ankles."

"Slanderous lies." Looking ahead, Seth crossed his leg over his knee, smoothing the tan linen and bouncing his foot, which was stylishly sheathed in a bicolored Oxford.

"Seriously, though," Oliver said cautiously.

Seth twisted back around, a look of worry creeping onto his face.

"There will be some water splashes, so if you stay to my right, you shouldn't get any wet drips or anything from my pole."

Seth put his face in his hands at his lap and his body shook with laughter.

"Oh my God... that's not what—" Oliver rubbed his face with his free hand and laughed at himself. He cleared his throat and tried to adopt a voice of authority. "Are you ready to take this seriously?"

Seth wiped all hilarity from his face and gave Oliver a salute. "Aye, aye, Captain!" He turned forward again and rested his elbows on the till near Oliver's feet.

Oliver grasped the long pole and pushed it down to the bottom of the river, using his feet to turn the boat as his arms used the pole for leverage. It took him a few strokes to get the hang of it: drop, push, hand over hand, let the pole float like a rudder behind the boat, repeat. The day was mostly overcast and a little chilly, but Oliver felt perfectly warmed by the activity as they made their way up the River Cam.

"It's so beautiful," Seth murmured as they passed under the Bridge of Sighs. They continued heading north toward a particular park Oliver favored at a slow but steady pace; the trees were leafing out in an almost neon green, the grass was lush, and a light breeze cast gentle ripples along the surface of the water that broke in the wake of their boat.

It really was one of the most beautiful ways to see the city, and with it being off-season and a weekday, it seemed as though they had the river to themselves. Oliver enjoyed the steady action of pushing them off, letting the pole drag behind the boat, and repeating the pattern over and over again, his mind free to take in the beautiful setting—mostly centered on the handsome man sitting by his knees, murmuring over the pretty sights.

"Just say when you'd like to eat and I'll dock us."

"Are you getting tired?" Seth asked. He let his head drop back between his elbows to smile up at Oliver.

Oliver almost forgot to push off on the pole and nearly dropped it. He cleared his throat and focused before answering, "No, not at all. It feels good to use my muscles for more than cracking books. I feel like I've been cooped up for months."

They floated on, past the end of the university grounds and farther on, where huge willow trees draped across the water. The steady sound of the water against the hull of the boat was soothing.

Seth dropped his head back again to look up at Oliver. "If you decide to go with Silver, are you going to miss this?"

Oliver held the pole so that it floated out behind the punt and ran his hand through his hair, a little damp at his temples from the exertion. "I... no. I mean, don't get me wrong, I've enjoyed it here. But it's just a place."

Seth sat back upright and nodded, looking out over the water. After a moment he said, "Can we pull over there?" He pointed to the right bank, where there were trees and not much else. It was where Oliver had been heading, anyway.

With a little effort, using his feet and the pole as leverage, he managed to run the boat alongside the stone barrier close enough to hop off easily. He dropped the pole on the ground, offered a hand to Seth to hoist him onto dry land, and they both tugged the boat up on the stone levee, sideways to keep it from drifting off.

The two of them got the blanket, cushions and hamper set up quickly and settled in. Fortunately the tree cover was thick enough that the ground wasn't too damp from the earlier rains, and the blanket was thick wool.

When the smell of the food hit Oliver, he realized just how hungry he'd gotten. Seth took a moment to lay everything out and held up the bottle of Pimm's with a questioning look.

"Is this soda? Or lemonade?"

"Pimm's, my dear boy," Oliver said with an ostentatious fake accent, "is the very essence of a British summer." He cracked the top and poured, saying in his normal voice, "Even though it's not summer. It's nice and has a bit of a kick to it. Like light beer, nothing crazy."

They dove into the food, Seth graciously thanking him for the suggestion that they eat now. Of all the good things packed in the hamper, Oliver was most excited for the scones and clotted cream. Seth made a face, saying, "I try to not eat foods with the word 'clot' in the name."

Oliver scooped up a small amount of cream with a bit of scone and held it out him. "Seth," he whined, "it's so good, though. It's like—hmm. It's not sweet butter, and it's not crème fraîche; it's in between. Just taste it." He made puppy eyes at Seth, wiggling the bite back and forth to tempt him.

Seth rolled his eyes and leaned forward, opening his mouth so Oliver could pop the bite in. Seth thoughtfully chewed it, closed his eyes as he swallowed and said, "Oh my *God.*"

"Good, huh?" Oliver said, smiling broadly and spreading more on another bite.

"Oh my *God.*"

Laughing, Oliver held out more, which Seth had no problem taking. Watching Seth with his eyes closed as he moaned was starting to have an effect on him, however. Oliver was growing increasingly aware of how handsome Seth was, how close they were to each other and how romantic the setting was. He needed to slow his thoughts and relax—well, as much as he could in present company; he lay down on his side, stretched out with his head propped on his hand and breathed slowly and deeply, the peace of the day beginning to creep in and settle him.

"Do we have to rush back, or anything like that?" Seth asked.

"Nope." Oliver sighed happily. Pleasantly full, a little tired, and here in solitude with Seth in a beautiful location: It was a great day. "We can take as long as we'd like."

"Oh, good." Seth stretched out alongside Oliver. "So," Seth asked, his voice soft and hesitant. "It's just a place?"

Oliver traced his finger along the lines that made up the plaid on the blanket, a little undone by how close Seth was to him just then. He forced himself to pay attention. "What's that?"

"Here. Cambridge. It's just a place?"

"I... well, yes. I'm not planning on growing old here; it's not my dream destination for my life, if that's what you mean?"

Seth sighed pleasantly and rolled on his back, hands behind his head. "That's what I mean."

Oliver watched as Seth's eyes closed and he breathed serenely, a small smile at the corners of his mouth.

"Seth, I... I realized something today. And you're going to laugh at me because it should have been obvious."

Seth turned his head and regarded him for a moment, and then smiled and rolled his head back where it had been and closed his eyes again. "It always did take you a bit to, um, process certain things."

"I've really been unfair to you."

Shaking his head, Seth reached out, holding his hand toward Oliver; he took it and sighed, shoulders dropping at Seth's smile.

"And I get it. I really do." Oliver rolled to his back, still clasping Seth's hand in his. "I just want to be with you. I'm willing to wait, to work for it, whatever I can do. But I shouldn't have expected *you* to be willing to wait." It was upsetting to realize how wrong he'd been on that count, to realize that he'd been unconsciously hurting the person who meant the most to him. "I want you to know that to me, you're always worth it."

He felt Seth drop his hand and his heart lurched until he sensed Seth moving beside him. He opened his eyes to find Seth leaning over him, propped on his elbow.

"I want to be with you, too," Seth sighed, drawing his knuckles gently down Oliver's cheek. "I don't think I ever stopped wanting that, honestly." Seth laughed softly, a little sadly, too. "I don't think I ever stopped hoping for it, Oliver, not for years. Up until now I think I've been upset with myself for wanting it to come true without any hope that it actually could. Nothing has hurt me like losing you did, Oliver. You were everything to me."

Oliver reached up to take hold of Seth's hand and kissed the backs of his fingers, drawing his lips lightly across the soft skin as he tried to control his breathing and racing heart. Watching Seth lean to kiss him made it seem as if everything had switched to slow motion, and he marveled at the dappled light behind Seth's head making a corona around his soft brown hair, the startling color of his eyes, his soft, pink lips barely parted as he moved closer, and then Oliver was lost in the sensation of kissing this man he loved with everything in him.

It should have felt ridiculously clichéd, the two of them in the woods on a blanket with a picnic, kissing, but for Oliver it was the furthest thing from it. It was Seth, there with him in every sense of the word, Seth who wanted *him* and was finally able to say it, Seth, kissing him and making tiny, needy noises at the back of his throat when Oliver's fingers sank into his hair, holding him close.

It was perfect.

Oliver drew one hand down Seth's back, applying a little pressure to let him know that it was okay to rest his weight on Oliver. He wanted Seth as close as he could get him. They kissed slowly, languidly, as if they had all the time in the world. Oliver wanted that to be true. He sighed and turned his head as Seth kissed along his jaw, splaying his hands against the soft fabric of Seth's sweater and nuzzling Oliver's hairline behind his ear. He cried out Seth's name in a needy gasp when Seth buried his hands in Oliver's hair and groaned softly against the tender skin of Oliver's neck.

"I want this, Seth, I want this *always.*"

Seth's breath stuttered warmly against Oliver's skin and Oliver tightened his hold, his arms crossing over each other at Seth's back, wanting to never let him go. The cold of the ground seeping through the blanket couldn't compete with the warmth of Seth's body. It stoked something inside of him. Desire, yes, but simple longing, too, to share every day between them; to have inside jokes, wordless conversations across rooms at boring parties, chores and routines and love—so much love that other people thought of them when they imagined what their own lives could be.

He wanted anniversaries and birthdays and bad days and days when they couldn't bring themselves to leave their bed because they hadn't loved each other enough to justify going out in the world just yet.

But it was still a want. It wasn't an assured thing, and that was pure agony.

They held each other as their breathing evened out, even though the passion still burned in Oliver's skin to have Seth, to kiss every inch of him while telling him that he was it, he was everything.

He drew his hand up the back of Seth's neck to hold him close. "I love you so much."

Seth pulled back, smiling even though hurt and longing both still shone wetly in his eyes, and said, "I know you do. I do." He kissed each corner of Oliver's lips and his cheek and lay back against him, arms sliding under his body to hold Oliver close. "I love you, too."

They stayed that way for some time, holding each other, trading soft kisses and quiet murmurs of affection and need until Oliver felt almost drunk with it. His back pocket vibrated; his smartphone.

"Seth?"

"Mm?" Seth asked, kissing along the tendon of Oliver's neck to end with him burying his nose in the tender crook of Oliver's neck.

Oliver's hands curled against Seth's shoulders, holding him there as he shivered. "Hmm, that tickles. I think I just got a reply email."

"Was that why your butt vibrated?"

Oliver nodded, and his laugh turned into a quiet moan as Seth dragged his teeth lightly along the edge of Oliver's ear.

"Do you need to get that?" Seth whispered, making the hairs on Oliver's arm stand up.

"Oh..." Oliver's leg twitched from the tickling sensation coursing through him at the touch of Seth's lips on his neck. "Well, it's just that it might be Silver—about me going back to New York?"

Seth kissed his neck once more with a loud smack and pulled back. "Yes, I'd say you do need to get that." He rolled off of Oliver and sat up as Oliver raised his hips to grab his phone from his back pocket. Spam, spam, department mixer invitation, and there it was: Dr. Jones's reply.

He scanned over it quickly, smiling as he read her excitement that he was going to take them up on the offer.

He smiled up at Seth and joked, "So... got a spare sofa I can crash on for a few days?"

Seth grabbed his forearm. "You get to come?"

"I get to come," Oliver said, smiling as Seth dropped back on top of him and kissed him breathless. Oliver wrapped his arms tightly around Seth, gave him a squeeze and rolled them over.

Seth laughed. He put his hands on Oliver's chest and working his fingers in little circles. "And no, I don't have a sofa that you can crash on. I have a loveseat, and even if I folded you in half you wouldn't be able to sleep comfortably."

"Oh. Okay, sure. Yeah, that's—"

"Oh my God, don't be stupid." Seth shook his head and pulled Oliver down for another kiss, this one less frenzied.

"But Mr. Larsen, wherever shall I—ah!—sleep?" Oliver tried to act suave and pulled together, but Seth knew how much Oliver loved to have his hair tugged to expose his neck. Which was what Seth had done, and where he was currently kissing.

Seth dropped his head back to the blanket and smiled slowly and sweetly, his eyes heavy-lidded. "Mm, the bathtub, of course."

Oliver dropped all of his weight onto Seth, earning an "Oof!" as Seth tried to draw in enough air to laugh. Still smiling, he pushed Oliver off and onto his side.

"So, what *do* you want to be when you grow up, Mr. Andrews?" Seth asked, pressing the flat of his hand over Oliver's heart and working his thumb back and forth over the smooth material of Oliver's shirt.

Oliver blinked a few times to shake off the haze of lust clouding his brain. He shook his head and laughed at himself.

"Well, I've thought a lot about taking what I've learned through research and using it to work one-on-one with people, you know? Counseling individuals and their families. But then I think that it might be better to work on a larger scale, like, run a facility that specifically targets communities where people who identify as LGBT don't feel safe, and work on changing that."

Seth hummed appreciatively. "Tough job."

Oliver nodded. "That's why I need a tough school."

Seth sat up, folding his legs neatly to the side and poured them both fresh drinks. "So you have to figure out which school is going to help you achieve that."

Oliver crossed his legs, leaning back on his hands, and sighed. "Yeah. I know what Cambridge has to offer; it's just a matter of finding out exactly what Silver can do for me."

"What *does* Cambridge have to offer?" Seth asked. "I want you to explain them both to me so I understand what you're going through."

Some of the weight that had been pressing down on Oliver lifted; Seth wanted to be a part of this. That was where Oliver had gone wrong, initially: keeping Seth out of the discussion. If they were going to come out together on the other side of this, they'd need to avoid making the mistakes they made the first time around.

Exhaling sharply through his nose, Oliver worried his bottom lip, trying to think of the best way to explain it. "Well, Cambridge carries huge prestige, so that's helpful no matter where I go. It's an excellent research facility. On the wobble list would be that I would mostly be on a computer. Not a lot of one-on-one or group work."

Seth was watching him intently, nodding his head.

"I'd be acting as an administrator for most of my time here, you know, managing the project, not doing as much fieldwork."

"And that's what you like?" Seth asked.

Oliver ran his hand through his hair. "I... don't know yet. On the one hand, it might be good to know how to run something this huge. It definitely could carry over."

He was silent for a moment. Did he want to be in charge of people doing the work, or do the work himself?

"So!" Seth said, drawing Oliver's attention back to the conversation. "Pros and cons for Silver?"

"For one, you're there," Oliver said, grinning.

Even though he blushed, Seth gave Oliver a "get serious" look. "Schools. We're talking about schools."

"Well, they want me because of this project I'm doing here."

"You'd kind of be like a rock star?" Seth asked, smirking.

It was Oliver's turn to blush. "I don't know about *that*, but it would get my foot in a lot of doors there. Plus, they're paying for all six years; I just have to work those last three. That's going to be tight financially, but not as tight as staying here, so that's a huge consideration. I really don't want to keep asking my father for money. The big difference is that I'd be working with kids and their families almost right away."

Seth looked off at the water, seemingly lost in thought.

After a few moments, Oliver said softly, "Hey, where'd you go?"

"Sorry," Seth apologized. "Just thinking. There's really just the one question you have to ask yourself, you know. Do you want to work in an office or do you want to work with people?"

"It's not that... hmm." Was it that simple? Sure, money was a big concern. He knew that his parents had invested his college money wisely and he had graduate school savings to pay for the basics, but still, he would have to live off of his savings carefully in England to pull it off. He could teach and earn a stipend, but that would seriously cut into time for his own study. That would be less of a problem in New York, as expensive as the city could be. He wouldn't mind moving into someone's closet if he could get a deal on rent.

"I'm just thinking of the first thing you told me about your studies when we talked in New York," Seth said.

"Oh?" A thrill raced through Oliver at the thought of Seth having listened that intently to him when neither of them knew what would happen.

"You said that it was hard not being able to talk to people because you had to be impartial. Is that how it would be at Cambridge?"

Oliver nodded slowly, thinking. That's exactly how it would be. He would be the face of the project, the go-between with the government. He could do that, easily. His father had made sure he was well groomed for any situation; he could put on a game face for any occasion that called for it.

But did he want to always be that person?

"Then it's like I said, isn't it?" Seth asked. "Direct contact or not?"

Oliver took a moment to breathe deeply; Seth was watching him carefully, a smile just beginning to blossom on his face. He seemed to be okay with all of this, acting as his friend, as someone to bounce ideas off of—not someone who could possibly be left by the wayside if Oliver didn't choose Silver. Oliver's heart ached painfully to see that Seth was still the boy who would wait for Oliver to choose him.

"I can see why you'd want to do either, honestly," Seth said, his head tilted to the side as he thought through his words. "And I can imagine that you'd be equally as good at either, too." Seth smiled and tapped Oliver's shoe with his own. "If you were just bad at something for once, this would be much easier for us."

"You're amazing, you know?"

Seth laughed softly. "Of course I know." Oliver didn't miss the blush creeping up Seth's face. It felt wonderful to know that Seth wanted them to make it work, and that he wanted to help him make the best choice for *him*, not Seth.

In a matter of a few days, he'd know for sure how all this would play out. As much as he wanted this time together to last forever, he was desperate to get to Silver and finally be able to make an informed decision.

"Do you want to stay for a while longer, or are you ready to shove off?" Oliver asked, nudging Seth's shoe.

Seth drained his glass with a flourish and got to his knees. "I think I'm ready for us to go. Besides, it's starting to get a little chilly."

Oliver hopped to his feet and pulled Seth up flush against him, running his hands over Seth's arms. It was something he didn't think he could ever get tired of—being allowed to touch him like that. Seth snaked his arms around Oliver's waist and said, "I forgot that you're like a human furnace."

Chuckling softly, Oliver kissed Seth gently on the lips. "Do you want to man the pole? That should warm you up."

Seth let out an almost strangled moan and laughed, laying his head on Oliver's shoulder. "There is no way to describe it without it being a double entendre."

Oliver blushed and shook his head. "You know I didn't mean—"

Seth shut him up with a soft kiss and pulled back to start packing the empty containers back into the hamper, still chuckling. As Oliver shook out the blanket and reloaded the punt, Seth stood on the shore with his hands on his hips, regarding the boat.

Oliver bumped his hip into Seth's and held the edge of the punt to keep it from wobbling as Seth climbed back in. He was about to step on the till when Seth gave him a saucy grin and asked, "Hey, sailor. Going my way?"

Leaning down, Oliver kissed Seth's lips softly, saying, "The face that launched a thousand ships. Well, this one, at any rate." He grabbed the pole, hopped onto the boat and pushed off.

* * *

Conversation was lighthearted and teasing for the rest of the afternoon; it was all out in the open, the choice that needed to be made and their feelings for each other. Oliver caught Seth glancing at him and smiling as they returned the punt.

"What?" Oliver asked, nudging Seth's shoulder as they made their way back to the apartment.

"Nothing," Seth grinned. "It's just been a really good day."

Oliver ducked his head, laughing softly. It was one of the best days he could remember. "Oh? Anything in particular?" he asked Seth.

"This really handsome guy planned an amazing outing for me that was terribly romantic, that's all."

"Hmm, better tell me who this guy is so I can tell him to back off," Oliver replied, giving Seth a wink as he unlocked the door and held it for him.

"Oliver! And his friend Seth! Come, come; meet my friends," Janos shouted from the sofa. Four other guys from the football team were in the house, watching a game on the television. So much for a continuation of the romantic afternoon.

"This is who I am telling you about," he said to the group, pointing at Seth. "His father is a giant biker—it's called that, yes?" he asked Seth.

Seth, a wary look on his face, replied, "Uh... sure?" He exchanged a confused glance with Oliver.

"He is badass giant on a Harley." Janos made the universal sign for engine-revving and hopped off the sofa. He ran around it to Seth, took him by the shoulders and led him into the room to talk to the other men. "He is... uh, what do I call him, Oliver? Your lover, or...?" He twisted around when asking Oliver, but Seth put his hands up: "enough."

"Janos? If I may?" Seth's voice was higher pitched but forceful. One of the guys narrowed his eyes at him, and Oliver's hand flexed at his side. Seth carefully extricated himself from Janos's hold. "You can call me Oliver's friend Seth. That's easy to remember, right?"

"Yes. Ah, Oliver! I remember you tell me that just because you are a homosexual, you are not in love with every man, okay," Janos said, nodding. He looked back at Oliver and Seth as if he was proud of himself. Well, baby steps. At least he'd been listening *that* night. "Seth, if you like, you come with us to the pub and show them your father's pictures, hmm? Tell some biker gang Hell's Angels stories?"

"I... thank you, but no," Seth replied, shooting Oliver a completely exasperated and dumbfounded look.

"Um, Janos? Seth is on vacation."

"Plus, you can see his custom bikes online on their website," Seth said. Oliver spied his laptop on the table near them, turned it on and pulled up Big Mike's website and the custom shop page. "Here you go. Be sure to check out Little Mike's Death Chopper."

Oliver passed Janos his laptop and pulled Seth into his room while the guys were all entranced and mumbling about the specialty.

"Holy shit, that guy is huge!" Oliver and Seth heard one of them saying. "That's *his* dad?"

Oliver closed the door and Seth started to crack up. "Well, I'm at least happy to see that he's making overtures to us. He's not a bad guy, just... well, ignorant in the actual sense of the word. I think I'm the first gay man he's ever interacted with."

Seth snorted. "First *out* gay man, I'm sure."

Oliver sat on the edge of his bed and held out his hand. "Come 'ere, you." His smile grew as Seth drew closer. Wrapping his arms around Seth's waist, he pulled Seth to stand between his legs and craned his head to look up at him.

"Hi."

Seth brushed Oliver's hair back off his forehead, smiling sweet and intimately. "Hello. I love your hair longer like this. Easier to get my hands into."

Oliver closed his eyes and pressed his cheek against Seth's abdomen as he ran his fingers through Oliver's hair.

"Thank you for today," Oliver said, his voice slightly muffled by the fabric of Seth's thin, soft sweater.

Seth carded both hands into Oliver's dark hair and tugged, getting Oliver to look back up at him. "What for?"

"For letting me do this." Oliver tipped his head back and tugged on Seth's torso, pulling him into a warm kiss.

Seth traced his thumb pads over Oliver's cheeks and said, "Oh, you're very welcome." Oliver was pleased to hear a little bit of a rasp in Seth's voice.

"Hey," Oliver said, straightening up. He toed off his shoes and moved back on the bed to rest against the pillows. He felt sleepy and warm and happy and wanted to feel Seth against him and just revel in this wonderful day they'd shared. Something to add to the other wonderful moments they'd shared. He patted the space next to him.

Grinning, Seth sat on the edge of the bed, untied his laces, carefully lined up his shoes and walked around the bed to lay next to Oliver. He propped himself up on one hand and drew his finger down Oliver's jaw-line, neck and chest, and then laced their fingers together.

"Sometimes I just don't believe you're real," Seth said, breathlessly.

Oliver kissed the back of Seth's hand. "Same here."

But he was: Seth was right there, gazing back at him adoringly, and it filled Oliver's heart with so much love and want that he thought he might burst if Seth didn't kiss him. Seth must have felt something similar as he moved the few inches it took for their lips to meet, soft and pliant. Oliver reveled in the sensation, warm and wonderful; Seth wanted him, wanted this, and the relief and joy he felt from knowing that was almost too much to bear.

That it wasn't certain they would be together from this time on put a damper on his elation, however. Eventually, Seth would go back home and back to work and Oliver would finish his degree, and all of it would happen with an ocean between them, and while he still had all of those years to make up for, all of those nights he hadn't told Seth he loved him, all of those days that didn't start and end with them together.

He rolled Seth onto his back, as if to pin him there and keep him as a permanent fixture in his life. He tilted his head, needing to kiss Seth more deeply, touch him more and feel his warm, solid body under his own. Seth clutched at him just as passionately, holding Oliver's face, his shoulders, sliding his warm, firm hands over Oliver's back. His mouth opened to let Oliver slip in his tongue and stroke against his.

Oliver's heart was racing—he could wake up and find that this was another painful dream where happiness bled into his worst fears. He buried his face against Seth's neck, holding on tightly as he tried to catch his breath. Seth stroked and soothed wherever his hands could reach, until he finally tugged Oliver up to look at him.

"I know," Seth said, softly, his eyes almost translucent in the low light. "I know. It's... me, too."

Oliver closed his eyes, the breath shuddering out of him. He just wanted this forever. He whined softly at the sensation of Seth petting his face, his hair. When he opened his eyes again, he saw that Seth's hazel eyes were swimming with unshed tears.

"I just..." Seth sighed and closed his eyes as he said, "I missed you *so much*, babe."

Oliver pressed their lips together firmly, needing contact, over and over: I'm here, I love you, don't go. They collapsed into each other's arms, simply holding each other. Seth was warm and firm and *right there*, and Oliver had him in his arms, and he just didn't want it to ever stop. Seth hummed something quietly under his breath as his hands worked through the hair on the back of Oliver's head, over and over, until they both felt calm and their breathing evened out. Oliver didn't want to move, he didn't want Seth to move; he wanted to stay there, wrapped up in their reclaimed love.

"Tuesday. Tuesday you go and meet with them, and then we'll know," Seth whispered against Oliver's ear, almost breathless from the weight of Oliver on top of him.

Oliver rolled them over, pulling Seth onto him. He needed his weight to anchor him here in the moment. Seth shifted to rest his cheek against Oliver's shoulder, his hand toying with the neckline of Oliver's shirt. "I love you," Oliver said, and kissed Seth's hairline, his eyes closing with the familiar scent and sensation, hoping he would never be in a position to forget what it was like.

"Tuesday. Until then, it's us, okay? We're here, and I just want to be with you this week, okay?" Seth buried his face in Oliver's neck and breathed deeply. Oliver tightened his arms, nodding; he gave a yelp a moment later when Seth poked him in the ribs, tickling him.

"And we're not going to spend it lying here moping," Seth said, looking down at Oliver with determination in his eyes. "Besides, there are far better things we could be doing."

The warmth in Oliver's chest began to pool lower. "Yeah?"

Seth swung his leg over, straddling Oliver and looking down with nothing less than pure mischief in his eyes. "Yeah."

He leaned forward, drawing the tip of his nose along Oliver's lips and cheek, exhaling over Oliver's earlobe and sending shivers through his limbs. Seth was kissing down Oliver's neck, pulling the collar of Oliver's shirt away with the tip of his finger, when the guys in the other room gave a cheer.

Seth collapsed to Oliver's side, laughing.

"No, no! They're just encouraging us!" Oliver whined, trying to pull Seth back on top of him.

Seth shook his head, still chuckling. "Oliver, I am not going to try to get you off with a group of homophobic soccer players in the other room. I don't think I've even imagined that particular scenario before."

Oliver pushed up onto his elbow and fixed Seth with a sour face. "Fine."

Seth grinned. "Come on. Up! Let's get something to drink and figure out all of the wonderful things you're going to show me while I'm here."

Oliver rolled on top of Seth and gave him a positively wolfish grin, but Seth pushed him off and sat up, laughing. "One-track mind... and later. When there's not an audience."

He smoothed his hair and shirt as Seth got to his feet and asked, "Promise?" He knew the word meant something more than just the intention to be together later that night.

Seth slipped his arms around Oliver's neck, smiling sweetly. "Promise."

Chapter Eighteen

"We could go to Piccadilly Circus; there's the rest of the West End—size up the competition for the next desperately hungry wannabe?" Oliver teased.

Seth kicked at Oliver's foot. "Funny. But yes to Piccadilly. I notice you didn't say anything about going to Buckingham Palace. Too touristy?"

They sat at the small table between the kitchen and living room, feet tangled together in the space underneath. They were leaning close to each other in order to hear themselves over the din of the guys shouting at the soccer game on the television. Apparently there was a massive drive to score happening, and the guys were practically screaming.

Seth glanced their way and snorted, "One to zero? They should change how many points a team gets for a goal to make it seem more exciting."

Oliver looked over his shoulders at Janos and his friends to make sure they didn't overhear. He'd been quickly and sternly informed, his first week in England, that he was *never* to disparage football (still soccer, to his American sensibilities).

"Anyway... oh!" Oliver smiled and took Seth's hand. "I could waltz you across Trafalgar Square?"

Seth glanced down at their hands and looked pleased.

"Oh, and the London Eye!" Oliver raised an eyebrow. "That's the huge Ferris wheel?"

"Can we?" Seth was positively incandescent with excitement, Oliver was happy to see.

They mapped out the remaining touristy things they could do as the guys wrapped up their commentary on the game.

"Seth, Oliver: we are going to the pub. Come with?" Janos asked.

Seth yawned hugely, stretching his arms out in an exaggerated manner. "Oh, thank you, but no. I'm exhausted. Still not used to the time change."

Janos nodded and clapped Oliver on the shoulder as he left.

Oliver turned to Seth, smirking as the group left the flat. "It should be the other way."

"Hmm?" Seth asked, smiling and leaning toward him with his chin propped on his hand.

Oliver laughed. "You should be wide awake, because it's not even dinnertime in New York yet."

"You're cute," Seth said. "Thick-headed, but very, very cute. So... I think I'm going to take a shower." He dropped his voice and purred, "I'd offer for you to join me, but it's hard enough not to slip and fall to my death in there on my own."

"I told you, claw-foot tubs are terrible as showers." Oliver tried to play it cool, but it was hard when Seth was running his toe up Oliver's instep, and higher, and offering to shower together.

"Is... Janos going to be gone for a while?" Seth's foot was halfway up Oliver's calf and his brain was starting to short out.

Oliver tried not to squirm as he answered, "He's usually gone for hours when he's out drinking after a game."

"That's convenient." Seth stood and ran his hand through Oliver's hair before walking off and tossing over his shoulder, "Meet you in bed."

Oliver's hand spasmed on the table. "Okay," he replied, barely able to find the breath to get it out as he watched Seth walk out of sight. He pushed away from the table and raced to Janos's bathroom. He didn't even care about getting a towel—he was hot enough that the water droplets on his skin would probably evaporate instantly. He hardly bothered to let the water heat up fully before jumping in, soaping up, shampooing and rinsing off.

He thought of their last time together as he watched the soap run down his legs and into the drain, how he'd really taken Seth for granted; he'd just... *taken* that night. He knew he still loved him; it had felt so *natural* to be together. He wanted Seth back in his life, but he'd had no idea how to *get* Seth back, or if that was even what Seth wanted. Oliver had just assumed that they were on the same page this whole time. Once again, Oliver had jumped in with both feet, not thinking things through.

He hadn't thought about anything but the moment: he was with Seth and all was well.

Right?

And then he remembered how, back in New York City, Seth had offered to leave right away, to get out of Oliver's way and not be a burden; had Seth thought it was just... what? Just that night, and nothing else? Something fun for Oliver to do while he was in town?

Oh my God, that's exactly what he thought.

Sick, burning shame roiled in his gut as he shut the water off and pulled aside the shower curtain. He dried himself off rapidly and thought of how special Seth had made that night, how tender and attentive he'd been. How he'd wanted Oliver to look at him. How he'd held everything that Oliver was between his two hands and had *loved* him that night.

And with absolutely no expectation of more. That was because Seth had thought it was all that *he* was going to be given: just that one night.

Could Oliver have done that? Just had one night with Seth and not have expected anything else? The thought of not having their New Year's together, their trip here in England... how could he not have seen just how far Seth was willing to go simply to be with Oliver for whatever time Oliver would give him, no matter the cost to his own aching heart?

It's like he's making up for not being willing when we were younger. Oh, my God...

With the towel wrapped around his hips and held in place with one hand, he quickly walked through the chilly house and back into his room. He slipped into bed and rested against the headboard with the sheets pooled at his waist and waited, with nothing but his thoughts about how selfless Seth had been.

Oliver could hear the sound of him happily singing in the shower; his obliviousness to Oliver's rising shame for his mistreatment of Seth over the past months went a long way toward easing it. He was so frustrated with himself for not realizing that he'd even been *doing* that.

But.

Seth was here, flirting and kissing and *singing*, and he knew without a doubt that for Oliver this wasn't just now. Oliver wanted always. Which meant Seth must want that, too. And he'd flown across an ocean just to be with Oliver on the *chance* that they might have an always. Feeling more humbled by the moment, Oliver flashed back to years before, and what Seth had said to him:

"If you wanted to be with me, then you would. It's that simple for me."

Seth wanted to be with him and so he was here. In England. Waiting for Oliver. Waiting *again.*

The door opened, releasing steam in curling tendrils as Seth stepped out, also in nothing but a towel. His body was strong and lean, and he was *there.* Seth walked to the dresser, but Oliver suddenly held out his hand across the mattress and said, "Seth. Please."

Seth walked to the edge of the bed, about to release his towel and slip in when Oliver stopped him by getting to his knees on the bed and grabbing Seth at the waist. Oliver tugged the towel off of Seth's hips and skimmed his hands slowly up Seth's ribs, across his chest and then up his neck to bury them in Seth's thick, soft, still-damp hair. He leaned in, drawing his lips lightly over Seth's but pulling back when Seth tried to deepen the kiss.

"Thank you," he said, not sure if it expressed everything in his heart, but unable to articulate any more than that through words.

Oliver moved backward on the bed to make room, smiling as Seth stretched out. Seth's body was almost otherworldly; he had long limbs and was well-muscled, but still managed to be lithe. He was strong, he moved effortlessly, he was everything Oliver found attractive in a man. But it was who Seth *was* that made him so attractive. Oliver traced his fingertips along the defined muscle of Seth's thigh, up and over his hip bone.

"You're so beautiful," Oliver murmured, pressing a kiss to Seth's solar plexus and drawing his lips lightly up Seth's body to suck gently at a spot just above his Adam's apple. "Just beautiful."

Seth let out a whine and tugged at Oliver's hair to get him closer. Oliver's fingers ghosted along the faint shadow of stubble at Seth's jaw.

"I'm so unbelievably lucky," Oliver whispered, kissing Seth's temple and nuzzling his cheek.

"What?" Seth's voice was breathy as he strained upward, bringing their bodies into closer contact.

Oliver settled his legs between Seth's, his eyes closing briefly at the sensation of Seth's cock against his belly, growing even harder. He cupped

Seth's face, thumb pad drawing lightly over Seth's high cheekbone. "I'm lucky that you'll let me do this, that I get to be with you."

Seth closed his eyes, shaking his head and pulling Oliver back to kiss him slowly and deeply, his hands gripping at Oliver's back. They rocked together, gasping into each other's mouths, legs twining together as if they couldn't get close enough.

Oliver mouthed along Seth's clavicle only to come back to kiss his lips again all the more fervently. He needed Seth, needed him to know how much this meant, that this was supposed to be how every night ended: Seth in his bed, their hands on each other and their love for one another filling them.

Seth's hands were buried in Oliver's hair and he tugged on it lightly. Oliver loved that Seth was so physical. Seth wasn't overly vocal in bed, surprising given that he was a performer and singer; but what Seth didn't say he made up for with his body language. He wrapped his legs around Oliver and splayed his hands across Oliver's back to hold them as close together as could be; he rocked their bodies languidly, he arched and gasped and clutched and dragged his lips over every inch of Oliver, and Oliver didn't think he could ever get enough of it.

He moved down Seth's body, taking his time, feeling in his bones that he *would* have time. This wasn't just a week with a former love; it couldn't be just this time, not with the way every part of his being burned with need for Seth back in his life.

He sank his mouth over Seth's cock and moaned at Seth's shuddering gasp of surprise. It had been four long months since he'd connected with Seth in this way, and years, before that. Oliver gave himself a moment to pull off and hold him, his eyes closing with the sensation of Seth stroking his hair and the sweet way he murmured Oliver's name. He mouthed along the sensitive tendon at the top of Seth's inner thigh and shuddered again with the realization that for him, this was it. Seth was the only one for him.

Oliver whispered the words, "I love you," somewhere near Seth's navel before sinking back over him again, flattening his tongue to taste every inch, to burn the memory of Seth's body into his mind. Every whine he pulled from Seth's lips, every tremor in his muscles as Oliver worked him with his mouth and hands, every cry of pleasure from Seth filled

Oliver with so much joy. He was the one who could do this, who could reduce Seth to this. On the heels of that triumph was a feeling of utter humility that Seth trusted him enough to be this way, even though it might not be forever for them.

It felt like a stab to his gut, the pain that thought caused him. He redoubled his efforts; he wanted this to be about Seth, not him. About him showing Seth that he mattered, and how honored and humbled and filled with need Oliver felt to be like this, together again.

Oliver flicked the tip of his tongue along the narrow groove on the underside of the head of Seth's cock, knowing how sensitive it was, remembering how much Seth had loved it when they'd discovered that particular spot years ago. Oliver was rewarded when Seth brokenly moaned his name as he grabbed the bedclothes near his hips, his hands curling tightly into the fabric. Seth arched his body, driving him deeper into Oliver's mouth, as deep as he could go. Oliver took it all, letting Seth work him as he needed, desperate to give all the pleasure he could.

"Please, I'm so close... please?" Seth carded his fingers through Oliver's hair over and over, his voice plaintive and desperate.

Oliver pressed his forearms on Seth's inner thighs to spread him open, wanting to hold him down and never let him go. He wanted it to be so good for him that Seth would cry out his name and forget how to say anyone else's. His mouth was tight and wet; he stroked and twisted with his hand in the manner he remembered—no, *knew* Seth loved. Seth's hand flexed once in his hair and Oliver looked up; Seth's head was thrown back, his mouth slightly parted as he softly panted Oliver's name with each exhalation as if it was something precious.

With a tiny whine, Oliver pulled himself to his knees, grabbing Seth's body under the hips and pulling the heated flesh up to meet his mouth as he hollowed his cheeks and sank down once, twice, three times more, and Seth arched again, climaxing while Oliver swallowed him down, petting every inch of skin he could touch as Seth's body shook with his release.

Seth collapsed, breathing heavily. After a moment in which he tried to catch his breath, and Oliver stroked his thighs and hips, kissing away the red marks where Oliver had held him tightly, Seth stretched a hand out to him. Oliver lay beside him and entwined their fingers as he placed soft kisses on Seth's flushed skin and under his chin. Seth quietly but fervently whispered, "I love you," as he ran his fingers through Oliver's hair.

It had felt amazing to be with Seth in December; he'd had no expectation of even speaking to Seth when he'd gone to New York, and every moment they'd shared talking and just being together was such a wonderful surprise that Oliver could hardly look past the moments as they happened. But now, knowing without a doubt that his love would never go away, knowing that Seth loved him too... being together like this was an absolute gift.

Oliver cupped Seth's cheek, taking in the gorgeous sight of him satisfied, pink-cheeked and breathless. Seth's eyes closed as he gave a breathy laugh.

"Good?" Oliver asked.

Seth rolled his head back, hands splayed and coursing over the wide expanse of Oliver's back. "So, so good."

Oliver nuzzled Seth's hair, a little damp and sweaty at his temples, coming undone at the undeniably unique and wonderful smell of him. It brought to mind so many memories of the two of them slipping away from family events, hiding from their friends, stealing moments to be with each other, their overwhelming need to connect physically. Oliver thought those memories were almost choking him; he needed more than just memories.

"Love you," he whispered in Seth's ear, growling low in his throat when Seth arched up against him, wanting their bodies to touch again. He hung his head and pressed his forehead into Seth's neck, shaking with need. It was beyond the physical; it was everything. He didn't just want to get off. He wanted Seth's love, his time, his future, all wrapped up with his, so tangled together that there was no question of ever separating them from one another again.

Oliver curled up against Seth; he didn't want to be away from him, even to cool off. Seth hummed happily at Oliver's side, his hand lazily stroking Oliver's shoulder and arm.

"I think I lost my last name and the year back there," Seth laughed.

Oliver laughed softly against Seth's neck and smiled with pride.

"Let me catch my breath, and then—"

Oliver silenced him with a slow, deep kiss. Seth melted against his lips as he took his time. "I just want you to hold me," Oliver said. "Is that okay?"

Seth looked into his eyes, a question on his face, so Oliver kissed him once more just to punctuate that it was what he wanted.

"Are you sure?" Seth asked. "Because believe me, it would be my pleasure."

Oliver curled back up against him, his nose just under Seth's chin so he could breathe him in. "I'm sure."

Seth wriggled a bit to pull the sheets and blanket up over them, then settled more comfortably into the bed, his arms wrapped around Oliver.

"But if you have the urge to do anything later, feel free to wake me up," Oliver murmured, already feeling tired from their day. He smiled against Seth's neck as Seth gently shook with laughter. Seth found his hand again, pressed it to his chest and drew lazy patterns on Oliver's arm until they both fell asleep.

* * *

They spent the next day taking the train into London and seeing the sights, holding hands and enjoying comfortable silences for stretches or chatting about anything and everything. In Trafalgar Square, Oliver stayed true to his word: a group of young musicians were busking near the fountain, and when they began to play Shostakovich's "The Second Waltz," Oliver held out a hand and gave Seth a small bow.

Seth laughed and continued tapping his toe to the rhythm; they were really good. A few people in the growing crowd swayed in each other's arms. Oliver cleared his throat, took Seth's hand and tugged him into his embrace with a cheeky grin.

Blushing and laughing, Seth allowed himself be waltzed through any open space Oliver could find in the square. Oliver hadn't taken cotillion and ballroom dance lessons all of those years at his mother's insistence for nothing, after all. A few other people—an older couple making up for their advanced years by staring lovingly at one another, and a young married couple who swayed rhythmically more than dancing—began to move around the musicians, spurring Oliver on. He moved them out of the main cluster of listeners and held Seth close and sure, his feet making the quick one-two-three steps as Seth easily kept up.

In fact, Seth was so adept that once he got over the initial shock and embarrassment—it seemed as if no one really cared, or if they did, they kept it to themselves—he laid his head on Oliver's shoulder, keeping his right arm in perfect position as they moved. Oliver flashed on another night of dancing with Seth in his arms, their last New Year's Eve as a couple, when they had slow-danced in the Larsens' garage; and he held Seth tighter, as tight as the ache in his heart had been. He could imagine the vision they made just then, Seth's light hair in stark contrast to Oliver's inky black mane, both of them long and lean, moving easily and competently across the open plaza in perfect sync. The song ended, the audience applauded, and a few people even nodded and smiled at them as they laughed and moved on. Seth slipped some bills from his pocket into the open violin case as they passed by.

They rode the London Eye, Oliver making a point, in the crowded car, to keep a spot right at the glass at the back so Seth would have the chance to look out over the city with an unobstructed view once they made it to the top, while Oliver hooked his chin over Seth's shoulder and wrapped his arms around him from behind, simply enjoying the time they had together.

Everything seemed so natural, as if they'd gone back in time: the ease of their companionship, their ability to talk or just be silent and share space together, the never-ending desire that evidently coursed through them both. Seth stole kisses as they took their seats on the train, ran his hand down Oliver's arm as he moved to take a seat in a restaurant. Oliver would look up from their map to see Seth breathing shallowly with a heated look in his eye.

They did their best to be quiet and respectful of Janos back at the apartment, but Oliver couldn't keep his hands off Seth. They made pleasantries with Janos until they could slip away and lock the door, Oliver pressing Seth into the bed, hands working quickly and surely to undress him as Seth did the same to Oliver. Oliver wanted to bring Seth off as quickly as possible just to show that he *could*, but always, always took his time, making a point of lavishing affection and attention on every inch of Seth's body, as Seth did to him.

It was if they both knew that there was still the chance that it wouldn't work out in their favor, that life would come between them once again.

Oliver stored up every caress, every kiss, not wanting to think about how it could be their last. There was almost an unspoken agreement not to discuss the decision facing them; they could feel the painful weight of it lingering in the background, a dull pain that they tried to cover with "I love you."

It was a heady few days of rebuilding the love they'd once shared, interspersed with trips to a museum here and there, forcing themselves to leave for food but coming back to the apartment as quickly as possible to wrap themselves up in their private world of lovemaking.

Now Seth, his hand stroking lower and lower on Oliver's body, breathlessly asked if Oliver would let him fuck him again; and before he'd finished asking, Oliver was already twisting and reaching for the bedside table.

He pulled out a small gray bottle and a few condoms and turned back to kiss Seth, who was looking down at him with a peculiar sort of half-smile.

"What?" Oliver asked, craning his neck up to kiss him again.

Seth shook his head as if to clear away a thought, murmured, "Nothing," and pressed their lips together.

This time it was Oliver who pulled back, laying his palm on Seth's chest. "Really. What?"

Seth settled his body over Oliver's, sighing and covering his cheeks with kisses. "It's ridiculous, and I have no right, but..."

"Seth. You can tell me anything."

"I just..." Seth pushed up on his elbows, dipping his head to kiss one of Oliver's temples and then the other. "I don't like the thought of you with condoms. Because that means you've been with someone else. And *of course* you have, I just, well, I don't like it." Seth looked at him, and the fire in his eyes sent a tremor through Oliver's body.

He thought he understood completely. He felt the same. "Say it."

Seth buried a hand in Oliver's hair, watching his fingers intently.

Oliver shook his head a little to get his attention again. "Seth. Say why." He needed to hear that this was real, that what they'd been to each other before was what they would always be.

Seth took a deep breath, his hand drifting down Oliver's body, loosely circling Oliver's cock, sliding lower and stroking. "Because you're mine," he whispered.

Oliver's eyes closed as he sighed, "Yes," and pulled Seth down to kiss him. He needed to feel every inch of their bodies touching, from tongues to fingers to toes. Seth barely missed a step in opening the top of the small bottle, to stroking inside Oliver with a finger, his lips ghosting over Oliver's, swallowing every exhaled "Seth" that Oliver could barely find the breath to say.

Seth took his time, seeming to relish every moan, every cry from Oliver as his fingers stroked deep, deeper. Oliver was grateful for the weight of Seth's body on his—he felt as if he could fly apart at any minute. Finally, *finally* Seth entered him, holding his body close as he curved his spine, driving in so slowly, pulling out to kiss him and drive back in. Every nerve ending in Oliver's body was on fire, tingling from the overwhelming sensation of Seth everywhere, inside him, on him, his every sweet breath flooding Oliver's body.

He could feel that deliciously intense sensation pooling low in his belly as Seth thrust into him relentlessly, holding his legs open and simply taking. He gripped himself, letting Seth's thrusts drive his cock through his own hand, and he pulled Seth in by the back of his neck and kissed him deeply, moaning, "Love you," as he climaxed, Seth gasping and following shortly after.

They stayed wrapped in each other, catching their breath, kissing wherever they could reach, still needing to touch, to connect, to belong to each other. All too soon the reality of life and their separate living situations would make itself apparent. For now, though, the world was just the two of them.

Chapter Nineteen

Monday came, a day they spent doing laundry and packing for the trip to the airport later that afternoon. Oliver agreed to wear the outfit Seth picked out for his meeting at Silver and finally handed over his laptop, giving Seth the chance to look up David Falchurch's reviews.

"I don't know why you're nervous. No one can compare with you, Seth."

"That's sweet," Seth said, twisting to give him a smile. "And ridiculous. Now hush, and get back to folding socks while I do damage control."

Oliver smiled to see their suitcases side by side on his bed as they packed.

"Oh my God."

"What?" Oliver asked, dropping his socks and rushing to Seth's side. Seth had his hand pressed to his mouth.

"Seth, *what is it?*"

Seth's face broke into a huge grin. "He sucked!"

Oliver looked over his shoulder at the computer screen as Seth did a little wiggly dance. "Where has our city's songbird gone?" Oliver read. "Falchurch may have originated the role, but Seth Larsen stepped in and made it his own. Having seen the chemistry between Larsen and Rogers, living and dying along with them as they performed, watching this usurper try to create an immortal love with Rogers was practically an insult.

"His voice may have gotten stronger during his time away, but his vocal range is painfully limited compared to that of Mr. Larsen. And again I ask: Where has Mr. Larsen gone? Thankfully I've heard from the production team that they intend to bring him back after this 'experiment.' Let's hope they never attempt another."

Seth was doing a rhythmic shoulder shake, singing, "Ha ha *ha*, ha ha *ha*." Oliver turned and swept Seth up in his arms, laughing. "They love you! See?" Oliver kissed him loudly on the lips. "I get to say 'I told you so' when it turns out okay, don't I?"

Seth threw his arms around Oliver's neck and kissed him back. "Yes."

Oliver pulled Seth off his feet in another bracing hug, held his face in his hands and beamed. "They want you! Told you so."

Seth rolled his eyes good-naturedly. "Oh my God, it really worried me, and I'm *so* relieved." He sighed and rested his forehead on Oliver's shoulder. "I can't wait to get back and call my dad. He told me the same thing you did, but I didn't want to get my hopes up just to have them squashed, you know?"

Oh, did he. "So you're a permanent fixture on Broadway, huh?" Oliver asked.

"Looks that way," Seth laughed, hopping up and carefully folding a pair of freshly washed jeans. He laid them inside his suitcase, sighed and turned to slip his arms around Oliver's waist and rest his cheek on his shoulder. "That's where I'll be," he said, both proud and wistful, as if he was telling Oliver where he'd be waiting, once again, for Oliver to choose him.

Oliver wrapped his arms around Seth, smoothing a hand up and down the flat planes of his back. His stomach was starting to twist into knots with anticipation for this trip and the meetings he had scheduled. He had no idea if Silver could meet his expectations, if it could truly compete with Cambridge. He didn't know what would happen if it *didn't* meet his needs and he found himself there in Seth's apartment, packing to leave. For good. He just had to keep telling himself that for now it was still the two of them. They'd tackle the future when they finally knew what to expect.

They finally got everything packed and set by the front door. Janos was elbow-deep in a sandwich, and looked up from his plate with both cheeks full as they gathered their things.

Janos held a finger up to them to get them to wait, swallowed and wiped his mouth. He stood and clasped Seth by the shoulders and said, "Seth, you are a good guy. It was good knowing you. Safe travels," and kissed him on both cheeks, letting him go with a squeeze.

"Oh, well. How... very continental!" Seth was positively flushed. "It was very good to meet you, as well." He shot Oliver a bewildered stare, but Oliver was too busy holding back a laugh.

"I'll be back in a few days, then?" Oliver said.

Janos gave him the same treatment: shoulder clasp and two kisses. He waved at them and went right back to his sandwich, eating it as if it held the secret to the meaning of life.

"Okay then, shall we?" Oliver said, suppressing laughter as they grabbed their luggage.

* * *

Traveling was fun, but traveling *with* someone was even better. They held hands during takeoff, smiled when pressed back into their seats from the gravitational force, and continued to smile once they'd leveled off at cruising altitude. It was too noisy to carry on a proper conversation, so Seth pulled the armrest up and tugged on Oliver's sleeve to get him to scoot closer so he could see the vast ocean out of Seth's window. They settled in with their books and zoned in and out of sleep for the duration of the flight.

They disembarked, sharing a few looks of exaggerated exasperation as they moved through customs. Seth quietly said, "This way," as he pointed Oliver to the direction of the cab stand.

Seth rested his head on Oliver's shoulder, sighing softly, as they stood in line. A very chipper man with a thick accent quickly took their bags and stowed them in the trunk of his cab as the two slid into the back seat. Seth gave him directions to his apartment in Brooklyn Heights and flopped back against the seat to be gathered up in Oliver's arms as they drove through traffic.

"I'm excited to see your place," Oliver said after several minutes of quiet.

"Well, it's not much, but at least it has an actual kitchen and not just a microwave and mini-fridge, like my first New York apartment."

They fell back into silence. Oliver rubbed soothing patterns into Seth's shoulder and arm and watched the city pass by. It was as if he'd gone through the looking glass and was stepping into their imagined future at last, except that everything was so unsettled. It wasn't a happy, elated homecoming, but a nerve-wracking "what if?"

Seth tried to pay the fare when they pulled up to his six-story apartment building, but Oliver waved him off. "They're paying my expenses, you know."

"At least we have an elevator," Seth said as they lugged their suitcases up the concrete stoop. Seth's place was on the fifth floor, and the ride was quiet. Even Seth's voice had steadily grown quieter; they reached his door and he said, "Here we are," quietly and opened the door.

He dropped his keys on the console by the front door—there was a small decorative bowl for just that purpose. Across from that was a shallow closet ("One of two! Very exciting.") for their coats, and as Oliver reached for the doorknob to open it, his heart gave a staggering thump. It opened to the right, just as the door in his dream had. There were pictures on Seth's wall, as well; pictures of him in different casts, and in every one of them he wore a joyous smile.

Seth was happy in these pictures. Seth had been happy before Oliver came in like a tornado, ripping up everything in his path. Maybe, if this whole situation didn't end up working in their favor, he would take away Seth's chance at being happy again.

"Oliver? Are there no hangers? If you see a wire one, don't use it. I keep the ones from the dry cleaner's in there to remind me to recycle them."

Oliver cleared his throat, forced himself to smile and replied, "No, it's fine, and thank you."

"Well?" Seth said, smiling and cocking his head to the side. "Don't you want a tour?"

Laughing, Oliver let himself be led a few feet into the center of the apartment. Seth stood behind him, hands on his shoulders and pointed him left. "That's the kitchen, and don't be jealous of the Formica counters. They're very chic." He turned Oliver ninety degrees to the left. "The entryway, but doesn't it look different from this angle?" Oliver laughed and let Seth turn him another ninety degrees. "I know it's only one foot long, but my realtor and I agree that this is my hallway. Bathroom on the right, bedroom on the left."

"I'll take a right, then, if you don't mind."

"I'll be in here when you're finished," Seth said, kissing Oliver on the back of his neck and rolling his suitcase into his bedroom.

Oliver took care of necessities and washed his hands, letting the soothing cool water run over his wrists. He glanced at the toothbrush holder next to the faucet. It had space for two brushes, but there was only one. The nerves that had been building slowly over the past few days were having a full-scale riot in his gut. It was all so close, everything he'd wanted. A cozy place for the two of them, a happy and fulfilling life, in which they were both achieving their dreams, and love waiting at home at the end of the day.

But what if? He couldn't bring himself to think about the alternative. To come home after his meetings and look at Seth's crestfallen face when he explained that he was sorry for getting Seth's hopes up *again*, but it just wasn't going to happen? He pressed his cool, damp palms over his eyes and tried to control his breathing.

First thing in the morning, he'd meet with the people at Silver. He'd get a better idea of what he needed to do; and if it was to stay in England, he would just have to come back to Seth's apartment and tell him. Maybe he could convince Seth this time... He clutched at his stomach and breathed deeply.

He had brought this on himself; he needed to make things as easy for Seth as possible, no matter what the outcome.

Since they were still on Cambridge time, it was close to midnight on their body-clocks and they decided to order in and get a good night's sleep before their big day. Seth—anxious to prove that he'd earned his role—wanted to work with his vocal coach all the next day to undo any damage from not performing for a week and come back with a splash.

Seth hadn't lied about his sofa, or rather, loveseat. ("They call it that because you have to love whoever you're sitting next to, since you'll practically be in their lap.") Oliver was grateful that he loved Seth, then, as he sat against the short, square armrest with Seth laying back against him, holding a takeout box of spicy noodles in one hand and a pair of chopsticks in the other. He fed them both while they caught up on the news.

It could end like this: shared food, shared space, shared *lives*. Oliver could come home after a long day, swing through a deli and pick up some of Seth's favorite things for dinner; maybe he'd come home to find that

Seth had done that for him. There could be bills and junk mail with both of their names on it.

Or he could ruin everything. He could shatter Seth's world again and spend six more years being intellectually fulfilled while his heart remained empty. His hand convulsed slightly on the armrest, and he ran it up and down Seth's bicep. He needed to hold on to the fantasy a little while longer.

Oliver offered to clean up while Seth took a shower and got ready for bed. He was bent over at the waist to retrieve an errant packet of duck sauce when he heard Seth make a pained noise in the bathroom. Quickly he dashed to the bathroom door, knocked and called out, "Seth? Are you okay?"

"Oh my *God*. I missed proper water pressure so, so much."

Oliver pressed his forehead to the door and rolled it from side to side. "I thought you were hurt!"

"No! Sorry! Just... you'll see when you get in here. But I'm going to need a moment alone with my shower head, thank you. "

Oliver laughed, his panic ebbing. He pressed the flat of his hand against the door and forced his breathing to settle. It was fine. It was all going to be fine, he told himself, and headed back to the kitchen before taking his turn in the bathroom to see if the shower lived up to the hype.

Feeling rather blissed out after a hot shower, Oliver entered Seth's bedroom, rubbing a towel over his hair with another one secured around his hips. Seth had a smug expression on his face, legs crossed at the ankle as he reclined back against his headboard, where he'd been reading.

"Holy shit."

Seth laughed. "I told you!"

"It's... oh my *God*."

"I didn't want to be rude while I was a guest in your home, but seriously, Oliver. Your shower... it's like being spit on by angry cats. You can't tell me you want that for another six years."

They both went still at that. Seth blushed, ducked his head and tucked a card into the book he'd been reading. Oliver's heart was racing, and that blissed out feeling had suddenly all but disintegrated. Seth looked down at the book in his hand and shook his head, as if he was mad at himself. He murmured, "Sorry," and then hopped off the bed to pull the blanket and sheets down.

"Get ready for your second 'oh my God' of the night," Seth said, a little too brightly.

Oliver cocked an eyebrow at him, waiting for Seth to finish that thought. Seth laughed, bent over at the waist and pressed his face into the mattress, his back shaking up and down. "*I meant the mattress,*" Seth said, his voice muffled by the downy bedding.

Oliver was determined to keep things positive on this last night before they had an idea of what was to come. He chuckled as he slipped into the cool, thick sheets and immediately closed his eyes and moaned, upon stretching out, "Oh my *God*. It's like sleeping on a flock of geese."

"If they were made of silk," Seth said as he shut off his bedside lamp.

"Got anymore 'oh my God' things for me?"

Seth's laughter melted into a hum as he settled into his fluffy pillows. They both turned on their sides to face each other. Seth reached out and ran his fingers through the hair over Oliver's ear; Oliver immediately felt the volume of his worries dial down just from the contact.

"So. We'll see how tomorrow goes, hmm?"

Oliver opened his eyes to find Seth just inches away, watching his fingers move through Oliver's hair. His heart clenched painfully with how much he loved Seth; everything was hanging in the balance, and here was Seth, soothing *him.*

"God, I love you so much," Oliver said, bringing their foreheads together. He wished that things had just gone perfectly all those years ago, so they wouldn't be in this mess now.

Seth lay back against the pillows and motioned for Oliver to snuggle close. "I love you, too," he said, kissing Oliver's hairline as his arms tightened around him.

As tired as he was from a long day of travel, Oliver couldn't fall asleep quickly. He watched the streetlights play across the bedroom wall, laid his palm on Seth's chest to feel the gentle rise and fall as he breathed, and hoped with everything in him that Silver would be the right choice.

* * *

Oliver woke up before Seth; his body was still used to a different time zone, so it seemed late. It wasn't so bad, though—just after six—so he quietly got out of bed, pulled the blanket up over Seth's shoulder to keep him warm, and went about making coffee. It took him a few moments of poking around to find all of the things he needed to make them breakfast.

While the coffee was brewing, he pulled out his laptop up to check his email. Dr. Jones had sent an itinerary for the day: meet her in her office off of Washington, tour the campus and meet with one of her colleague's students, who could give Oliver a more in-depth tour from the perspective of a doctoral candidate.

He was searching subway routes on Google maps when he heard a yawn; Seth was standing in the living room, stretching with sleep-mussed hair. Something warm and peaceful unfurled inside Oliver at the sight.

"Coffee?"

"Mm hmm," Oliver answered. "I didn't know which mug you liked best, so, I set out an assortment."

Seth snorted. "Excellent array of sizes and materials. I'm impressed." He dropped a kiss on Oliver's head and went about pouring a cup. "I don't care what it's served in as long as it ends up in me, to be honest."

"No special mug?"

Seth's eyes flicked to the mug next to Oliver's computer. "No."

Oliver looked at the ceramic travel mug he was using—he'd chosen it because it had reminded him of the paper cups from the Coffee Bean back in Atchison, where they went every day after school. His heart rate picked up at the thought that Seth might have bought it for the same reason. Oliver gave up the bar stool to Seth before he could protest.

"I'm making breakfast, silly."

"Oh! Well, then be my guest," Seth said, smiling as he sipped his coffee.

Simple scrambled eggs, toast and juice made a perfect breakfast; since Oliver was so nervous about the day, he didn't think he could stomach even that much, but Seth insisted he eat something.

Seth took his plate away and gave him a kiss. "Now go get ready so I can see how cute you look all dressed up again."

Oliver felt almost disconnected from reality as he cleaned himself up and dressed. In Seth's apartment. In New York City. While he prepared to interview a school so that *he* could possibly move here and they could actually have a life together, as they'd dreamed.

He tried to focus on the tasks at hand—brush teeth, wipe counter, comb hair, give up on hair, pick a tie—so he didn't have a full-fledged panic attack about the huge, looming "what if" hanging over their heads.

What if the school was wrong? What if the school was just okay? What if the school was perfect? Oh God, what if it was? Would they just pick up as if nothing had happened? Would Seth help Oliver find an apartment, or would Oliver convince Seth to maybe find a bigger place with him? Oh, *God*, if he decided to go back to Cambridge, would Seth even let him stay the night or would he kick—

Oliver hung onto the edge of the sink and shook his head, telling himself to get a grip. He rolled his eyes at his reflection and headed to the bedroom to finish dressing only to find a nice light-colored sport coat and coordinating button down-shirt waiting for him.

Seth popped his head into the bedroom and asked, "Casual but intellectual?"

Oliver couldn't help but smile, not when Seth's thoughtfulness helped take the edge off of his developing panic. "Perfect," he answered, his smile widening at the relieved look Seth gave him in return. He winked at him and backed out. Oliver looked around for the tie he'd packed and didn't see it.

"Seth? Have you—oh," Oliver said, coming up short at the sight of Seth, leaning against the kitchen counter with a tie around his shoulders.

"This?" Seth asked, smirking.

"Honestly, I don't think I can tie it; my hands are shaking too badly." Oliver looked down at his hands; they were trembling as though he had coffee jitters, even though he'd only had the one cup. Everything depended on today. On him.

"Here, let me," Seth murmured, draping the tie around Oliver's neck, flipping up his collar and tying the knot with deft fingers. Oliver closed his eyes as Seth worked, breathing deeply and slowly, letting Seth's calm allay some of his own fears. Seth smoothed his tie and collar, took Oliver by the lapels and pulled him in for a kiss.

Oliver sagged against Seth, holding him at the hips to keep himself upright. Seth pulled back, biting his lip and blinking rapidly. "It's going to be fine," he soothed. Oliver had the thought that Seth was trying to convince himself, too.

Sighing, Oliver laid his head on Seth's shoulder and let himself be held. If this was it... He understood better, now, why Seth had asked for them to just let the time in England be about them reconnecting and nothing else. It had been a vacation from their responsibilities, and now, faced with the big decision that would determine their relationship's fate, he just wanted to go back to the dream-world they'd let themselves hide in.

Seth didn't have to get to his appointment with his vocal coach until later that morning, so he was still in his pajamas. Oliver lifted the back of Seth's shirt with one hand, needing to feel his warm, smooth skin and using the contact as a touchstone that could center him. Seth melted against him with a sigh, holding Oliver tightly against him.

"Quit stalling." Seth pulled back after a moment, but there was no real aggravation in his voice. "I don't want you to be late and make a bad first impression."

Seth was being brave about this, so Oliver squared his shoulders and inhaled sharply, trying to smother the nervous butterflies and simmering panic that seemed to have taken up permanent residence in his gut and only intensified at the watery smile Seth gave him as he drew the flat of his hand down Oliver's blazer. Seth looked away after a moment and stepped back to lean against the loveseat.

Oliver exhaled slowly, grabbed his briefcase by the door and was just about to say goodbye when Seth spoke first.

"Oh! Wait just a second." Seth dashed over and rummaged through a drawer in the kitchen. "If you get finished early and I'm not here, or if you stay late and I'm at the theater." Biting his lip and suddenly looking a little shy, he pressed something metallic into Oliver's hand. A key. "It's the spare."

Oliver looked down at the small brass key; the actual weight was inconsequential, but it felt incredibly solid and monumental laying in the palm of his hand. "Thank you. And you're sure it's okay for me to just come in if you're not here?" He knew he was babbling; he couldn't help himself. "I can keep myself busy or go for a long walk, or meet you somewhere–"

Seth shut him up with a kiss and cupped his cheek, a soft smile on his face. "Just... make yourself at home while you're here."

Oliver pressed their foreheads together; he wanted to make this a home with everything in him, and he understood why Seth would be nervous. Oliver could never regret the time that he and Seth had shared since he stepped out of the shadows on Forty-fifth Street; and he couldn't imagine how empty his life would be had they not reconnected. But if Silver was wrong, if Oliver simply couldn't stay here when the better option was being offered overseas, he had no one to blame but himself for pushing things to where they presently found themselves.

There would be no question that this heartbreak would be his fault, and his alone.

He pressed a soft kiss to Seth's cheek, memorizing everything, his scent, the way he looked just out of bed, the feel of him against Oliver's hand. Just in case.

Oliver leaned in to kiss him one more time. "See you later?"

Seth nodded, biting the end of his thumb. "Babe?"

Oliver paused in the doorway and looked at Seth, his breath catching at the sight of him. Longing, want, fear; Oliver recognized all of Seth's emotions from his own reflection just moments before. "Yes?"

"I really hope this is the right place for you." Seth's voice was barely a whisper as he tried to keep himself composed—for Oliver.

Oliver's throat worked, trying to swallow the bitter, awful lump that kept him from saying anything more than, "Me, too." Seth looked away and nodded. Oliver stood there with the door open, forcing himself to breathe calmly. Part of him just wanted to pretend that they didn't have to be adults with responsibilities and stay there.

Instead, he turned to the open hallway, walked over the threshold and carefully shut the door behind him.

It was when the elevators shut, blocking the view of Seth's front door, that he realized Seth hadn't said goodbye. He clutched the key in his hand, eyes squeezed shut, and held onto it like an unspoken promise.

Chapter Twenty

Oliver checked his watch, tapping his foot impatiently as he waited for his train. He'd already wasted half an hour not paying attention to which direction the car that he'd boarded was going and ended up near Harlem before realizing his mistake. Seth said that he'd leave his apartment at five; it was just past four now. Oliver was tired after walking all day, talking with program directors, adjuncts, TAs and even meeting a young lady in one of Silver's programs for LGBT teens.

His mind was racing with all of the possibilities, coupled with the differences in the school's approach compared to Cambridge. Dr. Jones had hinted for a definitive answer but graciously agreed when Oliver politely said that he needed a night to sleep on such a big decision. She understood that this would be life-changing for him.

And Oliver would never make this call without Seth; he'd finally learned that. Although this choice was his to make, he wanted anything that had to do with their life to be decided upon when they were together. Even if it was something as simple as getting rid of that ridiculously small loveseat, he thought, grinning.

Sure, he knew he was giddy from the whole shiny-and-new aspect of Silver; but he still had to contend with the idea of giving up his project if he came here. He'd put so much into it, and the thought of just handing it over to anyone except Moira... he just didn't know if he was ready to do that. Talking to Seth would help get his thoughts straightened out.

The train pulled in, and Oliver did the on-off dance with the other passengers. The doors shut and the announcer came on. It seemed that they would have to wait for a new operator, so there would be a delay of eight minutes before they pulled out.

He groaned and covered his face with one hand. It was four-fifteen, and he had to get all the way to Brooklyn and then walk two blocks. He'd be cutting it close, but he was determined to see Seth and offer support before he left for his first performance back; it was the least Oliver could do.

*   *   *

He double-checked Seth's carefully-written instructions for getting to the apartment from the subway and walked swiftly to the building, sighing with relief when it came into view. It was just a few minutes after five; surely Seth had waited a few minutes? Oliver didn't bother waiting for the elevator but raced up the four flights of stairs, taking them two at a time as his briefcase banged against his leg. He fumbled out his key when he found the door locked and pushed in calling, "Seth?"

The apartment was dark, though.

"Damn it."

He set his briefcase down by the door, moved to drop his key in the dish on the console and felt a shiver of déjà vu race through him as he watched his hand pull back. He shook himself out of a false memory and crossed to where Seth had left him a note on the kitchen counter.

> *Oliver,*
>   *I'm so sorry we're not crossing paths, but I just can't be late. I'm feeling rusty and paranoid and need to get there and get into character. Call the theater—if you'd like to come back, I'll save a ticket for you at the front? Otherwise, I guess I'll see you when I get back, around 10:30?*
> *<3*
> *Seth*

Oliver smiled at the heart doodle, thinking of all the notes they had passed in French class or choir. God, he'd loved this boy—this man— since he was sixteen. And he realized with a pang that he would until he was sixty, and beyond.

He felt grimy, and took a few minutes to freshen up. After enough time had passed for Seth to make it to the theater, he called but was told,

"Mr. Larsen is in performance mode, and has said that he will mix rubber cement into my concealer if I even think of disturbing him."

"Just tell him that—"

"No, you don't understand," the woman said, getting almost hysterical. "He said *never.*"

Oliver breathed out sharply. "Okay, but... um, this is his—I'm Oliver? Oliver Andrews?"

"Oh! Oliver!" she sing-songed, embarrassing him. "Yeah, I got a ticket up here for you. You coming? If not, I know some people I can scalp—"

"Yes, I am," he said, cutting her off. "Thank you very much."

"No problem, sweetie."

He hung up the phone and sighed. It wasn't that he minded seeing Seth perform again, not at all; he just had wanted to wish him luck beforehand. Well, at least now he had plenty of time to clean up and change.

* * *

Oliver took his seat just as the lights were dimming, his playbill in hand. He'd tried not to take one but, then wondered if Seth had maybe changed his bio. Plus, now he could get the star of this particular show to autograph it a little more personally, he thought, smiling to himself. He squashed the thought that it still might end up yet another token of a relationship he'd once had with Seth.

After the applause died down and the orchestra began the opening number, Oliver forced himself to relax completely; he told himself to forget about his looming choice and the stress of the past several months and simply let himself enjoy the performance. There was time enough afterward to work through everything.

Seth was somehow even better than Oliver remembered. Now that Oliver was no longer having a panic attack from seeing his ex after several years, he was able to appreciate subtle touches to the performance, nuances he hadn't picked up on before.

And as before, Seth held the audience in the palm of his hand as he loved and lost and loved once again. Oliver realized at one point that he had been sitting with his mouth slightly open for some time and snapped his mouth shut, glancing around to see if anyone had noticed. Fortunately, they were all just as enthralled as he was.

During the intermission, Oliver took the opportunity to flip through his playbill. It was the same bio as before, the same picture of Seth looking sleepy and coy and so fucking sexy that Oliver couldn't wait for the show to be over and take him home and *show* him what that picture did to him.

He smiled as he skimmed the bio, his heart giving a tripping thump at "to his first duet partner, who made him believe he could finally get here." He was going to make a point of finding the answer to that mystery later that night.

As the second act drew to its emotional close, you could hear a pin drop. Oliver smirked to himself. He would bet all the money in the world that David Falchurch never had an audience like this, if the reviews he'd read were accurate. *This* was where Seth belonged; this was *his*. Seth had set his sights on Broadway and, through all of his hard work, had been able to make a name for himself. This was Seth's dream, and he'd achieved it.

Oliver was so proud of Seth and all that he'd accomplished. The dreams they'd had for themselves back in their little town—they mattered. Even though some of Oliver's dreams had changed, his still mattered, too. And Seth was the one person in his life who really understood that. He shook himself out of his thoughts as he realized the last lines, where they declared their undying love for one another, were being delivered by The Fair Youth and William.

"So long as men can breathe or eyes can see, So long lives this," William held Seth's hand to his lips for a fervent kiss, "and this gives life to thee."

They embraced, the curtain fell, and the audience rose to its feet, clapping and cheering. Oliver was pretty sure Seth had heard him whistle, if his looking over in Oliver's direction while laughing and shaking his head was any indication.

Oliver took his seat again as the rest of the audience filed out. He knew it would take a bit for Seth to wash the stage makeup off before he would be ready to go. Plus, he enjoyed hearing the audience say nice things about the show as they left. It made his heart swell with happiness. He was so unbelievably proud.

Oliver followed the tail end of the crowd as they left and made his way outside. It was a pleasant spring night; there was a bit of a queue already at the stage door, and since he knew he would be going home with one of the actors, he didn't mind crossing the street to be out of the way. Then he realized with a start that he was in the same alcove. It had a perfect view of the door; he watched the orchestra members file out, people from the chorus and then the one person who soured the experience: Brandt, a.k.a. Dough-Face.

It gave Oliver a mean spike of happiness to know that there weren't many people clamoring for his autograph, not when the actor who played Shakespeare was right on his heels. They barely said two sentences to each other, even though they appeared to be cordial. "William" was probably still mad about having David back for a week instead of working with Seth, someone with whom he had obvious chemistry onstage. If the audiences weren't responding to David, that meant they weren't responding for him, either.

Oliver shook his head at the unprofessionalism of sabotaging one's own show for the sake of bragging rights. He knew that he would never be able to tolerate Brandt, and it wasn't just because he'd tried to date Seth. Sure, a good seventy-five percent was because of that, but still. The guy was just a jerk.

And then there was Seth. He came out much faster than Oliver had anticipated; the crowd gave a little cheer and held out a jumble of things to be autographed. Seth took it all in stride: smiling, he thanked people for coming and signed his name, steadily moving down the line. He looked up and they locked eyes. Oliver could see Seth inhale sharply, and then visibly sigh in relief and smile.

Oliver grinned back, feeling centered and happy and really ready for autograph-signing to be finished so they could get out of there. He walked across the street toward him, taking his time to allow Seth a chance to see everyone who had waited to shower him with praise. Finally, Seth said loudly, "Thank you all so much for coming! It's great to be back."

As a few people in the crowd cheered, Oliver walked over to the partition and held out his arm. Seth beamed at him as he slipped his hand in the crook of Oliver's elbow, and Oliver wished he could do this every night.

"You were stunning." Oliver kissed Seth's cheek. Seth gave him an expectant look, but he just smiled and gave him a tiny shake of the head. "When we get back to your place, okay? It's still all about you tonight."

Oliver then pulled something out of the breast pocket of his sport coat, an origami flower he'd made from the tablet on Seth's counter.

Seth buried his face in Oliver's neck, his breath catching for a moment. Then Seth gave Oliver a kiss. "So sweet. Thank you."

Oliver kissed him back and said, "I have absolutely no idea where to go. Lead on."

Seth laughed and reversed their arms so he could pull Oliver in the right direction. For the duration of their twenty-minute train ride, Seth told him about the warm welcome he'd gotten. ("Liz hates everyone. *Everyone.* She kissed me on the *lips.* I had to check the news to make sure the apocalypse hadn't started.") How he and Jonathan, the actor who played William, had hugged tightly, Jonathan whispering that his girlfriend was glad that Seth was back so he'd quit pissing her off with his moodiness.

His arm around the back of Seth's seat, Oliver rested his cheek on his palm and listened happily to Seth talk all about the show and the cast and crew. He was so clearly in his element, so clearly meant to be here in New York. Seth was exactly where he should be, without question.

"I don't *honestly* wish David ill," Seth said, "I just wish him the best of luck on his next performance on a Carnival cruise."

"Maybe he can take Dough-Face with him. He could use some ocean air."

Seth laughed and squeezed Oliver's arm, the joy of a well-received performance still bubbling in him. Oliver wanted him to keep that feeling as long as he could, so he continued to say nothing about his day, even when Seth grew quiet and gently bumped their shoulders, hoping to coax something out of him. They started to walk the short distance to Seth's, but then Seth stopped short. "Oh, we should run in and grab something so we have actual food to eat tonight," he said.

"Don't worry about it. I had a little bit of time to kill after I got back from campus, so I ran down to the market at the corner and got a couple of things," Oliver said.

Seth tilted his head, a peculiar smile on his face. "You did?"

"Is that okay? I didn't want to be a bad guest."

"No! And of course! I just— " Seth shook his head and linked their arms again, leading Oliver around the street corner to his place.

"What?" He stopped, forcing Seth to stop and look at him.

He looked over Oliver's shoulder and worried his bottom lip with his teeth. "I used to have these little fantasies after we broke up. Us getting back together and things like that. You, showing up out of the blue and surprising me with cozy dinners. You'd make little gestures, like you used to when we were kids. Like the flower," he said, looking at the paper flower in his lapel.

"Seth, you're blushing!"

He folded his arms, looking slightly embarrassed but unable to stop grinning. "You can be very charming when you put your mind to it, Oliver."

Oliver wrapped his arms around Seth and pulled him into a warm embrace. He whispered in his ear, "I have a mind to be *very* charming tonight, I'll have you know."

Seth looked him in the eye. "Is that so?" Oliver couldn't tell if he was being coquettish or guarded.

Oliver gave him a quick peck and turned them back to the building. He was ready to get inside, get settled in and tell Seth all about his day so they could talk everything through. The anxiety of the past several weeks was building to a head and he just wanted to get everything out on the table.

He also wanted simply to be alone with Seth. It was amazing to hear that over the years Seth had longed for *him*, had thought about the affection he'd shown Seth when they were together and wanted more. He wrapped his arms around Seth from behind as they waited for the elevator and began softly kissing his neck.

Seth hummed and wrapped his own arms around Oliver's to keep him close. He seemed to be having difficulty making eye contact.

"What other sort of fantasies did you have, hmm?" Oliver asked, lightly dragging his teeth over Seth's earlobe.

Shivering slightly, Seth laughed as the door opened and a young man stepped out with his dog, giving them a curious look. Seth pushed the button to the fifth floor and draped his arms over Oliver's shoulders when the doors closed.

"Mm, one particular favorite had you giving me a foot massage that led... to other things."

Oliver drew his nose along Seth's cheek. "What things?"

Seth backed out of the opening door, towing Oliver along with a cheeky grin. "Maybe I'll show you later."

They got inside and dumped their things in the appropriate locations. Seth stopped in the middle of the room, clapped his hands together and said in a forced tone, "Kitchen? Living room? Where would be best for our life-altering discussion?"

Oliver held his hand for a minute. He needed to feel centered and calm. Maybe Seth could, too.

"Kitchen. I bet you're hungry; I know I am. We'll start here and see where the night takes us?"

Seth cocked his head and narrowed his eyes. "Hmm. That sounds like it could be ominous," he said softly.

Oliver saw worry creeping into Seth's expression so he leaned in and kissed him, whispering, "Don't close off, okay?"

Seth hopped onto the bar stool and watched Oliver pull containers of food from the refrigerator and heat up dinner.

Oliver had been so involved in Seth's performance that he'd almost forgotten about the other part of the day. Almost. Now he was trying to sort through all of his thoughts from earlier,

"So. Silver," he said, pushing a napkin and fork toward Seth, who put the napkin in his lap but left the food untouched as he waited with growing impatience for Oliver to elaborate.

Oliver sighed, but when Seth started, he grabbed Seth's hand and shook his head. "No, no bad sighs, that wasn't a bad sigh," he reassured him. He kissed the back of Seth's hand and softly on the lips over and over again until he felt Seth's body relax against him.

He leaned against the edge of the counter next to Seth and drew the tip of his finger along the prominent knob of bone at Seth's wrist. "It was... well, it was *great* today."

"Really?" Seth clutched at Oliver's hand, a nervous smile on his face.

"Yeah," Oliver exhaled, nudging Seth's plate toward him and pulling his own closer. "I met with the staff, and they're all pretty great—easy to get along with, you know? But that was what I'd expected."

"Mm hmm?"

"They all knew about TMMaT, which was surreal. I mean, it's a small world, but still. Pretty cool to be asked questions about it. Dr. Jones was impressed that the government had taken an interest in it so quickly."

Seth poked at his food, his eyebrows knitted together in concentration or worry, Oliver couldn't tell which. "That great, Oliver. You've worked hard on it."

Oliver ran a hand through his hair, still jittery and jumpy and unable to do more than push the food around on his plate. He *had* worked hard on it. He and Moira had poured their lives into the program and the *government* wanted it. It was incredibly flattering, and incredibly difficult to think of handing the keys over to someone else.

"Yeah, we did." It had been in the back of his mind all day—walking away from something that was so important to him. That applied to either choice, really, but wouldn't it be incredibly irresponsible to just walk away? To start something and not see it through?

He set his fork alongside his plate and watched Seth not watching him. He'd be doing that to Seth, too, if the tables were turned.

"So," Seth said, affecting nonchalance. "I was right about you being a rock star." He gave Oliver a smile and then looked back down at his plate. "Would you be one in Cambridge?"

"Well, I would certainly be doing important things, I don't know about rock star status. I would be in meetings and planning sessions; not very rock and roll," Oliver said, smiling lamely. "Important. Good stuff, for sure. Just... hmm."

Seth cocked his head in question.

"It would be a huge responsibility, Cambridge. Prestigious. I'd be the face of something important. Here I'm not that. And I just... I don't know." Oliver held on to the edge of the counter, chewing his lip. He'd been groomed since he was a child to want a certain type of respectable career that upheld the Andrews name. Cambridge would definitely do that.

"What would you be here?" Seth asked. Oliver looked up and saw that Seth was trying so hard to control his features, to be supportive and thoughtful. The sight just made his confusion twist and writhe in his gut.

"I wouldn't be a nobody, but I'd be a grunt. I wouldn't be the face of something huge; I'd just be one of the faces."

"Tell me about your day, then. Was anything about it satisfying?"

Oliver pushed off the counter and started pacing in the small room. "Yeah. Very. I mean, I really liked the people I talked to today, and they got me right in the mix on some ongoing programs, which was really cool."

Seth regarded him for a moment and inhaled slowly and nodded, as if agreeing to something he was thinking. He picked up his fork and said, "Tell me about that. The people from the programs and things."

"Well, there was one person who really put the bow on the whole day."

Seth looked back at him expectantly.

"Her name is Jen, she's fifteen, and she has serious attitude."

Seth's fork paused midway to his mouth. "Is she some kind of Doogie Howser? She's in the doctoral program?"

"No, no, she's a part of one of the social programs they have. When I introduced myself to her, she gave me the biggest bitch glare. I don't ever remember making an adult feel uncool and old when I was fifteen."

Seth bit back a laugh and patted Oliver's arm. "And? This hateful wretch of a girl was the *bow* on the day?"

"Oh, no, she was great. I knew the book she was reading, she didn't know there was a sequel, and then we became BFFs." Oliver laughed, thinking about her. It really had been a great visit. The more they'd talked, the more animated Jen had become. Her whole countenance began to glow with excitement as she told Oliver about the program she was in. It had been pretty amazing to see the energy and happiness that came just by virtue of having a place that accepted her.

"Oh!" He grabbed Seth's hand with both of his, his face also glowing with the excitement he'd felt earlier in the day. "Jen told me about the summer camp Silver runs that's focused on arts for underprivileged kids. Underprivileged *gay* kids."

Seth blinked. "I can't imagine what that would have been like when we were younger. Wait, yes I can," he said dryly. "There would have been you and me, and that girl with the pierced lip from the Coffee Bean. No one could make a latte like her, come to think of it."

Oliver laughed. "I said that to her, too. Well, not the latte part. Jen is training to be a peer counselor. She's a graduate of one of their other programs. The fieldwork they're doing here is amazing; it's all of the things I've wanted to get involved with, honestly. Not to mention that all of the other aspects I love—direct policymaking and implementation—are here, too."

Seth pushed back from the bar, his hands neatly folded in his lap as he thought. This was why Oliver needed to always include him. When Oliver got excited and his words began almost to trip over themselves, Seth could focus and think. And he knew that he could be that for Seth, too.

Seth seemed to be holding his breath. "So it seems like it comes down to that final question, doesn't it?"

Oliver rubbed his knuckles on his lower lip, trying to think it through. He owed it to Seth, hell, he owed it to himself to do that. "I can go the government route, which is awesome because you can effect change on a grand scale. I'd be rubbing elbows with important leaders, too. Or I can go the route of fieldwork, which is more of the hands-on stuff. One-on-one with families, schools, get involved directly."

Oliver paced back and forth in the small kitchen, his hands unable to settle anywhere as he talked about the different programs he'd visited during the day. The more he explained what was happening at Silver, the more energized he felt, as if he was waking up from a long sleep. He ran his hands through his hair, he paced, he occasionally grabbed Seth's arm to make sure he understood how big a deal a certain part of his day had been.

Seth watched with bright eyes as Oliver talked and talked, oh, God, probably boring him to death with details of social and behavioral intervention, the area he was especially interested in. It had been the driving force for his studies for the past five years, and he had seen it put to action today; it was just incredibly gratifying to finally see what could be accomplished.

He stopped abruptly, realizing that Seth was laughing quietly behind his hand. "What?"

Seth shook his head, still amused. "It's just... you're so excited."

"I know! I really am," Oliver said, his hand on his hip as he looked into the distance and smiled at the memory of his talk with Jen earlier and how the center had saved her life, how it made her want to grow up and be a counselor so no other kid felt isolated and wrong as she had when she came out to her family. It was how Bakerfield, and then Seth, had made him feel.

Seth pushed away from the counter and pulled Oliver into his arms. "Do you know the last time I saw you this animated?"

Oliver shook his head, beaming back at Seth. He felt really happy after such a busy and momentous day; he'd met some great people, had come even closer to realizing a dream he'd had for years, and now here he was in the circle of Seth's arms.

"The last time you performed for an audience," Seth answered. "You know that I was hopelessly in love with you the first time I watched you in action as Mr. Extemporaneous Speaker, right?"

Oliver hid his face in Seth's shoulder, feeling bashful and happy at the same time. Seth kissed his cheek and tightened his arms.

"You were so alive, so poised and confident. I'd just transferred and met you, this square-jawed, green-eyed boy, looking like you'd just stepped out of an Abercrombie ad, so painfully earnest and happy. And on my way to class I saw you addressing the entire lunchroom, trying to get volunteers for some charity fundraiser, which of course they all signed up for. You looked right at me, this scared new kid you'd inexplicably taken under your wing, you smiled and winked at me, and that was it. I was done for." Seth sighed and rocked their bodies side to side gently for a moment. "You were the most wonderful thing I'd ever seen. You have that same energy right now; do you realize that?"

Oliver's arms tightened at Seth's waist with the realization of how right he was; Oliver felt that bouncing, barely contained energy that used to course through him before a swim meet or before he walked onstage. As if something was about to happen, something amazing was just around the corner.

He tried to think about the last time he'd felt like this for something he was involved with. That first lecture of his freshman year at Brandeis; that was when he'd realized that someone just speaking to a crowd could command the same attention as they did singing at the top of their voice. That what a person said could move an audience as much as a turnaround from an underdog team or a perfectly executed note. And that the result could be sharing something that affected the world, beyond the room and the moment. He hadn't realized just how much *more* there was until then.

Seth rested his cheek against Oliver's, his warm breath tickling Oliver's ear. "You know what you want to do, don't you?" he asked quietly.

He'd thrived at Bakerfield as a teenager, a place that had a strict policy of tolerance and that fostered acceptance. At the time, it was just what he'd needed to help him become himself and not the closeted automaton his father would have preferred. The culture there had—without hyperbole— saved his life. Other kids' lives, too. But Bakerfield's students were the only ones benefiting from that forward-thinking attitude. What about other kids, at other schools in other states, who didn't have the chance to escape to a safe haven?

A kernel of an idea had begun to grow when he sat down with the boy he'd been assigned to mentor, a boy with angry tears on his face telling him about his former school, the one he'd been bullied out of because they had no policy in place to help him. No teachers, no administrative staff, no rule books had intervened on his behalf, just an angry father determined to make them do *something*. Oliver had wanted so badly to give him some of the comfort he'd enjoyed; Bakerfield was like a security blanket for him, a safe and nurturing environment he could wrap himself up in. He wished there were places like it for struggling kids everywhere. It wasn't fair that there weren't.

Before Bakerfield, he'd been a boy determined to hide himself, to be what was expected of him. Then he realized that it was okay to be himself, that no one was judging him. Not his peers, at least—he still had to pretend at home to appease his father. But until he reached out to Seth and watched him transform, Oliver hadn't understood what real strength was, what the power of support could do for a person.

Making a difference, helping others, giving them the tools to stand on their own and be strong individuals—*that* was what he wanted to do with his life. And it had all started with a simple moment of reaching out to a beautiful, hurting boy, taking his hand and just *listening* to him, just acknowledging that he was hurting. From that moment on, Seth had taught him the meaning of the word "brave," made him want to be better. Made him capable of being himself, even in front of his parents.

Standing here with him now and seeing him achieve everything because of that support? Oliver's whole life was different because of his connection with this one, special person. He loved working for major change and would always push for it, but he realized that the differences in his life— who he was becoming—were the result of his relationship with Seth.

Seth had asked him, "What would you be here?" His real self, that was what.

Seth was holding him lightly, as if a tighter embrace would fracture him. He was waiting for Oliver to make a decision. Oliver sighed, the palm of his hand at Seth's back, pulling him in. This was real; he really was holding the boy who set his life in motion.

"I... yeah. I know what I want," he replied, closing his eyes, his body thrumming with energy.

"And?" Seth asked, breathlessly.

"I told her that I needed to speak with you and sleep on it. But if I decided to take their offer, I'd come in just as soon as I knew and formally confirm."

Seth's arms began to tighten around him. "Really?" he asked, bouncing on his toes.

Oliver felt a little lightheaded. This was huge—this was his life, and he couldn't look away from how it would affect Seth. Interacting with that young lady earlier, seeing how strong and confident she'd become because of the tools she'd been given through the program, how she wanted to pass on her own confidence and learning... that was it. *That* was what he'd dreamed of doing himself since he was sixteen.

Being able to look into a person's eyes and know there was a difference, know that real change was happening, *that* was what he wanted.

"Really." He exhaled deeply as Seth pulled him back into a bone-crushing hug. After a moment he pulled back and held Oliver's face in his hands. His eyes were shining and his lip was trembling. Oliver tightened his hold at Seth's waist.

"This is the right place, Seth. It's..." He exhaled again and brought their foreheads together. "I want to be here."

"You're really coming here? You're not going to change your mind?"

Oliver nodded. "I'm really coming here." His chest felt tight, his limbs felt loose; he felt amazed and scared and excited and so in love and *happy*, all at once. "It's... perfect."

Seth sighed shakily. "And it's not for me, right? This is because it's—"

"Seth." Oliver pressed their lips together, just long enough to get him to stop talking and relax. "It's perfect. The school. The potential." He traced his fingers along the button placket of Seth's shirt, still thrilling at the sensation of the lean, strong chest under his hand. "And the best part is you."

"So it's decided, then?" Seth asked, practically vibrating under Oliver's hand. How did he get so lucky?

"It's still okay?" Oliver tipped Seth's chin up with his hand and stroked the backs of his fingers along Seth's jaw, his breath hitching when his touch made Seth sigh and close his eyes.

"Of *course*," Seth answered, kissing him. Relief and excitement raced through him in equal measure. He was doing this. Correction: *They* were doing this.

The thought of them as a *them* again hit him like a ton of bricks and he swayed in Seth's embrace. Then he held their foreheads together and he said quietly, "We decided, didn't we?"

Seth didn't seem to understand. Oliver smoothed his hand over the hair above Seth's ear, plunging his fingers in its thick lushness of it. "On there being a 'we.' Seth, I want this. I want the school, I want this city." His fingers tightened the slightest amount in Seth's hair. He was almost afraid that he would leave or disappear, that this wasn't actually happening. "I want *you*."

For a moment, Oliver wasn't able to breathe. Until Seth gave him a tiny nod of agreement, and the air rushed out of him in what was almost a pained whine. And then Seth was tentatively kissing him, and Oliver clutched at him, his arms, his back, until finally Oliver's hands settled, cradling Seth's face.

"I want you," he repeated. He wanted to make sure that Seth knew just how much he mattered; and something in his heart was fracturing at the hesitation he still felt from Seth. Loath as he was to stop kissing him, not be touching every inch of him that he could, Oliver pulled back, holding Seth's hands and looking down at them to stay grounded.

"Seth?"

"Really?" Seth asked. His voice sounded broken.

Oliver looked at him, then, and felt both so solid and sure of his decision and so upset with himself for fostering so much doubt in the man he loved; Seth should know to his core. And as he responded with an emphatic nod, Oliver said, "I am moving to New York City. I'm moving here, and first thing in the morning, I'm going to sign documents to make it official."

Seth sagged against him, his fists on Oliver's shoulders. Oliver held him, his hands warm and firm against Seth's body, further proof that as long as Seth would let him, he'd be here where he belonged.

"I want you in my life. My God," Oliver laughed, his arms squeezing tightly. "You *are* my life."

Seth breathed in relief and nuzzled his cheek against Oliver's, his arms over Oliver's shoulders and hands in his hair, holding him in place. It wasn't necessary; he wasn't going anywhere.

"Please. Let me love you," Oliver asked quietly.

Seth drew his hands from Oliver's hair to cup his face, a bewildered smile on his face. "Do you even remotely feel like eating?" he murmured, pressing his face against Oliver's neck.

"Not in the slightest."

Seth broke away, grabbed Oliver's hand and led him back to the bedroom. He sat on the edge of the bed and pulled Oliver to him, resting his face against Oliver's abdomen, just holding him. "I tried to not get my hopes up today, just so you know."

Oliver carded his fingers through Seth's hair. "I know. Well, I know *now*. I was my usual hopeful self."

Seth's breath was warm against Oliver's belly. "I know. I love that about you." He looked up at Oliver, his face no longer guarded, no hesitation to be seen. "It was nice to think you were seeing us with a future."

Oliver drew his fingertips along Seth's forehead and temple. "I don't think I know how to see one without you, to be honest."

"Fortunately, it looks like you won't have to," Seth said, smiling against Oliver's shirt even as his hands tightened their grip.

They were still for a few moments, holding each other as they let the reality sink in that this was going to happen, that they could move forward together. Seth gave Oliver's hips a squeeze and pushed him back a step. "Come on. I want to just hold you," he said, and he stood to undress.

It's how every night is supposed to end.

Another tidal wave of "this is really happening" threatened to knock Oliver off his feet; he took it as a sign to hurry up and lay down. They both stripped to their briefs, and soon enough Oliver was slipping into

Seth's opened arms, laying his cheek against Seth's shoulder, and letting himself truly relax.

Anchored—that's how he felt, laying there together; no longer adrift and going where the academic winds blew him, alone and wondering how he'd gotten himself where he was. The nervous twisting in his belly that had been with him ever since he first heard that video clip all of those months ago was melting away as Seth kissed his temple, stroked his hair, held him closer. To think that only a few months ago he was sitting in his bedroom with a ribbon-tied stack of letters, wondering how he'd gone so wrong—now, here, enfolded in Seth's arms, he wondered how he got so lucky and it could go so right.

"I love you. It doesn't seem like enough, but I do. I love you with everything I am," Oliver whispered, shivering as Seth's fingertips lightly trailed down his bare back and up again to his hair. Seth pulled gently until Oliver took the hint, moving up on the bed until he was leaning against the headboard and they were face to face.

Seth shook his head, his eyes closed. He inhaled deeply and leaned forward to kiss Oliver, breathing an "I love you" over his lips and into his mouth.

So much want, need and affection flowed through Oliver. He pulled Seth up against his body, his hand skimming over Seth's shoulder and down his arm, his fingertips drawing back and forth over the soft down on his belly. With a quiet moan, Seth opened to him, his own hands holding Oliver firm and sure, tilting his jaw to let Oliver kiss him deeper as they whispered each other's names into warm, bare skin.

The moon shone through the blinds, illuminating Seth's pale skin as he knelt over Oliver and kissed a trail down his chest and belly. It glinted off his hair as his mouth sank over Oliver's hard and straining cock, and the ever-present street noises were drowned out by the gasps forced from Oliver as Seth worked his fingers inside him.

Nothing could match the overwhelming passion and love that filled every inch of him when Seth finally entered him, his body curled protectively over Oliver's back, their fingers entwined and stretched overhead.

When Seth panted, "I love you," as he climaxed, his arms wrapped tightly around Oliver's waist and his face pressed against Oliver's shoulder blades, the moment was so gratifying and perfect that Oliver couldn't help but press their joined hands to his lips, feeling as if their love-making marked something official for them. They were in love. They were together. That would never change.

They had changed, though, had grown up, had moved past the road-blocks of their youth. Oliver had wandered through life trying to discover who he was and who he wanted to be. While he was still developing—and he imagined he would be for years to come—he knew that he wanted to *be* with Seth at his side, and that quite possibly he couldn't be that future self *without* Seth to challenge him and push him constantly to improve himself, if only to be worthy of Seth's love.

After cleaning up, they lay together in each other's arms, trading sleepy kisses in the dark. Seth yawned against Oliver's neck, sending goosebumps down his back. Oliver pulled the blanket up higher around them and happily nestled in the soft bed. He felt safe and connected and confident that they had the rest of their lives to make up for the nights they hadn't ended like this—together.

As Oliver began to fall asleep, he noticed that, with the moonlight softening his features, Seth looked just like the boy he'd met years before, the one who changed his life for the better.

Chapter Twenty-one

"Oliver, she's going to get suspicious."

"Mm, I don't care. One more."

Seth laughed and pushed Oliver away. "We are in *public*." He smoothed his hair, then seemed to think better of it and straightened Oliver's hair and collar instead. "Now go sign the whatever it is, and let's go celebrate."

Oliver propped himself up against the doorway to Dr. Jones' office, positively beaming at his boyfriend. They'd traded goofy, face-breaking smiles all morning as they rushed to dress and get breakfast and make it to Silver as soon as possible.

"And you're sure you're okay with this?" Oliver asked, even though he knew the answer.

"I'm about to change my mind if you don't cut it out," Seth said, rolling his eyes. He gave Oliver a quick peck on the lips. "Now get going. I spied a fascinating bulletin board down the hall that I think I'll occupy my time with while you take care of this." Seth shot him a big grin over his shoulder as he moved off, and Oliver stood there for a moment and watched him walk away. Seth paused at the corner and gave him an exasperated glare and a shooing motion before ducking around it.

Laughing to himself, Oliver rapped twice on the door and waited to be called in. This was it; once the ink was on the paper, there was no going back. Fortunately, he had no intention of changing his mind. This was where he was supposed to be; this was *who* he was supposed to be.

"Come in!" he heard. He took a deep breath, checked his hair one last time, and opened the door.

"Dr. Jones! Good morning." Feeling like he was practically floating, he walked in and shut the door behind him.

* * *

Oliver stared out the window of the cab, watching the city disappear behind him as they drove toward the Lincoln Tunnel; he could only get a flight out of Newark on such short notice. He caught sight of his expression in the glass as the darkness of the tunnel took over, the flickering reflective lights on the walls distorting his features. He was unbelievably happy to have a plan and that Seth featured so prominently in it; he couldn't deny how hard it was to leave, though. Just a few months until graduation, and then they would never have to be apart again.

At least that's what Seth had said to him as he held him on the sidewalk, the cab driver grumbling at the side of the vehicle. Seth had wiped away Oliver's tears, laughing at him for being so emotional, even though his cheeks were equally wet.

"Just a couple of months. They'll fly by," Oliver agreed.

"Call me when you get there? Or send me an email, I don't care which; just let me know you're there, okay?"

Oliver nodded and leaned into him. They held each other for another moment, neither wanting to let go. The cab driver threw his hands in the air. "You want to pay to stay? Okay, but I'm sitting down."

Seth shot him a sour look and dipped down for one last, quick kiss. "Love you."

Oliver closed his eyes and smiled. He would never, ever take those words for granted. And they felt so amazingly good to hear. "Love you, too."

"Call me," Seth had repeated, stepping back so Oliver could leave.

Now sunshine blasted through the windshield as they exited the tunnel; the grimy industrial area of Jersey was all there was to see, looking ahead. He twisted in his seat and saw the tip of Manhattan out of the back window, just barely visible; beyond it in the distance was the Brooklyn Bridge, Seth and where Oliver would be soon.

He turned back in his seat and let himself sigh just once. It was just a pause—he'd be back, and he wouldn't have to leave again.

April 13, 11:08 PM GMT
To: Seth Larsen

From: Oliver Andrews
Subject: I'm here and I miss you

Before I collapse, I wanted to let you know that I made it here safely, there were no crying babies on my flight, and I came home to find Janos being indecent with a young lady—not Moira—on the sofa.

Straight boys have no class.

I'm about to go to bed; it's going to be hard to not have you next to me, but in a few short months I'll have you forever. You already have me.

I love you.

Oliver

p.s. I hope you had yet another spectacular performance tonight. I'll bet that whoever your "first duet partner" was, he knows how stupid he was for ever letting someone as amazing as you go.

April 13, 10:21 PM EST
To: Oliver Andrews
From: Seth Larsen
Subject: :(

Legs were broken (figuratively speaking) and we had another great show. Apparently my "grief and loss" were "palpable." You always did push me to be my best in a performance.

I wish you were in my bed. I look forward to when it's our bed. Get some rest, dive into work, don't flunk out.

I love *you.*

Seth

p.s. I think he knows how stupid he was. Thank goodness he's getting so well educated now. I hope he never does something stupid like that again, but he shouldn't worry. I wouldn't let him. :)

* * *

April crawled by until they found a rhythm in communication. Oliver would Skype after dinner, which was before Seth's scheduled afternoon training sessions (either physical or vocal). Having that regular connection did wonders for Oliver's ability to sleep at night; no more fitful dreams woke him to an aching sense of loss.

They each threw themselves into work knowing that it would help occupy their minds. When it was clear that everything was going according to plan, Oliver sent graduation information to Seth, with the hope that he might be able to come in June.

"Summer is one of the busiest times on Broadway, though. And with my new contract... I wish I could come, I really do," Seth said sadly during one of their Skype sessions.

Oliver sighed and propped his chin on his hand, wishing that it weren't just a projected image. "I know. I sort of expected that, but I thought I'd ask anyway."

"Your family is coming, right?" Seth asked. The image briefly became grainy and distorted as he shifted to a more comfortable position on his tiny loveseat.

"Yes, they'll come out the day before and stay until just after."

"Are they going to record it?" Seth asked.

"I'll make sure they do," Oliver said, smiling.

"Good, because I've watched a few Cambridge graduations on YouTube, now, and it's like a coronation of royalty or something. You know how I love a good show."

One month. That's all he had to endure, just one more month.

Seth sent him an email exactly one month before his graduation with "Isn't this nice?" and a link to an apartment in the West Village: two bedrooms, one-and-a-half baths and three whole closets. Oliver whistled when he saw the listed rental price.

May 28, 7:31 PM GMT
To: Seth Larsen
From: Oliver Andrews
Subject: Have you learned to spin straw into gold, Rumpelstiltskin?

Great place! I can't believe that bathroom remodel—the shower looks like a dream. Do you have a friend moving there? Or are you just wishfully thinking?

Moira says hello, by the way. She's found clips on YouTube of bootlegged performances (sorry) and keeps singing some of your

numbers to me. Her strengths lie in other areas.
Love you!
Oliver

May 28, 2:44 PM EST
To: Oliver Andrews
From: Seth Larsen
Subject: Har har de har har.
Well, I'd like to think I had a friend moving there. :)
What do you think about that place, Oliver? Check it out on a map. Look at how convenient it is to the Washington campus!
I love you, even when you're being thick. Perhaps you need to read between some lines, Mr. Higher Education. ;)
Seth

Oliver blinked at the monitor. Then he pulled up a map to find that the apartment was a short walk to his campus, only a few blocks, and close to Seth's theater, too. He sank back into the pillows on his bed, biting his lip. He clicked the link to the details on the apartment again. Monthly rent was steep, but then, that was New York. He expected it to be. But he'd also expected to pay the full amount by himself.

Half of the rent would still be well within budget. Especially if all of the other costs were being shared. *Shared.* His heart started pounding as he clicked through the pictures listed on the realtor page. One of the bathrooms had been gutted and remodeled and had an amazingly huge shower. He clicked on the next picture of the living room. One wall was exposed brick. He flashed to one of their old fantasies of their first New York apartment together.

It was supposed to have an exposed brick wall and a shower large enough to "share."

This intensity of his longing, hope and excitement seemed as if it might cause him physical damage. He took a deep breath. Once he had himself under control, he typed a fast response to Seth.

You have more than a friend moving there. Tell me what I have to sign.

Oh my God. Seth!!
YES. <3

He sat back, staring at the screen with a huge lopsided grin on his face, and imagined them decorating the place. After a few minutes, Seth replied.

Okay. I had to take a minute to dance around. :) I emailed my realtor; she's jumping on it. We should be able to move in on July 1, should everything go according to plan. Oliver, I am excited and happy and so unbelievably in love with you, and if you were here, oh, the things I would do...
We're finally doing this!
Love you love you
Seth

Oliver stretched out on his mattress, grinning and running a hand through his hair. They'd definitely need to lose that tiny loveseat. Oh God, they were going to go furniture shopping together. Set up a house together. *Their* place, finally. He continued to sprawl there, staring up at the ceiling with his hands behind his head, beaming up at nothing. One more month.

* * *

A week later and he had a manila envelope waiting for him when he got home, containing a stamped and addressed envelope (with international postage paid) and a handwritten note.

Oliver,
I didn't think we'd be doing this long-distance, but then, a few months ago I didn't think we'd be doing this at all. I'm so glad we are.
Love you,
Seth

Oliver read over the paperwork briefly, smiling at Seth's familiar signature. He checked all of the appropriate boxes for "co-tenant" and signed his name with a flourish. He whistled as he walked to the end of the block to mail the envelope. There may have been an extra little spin with his arms stretched out wide as he turned back toward the almost-not-his-anymore apartment. There definitely was a sparkle in his eye. He hadn't been able to get rid of that for a few days, now.

Not that he was complaining.

* * *

After a long but good day, Oliver had gone back to his apartment so he could change out of his graduation gown, with the intent of meeting his parents at the pub in a short while. His parents seemed proud of him, and Moira surprised him with a full-mouth kiss as he turned to congratulate her; the memory of that was still making him blush and laugh, especially over the look of confusion on his father's face.

His room was mostly emptied, aside from the furniture that stayed with the house. He had a bag with clothes for tonight and tomorrow; the rest of his belongings had been sent ahead to the new apartment.

With a lot of cajoling on Oliver's part, he'd convinced Seth to leave the unpacking at the new place to do together. It was hard enough for him to be on the other side of the ocean—he wanted something of this monumental step to be done together.

Seth had sent him an email the night before with a very important picture: him, holding two keys. A thrill rocketed through him at the thought of what was to come. He was flying out the next afternoon; he didn't think he'd sleep a wink that night.

Saying goodbye to Janos had been surprisingly emotional. They didn't cry or anything; parting just left a void. They'd spent a significant amount of time together, Oliver learning how to block out unwanted noise, Janos doing the same—even if it was only during the week when Seth visited.

Janos had clapped him on the shoulders, pulling him in for a kiss on each cheek and a formal farewell. He in turn gave Janos a firm handshake and a sincere, "It's been good getting to know you."

Janos looked as though he wanted to say more, but instead he simply clapped Oliver on the shoulder again and said solemnly, "Oliver, you're a good man."

Though he couldn't understand why, it left him buzzing as if from the highest praise.

It had been harder with Moira, who met with him and his parents the night before for celebratory cocktails. He knew it was going to be bad when she barely had anything to drink. She laughed at herself when she began crying at the end of the night.

"Fook me, lad, but you're a hard one to let go of," she said, her voice breaking as she threw her arms around his shoulders.

He held her up off the ground and swung her legs back and forth to get her to giggle. "You'll always have a place to visit in New York, you know."

"Sure, and you'll go flaunting your dream life in my face," she scowled at him. "You and that beautiful boy of yours. Oh, Christ. I'm happy for you, Oliver, truly, just feeling a little sorry for myself is all. I got used to your gob, didn't I?"

* * *

His family pulled up in their rental car to collect him for the ride to the airport. His mother didn't like that he wasn't coming back to Kansas with them, but Oliver didn't have to push too hard to get her to back off.

It was just how his family was.

Thinking of that led his thoughts to the card he had slipped into the outside pocket of his carry-on bag.

> *Hey Kid—*
> *Hope your new degree don't mean you can't hang with us slobs no*
> *more.*
> *I'm real proud of you, Oliver. Graduating is something special.*
> *Looking forward to seeing pictures of you in that fancy cap and gown*
> *Seth keeps going on about.*
> *Love ya.*
> *Big Mike*

There had been another card that the rest of the gang had signed;

Natalie had kissed it with some garish lipstick and Little Mike wrote an especially nice message about how glad he was that Oliver and Seth were back together. It made Oliver choke up and required a walk around the block so the guys watching soccer in the other room wouldn't hear him cry.

He'd always known Seth was more to him than just someone to love; Seth was a family and a whole life, too.

He smiled at the stewardess as he declined a beverage and tuned out his parents as they debated the merits of white wine over red. Just a few more hours and he'd be home. He closed his eyes, resting his cheek against the cool glass of the airplane window, and imagined the sensation of flying was really the tether connecting his heart to Seth's, pulling him back to where he belonged.

* * *

He'd given his mother a kiss on her cheek, shaken his father's hand and accepted their "congratulations" as they stayed in their seats and he disembarked in New York City. He always got an excited happy feeling as he walked down the airway at an airport, knowing that he was almost home, and it had been no different this time. In fact, his excitement continued to build through customs and beyond, because he was coming home, to his real and proper home. He was rolling his bag through the terminal, heading toward the cluster of public transportation options, when his phone vibrated in his pocket.

Look up.

He read it again, then looked around the busy space. Seth was leaning against the glass wall by the exit, smiling at him. Oliver dropped the handle to his luggage and jogged the ten or so feet to where Seth was, picking him up in a crushing hug and kissing him anywhere he could reach.

Laughing, Seth pushed at his shoulder. "Your stuff's going to be stolen, babe."

Joyfully stealing one more kiss, Oliver said, "I don't care."

Seth rolled his eyes playfully, then swiftly walked over to grab Oliver's rolling bag and duffel.

"What are you doing here? I thought you had the mover earlier and the Sunday matinée today?" Oliver asked, snaking his arms around Seth's waist.

Seth kept the bags between them and hugged Oliver back one-handed. "First part is done, and as for the matinée, I gave it to the understudy because I just knew that you'd try to take a cab. It's time for you to learn how to get around the city like a proper New Yorker," he said, leading Oliver by the hand to the A train connection.

"Fifteen more minutes," Seth said, once they were aboard.

Oliver's excitement rose at the promise in Seth's voice.

The train was packed and they were pushed close together. Oliver held the overhead strap with one hand while the other was wound around Seth's waist. Oliver breathed him in, trying to absorb the fact that he was really here. *Finally.*

Seth gave his side a squeeze when it was their stop. They wrestled their things off the train, quiet as they held hands and climbed the stairs out of the subway. Instead of turning right as Oliver anticipated, Seth turned to him instead, dropping the duffel between his feet and twining his arms around Oliver's neck.

"Hey. I love you."

Warmth radiated through Oliver's body. He completely forgot that people were streaming past them on the street corner; all he could see was love looking back at him through clear hazel eyes.

"I love you, too," Oliver breathed.

Seth laughed softly under his breath and kissed Oliver gently. Then he pulled out his phone and snapped a picture of the two of them with their cheeks pressed together.

"Come on. Almost there," Seth said, towing him along the side street to their building. Oliver thought briefly that it was a good thing Seth knew where they were going, because he was feeling rather foggy from the combination of travel and being this close to his boyfriend again.

"This is it." Seth stopped in front of a charming red brick prewar building, dug into his pocket and pulled out a key ring; there was only one key on it. Seth held it out to Oliver, smiling, but as Oliver reached to take it, Seth snatched his hand back and gave him a kiss.

"Oliver." Seth cupped his cheek and quietly said, "I love you."

Oliver was feeling positively lightheaded at this point. He laughed and reached for Seth's hand. "I love you, too," he sighed, happy beyond telling.

Seth took out his phone again, but this time he snapped a picture as he pressed his lips to Oliver's.

While Oliver certainly had no problem with being kissed, he could tell something was going on. He tilted his head and gave Seth a skeptical look. "What are you up to?"

Seth shook his head, biting the end of his thumb to keep from laughing. "You're tired, aren't you?"

"A little, but—"

"Let's get you upstairs and comfortable."

They went inside the air-conditioned building. Oliver immediately felt a little more solid, less floaty and dreamlike.

They were the only ones on the elevator. As it climbed to the eleventh floor, Oliver took the opportunity to pull Seth into his arms. Their bodies touching reassured him that this was real, that this was not just an amazing dream. Seth ran his hand up and down Oliver's spine and hummed softly into his ear.

Stepping off the elevator, Seth led the way again down a short hallway to their door. "Would you be so kind as to do the honors?" Seth asked.

Oliver pulled out his key; it took him a second to steady his hand and actually get the key in the lock, but managed in the end, giving a tiny "Yay!" when the door opened. Seth held the door for him as they entered.

Boxes were still piled high against the walls, but that was to be expected. There was a new sofa, much larger than the loveseat; it even had chaise at one end. Oliver could already see them curled up on it, watching TV or reading books, and his heart flip-flopped and he couldn't stand it anymore—he dropped his suitcase, pulled the duffel off of Seth's shoulder and tugged him into his arms.

Seth breathed, "I love you so much," into Oliver's ear, sending chills down his spine.

He pulled back, then; Seth's eyes were positively shining.

"Don't you remember?" Seth asked.

Oliver lightly ran his thumb along Seth's jaw and shook his head, no. He wasn't fully capable of speech just yet, and his faculties for problem solving were clearly on vacation.

Seth ran his fingers up Oliver's sides. Oliver wrapped his arms around Seth's shoulders, trapping Seth's arms between them. Seth sucked lightly at a place just under Oliver's ear that got him to moan brokenly, "What?"

"When I first got to Juilliard I promised that when you finally got here, I could take you to any corner, to any place in the city and tell you that I love you." He kissed Oliver's neck again, saying, "And I'm a man of my word," against Oliver's overheated skin.

"Oh, *Seth*." Oliver hugged Seth so tightly that he gave a little squeak. Oliver held his face and kissed the corners of his mouth. "Your very first letter to me."

Seth made a happy noise. "I knew you'd get here eventually."

"Did you?" Oliver asked, fingers raking up Seth's spine.

"Well, in the very beginning I hoped you would," Seth said quietly. "You got me hoping again in England."

A pang shot through Oliver for all the years missed. He led Seth to the sofa, still holding his hands, keeping his eyes on them as his fingertip followed the prominent tendons and veins on the backs of Seth's elegant, strong hand.

"I am so sorry that I'm so... stupid. Foolish. I—" Oliver exhaled sharply, shaking his head. Seth leaned forward and rested his cheek on Oliver's shoulder.

"I'm sorry, too. But we're here now, right?"

Oliver nodded. He turned to place a firm, needy kiss on Seth's hair.

Seth said, "I'm going to make a rule: no more apologizing for the past. I think we've more than made up for it." He brought their hands up to his face and kissed Oliver's knuckles one by one. "Let's make happy memories, okay?"

The lump that had formed in Oliver's throat began to melt away at the sensation of Seth's mouth on his skin, at the determination in Seth's voice. He swallowed thickly and sat up, wanting Seth to look at him, to see just how much he meant it when he said, "I promise."

They held each other for a moment, rocking gently back and forth. Oliver shivered once, as if his subconscious was trying to shake off as much of the sadness from the past as it could.

Seth gave him one last squeeze and pulled back. "I've seriously got to get my hands on some of these boxes or I'm going to go crazy."

Laughing, Oliver let Seth pull him to his feet as he surveyed their new place. "What do you want me to do?"

Seth tapped his lip with his finger, thinking. "First, I need my clipboard; I think I left it in the kitchen with the last load from yesterday. It'll show you what each colored dot represents: bedroom, bathroom, kitchen, study—oh, that's what I'm calling the spare bedroom."

Oliver let Seth put him to work organizing stray boxes that hadn't been put in the right color-coordinated room. Seth seemed like a professional mover.

"Why am I surprised?" he said under his breath, impressed by the way Seth unpacked wine glasses from their bubble-wrap with incredible speed.

"Hmm?" Seth asked over his shoulder; he didn't slow down once.

"You're... how are you so good at this?"

"It's a gift. Summers spent reorganizing my dad's shop, I guess," Seth said, attacking a new box.

"If you would, please address the boxes of linens in our bedroom; I don't want to sleep on a bare mattress tonight." Seth shuddered at the thought, as did Oliver but for an entirely different reason, he suspected.

Our bedroom.

Every morning they would wake up together. Every night they would go to bed together. They weren't sleeping over. This wasn't a vacation or a weekend or a trial run: This was their place. He stood there watching Seth unpack a box of framed pictures and he would have sworn that he felt the world shift back into place.

"You said 'our bedroom.'" He could barely find the breath to say it.

"Hmm?" Seth asked over his shoulder, and did a double take. "Oliver? What is it?"

Surely his face was splitting from the sheer volume of joy that was pouring out of him. "You said 'our bedroom.' We have an 'our bedroom,' finally."

Seth went still and his hand dropped to his side as a smile slowly spread across his features, too. "I did say that, didn't I?"

Oliver stepped carefully around the open boxes and packing material and leaned in for a kiss. "You did."

Seth hummed happily against his lips after a lengthy second kiss, and then said, "Seriously. I love you, but sheets, Oliver. I need sheets."

Oliver bravely walked backwards through the chaos, loath to lose sight of Seth for a moment, even though Seth was rolling his eyes and laughing at him, until he was able to duck into the bedroom. There was Seth's magnificent mattress, thank goodness, and several boxes against the wall.

He found the one marked "Linens" and ripped it open. Inside were freshly washed sheets packed in tissue paper with a lavender sachet. He laughed, shook his head, and pulled them out, snapping them in the air to get the fold lines out.

After he put the bedroom in order, his body clock reminded him of how late it really was, and how grimy he felt from traveling all day. "Permission to skip unpacking until tomorrow so I can clean up?" he called out, opening a box marked "Toiletries."

"Sure. But you are on kitchen duty tomorrow. It's my one day off and I want everything in its place, mister."

"I won't take long," he said, leaning down to kiss Seth, who beamed back up at him.

"Take as long as you need. I'm going to finish unwrapping a few things while you shower."

Oliver made sure enough towels were unpacked for the two of them as the water in the shower heated. They hadn't installed Seth's magical shower head yet, but the water pressure was great, regardless. He made quick work of cleaning up, knowing that Seth's bed—correction: *their bed*—was waiting for him. Currently, he only knew where his underwear was, so he pulled on a nice striped pair of square-cut boxer briefs and slipped into the bedroom.

Seth was sitting on the floor on the right side of the bed, sorting through a box of small framed photographs. He turned when he heard Oliver enter the room, and his "oh, hello" smile turned into an "oh, *hello*" smile.

"Oliver?" Seth asked as his eyes raked over Oliver's bare chest.

"Mm?"

"I get to see this every single night." Seth rose gracefully to his feet and walked around the foot of the bed, skating the flat of his hand up Oliver's abdomen and chest, fingers raking the coarse, dark hair there against the grain. "Lucky me," he whispered, still watching his hand as it trailed over Oliver's body. Oliver shivered, but he wasn't cold.

"Seth?" Oliver hardly recognized his voice, it was so husky and filled with need. "How quickly can you get to bed?"

Seth's gaze made his breathing run shallow; it had been a long time since he'd been with Seth, able to hold him, kiss him.

"Ten. But I'll make it five."

Oliver moved in to kiss him, his eyes beginning to close and his pulse picking up speed, but Seth pushed him back gently, eliciting a pained whine. Oliver just needed Seth in his arms. Possibly under him. Over would be even better.

"You really need to give me five minutes. I won't be long." Seth raked his fingers over Oliver's damp scalp and tugged on the soft hair at his nape.

Oliver nodded. Speech seemed to be far too difficult all of a sudden. Seth started undressing as he left the room, and Oliver continued to stare at the spot where he had been, feeling more than a little frustrated that Seth had only started unbuttoning his jeans as he walked out. The least he could have done was take them off before leaving. The sound of the water broke his reverie, and he started frantically searching for his luggage.

He was glad that Seth took slightly longer than the promised five minutes, because Oliver almost sank to the floor in frustrated tears when he couldn't find his bag. He knew Seth placed a high priority on personal items, so where did he put it? The water shut off and it was like a light bulb—the closet!

Oliver raced back to their bedroom, almost slipping and losing his footing on an errant strip of bubble-wrap, jerked the closet door open and found his roll-away bag. *Oh thank God.* The bathroom door opened and Oliver, after grabbing the lube, barely managed to get the pocket zipped back up and himself artfully arranged on the bed by the time Seth came into the bedroom, stark naked and drying his hair. He had a second towel under his arm, which he dropped on the foot of the bed.

Oliver mindlessly ran his fingertips over his belly as he watched Seth slide the soft cotton over his thick hair and then wrap it around his shoulders to dry off his back; it accentuated his narrow waist and the breadth and strength of his shoulders. Oliver cleared his throat, but his voice still came out gravelly as he said, "You said five minutes; that was almost nine."

Seth draped the towel over the top of an empty box and crawled across the bed on his hands and knees, already half hard, a knowing, naughty grin on his face. "Mm hmm. Want to know why?"

He straddled Oliver's waist, using the headboard for leverage as he bent down to kiss Oliver, his mouth hot and wet and needy. Oliver's head was swimming; Seth's tongue slipped into his mouth, and his body was warm and still slightly shower-damp. Seth grabbed Oliver's hand and brought it down his body. When Oliver made to curl his fingers around Seth's cock, he laughed softly against Oliver's lips, saying, "No."

He slid Oliver's hand lower, dragging the pads of Oliver's fingers over his already-stretched entrance and exhaled over Oliver's parted lips as Oliver's brain caught up. Oliver groaned against Seth's mouth as two fingers slid in, hot and tight, but easily.

"Oh my *God,*" Oliver moaned.

Seth moved to lay next to Oliver, snapping the waistband of Oliver's striped briefs. "Very nice," he said, kissing Oliver thoroughly before saying, "Now get them off."

Not quite in control of all of his faculties, Oliver did manage to raise his hips to allow Seth to pull them down his legs. God, it had been months, and before that, *years*, since Seth bottomed. Oliver pulled Seth back flush against his body, his hands gripping Seth's round ass and kneading it, grinding their bodies together, not wanting to be apart for even a second.

Seth sucked Oliver's bottom lip between his teeth, pulling back with a wordless groan Oliver thought sounded quite intelligent, given that at the moment he would have had trouble remembering most of the alphabet. Seth had the tiny bottle of lubricant in his hand; he grabbed one of Oliver's and kissed the palm, his eyes closing on contact. Then he popped the lid off the bottle and squeezed a generous amount across three of Oliver's fingers.

"Jesus... I—" Seth stopped Oliver's brilliant soliloquy with another searing kiss while guiding Oliver's lubricated hand between his legs.

"It's been months. I need you," Seth exhaled, his voice high and breathy as he started to ride Oliver's fingers.

"I need you, too. Oh my *God,*" Oliver moaned, pressing his face into Seth's neck to anchor himself. The need to feel Seth's body against his radiated from the marrow of his bones. This was the sort of thing that must lead to people dying during sex, Oliver thought. He was pretty sure that his heart had stopped and he was incapable of breathing, and all he could focus on was the tight, slick heat currently engulfing the fingers of his right hand. That and the unbelievable image of Seth leaning over him, hair hanging down and tickling Oliver's face as he gasped and moaned.

"Hips."

"Hunh?" Oliver asked, arching up and trying to get Seth's lips back on his again, but Seth had twisted away, reaching for something.

He turned back and had a spare towel in his hands. "Hips," he said again, his voice becoming reedy and frantic as he pushed on Oliver's leg. Oh. Right. Oliver raised himself up enough for Seth to slide a towel under their bodies.

Thankfully, Seth came back to kiss him, his tongue sliding and stroking against Oliver's. "I want you, but I want to sleep on a clean bed, after." Seth kissed along Oliver's neck to his ear, whispering, "I really fucking want you right now, Oliver."

"You're going to *kill* me." Oliver pushed up on his elbows, sliding backwards to rest against the headboard. He held his hand out and pulled Seth into his lap, his breath rushing out all at once at Seth's moan when their bodies made contact again. Oliver held him close, kissing his neck and thrilling at the desperate, breathy noises he was making. He thrilled, too, at the fact that only he had the pleasure of getting Seth to make those noises.

"Please," Seth whined, pushing back with his hips and grinding against Oliver. He held himself still as Seth sank down slowly over him, overcome by the way their bodies fit together and how amazing Seth felt on top of him and in his arms, his sweat-slick muscles and skin moving under Oliver's hands.

He held Seth still for a moment, his forehead against Seth's sternum, willing his brain to catch up with his body. Seth ran his palms up Oliver's arms and shoulders, tipped his head back and drew his lips softly, back and forth, over Oliver's mouth.

"Are you with me?" Seth asked, his voice husky and desperate.

Oliver caught his breath. "Yes," he said, his hands gripping Seth's hips. He kissed Seth fervently, communicating that there was no question he was here not just for the moment, but for always.

As Oliver grabbed Seth's hips, rocking him up and down, angling his hips just so, Seth's chin dropped down and he inhaled sharply. "Oh, f-fuck, Oliver—just th—" Seth stammered.

Oliver's breath came out closer to a growl as he redoubled his efforts. God, he fucking loved it when Seth couldn't get a word out because of what Oliver was doing to him—he flashed to the first time he'd brought Seth off like this, years before, when Seth came home from New York and they were so desperate to be together.

That first time, Seth had said he wanted to feel Oliver inside of him, and Oliver, who had been wound up for weeks anticipating Seth's arrival, had almost come just when he asked for it. Once he had Seth over him, and he felt that incredible heat wrapped around him so fucking tight and amazing—he was inside his *boyfriend*—Seth had cried out his name, his voice breaking, and that image of Seth sweaty, completely undone to the point of not being able to say Oliver's *name* in the end, was burned into his memory.

Back then, Oliver was young and stupid and so, so in love.

Now, Seth's head dropped back and his Adam's apple worked as he rose and sank rhythmically over Oliver, and Oliver realized that nothing had changed. Well, he wasn't as young as he once was, but he was still so, *so* stupidly in love.

He tried to last, wanted to last as long as he could for him, but it had been months and Seth was there, in his arms, his face flushed with pleasure, his body slick with sweat, and it was just like that first time and it was just too much, the memories tripping over reality.

He held Seth's cock in his hand and sucked on the spot just to the right of Seth's Adam's apple that he knew—*learned in the back of Seth's car the summer before his senior year of high school*—was incredibly sensitive and was rewarded by Seth beginning to gasp, "Oliver," with every rock, felt Seth trembling under his hand at the small of his back—*the first time they had sex Seth had turned away to pull his shirt off and his undershirt rode up and Oliver could see one prominent freckle just above the waistband of Seth's jeans*—and it was just too much. He pressed his cheek against Seth's sternum, thrusting desperately up into Seth's body, his hand loose but still working around him.

His orgasm didn't have a slow build; it rocketed through his entire body as he clutched Seth's ass, his mouth working helplessly along Seth's collarbone. He gasped as Seth wrapped his arms around him, feeling completely enveloped by him and the memories of all the times they'd been like this. As he pulsed deep inside Seth's body, his hand jacked Seth more firmly, his thumb working back and forth over the groove on the underside of the head of Seth's cock—*I love it when you hold me tight, Oliver; oh my God, just there*—and it was enough to get Seth to join him as he cried out Oliver's name brokenly through his own orgasm.

They held each other as their breathing slowed to something closer to normal. Oliver wanted Seth's lips on his; fortunately Seth had the same idea, and his lips kissed Oliver's cheeks, eyelids, the corner of his mouth.

After a moment of reassurances, Oliver collapsed back against the headboard with a sated grin. It was a better view of his boyfriend, anyway.

Seth laughed, running the palm of his hand over Oliver's belly, his fingers raking through the come splattered in the dark hair below Oliver's navel. "I made a mess of you."

"Yeah?" Oliver saw amusement, exhaustion and a whole lot of satisfaction, thanks very much, when he looked up at Seth. "I can honestly say that I don't mind," Oliver chuckled.

Seth leaned in once more to press his lips against Oliver's, murmur, "Mm, love you, babe," and nuzzle his cheek against Oliver's. He pulled back and used the spare towel to clean them up quickly. Looking around the room, Seth sighed, made a face and tossed the towel into an empty box. "Remind me to get us a laundry hamper first thing tomorrow."

Oliver scooted down into the bedding, still feeling high and giddy from his orgasm, and said, "Check. We need a hamper."

We.

He didn't think he'd get tired of hearing that, ever. Seth crossed the room again to shut off the light, and that's when Oliver noticed the small, framed picture on the end table on Seth's side. Seth's graduation picture from Bakerfield, the one in which Oliver had his arms around him, kissing him passionately. The one Oliver had seen in Seth's bedroom on New Year's Day.

"Seth, that's—" Oliver felt something click inside him, like another piece of their relationship was falling back into place. "That picture."

"Hmm?" Seth turned to look, and turned back blushing and bashful. "Is that dumb? I know it's probably cheesy to have a high school graduation picture up."

Oliver pulled Seth to him and sighed happily into his hair. "No. Not to me. I love that picture."

Seth, his hand on the center of Oliver's chest, pushed up enough to look Oliver in the eyes. "You do?" He snuggled back down against him. "Me, too."

Oliver closed his eyes and pressed his nose into the crown of Seth's hair, just breathing him in. "Why that picture? I know why I like it; I just want to know why you do."

Seth was quiet for a moment, his fingers plucking gently at the dark hair on Oliver's forearms and then smoothing it. "That was my reminder. Well, proof."

"Proof?"

Seth sighed, pressing his lips just over Oliver's heart. "That we did love each other. That I hadn't imagined it."

The wistfulness in his voice made Oliver's arms tighten convulsively, and he kissed Seth's hair again. "We did. We do. Why do you think I kept every letter you ever wrote me?"

Seth hummed softly and said, "I know. I know *now*." His voice grew even quieter. "But I wondered back then, after—well. I wondered if you really had loved me, or if I had made it up. And when I felt like that, I would look at that picture and—God, it feels narcissistic to say why."

"No, please. I want to know," Oliver pleaded.

"I would look at that picture and know that you *had* really loved me: it's clear, don't you think? That someone loved me once. That it was you."

Oliver tipped Seth's chin so they were looking into each other's eyes. Seth's skin was almost luminescent in the moonlight. "I never stopped, Seth. I never will."

He kissed Seth so sweetly, then, the kiss serving as a promise that the love they'd had was still there and would only grow through the years. Seth pressed their foreheads together and nuzzling Oliver's nose with his own.

They settled back against the mattress, yawning and chuckling at how tired they were from such a long day.

"Tomorrow we can empty out the boxes your mother sent, if you like. I'm dying to know what Andrews treasures are about to adorn our home," Seth said, kissing just under Oliver's jaw and wiggling to get situated just right in Oliver's arms.

"She did?"

"You didn't see them? They're by your side of the bed against the wall."

He twisted slightly to see what Seth was talking about. A familiar box with shaky handwriting on it that read "Oliver's H.S. Things" was on the bottom.

Seth said around a yawn, "If it's your old school uniform, I demand that you put it on first thing in the morning and woo me."

Oliver sank back into the pillows, smiling. He caressed Seth's hair, feeling sated and sleepy and listening to the pleasant, fading murmurs from Seth as he fell asleep in Oliver's arms. The moonlight cast a thin beam of silver across their bed, running along Oliver's arm as it covered Seth's. He closed his eyes, rested his cheek on Seth's head and remembered a book that contained two dried, pressed flower buds that he'd put in that very box years before.

> For the one I love most lay sleeping by me under the same cover in the cool night.
>
> In the stillness in the autumn moonbeams his face was inclined towards me,
>
> And his arm lay lightly around my breast—and that night I was happy.

* * *

June, Six Years Later

Oliver pushed open the door to their apartment, glad to be finished with school and work for the week; he had big plans for the weekend, including enjoying the entirety of it with Seth. It wasn't that he didn't enjoy himself at Silver; it had proved challenging in the best of ways. It was just hectic, but coming home to Seth every night, well, Seth coming home to *him* every night was the icing on the cake.

He fished his wallet and phone out of his coat pocket and was about to drop them and his keys in the bowl on the console in the entryway when he realized that the bowl wasn't there. It was a blown glass plate. Well, Seth did like to change things around—it was something Oliver found both adorable and maddening. Just when he was getting used to a system, Seth decided the feng shui was off and swapped things around.

Feeling butterflies over the excitement he had planned for later, he called out coyly, "Seth?"

No answer. Well, he may simply have run to the market for something special for dinner, that wasn't unusual. Oliver pushed his satchel under the table with his foot and loosened his tie as he walked into the apartment.

"Can I help you?"

Oliver started, a creepy-crawly sensation running down his spine. Some strange guy was standing in the kitchen. In *Oliver's* kitchen.

"I think I can ask you that?" he said warily.

The guy tilted his head, a quizzical look on his face, and then a look of understanding washed over his features. "Right. You must be Oliver."

That was when Oliver noticed a toolbox in the kitchen by the sink and he let himself exhale.

"Yeah, your... what, boyfriend? He told me that an 'Oliver' might come home before he did, but I must have spaced." He turned back into the kitchen and continued, "Almost got this new disposal in for you; I'll be out of your hair in less than ten."

The guy crawled back under the sink, and Oliver took a moment to catch his breath. He had the eeriest sense of déjà vu. He shook himself and moved off to the bedroom where he toed off his shoes, put them on the cedar shoe racks Seth had insisted on and laid his jacket on the bed.

He laughed, wondering why he had felt weird all of a sudden. Perhaps he was just jumpy. He was home, though, and Seth would be home soon, and then Oliver could finally relax. He noticed that Seth had brought the mail into the bedroom but dumped it on the side table. He scooped it up and set it on the dresser to be sorted through later. Sitting on the foot of the bed to pull off his socks, he felt the lump in his jeans pocket and drew out a small velvet box; he looked around the bedroom and decided to hide it under the pillows on his side of the bed.

As he hung up his coat, he heard the front door open and felt a sense of peace and anticipation rush through him at the familiar sound of Seth's key ring jangling as he pulled it from the lock.

"Oliver? Oh, hi, Joe. Almost finished?"

Seth was home. Oliver felt a little giddy, thinking about his big plans for the weekend. He had talked to Big Mike on the phone the night before while Seth was at the workshop for his new musical, and both of them had gotten a little choked up.

"Seth? I'm in the bedroom," he called out, trying to keep his voice from giving away how excited he was.

He heard Seth thank Joe and then the front door opened and closed again and they were finally alone. Oliver lay down on the bed on his stomach, his eyes closing with the enjoyment of stretching out after his long day. He turned his head sideways and watched the doorway for Seth to appear.

Seth came in the bedroom, all smiles.

"Hi!" Seth said. "Done for the weekend?"

"Yep." Oliver patted the bed next to him with a smile to match Seth's. He never got tired of it—Seth coming home, maybe exhausted, sore, or frustrated, but always with a smile for Oliver, and Oliver had one for Seth in return. Always.

Seth stretched out with a groan, throwing his arms high above his head and arching his back. Then he flopped to the bed with a sigh. Oliver lifted his head enough to drop a kiss on Seth's mouth. Seth reached up with one hand and held him there a bit longer, giving him a more thorough kiss.

"Mm. Hello," Seth murmured against Oliver's lips.

Oliver pulled back a touch and said, "Thanks for calling someone for that."

Seth narrowed his eyes, even though he was still smiling. "Hmm. If I left it to you, it never would have been repaired. Joe told me that it looked as if you were using the disposal for a compost pile; you know we're lucky to even *have* one. How many times do I have to tell you that you can't put coffee grounds in there?"

Oliver pressed his forehead against the mattress next to Seth's shoulder and looked up at Seth with forgive-me eyes.

"Honestly, Oliver," Seth laughed. "The trashcan is *right next to the sink.*"

"Sorry."

Seth was so easy with his forgiveness. They both were. After these years of living together, their love had flourished and grown with the care and honor they both paid to it; they knew what it was like to live without that love, and Oliver could never imagine a day without this man in his life, cherishing him just as much as he cherished Seth.

"So, do we have any plans?" Seth asked, and kissed Oliver on the cheek.

Oliver propped himself on his side and smiled. Even though his insides were bubbling with excitement for what was to come, he also felt completely at peace with this man. Safe. Secure. So, so loved. Seth was the other part of him, one he could never do without again. He was looking forward to making it official.

He ran his hand down Seth's left arm, giving his hand a squeeze before bringing it to his lips and kissing the backs of his fingers. He lingered on one in particular, delighted by the laugh he got out of Seth.

"Oh, I have one."

THE END

Acknowledgements

This eponymous story would not exist if not for one of my favorite songs of all time, one of those beautiful epics that tells just enough of a story to get you wanting more. The book would not exist in its original form if not for the tireless encouragement from one of my dearest friends, F.M., and while it sucked getting back page after page bleeding with red, its original version is a better story for having been beaten up.

Huge thanks to Jenn, Chrissy, Kate and Jess for undertaking the Herculean task of reading this final draft and telling me their thoughts. (And a bigger thanks for the honesty.) To C.B., Annie, Candy and Lex: none of this would have happened without your belief this would work, and I thank you from the bottom of my heart.

Lastly, to friends and family and random strangers who read this even though it may not have been your cup of tea, I owe you a margarita. A good one, not one of those cheapy deals made from canned mix. I'm totally good for it, promise.

About the Author

A life-long fangirl, Laura Stone takes a leave of absence from the glamorous life of motherhood while the kids are in school, devoting her days to writing full-time. In the past she's worn the hat of actress, Master Gardener and computer geek, but now sticks mostly to a Texas Rangers' ball cap as she raises her children. They're not fully raised, but then again, she would say that she isn't either.

She began telling stories to her parents at the age of four. She was so successful in catching her parent's attention that her father actually dislocated his back, trying not to sit on her imaginary cat, Doka.

She lives in Texas as proof that it's not totally populated by hard-line right-wingers—and because that's where the good tamales are from.

Connect with Laura at laura-stone.com, on Goodreads at www.goodreads.com/Laura-Stone and on Twitter @stoneyboboney.

interlude **press**

A Reader's Guide
to
The Bones of You

Questions for Discussion

1. In romance novels, we often romanticize sacrifice. In The Bones of You, Seth and Oliver aren't willing to walk away from their respective careers on separate continents just to be with each other. Is their love any less romantic just because they won't relocate for the relationship?

2. How does Seth and Oliver's approach to a long distance relationship change with the passage of time?

3. Why do you think Seth waits so long to commit to a new relationship with Oliver?

4. If Oliver had decided to stay in England, how do you think their relationship would have progressed?

5. How does the role that Seth plays on Broadway mirror his early relationship with Oliver?

6. Oliver tends to focus on others. Does that make him a "people pleaser" and if so, how does it impact his decisions? What are the consequences of this character trait, and do you think they're worth it?

7. Oliver's friend Moira is also dedicated to her career, but is more of a risk taker and free spirit than Oliver. Does her approach to relationships and sex influence Oliver's decisions?

8. Are Oliver and Seth getting a do-over on their earlier relationship and if so, how does the passage of time influence this?

9. How does Big Mike continue to hold a space in their lives for Oliver differently than Seth?

10. Describe Seth and Oliver's viewpoints on work versus relationships. How do you think their family experience may have shaped their individual priorities?

Now available from

interludepress™

Bleeding Heart by Melissa Graves

While the public struggles to live side-by-side with vampires, medical student Brian Preston has dedicated himself to their care and study by working in a government-run clinic that monitors and feeds the resident vampire population. He has learned to expect the unexpected in his job, but his life takes a surprise turn late one night when a young, struggling vampire named Kyle stumbles into his clinic and his heart.

As they draw closer, can Brian come to grips with loving the elusive vampire, and can Kyle find the strength to share the secret that can separate them forever?

ISBN 978-1-941530-01-6

Platonic by Kate Paddington

Mark Savoy and Daniel O'Shea were high school sweethearts who had planned their forevers together. But when Mark goes to college in California rather than following Daniel to New York, he embarks on a decade-long search for independence, sexual confidence and love. When Mark lands a job in New York and crosses Daniel's path, they slowly rebuild their fractured friendship through texts and emails. If they finally agree to see each other, will they be able to keep it platonic? Or will the spark of a long-lost love reignite just as Daniel accepts a job overseas?

ISBN 978-1-941530-02-3

Pivot and Slip by Lilah Suzanne

Former Olympic hopeful Jack Douglas traded competitive swimming for professional yoga and never looked back. When handsome pro boxer Felix Montero mistakenly registers for his Yoga for Seniors class, Jack takes an active interest both in Felix's struggles to manage stress and in his heart, and discovers along the way that he may have healing of his own to do. Faced with the ghosts of his athletic aspirations, can Jack return to his old dream or carve out a new path, and will their budding romance survive the test of Felix's next bout in the ring?

ISBN 978-1-941530-03-0

Designs On You by Carrie Pack

If graphic designer Scott Parker has to design one more cupcake company logo, he might lose it. When tasked with retouching photos for a big fashion client, a stunning, lanky model mesmerizes Scott and occupies his fantasies long after the assignment is finished. When the model is assigned to one of Scott's projects, Scott discovers that the object of his desire is nothing like what he imagined. Despite Jamie Donovan's aloof and dismissive behavior, Scott struggles to forge a friendship with him, all the while trying to keep his attraction at bay. Will Jamie follow through on signals that he may be interested, or will he forever be the beautiful man in the photograph, an untouchable fantasy?

ISBN 978-1-941530-04-7

One **story** can change **everything**.

www.interlude**press**.com

interlude ✦ press

One Story Can Change Everything.

interludepress.com

*Twitter: @interludepress * * * Facebook: Interlude Press*
*Google+: +interludepress * * * Pinterest: interludepress*
Instagram: InterludePress

CPSIA information can
Printed in the USA
LVOW10s2353210815

451141LV000

530160